She can save her world...but only by risking the life of the man she loves.

A deadly virus attacks the inhabitants of Zephyria. Princess Aquatania, a sea dragon shifter and sorceress, also a brilliant scientist and doctor, is determined to combat the contagion that swiftly afflicts most lifeforms.

Aquatania devises a daring plan, harnessing various strains of dragon blood in her quest for a cure for the population. To find it, she must journey into the crushing depths of the ocean.

At her side is Kieran, the formidable fire dragon general of the royal legions. As they plunge into a perilous quest beneath the waves, their contrasting powers—her command of the sea, his mastery of flame—become their greatest weapon...and the spark of an unbreakable bond.

With the virus spreading and enemies closing in from above and below, Aquatania and Kieran must race against time, trust in each other completely, and risk everything.

I0598338

This book is a work of fiction. Names, characters, places, and incidents either are products of the author's imagination or are used fictitiously. Any resemblance to actual events or locales or persons, living or dead, is entirely coincidental.

Aquatania's Impetus
Copyright © 2025 Gabriella Bradley
ISBN: 978-1-4874-4353-5
Cover art by Martine Jardin

Published by Extasy Books Inc

Look for us online at:
www.extasybooks.com

Aquatania's Impetus

By

Gabriella Bradley

Chapter One

The sea-essence glowed an ethereal blue in the glass vial, pulsing with the ancient magic of the deep. Princess Aquatania squinted at the minuscule measurement markings as she tilted the dropper precisely three degrees, allowing exactly two drops to fall into the centrifuge chamber. Her breath caught in her throat, not from nerves, but from the practiced stillness that came with years of scientific precision. The wrong amount would render hours of careful work useless, and the rare compounds extracted from the twilight zone of the ocean were too precious to waste.

As she stepped back from the equipment, her gaze snagged on her reflection in the centrifuge's polished cover. There they were again—those golden markings, rising beneath her skin like living veins, curling into runes whenever tension or focus overtook her. They were remnants of the ancient bond she carried, an inheritance that stirred whenever her emotions slipped beyond her control, etching its script across her flesh. The bioluminescent solution pulsed in the chamber, its violet glow scattering across her platinum hair and tracing shifting patterns over her face.

The laboratory hummed with energy, both electrical and magical. Aquatania moved between workstations with practiced ease, her white lab coat billowing slightly in the gentle breeze that circulated through the high-ceilinged room. The lab was situated in the highest tower of Zephyria's sky island, offering panoramic views of the endless sky and glimpses of the distant ocean and land below through crystal-clear windows.

The space was a testament to her dual heritage. Advanced spectroscopy equipment shared countertops with ancient conch shells inlaid with spellwork that could detect toxins no machine could identify. Holographic displays projecting molecular structures hovered above tables carved from coral that had grown under the influence of sea dragon songs for centuries. It was neither entirely of the modern world nor completely ancient. It was hers, the perfect synthesis of who she was.

"Sample forty-two-B appears stable," she murmured, her voice automatically captured by the lab's recording system. She picked up a fountain pen — no digital device could replace the connection between thought and ink for her — and she made careful notations in a leather-bound journal.

Binding rate accelerated by twenty-eight percent with the addition of phosphorescent algae extract. Potential application for rapid wound healing, particularly for burns and abrasions with nerve damage.

Her handwriting flowed across the page, each character perfectly formed despite her excitement. This could be it…the breakthrough she'd been seeking for months. If the healing serum could be stabilized at various temperatures, it could revolutionize treatment for both humans and sea-folk.

Aquatania glanced at the row of crystal vials displayed on a shelf above her primary workstation. Each was uniquely shaped, some spiraling like nautilus shells, others faceted like deep-sea gems. They'd been passed down through seventeen generations of sea dragon royalty, each vial attuned to specific elements and energies.

She selected one that resembled a teardrop, its surface etched with wave patterns that seemed to move in the light. This particular vessel had been her great-grandmother's favorite, used to stabilize volatile compounds with its innate connection to water memory. Aquatania held it reverently, feeling the subtle vibration against her fingertips. It was a sensation only those with sea dragon blood could detect.

"Let's see if you can help me," she whispered to the vial, a

2

habit from childhood that she'd never outgrown. She carefully transferred a small amount of the processed serum from the centrifuge into the crystal container.

The reaction was immediate. The blue liquid shimmered, then deepened to a rich sapphire as the ancient magic of the vial interacted with her scientific compound. The temperature remained stable, but the molecular cohesion increased dramatically. It was the exact effect she'd been hoping for.

From a drawer beneath her workbench, she retrieved a large shell resembling a fan coral but with intricate whorls along its edge. This amplifier, when placed beneath the vial, would enhance the magical properties while allowing her to observe the scientific reactions without interference. It was an ingenious tool, developed by her ancestor Queen Mariana, who'd first bridged the gap between sea dragon intuition and methodical science.

Aquatania remembered her father teaching her to use these artifacts when she was barely tall enough to reach the laboratory counters. *"Feel it with both hearts,"* King Poseidronus had instructed, his deep voice patient but firm. *"Your human heart understands order and measurement. Your dragon heart knows the song of the sea. True mastery comes from listening to both."*

She looked up at his portrait hanging on the eastern wall of the laboratory. The painting captured his regal bearing — shoulders straight, his chin lifted, a crown of coral and pearls gleaming against his dark hair. But the artist had also captured something often overlooked in official portraits, the curious glint in his eyes that matched her own. For all his adherence to tradition, King Poseidronus had recognized and nurtured her scientific mind.

His stern gaze in the portrait seemed to follow her movements, a constant reminder of what awaited beyond these laboratory walls. Council meetings. Diplomatic negotiations. The weight of a crown she would one day wear.

3

Her fingers tightened around the crystal vial, then deliberately relaxed. Science was not an escape from her royal responsibilities but another facet of them. Every breakthrough here could benefit her people.

The centrifuge completed its cycle with a soft chime. Aquatania returned to it, carefully extracting the remaining serum and transferring it to labeled storage containers. Each movement was deliberate, and each container was precisely marked with its composition and date. Systematic work was satisfying in a way that royal protocols never were. Here, results came from method and insight, not tradition and hierarchy.

She placed several drops of the serum onto a culture plate containing damaged tissue samples and slid it under a microscope enhanced with both magnification technology and magical focusing crystals. Through the eyepiece, she watched cellular regeneration begin almost immediately. Healthy cells multiplied and migrated to the damaged areas, rebuilding what had been broken.

Tissue regeneration at triple the standard rate, she noted in her journal, unable to keep a smile from spreading across her face. *Minimal scarring pattern. No adverse reactions observed in the surrounding healthy tissue.*

Aquatania straightened, allowing herself a moment of pride as she surveyed her work. The glowing solutions, the precisely arranged equipment, and the ancient artifacts harmonizing with modern science. All of it represented hours of dedication, years of study, and generations of knowledge.

The healing serum wasn't perfect yet. It still needed testing for longevity, adaptability to different species, and resistance to varying environmental conditions. But it was a significant step forward. Perhaps the most promising version yet.

She began securing her samples in the temperature-controlled storage unit, her mind already racing with the next series of experiments. The work of a scientist, like the work of a princess, was never truly finished.

Aquatania closed her journal with a satisfied snap, allowing herself a brief smile at the promising results. The healing serum would need further refinement, but today's breakthrough marked significant progress.

She was reaching for her cooling tea when a harsh crimson light cut through the laboratory's serene blue glow. The urgent communication device on her desk, a spiral shell inlaid with pulsing crystals and silver circuitry, began emitting a low, rhythmic tone that sent a chill down her spine. In five years, she'd only seen it activate twice, and neither occasion had brought good news.

The device's pulse reflected off the glass vials and metal surfaces around her, painting the laboratory in flashes of blood-red warning.

This wasn't a scheduled communication or even a standard emergency. This was the royal emergency frequency, reserved for situations that threatened sky island settlements or sea kingdoms alike.

Aquatania moved swiftly, her scientific satisfaction evaporating like sea spray in desert heat. She finished securing the samples in a locked preservation chamber. Whatever the emergency, her breakthrough was too valuable to risk. With practiced motions, she shut down equipment that could become unstable if left unattended, her fingers flying across control panels and sealing mechanisms.

"Accept transmission," she commanded, her voice steady despite the apprehension building in her chest.

The shell's apex opened like a blossoming anemone, projecting a holographic image that hovered at eye level above her desk. The three-dimensional figure of a man appeared, his formal robes of office identifying him as an administrative official from Aethoria, the floating city known for its artisans and innovation. His normally immaculate appearance was disheveled, his hair askew, his robes

5

wrinkled, and his eyes wide with barely contained panic.

"Princess Aquatania," he said, bowing hastily. His voice wavered with strain. "Forgive the intrusion, Your Highness, but we face an unprecedented crisis."

"Councilor Thorne," she recognized him now. He was Aethoria's Minister of Public Welfare. "What's happening?"

"People are falling ill by the dozens, Your Highness. High fever, chills, and a strange red rash." His holographic hands trembled. "We've never seen anything like it. The illness manifested three days ago in the eastern quarter. We thought it was isolated, perhaps something brought by traders from the Midnight Isles, but it's spreading throughout the city with alarming speed."

Aquatania's mind immediately shifted into analytical mode, categorizing symptoms and considering vectors. "Describe the progression. How quickly from first symptoms to severe illness?"

"Alarmingly fast. Begins with fatigue and headache, followed by fever within hours. By the second day, the rash appears as raised red welts that spread from the neck downward. By day three, the victims are bedridden with muscle seizures." He swallowed visibly. "We've lost seventeen citizens already, mostly elderly and children."

"Containment measures?" she asked, already moving to a different workstation where she kept regional medical records and outbreak histories.

"We've established quarantine zones, but they're becoming overwhelmed. Our healers are distributing fever reducers and anti-inflammatory potions, but they barely manage the symptoms." The desperation in his voice deepened. "We've tried magical interventions, purification spells, health wards, but nothing slows the progression."

Aquatania's fingers traced patterns on a crystal interface, pulling up records of past illnesses reported in the floating territories. "Any connection between the initial cases?

Common activities, foods, water sources?"

"Nothing obvious. It's struck across social strata, different districts, various professions." He hesitated. "But there's one strange detail. The rash...it sometimes forms patterns. Not random welts, but almost...deliberate shapes. One healer swears she saw something resembling script on a patient's back."

That detail sent warning flares through Aquatania's mind. Disease didn't create patterns, but curses might. Or toxins with magical properties. She glanced at her recent experimental notes, wondering if her research on cellular regeneration might be adaptable to combating whatever this was.

"How many are currently infected?" she asked.

"Over two hundred confirmed cases. Potentially hundreds more incubating." The hologram flickered slightly as Thorne ran a hand through his hair. "Our healers are overwhelmed. We don't have your expertise in both scientific and magical medicine, Your Highness. Or your laboratories and resources."

His image leaned forward, the projection stretching slightly with the movement. "We need your expertise, Princess." His voice dropped, pride giving way to naked fear. "If this continues unchecked, we could lose half the city's population within a week."

Aquatania's dual nature stirred within her — the scientist curious about the pathology, the royal conscience awakening to responsibility. The healing serum she'd been developing wasn't ready for human trials, but its principles might apply to whatever was attacking Aethoria's people.

She studied the hologram of the desperate official, weighing obligations and possibilities. Her father would expect her to consult the Royal Council before taking action. Protocol demanded it. But protocol wouldn't save lives in the next crucial hours.

"Have you contacted the other sky islands? Or the sea kingdoms?" she asked.

"We've sent messengers, but—" He glanced over his shoulder as someone off-screen spoke urgently to him. When he turned back, his face had paled further. "Twenty-six new cases in the last hour. Three more deaths."

The decision crystallized in her mind. This wasn't just about science or royal duty. It was about her unique position to help. Her human intellect could analyze the disease scientifically. Her sea dragon heritage gave her resistance to most pathogens and the ability to travel swiftly. And her transformation abilities would allow her to transport necessary equipment without risking contamination.

"I'm coming to Aethoria immediately," she said, already mentally cataloging what supplies she would need. "Prepare your largest healing facility to serve as a command center. I'll need access to all patients, records of progression, and samples from the environment."

Relief washed across Thorne's face. "Thank you, Your Highness. I'll have everything ready for your arrival."

"One more thing," Aquatania added, her tone hardening with authority. "This illness may have magical components. Until I arrive, have your healers draw silver circles around the beds of the most severe cases. It won't cure them, but it might slow the progression."

As the hologram flickered out, Aquatania was already moving with purpose. Scientific curiosity and royal responsibility had merged into a singular focus. Whatever threatened Aethoria's people would face the full force of her dual nature, human science and dragon magic combined.

"I'm coming," she whispered to the empty air, as if the suffering citizens could somehow hear her promise. "Hold on."

Aquatania moved with practiced efficiency, her hands never hesitating as she gathered essential equipment. This wasn't the first crisis she'd responded to, though something about the strange illness made her stomach tighten with unusual apprehension. She pulled a waterproof satchel from beneath her workbench. It was specially designed with padded compartments to protect delicate scientific instruments during flight. The transformation to her dragon put considerable stress on anything she carried, but it had a harness designed to adapt to her changing form and would remain intact while she shifted. Only the most carefully secured items would survive the journey intact.

"Emergency protocol seven," she commanded, and throughout the laboratory, preservation fields activated over ongoing experiments. Sensitive compounds were automatically transferred to stasis chambers, and her digital notes locked themselves behind multiple layers of security. The laboratory would maintain itself for at least three days without her presence.

She selected tools with deliberate care. Her most sensitive diagnostic crystals, capable of detecting magical contamination in biological samples...a set of silver extraction needles for drawing infected blood safely, three vials of her partially completed healing serum, which might be adaptable to the mysterious illness, and a collection of rare reagents that could neutralize most known toxins, both natural and magical.

She placed each item carefully into its designated compartment in the satchel, cushioned against impact. She added her journal, several empty specimen containers, and a small but powerful microscope enhanced with both technology and magical enchantment. As an afterthought, she grabbed the teardrop-shaped crystal vial that had helped stabilize her healing serum. Its affinity for water memory might prove useful in identifying an unknown pathogen.

"Final additions," she murmured to herself, packing a set of protective gloves woven from silk and silver thread, effective barriers against both conventional contagions and magical corruption. She wouldn't need them in dragon form, but treating patients would require her human hands.

With the satchel secured, Aquatania activated the laboratory's highest security protocols and strode toward the eastern doors leading to the observation balcony. The doors recognized her biorhythm and slid open soundlessly, admitting her to the wide circular platform that extended from the tower like an outstretched hand.

The balcony offered an unobstructed view in all directions — the floating archipelago of the sky islands with their interconnected bridges and transfer platforms, the distant mainland shrouded in mist to the north, and the vast expanse of ocean to the south and east. Somewhere beyond the eastern horizon lay Aethoria, its crystal spires normally visible on the clearest days but now obscured by the gathering afternoon clouds.

Aquatania secured the satchel across her body. The winds at this altitude were brisk, tugging at her lab coat and whipping strands of her platinum hair across her face. She took a deep breath, centering herself for what came next.

The transformation began with a familiar tingling beneath her skin, like the prickling sensation of a limb waking from numbness, but spread across her entire body. She closed her eyes, focusing on the rhythm of her heartbeat as it began to change, growing stronger, more deliberate. The tingling intensified, becoming a wave of heat that surged outward from her core.

Her skin flushed, then began to change texture. It started at her hands, the smooth human skin rippling as iridescent blue scales pushed to the surface. The scales emerged in a pattern like spreading ripples in water, flowing up her arms and across her torso. Each scale caught the sunlight, reflecting it in shimmers of azure and turquoise. Where her human skin had been pale, dragon scales gleamed with the colors of

10

tropical waters.

The sensation was not painful, but neither was it comfortable, a stretching, pressing feeling as her body prepared for the dramatic change. Her clothes dissolved into mist, an enchantment woven into the fabric by royal tailors specifically for those with transformation abilities. Only the harness remained, expanding as her form changed.

The next phase came swiftly. Her bones began to shift, making soft cracking sounds as they elongated and reorganized. Her spine stretched, vertebrae multiplying and extending behind her to form a powerful tail. The pressure built within her chest as her rib cage expanded, making room for larger lungs and a heart that now beat with the force of ancient magic.

Aquatania gritted her teeth. This part always tested her concentration. Her height doubled, then tripled, her perspective shifting as she towered above the balcony floor. Her muscles thickened, density increasing as they wrapped around her transforming skeleton. Tendons pulled taut, then relaxed into their new configurations. Her hands and feet curved into powerful claws, each tipped with a talon that could slice through steel yet retain the dexterity needed for delicate work.

The sensations cascaded through her nervous system, pinpricks of intense heat followed by cooling relief as each body part completed its transformation. Her shoulders stretched outward, the bones hollowing even as they grew larger, preparing for flight. A pressure built between her shoulder blades, intense and insistent, until her skin split painlessly to allow massive wings to unfurl. The membrane stretched between elongated digits, thin enough for sunlight to pass through yet strong enough to bear her weight on air currents.

The final stage reached her face. Her jaw extended forward, teeth reshaping into points designed for gripping and tearing. Her nose and mouth merged into a powerful muzzle, nostrils flaring with enhanced capacity. Her ears elongated into fin-like appendages, capable of detecting the slightest atmospheric changes. Along her now-elongated spine, decorative fins unfurled in a ridge that ran from the base of her skull to the tip of her tail, each translucent membrane webbed with bioluminescent veins that would glow in darkness.

Throughout the metamorphosis, she knew her eyes remained the same sea-blue. It was the one feature unchanged in either form. The transformation complete, Aquatania stretched her massive body, adjusting to dimensions that dwarfed her human form. She was nearly sixty feet from snout to tail-tip, her wingspan twice that length when fully extended. Her scales caught the sunlight, sending flashes of blue-green across the balcony floor.

With the change came a rush of sensory information, scents carried on the wind from miles away, subtle variations in air pressure that foretold weather patterns, and the distant taste of salt brought to her by the slight breeze from the ocean far below. In this form, her connection to the sea remained strong despite her distance from it. She could sense the pull of tides, the movement of currents, the life teeming beneath the distant waves.

Most remarkable was her dual awareness. The scientific precision of her human mind remained intact, but was now complemented by the instinctual knowledge of her dragon heritage. Ancient memories stirred at the edges of her consciousness, migration routes used by her ancestors, hunting patterns, and territorial boundaries of sky and sea that had stood for millennia.

She moved to the edge of the balcony, her powerful muscles coiling in preparation. The satchel of equipment felt insignificant against her massive form, though she knew its contents were crucial to her mission. Aethoria lay approximately forty miles east, a journey that would take mere minutes in this form.

Aquatania spread her wings to their full extension, feeling the wind catch beneath the membranes. Her heightened senses detected the perfect moment when the air currents aligned. With a powerful thrust of her hind legs, she launched herself from the balcony, her massive body momentarily suspended in the open air before her wings caught the wind.

The first downstroke sent her surging upward, the second propelled her forward with gathering speed. Each powerful beat carried her higher and faster, her streamlined body cutting through the air with natural grace. She banked eastward, adjusting her trajectory toward Aethoria with instinctive precision.

Chapter Two

Aethoria emerged from the clouds, its once-gleaming crystal spires now dulled under a haze that hung over the floating city like a shroud. Aquatania banked her massive dragon form in a wide arc, her keen eyes taking in details invisible to human sight. Silver barriers glinted around sections of the city, makeshift quarantine zones hastily erected against the spreading illness. Where colorful banners would flutter between buildings and sky-ferries would dart like dragonflies, there was an unsettling stillness broken only by the movement of emergency personnel. The city was wounded.

She circled lower, following the beacon lights of the emergency landing platform at the city's western edge. The platform, generally reserved for diplomatic vessels, had been cleared of all traffic, surrounded by a ring of silver torches whose flames burned with unnatural brightness. Even from the air, she could sense the magical wards embedded in that silver fire, designed to purify any contagion that might pass through.

Aquatania tucked her wings close to her body and descended in a controlled spiral, her powerful body cutting through the afternoon air with precision. As the platform drew closer, she extended her wings to slow her approach, her powerful muscles adjusting to create the perfect amount of drag. Her claws touched down with surprising delicacy for a creature of her size, her talons clicking against the polished stone surface.

Guards in silver-embroidered uniforms stepped back instinctively, though they maintained their positions around the platform's perimeter. Each wore a face shield of clear crystal with thin silver wires woven through it. It was protection against both physical and magical contamination. Their hands rested on the hilts of swords that glowed faintly with enchantment.

Aquatania dipped her massive head in acknowledgment, then moved to the center of the platform where a large circular area had been designated for transformation. The intricate patterns carved into the stone would help contain and disperse the magical energy released during the change.

She closed her eyes, focusing inward. The transformation back to human form began with a subtle shift in her core temperature, a cooling sensation that spread outward from her heart. Her massive wings folded tightly against her body, then began to shrink, the membranes thinning and the bones contracting with soft sounds like distant waves breaking on the shore. Her tail shortened, vertebrae merging and retreating into her spine in a cascade of gentle pops.

The blue-green scales across her body softened, losing their metallic luster as they began to recede beneath the surface of her skin. They shimmered like underwater gems, catching the final rays of sunlight before disappearing. Her massive frame contracted, the bones reshaping with quiet creaks and sighs. The change was a dance of matter and magic, her body remembering its human shape with each passing second.

As her form diminished, a mist rose from her skin. It was part of the transformation process that would reconstitute her clothing. The enchanted fabric molecules, dispersed during her change to dragon form, now gathered and rewove themselves around her shrinking frame. Her claws retracted into fingers, talons softening into nails. The ridge of decorative fins along her spine flattened and disappeared, leaving only smooth skin in their wake.

Her face was the last to transform, the muzzle shortening, and teeth reshaping into human dimensions. The fin-like ears receded into rounded human ones. Only her eyes remained unchanged.

When the transformation was completed, Princess Aquatania stood tall in her human form, dressed in practical attire suitable for her work, fitted trousers, a deep blue tunic, sturdy boots, and a belt from which various scientific instruments hung. The satchel of medical supplies remained securely strapped across her body, the transformation harness having adjusted seamlessly to her human dimensions. Her platinum hair was pulled back in a simple braid, practical and unadorned.

"Princess Aquatania of Sky Island, Zephyria, and the Sea Kingdom of Oceana Prime," she stated clearly to the guards who approached with detection wands. "I've come at Councilor Thorne's request."

The guards swept their wands over her, thin rods of silver and crystal that hummed faintly as they detected magical signatures. It was standard protocol, even for royalty, especially during a contagion.

"Your credentials are confirmed, Your Highness," the lead guard said, lowering his wand and bowing. "Thank you for coming. The city is grateful."

Aquatania nodded, but her attention had already shifted beyond the platform. From this vantage point, she could see the sprawling emergency medical camp that had been erected in what was once Aethoria's central park. White tents stood in ordered rows, but the order ended there. Medical personnel in protective gear rushed between structures, carrying supplies and supporting stumbling patients. Even from this distance, she could hear cries of pain and the constant murmur of healers attempting to soothe the suffering.

"Princess." A familiar voice drew her attention.

Councilor Thorne approached from a small administrative tent at the edge of the platform. His appearance shocked her. In the mere hours since their communication, he seemed to have aged years. Deep shadows underlined his eyes, his usually impeccable beard was unkempt, and a slight tremor affected his hands as he bowed.

"Thank you for coming so quickly," he said, straightening. "The situation has deteriorated since we spoke."

"I can see that," Aquatania replied, adjusting the strap of her satchel. "How many cases now?"

"Over three hundred since yesterday." Thorne's voice dropped, as if speaking the number aloud might somehow worsen the situation. "The wards aren't holding. Whatever this is, it moves through magical barriers like they're nothing more than decorative curtains."

He gestured for her to follow, leading her toward a path that descended from the platform toward the medical camp. As they walked, Aquatania noted the city's unnatural quiet...the absence of children's laughter, of merchants calling their wares, of musicians in the squares. Instead, there was the distant sound of moaning patients and the hurried footsteps of emergency personnel.

"We're calling it the Red Death," Thorne said as they approached the perimeter of the quarantine zone. His hands trembled as he pulled a small vial from his pocket, purification drops that he applied to both their wrists before they passed through the first silver barrier. "For the rash, you understand. Although the name has taken on additional meaning. It spreads like wildfire. It's"—his voice cracked slightly—"it's killing us, Your Highness."

Aquatania absorbed this information with the clinical part of her mind while her heart registered the human toll reflected in Thorne's exhausted face. Ahead, healers in silver-embroidered robes moved between makeshift tents where patients lay on cots arranged in tight rows. Around each tent glowed a faint silver circle, a containment ward designed to prevent spread, though according to Thorne, these were proving ineffective.

"I'll need to examine patients immediately," she said, mentally categorizing the equipment in her satchel. "Starting with the oldest and most severe cases and then tracking the progression back to the first infections, if any have survived."

"Of course." Thorne nodded, leading her toward the largest tent at the center of the camp. "We've prepared a workspace for you with all the equipment we could gather. Our best healers are ready to assist."

As they approached the tent entrance, the sounds of suffering intensified. Labored breathing, whimpers of pain, the rustle of fever-ravaged patients turning restlessly on their cots. Aquatania took a deep breath, steeling herself for what lay ahead. Her dual nature — her scientific mind and royal compassion — would be tested in equal measure.

"Let's begin," she said, stepping through the silver-warded threshold into the crisis that awaited.

*

Inside the main treatment tent, the air hung heavy with the mingled scents of medicinal herbs, sweat, and the subtle metallic tang that Aquatania's enhanced senses identified as blood magic residue. Rows of cots stretched in orderly lines, each occupied by a patient in various stages of the illness. Silver containment circles had been painted around each bed, their dim glow occasionally flickering. It was a sign the wards were failing to contain whatever magic might be involved in the contagion. The sound of rattling breaths filled the space, punctuated by occasional moans and the hushed voices of healers moving between patients with determined efficiency despite their evident exhaustion.

A young woman in healer's robes approached, her face pale with fatigue. A silver pendant in the shape of Aethoria's healing glyph hung at her throat, marking her as a graduate of the city's prestigious medical academy.

"Your Highness, I'm Healer Sarabina. I've been assigned to assist you," she said, offering a quick bow. "We've prepared a workstation as Councilor Thorne instructed."

She led Aquatania to a cleared area at the rear of the tent where a table had been set up with basic medical equipment, glass vials, crystalline measuring tools, mortar and pestle, and a collection of healing potions in labeled bottles. Not as sophisticated as her laboratory on Zephyria, but it would suffice for initial diagnostics.

Aquatania unstrapped her satchel and began unpacking her specialized equipment with practiced movements. She arranged diagnostic crystals in a precise pattern, each glowing faintly with stored magical energy. She withdrew the silver extraction needles and placed them in a sterilization dish filled with purification solution.

"I'll need to examine patients at different stages of infection," she said, activating her crystal slate with a touch. The translucent surface glowed to life, ready to record her observations.

Healer Sarabina nodded. "I've identified representatives of each stage. The most recently infected is a dock worker. The first symptoms appeared just hours ago."

The patient lay on a cot near the workstation, a burly man with weather-roughened skin. His eyes were closed, and his face was flushed with fever. Aquatania approached, pausing at the edge of the silver circle surrounding his bed.

"May I?" she asked the conscious man, respecting his autonomy despite the emergency circumstances.

He nodded weakly. "Anything to stop this, Your Highness."

Aquatania stepped through the containment circle, feeling the slight resistance of the magical barrier as it recognized her presence. She placed her diagnostic crystal on the man's forehead, watching as it changed color from clear to amber, indicating elevated body temperature and disrupted energy flow.

"Temperature significantly above normal," she noted, her voice calm and professional as her words recorded automatically on the crystal slate. "Approximately one hundred and four degrees. Pulse rapid but regular."

She examined his neck, where the first signs of the distinctive rash were appearing...raised welts of angry red that seemed to spread downward like crimson vines seeking soil. Unlike ordinary rashes that spread in random patterns, these welts formed lines that almost resembled writing, though in no alphabet Aquatania recognized.

"The pattern is consistent with other cases?" she asked Sarabina, who stood just outside the circle.

"Yes, Your Highness. It always begins at the neck and spreads downward. By tomorrow, it will cover his torso. By the third day..." She hesitated. "If he survives that long, it will reach his extremities."

Aquatania gently pressed a silver extraction needle against the edge of a welt. The needle's tip filled with a sample of blood and interstitial fluid, which she transferred to a crystal vial. Through the container, she could see that the blood was darker than normal, not the healthy crimson of oxygenated blood but a deep, almost burgundy shade.

Moving methodically through the tent, Aquatania examined twelve patients in different stages of infection, collecting samples and documenting symptoms with scientific precision. Her crystal slate was filled with observations—muscle spasms that increased in severity with disease progression, elevated temperature resistant to cooling potions, and the distinctive rash that seemed to follow specific pathways across the skin rather than spreading outward from points of origin.

At the far end of the tent, a young child of perhaps six years lay curled on a small cot, whimpering with fever. The rash had already spread across his small chest, the red lines stark against his pallid skin. A woman sat beside him, his mother, Aquatania presumed, dabbing ineffectually at his forehead with a damp cloth.

"May I?" Aquatania asked softly, and the woman nodded, her eyes hollow with fear and exhaustion.

Kneeling beside the cot, Aquatania placed her hand gently on the child's burning forehead. She closed her eyes briefly, connecting with the sea dragon side of her nature. A subtle blue glow emanated from her palm as she called upon her innate ability to manipulate water. The moisture in the air condensed around her hand, cooling and soothing as it bathed the child's fevered skin.

The boy's eyes fluttered open, surprise momentarily overriding his discomfort. "Cold," he whispered, but not in complaint. "Nice."

"The fever is trying to fight the sickness," Aquatania explained gently, maintaining the cooling effect. "But sometimes it fights too hard. This will help you feel better while your body works."

She sustained the cooling effect for several minutes, her free hand taking samples from the rash on his chest with practiced care. When she finally withdrew, the child's breathing had eased slightly, his small body relaxing into a less pained posture.

"Thank you," the mother whispered, fresh tears tracking down her already tear-stained face.

Aquatania nodded, her scientific detachment momentarily challenged by the raw gratitude in the woman's eyes. She moved back to her workstation, where Healer Sarabina waited with the collected samples.

"Why isn't healing magic working?" Aquatania asked as she arranged the vials in order of infection progression. "What have you tried?"

Sarabina sighed, the sound weighed with professional frustration. "Everything in our repertoire. Standard healing

21

incantations appear to offer momentary relief but have no lasting effect. Purification spells, regeneration charms, vitality infusions, they all fail within minutes. It's as if..." She hesitated, searching for words. "It's as if the illness absorbs the magic and uses it to grow stronger."

As if to punctuate her statement, a nearby containment ward hissed and flickered, its silver light dimming before stabilizing at a weaker intensity. The sound was repeated throughout the tent, magical barriers struggling against an unseen force.

Aquatania calibrated a small, portable microscope enhanced with both magical crystals and precise lenses. She placed a drop of blood from the most severely infected patient onto a slide and bent to examine it.

What she saw confirmed her growing suspicion. The blood cells themselves were malformed, their membranes distorted into shapes that echoed the patterns of the external rash. More concerning was the faint glow that pulsed through the sample, visible only because of her enhanced draconic vision.

"The pattern is consistent," she said, straightening from the microscope. "But the speed of progression is unlike anything I've encountered. This isn't behaving like a natural disease."

She methodically compared blood samples from patients at different stages. Each showed the same abnormalities, differing only in intensity. The progression was mathematically precise, too precise for a naturally occurring pathogen.

The tent's heavy atmosphere pressed in around her, the smell of sweat and fear, the rustle of fever-victims shifting restlessly, the constant low hum of pain. A healer across the room murmured comfort to a writhing patient whose muscles had locked in spasm. Nearby, the hiss of another failing containment ward punctuated the background noise like a whispered warning.

"Have you identified any common factors among the first

victims?" Aquatania asked, making notes on her crystal slate. "Shared locations, foods, activities?"

Sarabina shook her head. "Nothing conclusive. The first cases appeared in various districts and among different social classes. The only commonality was timing, all within the same twelve-hour period."

That detail sent a chill through Aquatania that had nothing to do with the tent's temperature. Natural outbreaks didn't begin simultaneously across disparate populations. They spread from a point of origin, following contact patterns.

"This is deliberate," she murmured, too quietly for anyone but herself to hear. The implications were disturbing. If this was an engineered contagion — magical, scientific, or both — then someone had unleashed it intentionally.

She looked up at the rows of suffering patients, her scientific mind calculating infection rates and progression patterns while her heart registered the human cost of each number. Whatever this *Red Death* was, its precision and resistance to treatment pointed to a sophisticated design rather than natural evolution.

The question was no longer just *what*, but *who and why*.

Aquatania bent over the cot of a merchant in the final stages of infection, his body wracked with muscle spasms so severe the healers had secured his limbs with padded restraints. The rash had spread to cover nearly his entire body, the red lines forming intricate patterns that seemed almost deliberate in their arrangement. As she carefully extracted a blood sample from the crook of his arm, a flash of movement caught her eye. On a nearby supply crate, a small green lizard sat perfectly still, its jewel-like eyes reflecting the silver light of the containment wards. What struck her as unusual wasn't the creature's presence, small reptiles were common enough in Aethoria's warm climate, but its complete lack of concern at being in a tent full of severely ill humans.

Placing the merchant's blood sample in a secured vial,

Aquatania approached the crate with measured steps. The lizard watched her advance without fear, its throat pulsing with calm breaths. It made no move to flee even as she extended her hand.

"You're rather confident, aren't you?" she murmured, her scientific mind already calculating possibilities. With a swift, gentle motion born of years of handling delicate laboratory specimens, she captured the small reptile, cradling it in her cupped palms.

The lizard remained docile, its scaled skin cool against her fingers. Aquatania scrutinized it. No signs of distress, no abnormal coloration, no evidence that it had been affected by whatever filled the air of this tent. Its eyes were clear, and its movements when it shifted in her hands were fluid and natural.

"Your Highness?" Sarabina approached, eyebrows raised at the sight of the princess holding a common lizard.

"How long has this treatment center been operational?" Aquatania asked, still studying the reptile.

"Four days. We converted the community hall when the first dozen cases appeared."

"And have you noticed any animals becoming ill? Birds, mammals, insects?"

Sarabina considered the question. "Now that you mention it, no. We've been so focused on the human cases..." Her voice trailed off as she realized the implication of Aquatania's question.

A guard standing near the tent entrance cleared his throat. "Begging your pardon, Your Highness, but that reminds me of something strange. My household has fallen ill, my wife and both children. But my pet crocodilian is perfectly healthy, despite sleeping at the foot of our bed."

Aquatania's attention sharpened. "A crocodilian? You're certain it shows no symptoms? No lethargy, no loss of appetite, no discoloration of scales?"

"None, Your Highness. In fact, he seems livelier than usual, if anything. Been a comfort to the children during their fever spells."

"Reptilian immunity," Aquatania murmured, her mind racing with implications. She returned to her workstation, the lizard still secured gently in one hand while she prepared a small collection tube with the other. With practiced precision, she used a microneedle to draw a tiny blood sample from the reptile's tail, just enough for testing, not enough to harm the creature.

The lizard's blood gleamed ruby-red in the crystal vial, healthy and vibrant compared to the dark, sluggish samples from human patients. Aquatania placed the lizard in a small, ventilated specimen box where it could remain comfortable while she worked.

"I need more reptilian samples," she announced. "Different species, if possible. And I need them quickly."

While Sarabina dispatched assistants to capture reptile specimens from around the city, Aquatania prepared a series of test slides. On each crystal plate, she placed a drop of infected human blood. Beside that, she added a drop of the lizard's blood, then carefully encouraged the samples to merge using a silver probe.

Under her enhanced microscope, the reaction was immediate and visible. Where the two blood samples mixed, the malformed human cells seemed to recoil from the reptile cells. More remarkably, the faint magical glow she'd detected in the infected blood dimmed significantly where it made contact with the reptilian sample.

"Fascinating," she whispered, adjusting the focus to examine the boundary between the samples. The reptile blood wasn't destroying the infection, but it *was* repelling it, creating a barrier that the diseased cells couldn't penetrate.

Aquatania straightened, her dragon-trained senses detecting something the microscope couldn't fully reveal.

There was a subtle magical residue in the infected blood. Not simply the byproduct of a disease process, but something deliberately woven into the contagion itself. It carried a signature that her sea dragon heritage recognized, ancient, complex, and intentionally crafted to affect humans but not reptilian species.

"This is a weaponized curse," she said quietly, the pieces falling into place. "One that's been magically engineered to specifically target humans."

When additional reptile specimens arrived, a snake from the city gardens, a turtle from a nearby fountain, and samples from two pet lizards belonging to city officials, Aquatania repeated her tests with each. The results were consistent. No reptilian blood showed signs of infection, and each sample demonstrated the same repelling effect when introduced to infected human blood.

She documented her findings on her crystal slate, the implications sending a chill through her that had nothing to do with the tent's temperature. If the disease was engineered to affect only humans while sparing reptilian species, it suggested a creator with not only advanced knowledge of magical pathology but also a specific agenda.

"Healer Sarabina," she called, "I need to test a theory. My blood may provide additional insights."

Sarabina looked startled. "Your Highness, is that wise? If you were to become infected—"

"My dual nature provides certain immunities," Aquatania assured her, already preparing a silver extraction needle. "Half sea dragon, remember? Reptilian ancestry."

She pricked her fingertip, allowing several drops of blood to fall onto a fresh slide. Under the microscope, her blood displayed unique characteristics, cells that appeared mostly human but with subtle differences in membrane structure and density. When she introduced a sample of infected blood, the reaction was even more pronounced than with the lizard's blood. The infected cells didn't just recoil; they seemed to lose cohesion entirely, the magical signature within them disrupted by contact with her dragon-influenced blood.

"This confirms it," she said, making rapid notes. "The contagion is specifically designed to affect human physiology while leaving reptilian systems untouched. My hybrid blood creates an even stronger repelling effect." She looked up at Sarabina, who was watching with fascinated attention. "This could be the key to developing a treatment."

Councilor Thorne entered the tent as she was completing her documentation, his face drawn with exhaustion but showing the first hint of hope since her arrival.

"Your Highness, the healers tell me you've made a discovery?"

Aquatania nodded, quickly explaining her findings about reptilian immunity and the magical engineering evident in the disease. "It's not a natural contagion," she concluded. "Someone created this specifically to target humans while sparing reptilian species. With this knowledge, I believe we can develop a treatment using reptilian blood components to neutralize—"

A young messenger burst through the tent flaps, interrupting Aquatania's explanation. His uniform marked him as part of Aethoria's communication corps, his face flushed with exertion and alarm.

"Your Highness! Councilor!" He gasped, bowing hastily. "We've just received reports of identical outbreaks on three other sky islands and in Oceana Prime!"

The tent fell silent, the implications of his words hanging in the air like a thunder cloud. Aquatania felt her blood run cold.

"Which islands?" she demanded, her royal authority cutting through the stunned silence.

"Nimbus, Cirrus, and Stratus, Your Highness," the messenger replied. "All reporting the same symptoms, the same progression pattern. The cases in Oceana Prime are concentrated in the coastal cities, which are mostly engaged in trade with the sky territories."

Aquatania's expression hardened as she processed this information. *Strategic targets, all major centers of commerce and governance.* This wasn't just an outbreak…it was an attack on the foundations of their allied civilizations.

"This is no coincidence," she said, her voice low but carrying the weight of certainty. "Someone has launched a coordinated biological assault against our kingdoms."

The reptilian connection suddenly took on new significance. Who would benefit from a contagion that spared reptilian species while devastating human populations? The list of potential perpetrators narrowed considerably.

"I need to establish communication with my father immediately," she told Thorne. "And I need larger quantities of reptilian blood for testing treatment protocols. If this is happening simultaneously across multiple locations, we're facing something far more dangerous than a local outbreak."

Her mind was already calculating what this meant for containment efforts, for treatment development, and for the political stability of the allied kingdoms. But beneath the strategic considerations lay a more personal conclusion — her people, both human and sea dragon, were under attack. And she possessed the unique combination of scientific knowledge and magical heritage that might save them.

"This is a deliberate attack," she muttered, gathering her equipment with renewed urgency. "And we will respond accordingly."

Chapter Three

Aquatania strode through the alabaster corridors of the royal palace, the rhythmic tap of her boots against polished stone echoing like a heartbeat. The crystal vials of blood samples clinked softly in her satchel, human and reptilian, infected and clean, scientific evidence of the deliberate attack spreading through Aethoria and beyond. Her mind still raced with implications, calculations, and theories, but she remained composed. Years of royal training had taught her to mask her emotions, even as the weight of her discovery pressed against her chest like a stone. Someone had engineered this contagion with precision, sparing reptilian species while devastating human populations. And now she had to tell her father.

The massive doors to the royal audience chamber loomed before her, carved from ancient driftwood salvaged from the depths and inlaid with mother-of-pearl that caught the light in iridescent flashes. Two guards flanked the entrance, their silver-tipped spears crossing as she approached, then parting in recognition.

"Her Royal Highness, Princess Aquatania of Sky Island Zephyria and the Sea Kingdom of Oceana Prime," the herald announced, his voice carrying through the vast space beyond.

The audience chamber opened before her like the interior of a massive shell, vaulted ceilings arched overhead, supported by pillars of living coral that had been coaxed into intricate spirals by generations of sea dragon magic. Glowing spell-wards twined around these columns in pulsing blue patterns, simultaneously decorative and defensive. Panoramic windows lined the eastern wall, offering breathtaking views of the endless ocean below, a strategic reminder to all visitors that Zephyria maintained dominion over both sky and sea.

King Poseidronus sat upon the Wave Throne, an imposing seat carved from a single piece of azure crystal that seemed to capture the essence of the ocean within its depths. Even in his human form, her father radiated power...broad-shouldered and straight-backed, his silver-streaked dark hair was crowned with a circlet of coral and deep-sea pearls. His sea-blue eyes, so like her own, were grave as they tracked her approach across the polished floor.

"Father," Aquatania said, dropping into a formal curtsy despite the urgency of her news. Protocol mattered, especially now.

"Rise, Daughter," he replied, his deep voice resonating through the chamber. "We have received preliminary reports from Aethoria. Your findings are concerning."

Aquatania straightened, for the first time noticing the two advisors standing to the right of the throne. One was elderly, with a wispy white beard and robes embroidered with the swirling patterns of Sky Island aristocracy. The other was younger, broad-shouldered, his facial features reminiscent of the eastern territories. Both watched her with expressions that betrayed nothing.

"My findings are worse than concerning, Father," she said, removing a crystal slate from her satchel and activating it with a touch. Holographic data projected into the air between them, charts showing infection rates, diagrams of the rash patterns, and microscopic images of blood samples. "The contagion spreading through Aethoria is not a natural disease. It bears all the hallmarks of deliberate engineering."

She stepped forward, her voice shifting into the precise cadence she used when presenting scientific findings.

"The illness progresses through three distinct stages, each mathematically precise in duration and symptomatology. First, fever and fatigue for exactly twelve hours. Second, the distinctive rash appeared at the neck and spread downward over forty-eight hours, forming patterns consistent with magical manipulation rather than natural spread. Finally, severe muscle spasms and neurological deterioration leading to death within seventy-two to ninety-six hours from initial infection."

King Poseidronus leaned forward, his eyes narrowing as he studied the projected data. "The mortality rate?"

"Nearly sixty percent, with higher percentages among the very young and elderly." Aquatania's voice remained clinical, though a muscle in her jaw tightened briefly. "Recovery, when it occurs, leaves significant neurological damage. Aethoria's healers have attempted all standard magical and medicinal treatments without success."

She advanced to the next set of data, displaying side-by-side comparisons of blood samples.

"The most significant finding is this…the contagion affects only humans. All reptilian species I tested, from common lizards to sea dragons, show complete immunity." Her eyes met her father's directly. "My own blood, carrying both human and sea dragon properties, demonstrates a unique repelling effect on the pathogen."

The elderly advisor stepped forward, his eyes narrowing. "You suggest this is targeted biological warfare? Against humans specifically?"

"The evidence supports no other conclusion," Aquatania replied. "The simultaneous outbreak across four sky islands and the coastal cities of Oceana Prime indicates coordination. The specificity of the target population, humans only, indicates intention."

She scrolled through her findings to a map showing the affected territories. "All major centers of commerce and governance have been targeted. The contagion bypasses magical containment wards with concerning ease, suggesting it was designed with knowledge of our defensive measures."

31

King Poseidronus's knuckles whitened as his hands gripped the armrests of his throne. "You have developed countermeasures?"

"Preliminary ones," Aquatania said, grateful to offer some hope among the dire news. "The reptilian immunity provides a pathway for treatment. I've begun synthesizing a serum using components from reptilian blood that neutralize the pathogen on contact. Initial tests in laboratory settings are promising, but production at a large scale will require significant resources."

The younger advisor cleared his throat. "How long before an effective treatment could be deployed?"

Aquatania assessed him carefully. Something in his tone struck her as odd, not quite concern, but something closer to calculation.

"With appropriate resources, perhaps three days for initial treatment batches. Full-scale production would take longer."

"Three days," the elderly advisor murmured. "By then, hundreds more will have fallen ill."

"Thousands," Aquatania corrected, letting the grim reality settle in the chamber. "The rate of spread is accelerating. Aethoria has established quarantine zones, but they're failing. I suspect similar situations across all affected territories."

King Poseidronus rose from his throne, his expression hardening into the look she recognized from times of crises when storms threatened the sky islands or diplomatic tensions rose with neighboring kingdoms.

"We will commit all necessary resources to your research, Daughter. Isolation wards will be established immediately throughout Zephyria. Trade vessels will be inspected before docking." He turned to the advisors. "Summon the Council. We must coordinate our response with the other unaffected territories."

The advisors bowed in unison. "At once, Your Majesty."

As they turned to leave, Aquatania's enhanced hearing, a

gift from her sea dragon heritage, caught a whisper between them, too low for human ears to detect.

"The plan is proceeding as expected," the younger one murmured, his lips barely moving.

Ice flooded Aquatania's veins, but her expression remained unchanged through years of royal discipline. She continued her report, detailing the resources she would need for her laboratory work, but her mind raced with this new information. The suspicion that had begun to form in Aethoria crystallized into certainty.

This wasn't just an attack from outside. The enemy was already within their walls, within the royal court itself. And they'd just revealed themselves to the one person uniquely equipped to stop them…a princess with the scientific mind to develop a cure and the sea dragon heritage to survive what was coming.

"I will return to my laboratory immediately, Father," she concluded, gathering her materials with steady hands that betrayed none of the turmoil within. "Time is our most precious resource now."

King Poseidronus nodded, his eyes reflecting concern not just for his kingdom but for his daughter. "Proceed with all haste, Aquatania. The kingdom depends on you."

More than you know.

She curtsied once more before turning to leave, her mind already formulating her next move.

Aquatania nodded to the guards as she exited the audience chamber, her posture suggesting she was headed directly to her laboratory as stated. She maintained this pretense until turning the corner, where she paused, her back pressed against the cool stone wall. A calculated risk formed in her mind with the precision of a chemical equation. If the advisors were indeed involved in the contagion's spread, they would likely discuss their *plan* further now that the king had called for council. Scientific method demanded investigation of this hypothesis. With a silent breath, she slipped off her boots, tucked them into her satchel, and pivoted on bare feet back toward the audience chamber's side exit, the one the advisors would most likely use.

She positioned herself behind a flowering coral sculpture, its branches providing adequate visual cover while allowing her to observe the ornate side door. The minutes felt like hours, her trained mind maintaining perfect stillness despite the adrenaline pulsing through her veins. Finally, the door opened, and the two advisors emerged, their heads bent close in conversation.

Aquatania waited until they'd advanced precisely fifteen meters, close enough to track, far enough to remain undetected. She moved from her hiding place with deliberate steps, placing each foot with the same care she used when handling volatile compounds in her laboratory. Years of precision work had taught her how to control every muscle and measure every movement.

The advisors maintained a brisk pace through the main corridors, nodding to passing courtiers and guards. Aquatania followed at a measured distance, using other palace denizens as cover, pausing behind a group of chattering nobles, bending to adjust her satchel as a servant passed with linens, examining a wall tapestry with false interest when one advisor glanced back.

Their path turned away from the bustling main halls, following a sequence of increasingly narrow corridors. The polished marble of the frequented passageways gave way to older stonework, the walls bearing the slight erosion of centuries of sea spray before Zephyria's weather wards had been perfected. The ambient light dimmed as magical illumination crystals appeared less frequently, spaced farther apart, their amber glow creating pools of light separated by stretches of shadow.

The advisors' shadows stretched along the walls, distorted

by the uneven lighting into elongated shapes that seemed almost too tall, too angular to belong to human forms. Aquatania cataloged this observation even as she dismissed it as a trick of the light.

She pressed herself into an alcove as they paused at an intersection, their whispers too distant to hear even with her enhanced senses. Her pulse remained steady, controlled by the same discipline that allowed her to hold a dropper motionless for minutes while measuring volatile compounds. When they moved again, she followed, maintaining exactly seven seconds of delay, enough time for them to turn a corner before she reached it, minimizing the risk of detection.

The corridors grew narrower still, the ceiling lower. These passages dated back to the original construction of the palace, when Zephyria was a smaller settlement, before it had grown into the floating metropolis it was today. Few had reason to venture here. The administrative functions had long since moved to the newer, grander wings. The moisture in the air increased, bringing with it the faint scent of salt and algae that permeated the oldest parts of any sky island structure.

The advisors stopped before a heavy wooden door reinforced with tarnished silver bands. It was an unused storage chamber, if Aquatania's mental map of the palace was correct. The younger advisor produced a key from within his robes, its teeth gleaming with an odd greenish tint that didn't match any metal Aquatania recognized. The lock turned with a dull click, and the two slipped inside, pulling the door closed behind them.

Aquatania counted exactly thirty seconds before approaching, each footfall precisely placed to avoid the creaking boards her analytical mind had noted and mapped during their passage. She pressed her ear to the door, but the ancient wood was too thick for even her enhanced hearing to penetrate clearly. Only murmurs reached her, the words indistinct.

Her gaze fell to the keyhole, an ornate opening carved in the shape of a spiral shell, large enough to offer a limited view of the chamber beyond. Her royal mind noted the inappropriate curiosity of such an action even as she lowered herself to peer through the opening. *Data collection requires observation,* she reasoned, silencing her royal etiquette training.

The chamber beyond had once been grand. Remnants of coral pillars rose from the floor, their once-vibrant colors faded to ghostly pastels. A table of weather-worn driftwood stood at the center, illuminated by a single light crystal that cast harsh shadows across the advisors' faces as they bent over what appeared to be a map.

"The contagion spreads faster than anticipated," the younger advisor said, his voice different now, deeper, with a hissing quality that raised the fine hairs on Aquatania's arms. "The humans will be eliminated within weeks."

"The timing is fortuitous," the elder responded, his own voice similarly altered, resonating with harmonics impossible for a human vocal tract. "Their defenses are focused outward, never suspecting the threat lies within their precious council chambers and throne rooms."

"The reptilians remain resistant, but they are few," continued the younger one, rolling up the map with jerking movements that seemed too fluid, too continuous for human joints. "Soon this world will be ours."

Aquatania controlled her breathing, her scientific mind calculating possibilities even as dread pooled in her stomach. Then the younger advisor turned toward a shelf of ancient scrolls, and the light struck his face at a new angle. The change began at his eyes, the pupils expanding until no white remained, then shifting from circular to vertical slits. His skin rippled like water disturbed by a stone, the texture changing from smooth human epidermis to something resembling fine scales, but not like any reptile native to their world.

The elder's transformation followed, more subtle but equally disturbing. His fingers elongated, the joints bending in impossible directions as the digits stretched to nearly twice their human length. When he spoke again, his lips didn't move in synchronization with the words, as if the sound came from somewhere else within his body.

"The king suspects nothing. His precious daughter's scientific mind sees the disease as an external threat, not an internal colonization."

Aquatania fought to keep her breathing silent, her training automatically cataloging details…the unnatural flexibility of their movements, the altered vocal patterns, the physiological changes that defied known biology. Not shapeshifters as she knew them, not sea dragons or any other species recorded in royal archives. These were something else entirely. Something not of their world.

"The samples she collected will lead nowhere," the younger one said, a sound like clicking beetle wings underlying his words. "By the time she realizes the contagion is merely phase one, the spores will have matured within the infected. Then the true transformation begins."

Their skin now glowed with a faint bioluminescence, pulsing in patterns that reminded Aquatania of deep-sea creatures, but wrong somehow, the rhythm too mathematical, too precise. She'd witnessed enough. Any more data would come at the risk of detection.

With the same careful movements that had brought her there, Aquatania began to back away from the door, her mind racing faster than her pulse. The pieces assembled in her thoughts like complex molecules forming a new compound — the contagion targeting only humans, the advisors' strange transformations, their talk of *colonization* rather than conquest. This wasn't just an attack…it was an infiltration. An invasion from beings capable of mimicking human form while harboring capabilities far beyond terrestrial biology.

37

The scientific hypothesis she'd followed to this door had yielded results far more terrifying than she had anticipated. But data, no matter how alarming, was still data. And data could be analyzed, understood, and used to formulate a response.

Aquatania retreated from the keyhole, her movements liquid and silent despite the tremor that threatened to emerge from her core. Scientific observation had prepared her for many discoveries, but never this...entities that wore human skin like borrowed clothing while plotting extinction. She flattened herself against the wall adjacent to the door, calculating the safest retreat path. The narrow corridor offered few hiding places should the door suddenly open. Time was critical. She needed distance between herself and these creatures before they sensed her presence or, worse, detected the faint sea dragon essence that permeated her hybrid blood.

She moved with deliberate precision, placing each bare foot exactly where the aged floorboards seemed least likely to creak. Her mind worked on dual tracks, one mapping her escape route through the palace's forgotten corridors, the other processing the horrifying implications of what she'd witnessed.

The contagion wasn't merely a weapon; it was a vector for something worse. The aliens had mentioned spores maturing within the infected, a *true transformation* to follow the disease. A colonization strategy requiring the elimination of the current dominant species.

The amber light from the sparsely placed crystals cast her shadow before her as she moved, a distorted silhouette that seemed to dance along the ancient stone walls. Each intersection required a pause...a moment to listen for approaching footsteps, to scent the air for unfamiliar presences. Silently, she cataloged every sensory input even as her royal training maintained her outward composure.

The sound came without warning, the rhythmic tap of boots against stone, approaching from an adjoining corridor. *Palace guard*, her mind instantly categorized based on the cadence and weight of the footfalls. Not one of them. The aliens moved differently, with that unsettling fluidity. But a guard would question why the princess was wandering barefoot in the oldest section of the palace, far from both the royal chambers and her royal laboratory.

Aquatania's gaze darted to a recessed alcove three steps ahead, once housing a statue, now empty save for shadows and ancient dust. Three seconds until the guard reached the intersection. Two strides to the alcove. She moved, swift and silent, pressing herself into the darkness just as the guard's shadow stretched around the corner.

She held perfectly still, controlling her breathing with the same precision she used when handling volatile compounds that might react to the slightest atmospheric change. The guard paused at the intersection, his lantern held high, its light stopping just short of her hiding place. She could see him clearly. Young, vigilant, his uniform bearing the insignia of the royal house. Human, her heightened senses confirmed. Not one of them.

For a moment, she considered revealing herself, enlisting his help. But caution overrode impulse. How deep did the infiltration go? How many others among the palace staff had been replaced? Without knowing who to trust, approaching anyone might alert the aliens to her discovery. The guard continued his patrol, passing her hiding place with no indication he'd sensed her presence.

Aquatania counted to thirty after his footsteps faded before emerging from the alcove. She moved with renewed purpose now, taking a circuitous route that avoided the main corridors where she might be observed. The older sections of the palace connected in ways forgotten by most...servants' passages, emergency evacuation routes, hidden staircases that her explorer's mind had mapped during childhood adventures.

She reached her private quarters without further encounters, pressing her palm against the door's recognition plate. The lock disengaged with a soft click, recognizing her unique biorhythm, a security measure that suddenly seemed inadequate. If these beings could mimic human form so precisely, what other biological signatures might they replicate?

Her chambers welcomed her with familiar comfort...the outer sitting room with its panoramic windows overlooking the eastern sky, shelves lined with rare books on both science and ancient sea dragon lore. The adjacent laboratory, smaller than her main research facility but equipped for preliminary work, gleamed with meticulously arranged equipment. Her sleeping chamber remained closed, the carved coral door inlaid with protective spells woven by her grandmother.

Aquatania locked the main door and activated the privacy wards with a gesture. Only then did she allow her composure to fracture. She pressed her back against the wall, sliding down until she sat on the cool floor, her satchel still clutched against her chest like a shield.

"Invasion," she whispered, the word hanging in the air like poison.

Her pulse quickened as the implications cascaded through her mind. The anger rose simultaneously...hot and primal, the dragon part of her nature responding to the threat. A shimmer of iridescent blue scales rippled across the backs of her hands, her emotions triggering an involuntary partial transformation. She stared at her changing skin, watching as delicate scales emerged and caught the light in flashes of azure and teal.

With deliberate effort, she closed her eyes and regulated her breathing, forcing the transformation to recede. She needed her human mind clear now, needed the scientific precision that had led her to discover the reptilian immunity to the contagion. The scales faded back beneath her skin, leaving no trace of their emergence.

Aquatania rose and moved to her private workstation, retrieving a secure crystal slate from a locked drawer. This device was isolated from the palace's main communication network, a precaution she'd taken for sensitive experiments, now serving a far more crucial purpose. She began making rapid notes, her fingers flying across the interface as she documented everything she'd observed.

The pattern clarified as she worked, connecting the disease's specificity to humans with the aliens' infiltration strategy. They'd placed their agents in positions of power across multiple kingdoms, engineered a contagion that would eliminate human populations while leaving reptilian species intact, and now waited for the *true transformation* to begin in those already infected.

But why spare reptilians? Was it inability to affect reptilian biology, or something more strategic? Her own hybrid nature had shown remarkable resistance to the contagion. Perhaps the key to creating an effective treatment lay not just in her preliminary findings in Aethoria, but also in understanding why these invaders had designed their weapon with this specific limitation.

She paced the length of her chambers, bare feet silent on the polished stone floor. The scope of the threat expanded with each logical progression. Not just Aethoria, not just the sky islands and coastal cities, all human civilizations stood at risk. And the infiltration had reached the highest levels of governance, compromising the very infrastructure that should be mounting a defense.

"I can't trust the established channels," she murmured, thinking aloud as she often did when working through complex problems. "Not the Royal Council, not the kingdom's military, not even palace security."

She needed allies, individuals whose humanity she could

verify, whose skills would complement her own. Her mind ran through possibilities. Master Healer Lyra from the Eastern Academy, whose expertise in magical pathology was unparalleled. Admiral Thane of the Sky Fleet, whose strategic mind was matched only by his unwavering loyalty to her father. Professor Carus from the Crystal University, whose understanding of extraterrestrial phenomena had been dismissed as theoretical until now.

Aquatania returned to her workstation, formulating a plan with the same methodical precision she applied to her experiments. She would need to leave the palace undetected, establish secure communication with potential allies, and continue developing the treatment for the contagion while working to expose the infiltration.

"This is no longer just a medical crisis…it's an invasion," she whispered. Her dual nature had never been more valuable…the scientific mind to develop a cure, the sea dragon's resilience to survive what was coming, and the royal determination to protect both her kingdoms.

She began gathering essential supplies, her movements precise and purposeful. The contagion had been explicitly engineered against humans by beings who'd studied their defenses and exploited their vulnerabilities. But they'd made one critical miscalculation. They'd failed to account for Aquatania…neither fully human nor fully sea dragon, but uniquely equipped to stand against them.

Night would provide cover for her departure, darkness becoming her ally as she moved to counter the threat none but she yet understood. The aliens believed their plan was proceeding undetected.

They were wrong.

Chapter Four

Aquatania arranged the crystal slides in perfect order, each labeled with meticulous script that detailed the progression of infection. Her private laboratory in the eastern wing of the palace gleamed, silver instruments catching the light from enchanted orbs that hovered near the ceiling, ancient scrolls unfurled beside state-of-the-art microscopes, containment vials etched with protective runes lining shelves of polished wood. She checked the time on the mechanical chronometer, its gears whispering behind etched glass. General Kieran would arrive in precisely seven minutes, assuming military punctuality. She had seven minutes to decide exactly how much to reveal and how quickly.

The general had been her fifth choice, not her first. However, the four individuals she trusted the most were all currently unavailable—three were stationed off-island, and one was hospitalized with a broken leg. Kieran was here, and more importantly, he had access to the military's secure communication channels, specialized equipment, and personnel. He had also been away on a northern expedition when the first advisors had arrived at court. He couldn't have been replaced. Not yet.

She activated the projection sphere at the center of her workstation, watching as it hummed to life with a pale blue glow. The enchanted crystal responded to her touch, displaying magnified images of blood samples, human cells under attack from the engineered pathogen, the alien influence visible as unnatural geometric patterns forming within the cellular membranes. She adjusted the resolution, ensuring the evidence would be undeniable even to a skeptical military mind.

Three sharp knocks on her laboratory door announced his arrival, exactly on time.

"Enter," she called, straightening her posture into the royal bearing expected of her public role.

General Kieran stepped through the doorway, his movements precise as machinery. He was exactly as she remembered from council meetings, tall and broad-shouldered with the coiled tension of a predator at rest. His dark hair fell just above regulation length, contrasting with fair, slightly tanned skin that suggested northern ancestry. His eyes, the color of sparkling amber, swept the laboratory in a practiced security assessment before settling on her, causing a strange tingling of her skin. She shrugged it off. She'd seen Kieran often, but it wasn't until now that she noticed his perfect features...and those eyes...

"Your Highness," he said, bowing with perfect formality. "You requested my presence with some urgency."

Aquatania studied him carefully, looking for any sign of the unnatural movement she'd observed in the false advisors. His joints bent normally, his breathing followed human patterns, and his eyes retained their whites and round pupils. No bioluminescent pulse disrupted his skin tone. He appeared completely human, but she needed to be certain.

"General Kieran," she responded, reaching for a small crystal vial on her workbench. "Before we begin, would you place a drop of your blood on this slide? A security measure, given the circumstances."

His eyebrows lifted slightly, but military discipline kept any further surprise from his expression. "Of course, Your Highness, though I confess I don't understand the necessity. I show no signs of illness."

She handed him a silver extraction needle. "You will shortly understand why."

He pricked his finger without hesitation, allowing a single drop of blood to fall onto the crystal slide she held beneath it.

Aquatania placed it immediately under her microscope, adjusting the focus with practiced ease. The cells displayed normal human and dragon morphology, with none of the geometric patterns present in infected samples. More importantly, they showed no trace of the alien cellular markers she'd begun to identify in her research.

"Satisfied?" he asked, a hint of dryness in his tone.

"For now." She gestured to the stool across from her workstation. "Please, sit. What I'm about to share must not leave this room."

He remained standing, his posture rigid. "I prefer to remain on my feet, if it's all the same to you."

Aquatania nodded, unsurprised. "The Red Death is not a natural contagion," she began, activating the projection sphere. It expanded its display, filling the space between them with three-dimensional images of blood samples. "It's an engineered weapon designed specifically to target humans while sparing reptilian species."

The general's expression remained neutral, though his jaw tightened almost imperceptibly. "We've suspected biological warfare. Our intelligence suggests involvement from the Southern Confederacy. They've been developing prohibited alchemical agents for years."

"It's not the Southern Confederacy," Aquatania said, manipulating the projection to show cellular degradation in real-time. "It's not from our world at all."

She explained what she'd witnessed in the abandoned storage chamber...the advisors' unnatural transformations, their revealing conversation, the mention of spores maturing within infected humans. As she spoke, she displayed evidence gathered from her research, the mathematical precision of the disease progression, the strange script-like patterns in the rash, and the resistance of reptilian blood to infection.

Kieran crossed his arms over his chest, his eyes narrowed

as he studied the projections. "With respect, Your Highness, that's quite a leap. Alien infiltrators? It sounds like something from a sensationalist pamphlet."

"I understand your skepticism," she replied, maintaining her composure despite the frustration building in her chest. "But the evidence supports no other conclusion. Look here." She manipulated the projection to highlight a cellular membrane under attack. "These geometric formations aren't random mutations. They're designed, General. Programmed to rewrite human cellular structure while leaving reptilian biology untouched."

"Even if I accept your analysis of the disease itself, the jump to extraterrestrial infiltrators requires significant imagination."

"I saw them transform," she insisted, her voice hardening. "These beings can pass as human until they choose not to. They're already within our government, within every major government. And they're using the Red Death as the first phase of a colonization strategy."

Kieran paced a short line, his military boots making soft sounds against the stone floor. "Let's say, hypothetically, I accept this premise. What's your proposed response? Accuse court officials of being alien impostors? Start a panic?"

"We develop a treatment first," Aquatania said, shifting the projection to show her experimental results. "My research in Aethoria demonstrated that reptilian blood components can neutralize the pathogen. More specifically, dragon blood shows remarkable effectiveness."

She displayed side-by-side comparisons, infected human cells deteriorating rapidly, while identical samples treated with dragon blood components showed the infection halting, and then reversing.

"I've begun synthesizing a treatment, but I need more dragon blood samples. Different types in significant quantities." She met his eyes directly. "That's where you come in and why I chose you to assist me. You have a scientific background, and as commander of the royal military, you have access to the dragon pens and the authority to requisition what I need without arousing suspicion."

Kieran studied the projection, his expression shifting subtly as the evidence accumulated. She could sense his military mind calculating, weighing probabilities, assessing threats, and considering contingencies.

"Assuming all this is true, we're facing an unprecedented threat with unknown capabilities, already embedded within our power structures." He turned to face her fully. "Why trust me with this information? What makes you certain I'm not one of them?"

"Three reasons," Aquatania replied. "First, your blood sample shows no signs of alien cellular structure. Second, you were off-island during the initial infiltration period. And third" — she hesitated — "dragon sense. It's subtle, but those with sea dragon heritage can detect certain...inconsistencies in the aliens' presence."

The admission of using her draconic senses seemed to surprise him more than the talk of alien invasion. His posture shifted, almost imperceptibly loosening.

"I can provide the access you need," he said finally. "But I want to see more evidence. Direct observation of these cellular interactions, not just projections."

Aquatania gestured to her microscope. "Then let's begin now. I'll show you exactly how dragon cells repel the infection."

She prepared a fresh slide, mixing a drop of infected human blood with a sample of her own. Under the microscope, the reaction was immediate and visible. The infected cells recoiled from contact with her dragon-influenced blood, the alien patterns disrupting and dissolving where the samples merged.

"See for yourself," she said, stepping aside.

Kieran bent to look through the eyepiece, his shoulder nearly brushing hers as he adjusted the focus. She watched his expression change as he observed the real-time evidence of her theory, the subtle relaxation of his brow, the slight parting of his lips as scientific reality overrode ingrained skepticism.

"This is..." He straightened, meeting her eyes with new intensity. "This changes everything."

"Will you help me?" she asked simply.

He nodded once, a decisive military gesture. "I'll arrange access to the dragon pens. Tonight."

*

The royal dragon pens lay deep within Zephyria's core, a vast network of caverns naturally formed when the island first rose from the sea centuries ago. Aquatania felt the temperature rise as she and Kieran descended the wide spiral staircase, the cool palace air giving way to the warm, slightly sulfurous atmosphere that dragons preferred. Torches lined the stone walls at carefully measured intervals, their flames protected by crystal housings designed to prevent accidental ignition of fire dragon breath. The distant sounds of massive bodies shifting against stone, occasional hisses, and the distinctive rustle of scales created an ambient chorus that grew louder with each step they took.

"How many dragons are kept here?" Kieran asked, his voice deliberately low as they reached the bottom of the staircase.

"Twenty-three at present," Aquatania replied. "Most are diplomatic residents, dragons belonging to visiting dignitaries or ambassadors from the reptilian territories. A few are part of Zephyria's defense force, and three are from my father's personal bloodline."

They approached a checkpoint where two guards stood at

attention, their armor reinforced with heat-resistant scales harvested from molted dragon skin. Kieran presented his military insignia, and the guards saluted crisply.

"General Kieran and Her Royal Highness Princess Aquatania," Kieran stated formally. "We are here on classified research business with full authorization from the throne."

The guards exchanged surprised glances. The princess was a known visitor to the pens, but rarely in the company of military personnel.

"Of course, General. Your Highness," the senior guard said, pressing his palm to a crystal panel that caused the massive stone doors behind him to swing inward with a grinding rumble.

The cavern beyond took Kieran's breath away. Aquatania could see it in the momentary widening of his eyes before military discipline reasserted control over his expression. Even for her, who'd visited countless times, the sight remained impressive. The space stretched nearly half a mile in each direction, its ceiling lost in shadows despite the countless light crystals embedded in the walls. Stone walkways crisscrossed the cavern, connecting specialized habitat areas designed for different dragon species. Some sections glowed with heat for fire dragons, others contained pools of seawater for aquatic varieties, and still others featured open-air sections where sky dragons could stretch their wings.

"We'll start with the sea dragons," Aquatania said, leading the way along the main walkway. "Their blood has shown the strongest neutralizing effect on the pathogen, likely due to their natural healing properties."

She approached a large section where artificial tide pools had been created, filled with enchanted seawater that maintained perfect salinity despite the altitude. A sea dragon lounged half-submerged, its massive body stretching nearly forty feet from snout to tail-tip. Iridescent blue scales shimmered in the torchlight, creating rippling patterns of azure and teal that seemed to flow like water across its form.

"This is Sapphira," Aquatania said softly. "She belongs to the Oceanic Ambassador. I've worked with her before."

Aquatania approached the edge of the pool, her movements deliberate and unhurried. She removed a small shell from her pocket and blew into it, producing a three-note melody that caught the dragon's attention. Sapphira's massive head lifted from the water, intelligent eyes focusing on the princess with obvious recognition.

"She remembers you," Kieran observed, staying several paces back.

"Sea dragons never forget a scent," Aquatania confirmed. She extended her hand, palm downward, and waited as the massive creature moved closer, its nostrils flaring as it took in her unique half-dragon essence.

Sapphira dipped her head in what appeared to be a gesture of respect, then moved to the edge of the pool where Aquatania stood. The princess placed her hand gently on the dragon's snout, establishing contact and trust. From her satchel, she withdrew a silver extraction needle, specially designed for dragon hide, its tip enhanced with both enchantment and technology to penetrate between scales without causing pain.

"I'll need to access the soft spot behind her left foreleg," Aquatania explained. "That's where the scales are thinnest and the blood vessels closest to the surface."

She began to move alongside the dragon's body, maintaining contact to keep Sapphira calm. Unexpectedly, the sea dragon shifted, a ripple of muscle moving beneath the gleaming scales as she twisted her massive neck to look at Kieran. A low rumble emerged from her throat, not quite threatening, but certainly wary.

Before Aquatania could react, Kieran stepped swiftly

between her and the dragon, his hand moving instinctively to the sword at his hip. The motion was purely protective, his body creating a barrier between the princess and potential danger.

"No...don't!" Aquatania caught his arm. "Quick movements trigger defensive responses. She's just curious about you."

Kieran froze at her touch but didn't relax his defensive posture. "She was showing aggression."

"Not aggression. Assessment." Aquatania kept her voice calm, though she was acutely aware of her hand still on his forearm, feeling the tension in his muscles. A strange flutter moved through her chest, unexpected and distinctly unscientific, at his instinctive move to protect her. She withdrew her hand quickly, attributing the reaction to the heightened circumstances.

"Sea dragons evaluate new presences," she explained, stepping around him. "They're extremely territorial about their handlers. Stand still and let her scent you."

Kieran remained motionless as Sapphira extended her neck, bringing her snout within inches of him. Her nostrils flared, taking in his scent with deep inhalations. After a moment, she made a soft clicking sound and returned her attention to Aquatania.

"You've been accepted," the princess said with a small smile. "Now, observe carefully. This technique works for all dragon species, though the precise location varies."

She moved to Sapphira's side and gently pressed her fingers along the junction where the dragon's foreleg met her body. The scales there were smaller, more flexible, with tiny gaps between them. Aquatania located a specific spot and inserted the silver needle with precise pressure, firm enough to penetrate between scales but gentle enough to avoid discomfort.

"The key is finding the natural seam," she explained as

dark blue blood flowed into the attached vial. "Push too hard or at the wrong angle, and you'll meet resistance. Dragons have remarkable pain tolerance, but they never forget being hurt. A perfect extraction leaves no pain memory."

Kieran watched with intense focus, his gaze tracking every movement of her hands. "How much do you need from each dragon?"

"Fifty milliliters is ideal. Enough to analyze the specific properties of each subspecies without taxing the donor." She withdrew the needle once the vial was filled, then pressed a small patch of healing algae to the extraction site. "The algae seals the puncture and prevents infection, though dragons rarely suffer from such things."

Their next subject was a fire dragon, its ruby-red scales radiating heat that made the air around it shimmer. Unlike the relatively docile sea dragon, this creature watched them approach with unmistakable wariness, smoke curling from its nostrils in warning puffs.

"Pyronis has a reputation," Aquatania warned. "He's part of our defense force, trained for combat. His handler was injured last month, so he's particularly suspicious of humans at the moment."

Kieran studied the creature with a professional assessment. "What's your approach with him?"

"Direct and respectful. Fire dragons respond to confidence and clear intent." She handed Kieran a pair of heat-resistant gloves. "You'll hold this cooling rod against his neck ridge while I extract the sample. It creates a pleasant sensation that distracts from the needle."

Together they approached the fire dragon's enclosure, a depression in the cavern floor lined with obsidian and filled with smoldering coals. Aquatania announced their presence with a formal draconic greeting, the words harsh and guttural in her throat. Pyronis responded with a blast of hot air that ruffled their clothing but stopped short of actual flame, a warning rather than an attack.

Working in tandem, they managed the extraction with minimal difficulty. Kieran applied the cooling rod exactly as instructed, his movements careful but confident. The fire dragon's blood glowed with internal heat as it filled the specialized containment vial, designed to maintain the sample's natural temperature.

Their final subject presented the greatest challenge, a sky dragon with feathered wings in shades of silver and white, its slender body more avian than reptilian in appearance. This creature perched nervously on a high stone outcropping, wings half-extended in preparation for flight.

"Stratus is young," Aquatania explained. "Barely mature, and not yet accustomed to handling. Her blood will give us insight into how age affects the neutralizing properties."

"How do we approach without triggering flight?" Kieran asked, already analyzing the problem.

"From above," Aquatania said, pointing to a narrow walkway that extended over the sky dragon's perch. "Sky dragons feel threatened when approached from below. It mimics predator behavior. From above, we're perceived as potentially dominant, but not necessarily dangerous."

They ascended to the upper walkway, moving in perfect synchronization now, their earlier tension replaced by professional focus. When Stratus shifted nervously, Kieran responded without prompting, using a technique he'd observed Aquatania employ with the sea dragon, a soft, consistent tone combined with slow, predictable movements.

The extraction required perfect coordination. Aquatania secured the delicate junction where wing met shoulder while Kieran distracted the dragon with a reflective crystal that cast fascinating light patterns across the stone. Aquatania worked swiftly, collecting the sample of silvery blood before the creature could grow too restless.

"Impressive adaptation, General," she said as they

descended from the walkway, the final sample secured in her satchel. "You learn quickly."

"Basic military principle," he replied, though she detected a hint of satisfaction in his tone. "Observe, adapt, execute. Though I admit, dragons require more finesse than most military operations."

As they made their way back toward the entrance, Kieran cast a final glance over the magnificent cavern with its diverse dragon inhabitants. His expression had softened from his earlier skepticism, replaced by something approaching respect. "You handle them as if you were born to it," he observed. "Not just your sea dragon heritage, but an understanding that goes beyond instinct."

"Science and instinct aren't as separate as people believe," she replied. "Both require careful observation and respect for the subject." She secured the satchel containing their precious samples. "Ready to see what these can do against our alien pathogen?"

He nodded, opening the massive door for her with newfound deference. "Lead the way, Your Highness."

*

The dragon blood samples glowed with subtle energy, each vial exhibiting distinct properties. The sea dragon's blood was a deep sapphire that seemed to pulse with tidal rhythms. The fire dragon's was a brilliant ruby that radiated warmth even through the specialized glass. And the sky dragon's was a mercurial silver that caught and refracted light like morning dew on spider silk.

Aquatania arranged them in precise formation on her workstation, her movements efficient as she prepared slides, reagents, and testing apparatus. Kieran stood at her side, his earlier skepticism visually giving way to focused attention as she explained each step of the process they were about to undertake.

"The principle is straightforward," she said, selecting a crystal pipette designed for handling reactive substances. "We introduce measured amounts of dragon blood to infected human samples, then observe the cellular interaction through both scientific and magical monitoring."

"You believe different dragon species will produce different results?" Kieran asked, watching as she labeled a series of crystal testing plates with meticulous precision.

"Almost certainly. Sea dragons possess natural healing properties tied to water memory. Fire dragons carry purification elements in their blood that neutralize most known toxins. Sky dragons have exceptionally adaptive immune responses." She looked up from her work, momentarily distracted by his proximity. "Could you stabilize that centrifuge while I prepare the base solution?"

Kieran moved to the apparatus she indicated, his hands surprisingly deft as he adjusted its settings. "Like this?"

"Perfect." She nodded, impressed by his quick adaptation to laboratory work. His military training evidently extended to following technical instructions with precision. "Now activate the stabilization field with that switch there. It prevents magical contamination during processing."

They fell into a rhythm as natural as breathing. Aquatania directing, Kieran responding, each movement becoming more fluid as they established a wordless communication. She prepared slides while he maintained the delicate temperature balance required for the samples. She mixed reagents while he recorded initial readings from the monitoring crystals. The tension that had characterized their earlier interactions gradually dissolved, replaced by the focused harmony of two professionals united by common purpose.

"The infected blood needs to be precisely measured," Aquatania explained, transferring dark crimson liquid to a series of testing chambers. "Too much, and it might overwhelm the dragon blood compounds before we can observe the interaction. Too little, and we won't get accurate results on efficacy."

She bent over her microscope, adjusting the focal crystals to achieve perfect resolution. Kieran moved behind her to retrieve a stabilization rod, and suddenly she became acutely aware of his presence...the warmth radiating from his body, the subtle scent of leather and something uniquely his own, like pine trees after rain. Her fingers hesitated momentarily on the adjustment dial, her scientific concentration fracturing as some other, more primal awareness asserted itself.

"Is something wrong?" he asked, noticing her hesitation.

"No," she replied, perhaps too quickly. "Just ensuring precise calibration." She straightened, putting necessary distance between them, puzzled by her own reaction. She'd worked alongside colleagues countless times without such distractions. Perhaps it was merely the stress of their circumstances, the heightened awareness that came with danger.

Aquatania refocused on their work, transferring the first dragon blood sample, the sea dragon's sapphire essence, to a crystal plate containing infected human cells. She placed the plate on the observation platform, activating the crystal display panel that would project a magnified image of the cellular interaction.

"Observe closely," she instructed, adjusting the final settings. "The reaction should begin almost immediately."

The display came to life, showing infected human blood cells in distressing detail. The alien influence was clearly visible...geometric patterns forming within and between cells, distorting their natural shape and function. As they watched, she introduced the sea dragon blood to the sample.

The effect was immediate and dramatic. The infected cells seemed to recoil from the dragon blood, the alien patterns within them disrupting upon contact. Where the two substances merged completely, the infection appeared to reverse, cellular structures returning to normal configurations, the geometric patterns dissolving like salt in water.

"Look!" Aquatania exclaimed, grabbing Kieran's arm in spontaneous excitement. "The neutralizing effect is even stronger with pure dragon blood than with my hybrid samples!"

Their eyes met in a moment of shared triumph, both registering the significance of what they were witnessing. Aquatania became suddenly conscious of her hand on his arm, feeling the solid muscle beneath the fabric of his uniform. She withdrew her touch quickly, but something had changed in that brief connection…a current passing between them that had nothing to do with science or aliens or the fate of their world.

She cleared her throat, directing their attention back to the display. "Let's try the fire dragon sample next. It should demonstrate different neutralizing mechanisms."

The ruby blood produced a distinctly different reaction. Rather than repelling the infection, it seemed to burn through it, leaving healthy cells untouched while destroying the alien influence in a process that resembled controlled combustion at the cellular level.

"Fascinating," Kieran murmured, leaning closer to the display. "It's targeting the infection specifically, not just blocking it."

"Yes," Aquatania confirmed, pleased by his accurate observation. "Each dragon species appears to counter the pathogen through different mechanisms. This gives us multiple pathways for treatment development."

The sky dragon blood presented yet another variation, forming protective barriers around healthy cells that prevented the infection from spreading further. While it didn't reverse existing damage like the sea dragon blood, it created what appeared to be perfect immunity for uninfected cells.

"These results confirm my theory," Aquatania said, making rapid notes on her crystal slate. "Dragon blood contains compounds that directly counter the alien pathogen. With proper refinement, we could develop a treatment that combines the best properties of each type."

Kieran's expression had transformed completely from his earlier skepticism. He studied the display with intense focus, his military mind clearly processing the strategic implications of their discovery.

"What's our next step?" he asked, the word *our* marking a subtle but significant shift in his perspective. No longer was this her theory that he was humoring; it had become their shared mission.

"We need to test combinatorial effects," she replied, already preparing new slides. "See if mixing different dragon blood types enhances or diminishes efficacy. Then we'll need to determine minimum effective dosages, stability factors, and delivery methods."

"And time is critical," Kieran added, his expression grave. "If what you overheard is correct, we don't know how long before the spores mature in those already infected."

Aquatania nodded, the weight of their task settling back onto her shoulders after the brief elation of scientific discovery. "We'll need more samples. Different dragons, if possible, to ensure we're not seeing individual variations rather than species-specific properties."

"I can help with that," Kieran said. "There's a unit of dragon warriors under my command, humans with trace dragon ancestry who've developed certain compatible traits. Not full transformation abilities like yours, but enough dragon essence in their blood to potentially be useful. They're stationed at the eastern garrison, outside the palace's political influence. Men and women I trust completely."

The offer surprised her. Dragon warriors were an elite military unit, rarely involved in scientific research. More significantly, Kieran was offering resources under his direct command, a clear indication of his commitment to their cause.

"That would be invaluable," she said. "Especially if their dragon ancestries are varied. Different bloodlines might show different effectiveness against the pathogen."

"I'll send for them immediately," he said, moving toward the door with renewed purpose. "I'll summon four of my most trusted officers. They can be here by dawn, bringing additional blood samples from the military dragon pens as well."

"Kieran," she called as he reached the door. He turned, his pale eyes questioning. "Thank you. For believing me."

His expression softened almost imperceptibly. "The evidence is compelling, Your Highness. And in my experience, ignoring uncomfortable truths doesn't make them less true." He gave a precise military bow. "I'll return with my officers as soon as possible."

Aquatania watched him leave, her scientific objectivity momentarily compromised by a complex emotion she wasn't ready to analyze. She turned back to the test samples, forcing her focus to the work at hand. There would be time later to examine the curious effect General Kieran had on her carefully ordered thoughts. For now, the fate of their kingdoms depended on the solutions they could derive from these glowing vials of dragon blood.

Now, at least, she had the beginning of a solution, and an ally she was increasingly certain she could trust.

CHAPTER FIVE

Dawn filtered through the crystal windows of Aquatania's private laboratory, casting prismatic patterns across workstations etched with protective runes. She arranged the vials of dragon blood in a semicircle before her, sea dragon sapphire, fire dragon ruby, sky dragon silver, each glowing with its own internal light. The samples from Kieran's dragon warriors had arrived as promised, the additional vials now nestled alongside her original collection, expanding their research possibilities exponentially. Aquatania felt a flutter of scientific excitement as she prepared her enhanced microscope, its base carved from a single piece of focusing crystal, the viewing apparatus ringed with magical sigils that would amplify both visual and magical perception.

Kieran stood at her shoulder, close enough that she could detect the faint scent of leather and steel that clung to him. "And your blood?" he asked, watching as she prepared a crystal slide with meticulous precision.

"Half human, half sea dragon," she replied, pricking her finger with a silver needle. A drop of blood, darker than human, lighter than pure dragon, welled on her fingertip. "My dual nature provides unique insight into both vulnerabilities and immunities."

"As we witnessed last night, the contagion doesn't destroy cells," Aquatania said, her voice taking on the measured cadence she used when presenting scientific findings. "It reprograms them. Look at the mathematical precision of those patterns. They're not random mutations. They're code."

Kieran leaned closer to the projection, his brow furrowed in concentration. "Like military signals. Coordinated attack patterns."

"Exactly." She felt a brief surge of appreciation for his quick understanding.

"So we're vulnerable as humans, but immune as dragons," he concluded, his voice revealing newfound respect for her scientific approach. "That explains why reptilian species haven't been affected."

"And why my hybrid nature provides partial resistance," she added, trying to refocus on the science rather than her unexpected awareness of him. "It's not complete immunity. The human aspects of my biology can still be affected. But the dragon elements slow progression significantly."

Kieran straightened, his tactician's mind visibly processing implications. "Can you isolate the protective factor? The specific element in dragon blood that repels the pathogen?"

"That's exactly what I've been working toward." Aquatania manipulated the projection to highlight cellular structures within dragon blood that appeared to generate the protective effect. "Each dragon type uses different mechanisms, but they all produce similar results. If I can identify the common protective factor and synthesize it..."

"You could create a treatment for humans," Kieran finished, the excitement in his voice matching her own.

"More than that," she said, switching rapidly between samples to illustrate her point. "By combining elements from different dragon species, I might create a compound that not only prevents infection but reverses damage in those already affected."

Kieran studied the simulation with intense focus. "How soon could you produce a viable treatment?"

"With these additional samples from your warriors, I can begin synthesis immediately." She gestured to the new vials he'd brought to her at dawn. "Having diverse dragon lineages represented gives me a broader spectrum of protective factors to work with."

She began preparing extraction chambers, silver

instruments gleaming in the laboratory's enchanted light. Each chamber would isolate specific components from dragon blood samples, separating magical essence from physical properties, defensive factors from regenerative elements.

"The process requires precision," she said, calibrating a crystal separation array with delicate adjustments. "Rush it, and we risk losing potency. Take too long..."

"And more people die," Kieran finished grimly. "How can I assist?"

The offer surprised her. Generals didn't typically volunteer for laboratory work. She glanced at him, reassessing. His hands, though trained for weapons, possessed a steadiness that might serve well for scientific tasks.

"Monitor these stability readings," she decided, indicating a crystal panel inscribed with fluctuating runes. "Alert me if any pattern shifts from blue to amber. That would indicate degradation in the sample integrity."

He took a position at the panel without hesitation, adapting to this new battlefield with the same focus he would bring to military strategy. Aquatania returned to her extraction preparations, her mind racing with formulations and calculations.

Between them, the projection sphere continued displaying its simulation, dragon blood components gradually overwhelming and neutralizing the alien contagion, restoring health to infected cells. It was just a simulation, a theoretical model of what might be possible. But as dawn strengthened into morning beyond the crystal windows, it offered something that had been in desperately short supply...hope.

*

The crystal sensors along the laboratory walls flashed from serene blue to angry crimson without warning. Aquatania's head snapped up from the microscope as protective wards flared to life around the perimeter of the room, their silver light pulsing with increasing urgency. The containment field surrounding their precious samples flickered, its magical barrier destabilizing as something powerful pressed against the outer defenses of her sanctuary. She felt it before she could name it…a wrongness seeping through the palace walls, alien and cold and calculating.

"Someone's breached the outer wards," she said, already moving toward the wall of preservation cabinets. The magical locks responded to her touch, mechanisms clicking open as she gathered the most critical vials of synthesized treatment. Each crystalline container held the potential salvation for thousands, irreplaceable hours of work distilled into glowing liquid.

Kieran abandoned the monitoring station, his body language transforming instantly from that of a scientific assistant to a military commander. His hand moved to his belt, drawing a blade that seemed too elegant for its lethal purpose, silver etched with runes that caught the pulsing red warning light from the sensors.

"How many?" he asked, voice clipped as he positioned himself between her and the laboratory door.

"At least three distinct energy signatures," she replied, placing the last vial in a locked cabinet reinforced with protection spells. Her fingers traced activation patterns across its surface, triggering additional safeguards. "They're moving too quickly for regular palace guards."

The magical alarm intensified, crystal sensors vibrating at a frequency that made her teeth ache. Outside the laboratory, she heard the distant sound of something heavy striking stone, followed by the distinctive crack of protective spells failing.

"Stay behind me," Kieran ordered, his stance widening as he readied himself before the door.

She'd barely moved to comply when the laboratory door crashed inward with such force that splinters of enchanted wood scattered across the stone floor. The silver reinforcement bands that had sealed the entrance now hung twisted from a single hinge, their protective runes flickering and dying.

Three figures burst through the shattered doorway. Humanoid in their general outline but wrong in every particular aspect. Their movements were too fluid, their joints bending at impossible angles as they flowed into the room with predatory grace. They wore the uniforms of palace staff, a guard, a court scribe, and what appeared to be one of the kitchen servants, but their disguises were slipping, unable to maintain perfect cohesion under the stress of action.

The false guard's skin rippled across its face like water disturbed by underwater currents, momentarily revealing a glimpse of something beneath, not scales or flesh but a surface that resembled metallic gel, iridescent and constantly shifting. Its eyes, maintaining human appearance in shape and position, had lost their whites entirely, becoming obsidian pools that reflected the laboratory's lights in fractured patterns.

"The research," hissed the one disguised as a scribe, its voice producing harmonics impossible for a human vocal tract. "Destroy it all."

They separated with coordinated efficiency, the false guard moving directly toward Kieran, the kitchen servant heading for the racks of samples on the central workstation, and the scribe making straight for Aquatania's crystal slate containing her research notes.

Kieran moved with unexpected speed, grabbing a high-backed laboratory chair and shoving it into the path of the approaching false guard. "Get to the emergency containment switch!" he shouted to Aquatania, his voice steady despite the chaos erupting around them.

The false guard collided with the chair, its body bending around the obstacle in a way that defied anatomy. Where its sleeve rode up, Aquatania glimpsed an arm transforming, human skin peeling back like a shed garment to reveal a limb composed of segmented, chitinous material that tapered into a serrated edge.

The kitchen servant reached the sample rack, sweeping an arm across the carefully arranged vials. Glass shattered against stone, precious dragon blood samples mixing with infected human tissue, hours and hours of work destroyed in seconds. The sound of breaking crystal barely registered before Kieran launched into action, his movements betraying years of combat training that his courtly demeanor had concealed.

He kicked the approaching scribe squarely in the chest, the impact sending it stumbling backward into a shelf of reagents. Glass containers rained down, shattering and mixing, filling the air with acrid chemical scents and clouds of colored vapor. Without pausing, Kieran pivoted toward the false guard, whose arm had now fully transformed into a weapon, not quite a blade, not quite a tentacle, but something that combined the worst aspects of both.

"The southwest wall," Kieran called to her as he slashed at the approaching appendage. His blade connected, drawing a splash of liquid that steamed where it struck the floor. "Silver panel behind the auxiliary containment field!"

Aquatania processed his instructions instantly, her eyes finding the emergency containment switch across the laboratory. Between her and the switch stood the false kitchen servant, now fully engaged in the systematic destruction of her research materials.

She ducked low beneath a workstation as the scribe recovered and lurched toward her, its movements becoming less human with each passing second. Its fingers had elongated to twice their natural length, joints reversing direction as they reached for her crystal slate. Aquatania snatched the device from its stand, clutching it to her chest as she scrambled toward the far side of the laboratory.

Kieran engaged both the false guard and scribe simultaneously, his combat style economical and precise. He blocked a strike from the guard's weapon arm with his blade, the metals meeting with a sound like crystal chimes. His free hand caught the scribe's elongated fingers, bending them backward until something snapped with a wet, splintering sound. The creature emitted a high-pitched tone that bore no resemblance to a human scream.

"They're after the treatment formula," Aquatania called, diving beneath another workstation as the kitchen servant abandoned the sample destruction to intercept her. She rolled to her feet on the other side, closer to the emergency switch, but still separated from it by a testing station covered in delicate equipment.

The kitchen servant's disguise was failing rapidly now, its form fluctuating between human appearance and something altogether different. Its torso stretched and contracted with each movement, the skull elongating momentarily before snapping back to human proportions. It reached for her with hands that flickered between five fingers and something resembling jointed pincers.

Kieran had maneuvered the false guard into a corner, driving it back with a series of precise strikes. His blade left silver trails in the air as it moved, the enchanted metal reacting to contact with alien physiology. "Whatever you're going to do, do it now!" he shouted, blocking another attack from the scribe with his forearm.

Aquatania vaulted over the testing station, equipment crashing to the floor in her wake. The emergency containment panel loomed ahead, a silver plate embedded in the wall, etched with concentric circles of protective runes. She lunged for it, fingers outstretched, as the kitchen servant's arm elongated impossibly to grab her ankle.

She felt cold, alien fingers close around her leg, the touch sending a chill through her body that had nothing to do with temperature. The creature pulled, its strength inhuman, dragging her backward across the smooth stone floor. Her fingers scrabbled for purchase, finding none on the polished surface.

Across the laboratory, Kieran slammed the false guard into a wall of enchanted crystal. The material flashed with brilliant light upon contact, magical wards activating to immobilize the intruder. The creature froze in mid-motion, its partially transformed body locked in a contortion of limbs and weapon-appendages.

"Hold on!" Kieran called, already pivoting toward her, but the scribe intercepted him, its body flowing like liquid metal to block his path.

The kitchen servant continued pulling Aquatania away from the containment switch, its grip tightening until she felt bones grinding together in her ankle. Pain shot up her leg, but with it came something else...anger, hot and primal, surging through her blood. The dragon part of her nature responded to the threat, scales rippling beneath the surface of her skin in patches of iridescent blue.

With a growl that held nothing human, she twisted in the creature's grip, bringing her free foot down with all her strength on its elongated arm. Her heel connected with an unnatural joint, and the limb buckled, momentarily loosening its grip. It was enough. She tore free, scrambling forward on hands and knees toward the containment switch.

The laboratory had descended into chaos. Shattered glass crunched beneath her palms, spilled chemicals mixing to create noxious fumes, the air thick with the alien sounds of creatures shedding their human disguises. Behind her, Kieran fought with controlled ferocity, his blade a silver arc as he battled to keep the remaining infiltrators from reaching her.

"Aquatania! Now!" he shouted, his voice strained with effort.

Her palm slammed against the silver panel, fingers spreading to cover the activation runes. The metal grew warm beneath her touch, responding to her unique biorhythm, to the royal blood that commanded the palace's deepest defenses. Silver light erupted from the panel, racing along channels etched into the walls and floor, forming a complex web of protective magic that enveloped her most valuable research.

Secondary wards sprang to life around specific cabinets and storage units, layers of protection folding over her treatment formulas and remaining samples. The containment field wouldn't physically stop the infiltrators. They were already inside the laboratory, but it would prevent them from accessing or destroying the most critical components of her research.

The kitchen servant lunged for her again, its form now barely recognizable as humanoid. Aquatania turned to face it, her back pressed against the wall, the containment panel still warm against her shoulder. Across the room, Kieran battled the scribe with increasing desperation, his movements slowing fractionally as the extended combat took its toll.

The infiltrators had breached her sanctuary, destroyed irreplaceable samples, and threatened everything she'd worked to create. But the core of her research remained protected, sealed behind wards that even these alien entities couldn't penetrate. Now they just had to survive long enough to use it.

Glass crunched beneath Aquatania's boots as she pushed away from the containment panel, and the acrid scent of alien blood mixed with spilled reagents to create a noxious cloud that stung her eyes and throat. The laboratory, once an ordered sanctuary of scientific precision, had devolved into a battlefield of shattered equipment and overturned workstations. Delicate instruments lay in ruins, crystal vials leaked their precious contents across stone surfaces where they hissed and smoked upon contact, and the projection sphere had rolled into a corner, its surface cracked but still emitting a feeble glow as it displayed fractured images of cellular structures.

The kitchen servant-thing lunged at her again, its form now barely maintaining humanoid proportions. Its arms stretched to impossible lengths, its fingers fusing and separating in rhythmic pulses as they reached for her. Aquatania ducked beneath a workstation, crawling through a narrow space between equipment stands. A beaker crashed to the floor inches from her hand, splashing corrosive solution that ate through the stone in bubbling furrows.

Across the laboratory, Kieran moved with lethal grace, his body seeming to anticipate the scribe-creature's attacks before they came. He'd positioned himself to prevent the infiltrators from reaching the preservation cabinets where the most promising treatment samples were stored. His blade caught the light from the warning crystals, leaving luminous trails in the air as he parried and struck with precise economy of movement.

"The northeastern cabinet," she called to him, pointing to a storage unit across the room. "It contains unstable compounds that might—"

She didn't finish as the kitchen servant's elongated arm swept across a shelf above her, sending glass containers raining down. Aquatania rolled sideways, feeling something sharp slice through her sleeve and graze her arm. Warm blood trickled down to her wrist, but she ignored it, scrambling toward a table covered with experimental apparatus.

Kieran had heard her incomplete instruction. He backed toward the cabinet she'd indicated, drawing the scribe-creature after him with calculated movements. When his shoulder blades touched the cabinet doors, he dropped suddenly to one knee. The creature's strike passed over his head, its elongated fingers puncturing the thin metal of the cabinet door.

The reaction was immediate. The cabinet contained reactive elemental essences, unstable compounds that responded violently to foreign energy signatures. A flash of blue-white light erupted from the punctured door, accompanied by a sound like ice cracking on a frozen lake. The scribe-creature's arm froze in mid-extension, crystals forming rapidly along its unnatural limb, spreading upward toward its torso.

"Fire and ice," Kieran said with grim satisfaction, rising and pivoting away from the partially crystallized infiltrator. "Classic combination."

The kitchen servant abandoned its pursuit of Aquatania, flowing across the laboratory floor with unnervingly fluid movements to join the attack on Kieran. Its lower body seemed to merge with the stone itself as it moved, leaving an oily residue in its wake that smoked faintly.

Aquatania took advantage of the momentary reprieve, diving toward her primary workstation where one critical cabinet remained unsealed. Inside lay a potential weapon, a solution of volatile dragon fire essence she'd been experimenting with as a purification agent. Too unstable for medical use, but perhaps perfect for their current situation.

Kieran engaged both remaining infiltrators simultaneously, keeping them at bay with a series of precise strikes. The false guard, having freed itself from the enchanted crystal wall through some unknown means, rejoined the attack. Its weapon arm had partially crystallized from contact with the wall's magic, making it move with jerking, spasmodic motions, but no less dangerous for the impairment.

"Behind you!" Aquatania shouted as the kitchen servant

circled around, attempting to flank Kieran.

He responded instantly, pivoting to slash at the approaching threat while kicking a toppled chair into the path of the guard-creature. His movements flowed from one to the next with practiced precision, each defensive action immediately followed by an offensive counter. This was not merely combat training, Aquatania realized. This was mastery born of experience. Kieran fought as he did everything else, with methodical efficiency and perfect control.

The scribe-creature, its arm still partially crystallized, retreated toward the shattered doorway. For a moment, Aquatania thought it might flee, but instead, it began to change more dramatically. Its human disguise sloughed away like a discarded cloak, revealing a form composed of overlapping segments that resembled neither insect nor reptile but something wholly alien. From its central mass, new appendages emerged, not arms but weaponized protrusions that gleamed wetly in the laboratory's fractured light.

"They're adapting," Kieran called, backing toward the center of the room to maintain sight lines to all threats. Sweat beaded his forehead, his breathing controlled but labored. "We need to end this quickly."

Aquatania's fingers closed around the dragon fire vial, its contents glowing orange-red through the crystal, pulsing like a captive heartbeat. The solution was untested in combat applications, its volatility making it too dangerous for casual handling. But desperation outweighed caution.

Kieran drove the guard-creature back with a flurry of strikes, his blade connecting with its partially transformed torso. Where the enchanted metal touched alien flesh, silver light flared, and the creature emitted a high-pitched sound that vibrated the remaining intact glassware. It retreated, a weapon arm held defensively before it, dark fluid leaking from multiple wounds.

The kitchen servant, seeing an opening, flowed around a toppled storage chest and approached from Kieran's blind side. Its body had abandoned any pretense of human form, reshaping into something low and predatory, multiple limbs propelling it across the floor with unsettling speed.

"Kieran!" Aquatania shouted, but her warning came a fraction too late.

The creature's arm elongated with explosive speed, the limb stretching across the intervening space like liquid metal reforming itself. Its appendage transformed mid-extension, the tip hardening into a serrated edge that slashed across Kieran's side before he could fully turn to defend himself.

The general's face contorted in pain, his free hand instinctively pressing against his side where blood immediately began to soak through his shirt. The wound didn't slow his reaction. He pivoted, bringing his blade down in an arc that caught the still-extended limb and severed it with a spray of dark fluid.

The kitchen servant recoiled, its severed appendage dissolving into smoking residue on the laboratory floor. It retreated momentarily, seemingly reassessing the threat Kieran posed despite his injury.

Aquatania saw her opportunity. With the creatures momentarily separated, she could target them more effectively. She uncorked the dragon fire vial, the sudden release of pressure sending wisps of orange vapor curling upward from its mouth.

"Kieran! Cover!" she shouted, then hurled the vial toward the space between the remaining infiltrators.

The crystal container shattered on impact with the stone floor, its contents igniting instantly upon exposure to air. But it was no ordinary fire...dragon fire essence burned with magical as well as physical properties. Flames erupted in a perfect circle, the conflagration rising to the ceiling in a column of intense heat and magical energy. The fire didn't spread beyond its initial boundary, contained by the essence's inherent magical properties, but within that circle, it burned with supernatural intensity.

The kitchen servant was caught directly in the blast, its fluid form instantly engulfed in orange-red flames that clung to its alien substance like living things. It thrashed wildly, appendages lengthening and retracting in spasmodic movements as the dragon fire consumed it from the outside in.

The false guard and the scribe-creature retreated from the heat, backing toward opposite walls of the laboratory. The distraction gave Kieran the opening he needed. Despite his bleeding side, he launched himself toward the false guard, blade extended in a perfect thrust that caught the creature where a human's heart would be.

The enchanted metal sank deep into the alien form, silver runes flaring with brilliant light upon contact. The false guard convulsed, its weapon arm crystallizing entirely before shattering into fragments that dissolved into steam before hitting the floor. Its form collapsed inward, its human disguise falling away completely to reveal the alien architecture beneath, all angles and segments that made no biological sense, before that too dissolved into a puddle of rapidly evaporating fluid.

Kieran wrenched his blade free, turning to face the final infiltrator. Blood soaked the entire left side of his shirt now, dripping onto the stone floor in a steady pattern, but his stance remained balanced, his grip on his weapon unwavering.

The scribe-creature assessed its position...two companions destroyed, dragon fire blocking one escape route, and a wounded but still dangerous opponent between it and the other. It made a sound like metal scraping against crystal, then suddenly flowed upward, its body extending toward the high ceiling of the laboratory where ventilation shafts provided access to the palace's air circulation system.

Kieran's reaction was immediate and desperate. He reversed his grip on his blade and threw it with remarkable accuracy. The weapon spun through the air, enchanted metal gleaming as it rotated, and struck the ascending creature at what appeared to be a junction point in its segmented body. The blade embedded itself deeply, pinning the creature to the stone wall just below the ventilation shaft.

Dark fluid poured from the wound, smoking where it hit the floor. The creature's form convulsed, appendages thrashing wildly before gradually slowing. Its body began to lose cohesion, segments separating and dissolving until only Kieran's blade remained, embedded in the wall with a slowly evaporating stain beneath it.

The sudden silence felt deafening after the chaos of battle. The dragon fire continued to burn in its perfect circle, illuminating the laboratory's destruction with its otherworldly light. Aquatania picked her way through the wreckage toward Kieran, who had finally allowed himself to lean against a partially intact workstation, one hand pressed firmly against his bleeding side.

"Are they dead?" she asked, eyes scanning the various puddles and stains that were all that remained of the infiltrators.

"Not dead," Kieran replied through gritted teeth. "Dispersed. There's a difference." He attempted to straighten, then winced, his face paling beneath its usual tan. "Their physical cohesion is disrupted, but their essence…" He didn't finish the thought, his knees suddenly buckling as the adrenaline that had sustained him began to ebb.

He collapsed against the workstation, sliding down to sit on the floor, his back against its base. Blood pooled beneath him, staining the white stone in an expanding circle that reflected the orange glow of the still-burning dragon fire.

"They came prepared," he said, his voice growing fainter. "They knew exactly what to target."

Aquatania knelt beside him, her scientific mind already calculating blood loss rates and treatment options even as her heart raced with a fear that had nothing to do with the alien attack and everything to do with the paleness of Kieran's face.

"Stay still," Aquatania commanded, her voice steadier than her hands as she knelt beside Kieran. Blood seeped between his fingers where he pressed them against the wound, the fabric of his shirt torn in a clean line that revealed the damage beneath. The slash was deep, exposing layers of muscle beneath torn skin, but what concerned her more was the unnatural discoloration spreading outward from the edges. This faint purplish tinge suggested alien toxins already at work. She pressed her palm against his forehead, feeling the clammy coolness of his skin, shock setting in, blood pressure dropping. Time was not their ally.

"Why didn't you shift?" she demanded again, tearing strips from the bottom of her lab coat with practiced efficiency. The white fabric, stained with chemical splatters and alien residue, would make a poor bandage, but it would have to suffice until she could access proper medical supplies. "Dragon form would have made you invulnerable to their weapons."

Kieran grimaced as she gently moved his hand away from the wound to assess the full extent of the damage. "No time," he said through gritted teeth. "Had to keep them away from your research." His eyes, though clouded with pain, remained alert and focused on her face. "The treatment formula is worth more than one soldier."

"Worth more than your life?" she asked sharply, pressing the makeshift bandage against the wound to slow the bleeding. The fabric immediately darkened with blood, the stain spreading outward in a perfect circle.

"If it saves thousands? Yes." His matter-of-fact tone held

no self-pity, only the pragmatic calculation of a military mind. "Besides, I'm not dead yet."

The ghost of a smile that accompanied his words did something peculiar to Aquatania's heart, a flutter that had no place in scientific methodology. She pushed the sensation aside, focusing instead on the immediate medical needs before her.

"I need to move you to the auxiliary medical station," she said, glancing toward a corner of the laboratory that had largely escaped the destruction. A small examination table stood against the wall, surrounded by cabinets containing basic medical supplies. "Can you stand with support?"

Kieran nodded, though the effort of pushing himself upright caused fresh blood to seep through the makeshift bandage. Aquatania positioned herself beneath his uninjured arm, taking his weight as he rose unsteadily to his feet. His height and solid frame made him substantially heavier than she'd anticipated, but determination compensated for the physical disparity as she guided him across the debris-strewn floor.

"The wound needs cleaning before I can apply healing agents," she explained, helping him onto the examination table. "Alien residue in the bloodstream could cause complications we can't predict."

"I've had worse," he said, though the pallor of his face suggested otherwise.

Aquatania worked methodically, cutting away his blood-soaked shirt with silver scissors to fully expose the wound. The gash ran diagonally across his ribs on the left side, approximately six inches long and deep enough to reveal muscle beneath. The edges of the wound showed the purplish discoloration she'd noticed earlier, now spreading visibly into the surrounding tissue. The alien weapon had left more than a physical injury; it had introduced some form of toxic agent into his system.

From a cabinet that had survived the chaos, she retrieved medical supplies, purification crystals, healing salve infused with dragon bone powder, and silver-threaded bandages designed to draw out magical contaminants. Her hands moved with practiced precision despite the urgency of the situation. Science required calm, even when treating a wound that grew more concerning with each passing minute.

"This will burn," she warned, uncorking a crystal vial containing clear liquid that emitted faint blue vapors. The purification solution, distilled from rare mountain springs and enhanced with sea dragon tears, would neutralize conventional toxins and some magical contaminants. Whether it would affect alien biologicals remained to be seen.

Kieran's jaw tightened as she poured the solution directly into the wound, but he made no sound beyond a sharp intake of breath. The liquid hissed upon contact with the purplish discoloration, creating wisps of steam that carried an unusual metallic scent. Aquatania watched carefully, noting that while the solution seemed to halt the spread of the discoloration, it didn't reverse the damage already done.

"Interesting," she murmured, her scientific mind automatically analyzing the reaction even as her hands continued working to save him. "The purification agent neutralizes the toxin but can't eliminate it completely. That suggests a biological component rather than purely chemical or magical."

"Is that your clinical way of saying I'm still poisoned?" Kieran asked, his voice strained but steady.

"For now," she acknowledged, reaching for a jar of healing salve. The thick, green-tinted substance gleamed with embedded particles of crushed crystal and dragon bone. "This should slow the toxin's progress until I can synthesize a more specific antidote."

She applied the salve with gentle fingers, coating the entire length of the wound. The medicinal scent of herbs mingled with the sharper tang of dragon bone powder, temporarily overpowering the acrid smell of chemicals and alien blood that permeated the laboratory. Where the salve touched the wound's edges, the angry red of inflamed tissue softened slightly, blood vessels constricting to slow the bleeding.

"This proves our theory," Kieran said as she worked, his eyes following her movements with scientific interest despite his pain. "If I'd been in dragon form, their weapons couldn't have pierced my scales."

"The evidence does support that conclusion," she agreed, carefully applying a layer of silver-threaded bandages over the salve. The enchanted threads would draw out magical contaminants while the healing agents worked. "Though I would have preferred a less personal demonstration."

His quiet laugh ended in a wince as the movement disturbed his wound. "Science often requires sacrifice."

"Not this kind," she said, securing the bandage with practiced efficiency. Her fingers lingered perhaps a moment longer than necessary against his skin, feeling the warmth returning as the healing salve began its work. "And it proves we need to work faster. They're getting desperate to stop us."

"Desperate enough to risk exposure," Kieran noted, his tactical mind functioning despite his injury. "They abandoned subtlety for direct action. That tells us they fear what you're developing."

Aquatania gathered the used medical supplies, placing them in a containment unit for later analysis.

"Can you detect any change in the wound's sensation?" she asked, returning to Kieran's side to check his pulse. His heartbeat had stabilized, the rhythm stronger than before. "Numbness, burning, unusual pressure?"

"Numbness radiating outward," he reported with clinical detachment. "And an odd sensation like...electrical current beneath the skin. Intermittent, not constant."

She nodded, recording these symptoms in her mental

catalog. "The toxin appears to target the nervous system. I've seen similar effects in sea creature venoms, though the progression is different."

Kieran attempted to sit up straighter, grimacing with the effort. "How long before I'm combat-ready again?"

"You're not leaving this laboratory until that toxin is neutralized," she said, gently but firmly pressing him back down. "Even with accelerated healing, the wound itself requires at least twenty-four hours to close. The toxin complicates matters. Without a specific antidote, I can't predict its course."

The laboratory's magical lights flickered, the damage from the battle affecting their power source. In the momentary dimness, shadows swept across Kieran's face, emphasizing the sharp angles of his cheekbones. When the light stabilized, she found him watching her with an expression she couldn't immediately categorize…respect mingled with something warmer, more personal.

"They'll come again," he said quietly. "In greater numbers, with better preparation. This was a probing attack, testing our defenses."

"Then we'll be ready," she replied, her voice matching his in intensity if not volume. "The containment field protected my most critical research. I can restart synthesis with the remaining samples."

Their eyes met in the flickering light, a moment of shared understanding passing between them. The stakes had shifted from theoretical to immediate, from scientific curiosity to survival. Kieran's blood on her hands made the threat visceral in a way that microscopic observations never could.

"We need to accelerate production of the treatment," she continued, moving to salvage what equipment remained functional. "And distribute what we have to key personnel immediately. You'll be the first recipient, once I've refined the formula to address the alien toxin."

Kieran watched her movements, his military mind visibly assessing their situation. "We should relocate to a more secure facility. This laboratory is compromised."

Aquatania surveyed the destruction around them. Shattered glass, spilled chemicals, broken equipment, scorch marks from the dragon fire, and dark stains where alien infiltrators had been dispersed. Her scientific sanctuary had been violated, transformed from a place of discovery to a battlefield. Yet the core of her research remained intact, protected by the emergency containment field she'd activated.

"Not yet," she decided. "Moving now would delay production. We fortify this position while continuing work." She gestured to the partially intact projection sphere, which still emitted a feeble glow from its cracked surface. "The treatment formula is nearly complete. With the data from this attack, including samples of alien tissue and the toxin in your wound, I can refine it further."

The laboratory's lights flickered again, longer this time, casting dramatic shadows across the debris-strewn floor. In that moment of semi-darkness, Aquatania made a silent vow. She would complete her work before more lives were lost...before the wound in Kieran's side could claim him, before the alien infiltration could spread further through the kingdoms they had sworn to protect.

When the lights stabilized, she was already in motion, retrieving viable samples from the containment field, mentally recalculating synthesis procedures based on their reduced resources.

"Rest," she instructed him without turning around, her hands already busy preparing a fresh batch of reagents. "Your body needs to focus energy on fighting the toxin. I'll wake you when the first treatment dose is ready."

"Aquatania," he said, her name spoken with unexpected gentleness. She paused in her work, looking back at him.

"Thank you."

The simple words carried weight beyond their syllables...acknowledgment of her skill, appreciation for her care, recognition of their shared goal. She nodded once, accepting what was offered and what remained unspoken between them.

"We'll defeat them," she promised, in a tone that left no room for doubt. "Not just their weapons and their infiltrators, but their entire invasion."

Chapter Six

The submersible craft shuddered as it entered the transport tunnel, its enchanted hull creaking under the pressure of the deep. Aquatania steadied herself against the control panel, feeling the water's resistance through her fingertips...a language she understood in her bones. The descent to Oceana Prime always tested her connection to her sea dragon heritage, demanding precision and respect for the ocean's might. She glanced at Kieran, noting the tightness around his eyes despite his composed expression. Three days had passed since the laboratory attack, and though his wound was healing faster than a typical human's would, she knew the alien toxin still lingered in his system.

"Current shift ahead," she warned as the navigation crystals pulsed with increasing frequency. "The tidal patterns have been irregular since the outbreak began."

Kieran nodded, bracing himself against the bulkhead. His hand moved instinctively to his side, where silver-threaded bandages still covered the healing wound. "Nothing we can't handle," he said, though his knuckles whitened as he gripped the safety rail.

The craft lurched violently as they passed through the outer wards protecting the underwater kingdom. Magical barriers designed to keep Oceana Prime hidden from surface dwellers manifested as visible ripples in the water, sheets of translucent energy that distorted light and disrupted currents. The submersible pitched sharply to the left, instruments flashing warning signals across the control panel.

Aquatania closed her eyes, extending her awareness beyond the craft's hull. She felt the water's chaotic movements...a confluence of natural currents and magical interference creating a maelstrom that threatened to push them off course. With practiced concentration, she extended her hand, her fingers splayed toward the viewport. The sea dragon part of her nature responded, her scales briefly shimmering beneath the skin of her forearm as she exerted her will upon the surrounding water.

The violent rocking gradually subsided, the craft finding stability within a pocket of calmer water that moved with them like a protective bubble. Sweat beaded on Aquatania's forehead despite the chamber's cool temperature. Manipulating water at that depth required significant energy, especially while maintaining such precise control.

"You're getting better at that," Kieran observed, his eyes tracking the unnatural smoothness of their passage through what should've been turbulent waters.

"Practice makes perfect," she replied with a tight smile, maintaining her focus on the currents. "Though I'd prefer less urgent applications."

The tunnel widened as they approached its terminus, darkness giving way to a soft, diffuse glow that strengthened with each passing moment. Kieran moved to the rear compartment, methodically checking the specialized containers that held their equipment and the empty vials awaiting dragon blood samples. Each container was etched with protective runes and reinforced with silver filigree. They were precautions against both the pressure of the deep and any attempt at magical tampering.

"Seals are holding," he reported, returning to the pilot's chamber. "But we should verify the integrity of the warding spells before we collect the first sample. If the aliens have found a way to corrupt magical protections…"

"They haven't managed to break my laboratory containment fields," Aquatania said, though she appreciated his caution. "These vessels were enchanted using the same principles."

The submersible emerged from the tunnel into open water, and Oceana Prime spread before them in a breathtaking panorama. Aquatania felt a familiar tightness in her chest at the sight, a complex blend of homecoming and scientific appreciation.

The underwater metropolis sprawled across the ocean floor in concentric rings, each circle rising higher than the one before, creating a spiraling city that ascended toward the distant surface. Buildings crafted from living coral glowed with bioluminescent light, blues and greens predominating near the outer rings, shifting to purples and soft reds toward the center. Glass domes of varying sizes housed air-breathing residents and visitors, connected by transparent tunnels that resembled crystalline veins threading through the aquatic body of the city.

Water-dwelling species moved freely through open archways and designated current paths, their forms silhouetted against the glowing structures. Schools of enhanced fish bred for their luminescent qualities traced patterns through the water like living constellations, providing both beauty and practical illumination to the underwater kingdom.

"It's easy to forget what we're fighting for," Kieran said quietly, watching a group of children, some human, some clearly from aquatic species, dart through a coral playground, their movements blurring the distinctions between them. "Until you see it like this."

Aquatania nodded, guiding their craft toward the outermost ring of the city. "We need to be careful," Kieran warned, his eyes scanning the patrol patterns of guards in sleek armor moving along the city's perimeter. "If the aliens have infiltrated here like they did Zephyria, they'll be watching the medical facilities."

"Which is why we're not using the main entry points," she replied, directing their vessel toward a seemingly unremarkable section of coral reef that flanked the city. "This access point is used primarily for maintenance and emergency medical transport. Limited traffic means fewer opportunities for infiltration."

Kieran studied the approaching reef with new interest. "How many secret entrances does Oceana Prime have?"

"More than appears on any official chart," she said with a small smile. "My father believes in contingency planning."

She guided the submersible into a narrow crevice between coral formations, revealing a hidden passageway just wide enough to accommodate their craft. Bioluminescent markers glowed at irregular intervals, visible only to those who knew what to look for…a navigation system for trusted visitors.

A particularly violent current caught them as they entered the passage, sending the submersible into a sideways drift that threatened to slam them against the coral walls. Aquatania reacted instantly, her hands moving in a fluid gesture that redirected the water's force around their vessel rather than against it.

"Something's wrong with the currents," she muttered, her brow furrowing with concentration. "They're not following natural patterns. Almost as if…"

"As if they're being manipulated," Kieran finished, his expression darkening. "Like the contagion itself."

They navigated the hidden passage in tense silence, finally emerging into a small enclosed docking area illuminated by soft blue light. Three other vessels were moored to coral pillars, each bearing the insignia of Oceana Prime's medical corps, sleek shapes designed for rapid transport of patients or supplies.

As their submersible settled against an available mooring post, Aquatania performed a final check of their equipment. "We need samples from at least three different ocean dragon subspecies," she said, securing her collection kit in a waterproof satchel. "The reef dragons have unique

85

immunological properties we haven't seen in the sky breeds."

Kieran nodded, buckling on his weapons belt, the silver-runed blade that had proven effective against alien physiology now complemented by a trident of oceanic design, gifted by King Poseidronus himself. "Let's hope they're feeling cooperative."

A figure emerged from an underwater airlock at the edge of the docking area, a thin man in the blue robes of Oceana Prime's healing order. Even through the distortion of water, Aquatania could see the nervous energy in his movements as he approached their vessel. His head turned constantly, his gaze darting to check the shadows between coral formations.

"That's our contact," she said, activating the airlock sequence that would allow them to exit the submersible without flooding its interior. "Healer Verin, if I'm not mistaken."

The outer hatch opened, water rushing in to fill the small chamber between the inner and outer doors. Aquatania felt the familiar embrace of ocean pressure as it enveloped her, her gills activating instantly along the sides of her neck, another manifestation of her sea dragon heritage. Beside her, Kieran activated the enchanted coral pendant that hung around his neck, a temporary adaptation that would allow him to breathe underwater for up to twelve hours.

They exited the craft to meet the waiting healer, who bowed deeply upon recognizing Aquatania.

"Your Highness," he said, his voice clear despite the underwater environment, another magical adaptation common among Oceana Prime's residents. "Thank you for coming so quickly." His eyes darted over Kieran, noting the military bearing and weapons with a flicker of both relief and concern. "Please, follow me. We must hurry."

He led them toward the airlock, glancing repeatedly over his shoulder as if expecting pursuit. "The situation has deteriorated since your father's message," he whispered as they entered the small chamber. "We lost an entire healing ward yesterday. The patients, the healers...all of them."

"Lost?" Kieran asked sharply. "To the disease?"

The healer's eyes widened with unmistakable fear. "No. They disappeared. The entire section of the facility...emptied. No bodies, no signs of struggle. Just...gone."

The airlock cycled, water draining away as air filled the chamber. Aquatania felt her gills recede, her lungs resuming their primary function. The healer's words settled in her stomach like ice, confirming her worst fears. The aliens weren't just spreading disease...they were harvesting victims.

The healing ward's doors sealed behind them with a soft hiss, the enchanted coral automatically adjusting to maintain the delicate balance of humidity and temperature necessary for treating both air and water breathers. Aquatania's senses were immediately assaulted by the mingled scents of medicinal algae, purification salts, and beneath it all, the unmistakable metallic tang of blood. Rows of beds stretched before them, each occupied by a patient in various stages of the Red Death, their skin marred by the distinctive crimson patterns that gave the disease its name. The ward hummed with the constant movement of healers in blue robes, their faces drawn with exhaustion as they worked against an enemy they couldn't defeat.

"We've converted three additional chambers to treatment space in the past week," their guide explained, leading them deeper into the facility. "It's still not enough."

Aquatania moved between the beds, her scientific gaze cataloging symptoms with practiced efficiency. The patterns of the crimson rash differed slightly from what she'd observed in Aethoria. Here, the lines followed paths reminiscent of ocean currents rather than the more angular formations she'd documented previously. The alien contagion was adapting to its environment, evolving to mimic the natural patterns of its surroundings. The implication sent a chill through her that had nothing to do with the ward's cool air.

A man in a nearby bed thrashed against the restraints, his body arching in the distinctive muscle spasms of late-stage infection. The rash covered his torso completely, the red lines pulsing with each labored heartbeat. A healer pressed a cloth soaked in blue liquid to his forehead, murmuring incantations that seemed to offer momentary relief before the spasms resumed with renewed intensity.

"How long has he been in this stage?" Aquatania asked, approaching the bed.

"Two days," the healer replied without looking up, her voice flat with exhaustion. "Longer than most. He's strong. He was a pearl diver before the sickness took him."

She looked back at Kieran, who remained near the entrance, his posture alert as he studied each person entering or exiting the ward. His hand rested casually on his weapon hilt, ready to respond to any threat. Though he maintained his vigilance, Aquatania could see the tension in his jaw as he witnessed the suffering around them.

A young girl, no more than twelve years old and wearing the light blue robe of an apprentice healer, stumbled as she carried a tray of medicine vials between beds. Exhaustion had her face pallid with dark circles beneath her eyes, making her appear much older. As Aquatania watched, the girl's knees buckled, the tray slipping from her grasp. Glass vials tumbled toward the floor in what seemed like slow motion.

Aquatania reacted instinctively, her hand extending in a fluid gesture. Water particles in the air condensed instantly around the falling vials, creating a cushioning bubble that halted their descent inches from the stone floor. With her other hand, she reached for the collapsing child, catching her before she struck the ground.

"Easy," she murmured, lowering the girl gently to a sitting

position. The apprentice's skin burned with fever, her pulse racing beneath Aquatania's fingertips. "How long have you been working without rest?"

"Two…two days, I think," the girl whispered, her voice cracking with dehydration. "There aren't enough of us left."

Aquatania pressed her palm to the child's forehead, calling upon her water manipulation abilities. Moisture gathered from the surrounding air, cooling and condensing against the girl's fevered skin. The water molecules responded to her will, carrying away excess heat while delivering hydration directly through her pores.

"You're showing early symptoms," Aquatania said softly, noting the faint redness at the girl's neckline, the first indication of the telltale rash. "You need treatment, not more work."

"Can't," the apprentice protested weakly. "Too many need help. Not enough healers."

"You can't help others if you become a patient yourself," Aquatania replied, guiding the girl toward an empty chair against the wall. "Rest here. That's an order from your princess."

Recognition flickered in the apprentice's exhausted eyes. "Princess Aquatania? You came yourself?"

"Of course I did." She completed the cooling treatment, then carefully lifted the suspended vials with another gesture, guiding them back onto the tray. "This is my kingdom, too."

A woman in the deeper blue robes of a senior healer approached, her movements efficient despite obvious fatigue. Silver threads woven through her collar marked her as a master of water-based healing arts. Her eyes widened slightly at the sight of Aquatania.

"Your Highness," she said, bowing briefly. "I am Healer Sarabina. We received word of your possible arrival, but with communications so disrupted…" She glanced at the apprentice with concern. "Lina, you should've told someone you were feeling ill."

"There was no one to tell," the girl mumbled, her eyelids drooping as Aquatania's cooling treatment eased her discomfort. "Everyone was busy."

Sarabina pressed her lips together, then turned back to Aquatania. "Thank you for catching her, both literally and diagnostically. We've lost too many healers already."

"How many cases now?" Aquatania asked, releasing the apprentice into Sarabina's care.

Sarabina's expression darkened. "Over eight hundred confirmed. We've lost seventeen just today," she whispered, glancing around at the rows of suffering patients. "Nothing works. Not traditional medicine, not magic, not even the ancient healing corals from the deep trenches."

Kieran approached, having completed his initial assessment of the ward's security. "Any pattern to the progression? Any commonalities among those who survive versus those who don't?"

"Water-dwellers last longer than air-breathers," Sarabina replied, guiding them toward a quieter corner of the ward where they could speak more privately. "And those with even trace amounts of reptilian ancestry show greater resistance. But ultimately, the disease claims nearly everyone it touches." She rubbed her eyes, leaving smudges of exhaustion beneath them. "And then there are the disappearances."

"Your colleague mentioned an entire ward," Aquatania said, keeping her voice low.

Sarabina nodded, her expression haunted. "Thirty-two patients, seven healers. There one moment, gone the next. The ward was sealed. No one entered or left through conventional means. The guards swear no one passed them."

"Conventional means being the operative phrase," Kieran noted grimly.

Aquatania removed the crystal slate from her satchel, activating it with a touch. The device hummed to life, displaying her research findings in glowing projection above its surface. "We've made progress understanding the contagion's mechanisms," she said. "And more importantly, we've identified a potential treatment approach."

Sarabina leaned forward, hope flickering across her exhausted features. "You have a cure?"

"Not yet a cure," Aquatania clarified, manipulating the projection to display microscopic images of infected blood cells alongside dragon blood samples. "But we've confirmed that dragon blood contains compounds that neutralize the pathogen. Different dragon species provide different protective effects, but all demonstrate some level of immunity."

The senior healer studied the projection with intense focus, her professional training momentarily overriding her exhaustion. "The cellular structure is disrupted at the point of contact," she observed, pointing to where the red geometric patterns broke down upon exposure to dragon blood. "Complete neutralization."

"Exactly," Aquatania confirmed. "We've synthesized preliminary treatments using sky and fire dragon blood, but our tests indicate that ocean dragon subspecies likely possess even stronger neutralizing properties, particularly against the strain affecting Oceana Prime."

"Which is why you're here," Sarabina concluded, understanding dawning in her tired eyes. "You need samples from our dragon populations."

"At least three different subspecies," Aquatania confirmed. "Particularly the reef dragons. Their proximity to coral ecosystems has produced unique immunological adaptations we haven't observed in other species."

Kieran moved closer, his voice dropping to ensure only the three of them could hear. "We need to move quickly. If the aliens realize what we're developing…"

"The Abyssal Cavern houses our oldest reef dragons,"

Sarabina told them, lowering her voice to match Kieran's. "A mated pair and their juvenile offspring. They've lived in symbiosis with the ancient coral formations for generations."

"That's perfect," Aquatania said, already calculating the specific properties their blood might contain. "How do we reach them?"

Sarabina hesitated, glancing toward the ward's crystal windows that looked out into the oceanic depths beyond. "That's the problem. The currents around the Abyssal Cavern have been treacherous since the outbreak began, almost as if the water itself is infected." She shuddered slightly. "Three retrieval teams have tried to reach the cavern for medicinal coral. None returned."

Kieran and Aquatania exchanged glances, a silent communication passing between them. If the aliens were manipulating water currents to isolate specific locations, it suggested they understood exactly which resources might pose a threat to their plans.

"I can navigate the currents," Aquatania said with quiet confidence. "My sea dragon heritage gives me advantages the retrieval teams didn't have."

"And I'll ensure you have the time and space to work," Kieran added, his hand moving unconsciously to the healing wound at his side.

A commotion at the far end of the ward drew their attention. A patient had broken free of his restraints, his body contorted by muscle spasms as he thrashed against the healers attempting to subdue him. The rash across his chest pulsed with unnatural light, the red patterns shifting and realigning like writing being continuously rewritten.

"The later stages have been becoming more...violent," Sarabina explained grimly. "As if something is trying to emerge."

Aquatania watched as the healers finally managed to restrain the man again, administering a sedative potion that gradually eased his thrashing. The implication of Sarabina's observation aligned too perfectly with what the aliens had discussed in the abandoned storage chamber. Spores maturing within the infected, preparing for *true transformation*.

"We need to reach those dragons immediately," she said, turning back to Sarabina. "Can you provide us with maps of the underwater passages leading to the Abyssal Cavern?"

"I can do better than that," the healer replied, removing a small coral pendant from around her neck. "This will guide you through the old maintenance tunnels. They run deeper than the main thoroughfares. Possibly deep enough to avoid whatever's affecting the currents."

Aquatania accepted the pendant, feeling the faint magical pulse within the living coral. It was a beacon attuned to specific locations within Oceana Prime's complex network of passages.

"Be careful," Sarabina warned, her voice dropping further. "Since the disappearances began, we've noticed changes in some of the guards and officials. Subtle things, movements too precise, voices without inflection, eyes that don't quite…react properly."

"We've encountered their kind before," Kieran said grimly. "And we know how to recognize them."

As they prepared to leave, Aquatania cast a final glance at the rows of suffering patients. The apprentice healer had fallen asleep in the chair, her young face momentarily peaceful despite the faint rash now visible at her collar. Time was running out, not just for the patients in this ward, but for all human civilizations across their world.

"We'll return with the samples," she promised Sarabina. "And then we'll show you how to begin production of the treatment."

The senior healer nodded, determination briefly overcoming exhaustion in her expression. "We'll be ready.

Just...hurry."

*

They descended through levels of Oceana Prime that Aquatania had rarely visited, following Sarabina's coral pendant as it pulsed with stronger luminescence whenever they turned in the right direction. The grand architecture of the upper city gave way to utilitarian passages carved through ancient bedrock, reinforced with coral growths that had been explicitly cultivated for structural integrity rather than beauty. The water grew colder as they swam deeper, carrying the mineral scent of undisturbed depths. Kieran moved beside her with surprising grace for someone not born to the water, his borrowed gill-enchantment functioning perfectly as he scanned their surroundings with military precision.

"These districts were evacuated three weeks ago," Aquatania explained as they passed through what had once been a thriving marketplace. Abandoned stalls swayed in the gentle currents, merchandise still displayed as if frozen in time, pearl-inlaid combs, bottles of luminescent ink, preserved delicacies from the deep trenches. "When the first cases appeared, my father ordered all non-essential personnel to relocate to the upper levels."

A child's toy, a carved figure of a sea dragon with articulated wings, drifted past them, carried by the current. Kieran caught it with a swift movement, examining the craftsmanship before carefully placing it back on an abandoned counter.

"Smart containment strategy," he observed. "Though it clearly wasn't enough."

They swam through a residential section where homes had been carved directly into coral formations, doorways hanging open, personal belongings still visible inside. The absence of

94

life created an eerie stillness broken only by the ambient sounds of water flowing through empty passages.

"Look there," Aquatania said softly, pointing to a dwelling where crimson markings stained the entrance, the universal symbol for quarantine in Oceana Prime. Similar markings adorned dozens of homes throughout the district, a silent testimony to how quickly the contagion had spread.

A faint vibration passed through the water, barely perceptible but distinct enough to make them pause. Kieran's hand moved to his weapon as they both turned toward the source of the disturbance, a cross-passage ahead where the water seemed to shimmer with slightly different density.

"Someone's coming," he whispered, his eyes narrowing as he focused on the shimmer. "Multiple someones."

They pressed against the wall of the passage, partially concealed by an overhang of fossilized coral. Six figures in the distinctive armor of Oceana Prime's guard patrol emerged from the cross-passage, their movements causing the strange disturbance in the water. Even from a distance, something about their swimming pattern struck Aquatania as wrong, too synchronized, too mechanical, lacking the natural flow that water-dwellers developed from birth.

"Those aren't regular guards," Kieran whispered, his mouth close to her ear to minimize the vibrations his voice created in the water. "Look at how they move...too synchronized."

Aquatania nodded, recognizing that Kieran was able to see the alien infiltrators' distinctive behavior patterns. The patrol moved with perfect spacing between each member, turning simultaneously as they scanned the abandoned district. Their movements lacked the subtle adjustments to current and pressure that came instinctively to true water-dwellers.

Kieran touched her arm, pointing to a narrow maintenance tunnel half-hidden behind a growth of filter coral. Without hesitation, he pulled her toward it, their bodies slipping into the tight space moments before the patrol turned in their direction.

The tunnel was barely wide enough for one person, forcing them to press against each other as they waited in tense silence. Aquatania found herself pinned between the rough coral wall and Kieran's solid form, acutely aware of the rhythm of his breathing through the enchanted gills at his neck. His arm remained protectively around her waist, ready to pull her deeper into the tunnel if necessary.

The patrol paused at the intersection near their hiding place. Through the filter coral, Aquatania could see their silhouettes hovering in the water, helmets turning with mechanical precision as they conducted their search. One guard drifted closer to the tunnel entrance, close enough that she could see the unnatural stillness of its eyes through the helmet's viewport, no blinking, no minor adjustments of focus, just fixed and emotionless observation.

Kieran tensed against her, his free hand moving to the hilt of his weapon. The moment stretched, water seeming to thicken around them as they remained perfectly still. Aquatania could feel his heartbeat against her back, steady despite the danger. After what seemed like an eternity, the guard rejoined its companions, and the patrol continued down the main passage.

They waited until the vibrations faded completely before easing out of their hiding place.

"They're patrolling abandoned districts," Kieran observed, his voice low. "Why waste resources on empty sections of the city?"

"They're searching for something," Aquatania replied, the coral pendant in her hand pulsing more intensely as she oriented it toward their destination. "Or someone. Survivors, perhaps, or..."

"Or they know what we're after," Kieran finished, his expression grim. "The reef dragons."

They continued their journey with heightened caution, using smaller maintenance passages and service tunnels whenever possible. The coral pendant led them ever deeper, past the lowest inhabited levels of Oceana Prime and into the ancient foundations of the underwater city. There, the distinction between natural and constructed environments blurred, corridors that might have been carved by tools or gradually formed by centuries of current erosion, their surfaces encrusted with varieties of deep-water life that thrived in darkness.

As they approached the region Sarabina had indicated, the water began to behave strangely. Currents that should've flowed smoothly now twisted in unnatural patterns, creating sudden eddies and violent cross-currents that threatened to separate them. The temperature fluctuated wildly. Patches of near-freezing water were interspersed with currents so warm that they left visible heat distortion.

"This isn't natural," Aquatania said, struggling against a particularly strong eddy that attempted to pull her off course. "These patterns are deliberate."

Kieran fought his way to her side, the enchantment allowing him to breathe underwater now seemingly working at its limits as the pressure increased. "Can you counter it?"

Aquatania studied the chaotic water movements, her sea dragon senses detecting the underlying pattern beneath the apparent randomness. "I think so. But it will take significant energy."

They reached what appeared to be a dead end, a wall of solid rock blocking the passage. The coral pendant in Aquatania's hand pulsed urgently, indicating their destination lay beyond this barrier. Upon closer examination, she could see a thin crack running vertically through the stone, barely wide enough to slip fingers into.

"The entrance to the Abyssal Cavern," she said, running her hand along the crack. "Sealed by these disrupted

97

currents."

Before them, the water writhed like a living thing, currents colliding to create a barrier as effective as any physical wall. To attempt passage would mean being torn apart by opposing forces, precisely the fate that had likely befallen the previous retrieval teams.

Aquatania closed her eyes, centering herself as she connected more deeply with her sea dragon heritage. Scales shimmered briefly across her forearms as she extended both hands toward the chaotic currents. She felt the water's movements, natural flows disrupted by an alien influence that pulsed with cold mathematical precision, lacking the organic rhythm of natural currents.

"Whatever happens, stay close to me," she instructed Kieran. "Within an arm's reach at all times."

She began to move her hands in flowing patterns, fingers tracing complex geometries through the water. Each movement countered a specific current, her will imposing natural order upon artificial chaos. The effort was immense. The competing currents resisted her control, pushing back against her influence with what felt almost like conscious opposition.

Kieran watched in silent amazement as the water before them gradually calmed, the violent forces subsiding under Aquatania's persistent manipulation. A tunnel of still water began to form through the chaos, a protected pathway just wide enough for them to swim through single file.

"Now," she said, her voice strained with effort. "Quickly. I can't maintain this for long."

Kieran moved first, positioning himself slightly ahead as they entered the corridor of calm water. Aquatania followed, maintaining her concentration on holding back the currents that pressed against her, creating a pathway from all sides. The crack in the stone wall widened as they approached, revealing itself as the true entrance to the Abyssal Cavern, previously hidden by the turbulent water.

They slipped through the opening, Aquatania's control faltering as they passed the threshold. The chaotic currents rushed back together behind them with a sound like thunder, sealing the entrance once more. She sagged slightly with exhaustion, and Kieran's arm encircled her waist, supporting her as they surveyed their surroundings.

The Abyssal Cavern opened before them in breathtaking expanse, a massive underwater chamber where ancient coral formations grew in impossible sculptures that defied gravity. Bioluminescent organisms pulsed in gentle rhythm along the walls, bathing the space in shifting blues and greens that created the impression of swimming through an underwater aurora. The cavern floor dropped away into darkness, a trench of unknown depth bisecting the space.

From that darkness, something moved. A massive shape rising with deliberate grace, scales catching the bioluminescent light and reflecting it in iridescent patterns. The reef dragon was unlike any dragon Aquatania had seen before, its body longer and more sinuous than sky or fire dragons, adapted perfectly to underwater movement. Coral-like growths extended from its spine in delicate formations that mimicked the surrounding environment, and fins rippled along its sides like translucent silk in water.

Two more shapes emerged behind the first, another adult of similar size and a smaller juvenile, their movements perfectly synchronized as they approached. Their eyes, large and luminous in the dim light, focused immediately on Aquatania, recognition evident in their intelligent gaze.

"They're magnificent," Kieran whispered, his expression showing rare awe. "I've never seen anything like them."

The largest dragon, clearly the elder of the group, moved closer. Its movements through the water were poetry, neither swimming nor flying but something uniquely draconic, simultaneously powerful and delicate. It circled them once, its massive body creating a gentle current that carried the scent of ancient ocean depths.

When it completed its circuit, the dragon extended one foreleg toward Aquatania, webbed claws unfurling to reveal the soft spot where scales thinned near the joint, precisely the location where blood could be safely drawn.

"They know," Aquatania whispered in awe, reaching for her collection kit. "They understand what we're trying to do."

The dragon remained perfectly still as she approached with her silver extraction needle, its enormous eyes watching her with what could only be described as solemn purpose. When the needle penetrated the thin skin between scales, the dragon didn't flinch, its gaze never leaving her face as the crystal vial filled with deep blue blood that seemed to capture the very essence of the ocean within its fluid.

"Thank you," she said, addressing the dragon directly as she withdrew the needle and applied healing algae to the tiny wound.

The dragon dipped its massive head in what was unmistakably a gesture of acknowledgment before moving aside to allow its mate to approach. The second adult positioned itself similarly, offering the same access point with equal dignity and purpose. The juvenile remained slightly behind, watching the procedure with evident curiosity.

"They're not just allowing this," Kieran observed quietly. "They're volunteering."

"Dragons have always understood more than humans give them credit for," Aquatania replied, carefully collecting a sample from the second adult. "Especially the ancient lineages like these reef dragons."

When she'd collected samples from all three dragons, Aquatania secured the vials in her specialized container. The blood glowed with subtle power, its deep blue color shot through with threads of bioluminescence that pulsed in rhythm with the cavern's ambient light.

The elder dragon circled them once more before retreating toward the dark trench with its family. Before descending, it turned back, fixing Aquatania with a penetrating gaze that seemed to communicate volumes without words. Then, with a powerful sweep of its tail, it disappeared into the depths, followed closely by its mate and offspring.

"Did you feel that?" Kieran asked, still staring at the spot where the dragons had vanished. "It was like it was trying to tell us something."

"I felt it," Aquatania confirmed, securing the sample container in her satchel. "A warning, I think. And perhaps something else...an offering of alliance." She turned toward the sealed entrance, already gathering her strength for the water manipulation that would be required to exit. "Now we need to reach the Kelp Forest Sanctuary for the second subspecies."

Kieran nodded, his expression returning to its vigilant assessment. "And hope those patrols aren't waiting for us when we leave."

Exiting the Abyssal Cavern proved less challenging than entering it, as if whatever force had manipulated the currents to create a barrier was now focused elsewhere. Aquatania still needed to part the chaotic waters, but the resistance she encountered felt diminished, the alien influence less concentrated. The precious vials of reef dragon blood were nestled securely in her satchel, their bioluminescent glow occasionally visible through the reinforced fabric. Kieran swam close beside her as they emerged into the abandoned districts once more, his eyes constantly scanning their surroundings, his body tensed for immediate response to any threat.

"The Kelp Forest Sanctuary lies northwest of here," Aquatania said, consulting Sarabina's coral pendant. The living navigation tool pulsed with a different rhythm now, its glow shifting toward green rather than the blue that had led them to the Abyssal Cavern. "We should be able to reach it through the agricultural sector. It's likely to be less patrolled than the main transit corridors."

Kieran nodded, adjusting the enchanted coral at his throat that enabled his underwater breathing. "The pendant, can it be tracked? Could the aliens use it to follow our movements?"

"It's bound to my bloodline," she replied, tucking the coral more securely into her palm. "It responds only to sea dragon essence. To anyone else, it would appear dormant."

They swam through narrow passages that wound between abandoned aquaculture farms, vast underwater fields where specialized crops had once been cultivated in perfect rows. Now the careful organization had given way to wild overgrowth, untended plants spreading beyond their designated areas, some species clearly dominating and choking out others in the absence of human management.

As they passed through what had once been a sea cucumber cultivation area, Kieran suddenly tensed, his hand signaling for Aquatania to stop. He hovered motionless in the water, his head tilted slightly as if listening for something beyond normal hearing range. After a moment, he gestured toward a dense growth of kelp that had escaped its containment nets and now formed a natural blind.

"Wait here," he whispered, his voice barely disturbing the water between them. "Something doesn't feel right."

Before she could protest, he slipped away, his movement through water surprisingly stealthy for someone not born to it. The enchanted weapons at his belt remained secured, his hands free for maximum maneuverability as he disappeared into the forest of swaying kelp stalks.

Aquatania pressed herself into the natural alcove formed by overgrown cultivation racks, her senses extended to their limits. The water carried subtle vibrations, movements too distant to see but perceptible to her enhanced awareness. Multiple sources, moving in formation. Not the chaotic patterns of natural swimmers, but the precise, coordinated movements she'd come to recognize as alien.

Minutes passed with excruciating slowness, each small sound or movement in the surrounding water sending a jolt of tension through her body. The vials of reef dragon blood seemed to pulse against her side, their vital cargo representing both hope and danger...salvation for thousands if they succeeded, a target that would draw every alien infiltrator within Oceana Prime if discovered.

Finally, Kieran reappeared, moving through the kelp with silent efficiency. His expression was grim as he rejoined her in the sheltered alcove.

"We're being followed," he confirmed, his voice barely above a breath. "Two divers, moving like the others, too synchronized, too precise for human movement. They're sweeping the agricultural sector in a search pattern."

"How far to the Kelp Forest Sanctuary?" she asked, already calculating alternatives.

"Maybe half a mile through this sector. But we'll have to cross an open transit hub to reach it." His eyes met hers, the concern in them tempered by strategic focus. "They're between us and our destination, moving perpendicular to our path. If we time it right, we might slip past, but one wrong move..."

Aquatania considered their options, mentally mapping the underwater geography of this section of Oceana Prime. "The agricultural sector connects to waste processing through maintenance tunnels," she said, recalling blueprints she'd studied during royal education on city infrastructure. "We could bypass the transit hub entirely."

"And the two trailing us?"

She studied the surrounding environment, the overgrown sea plants, the accumulated silt on abandoned equipment, and the natural currents flowing through the open-sided structures. "I have an idea."

Carefully, they made their way to a junction where several cultivation corridors intersected, positioning themselves where they would be visible to the searching divers but not immediately within reach. Aquatania focused her concentration on the water around them, feeling its movements, its suspended particles, its potential energy.

"When I give the signal, swim hard for that service tunnel," she whispered, indicating a small opening partially hidden by hanging nets.

The vibrations in the water intensified as the alien divers approached, their movement patterns betraying their inhuman nature even before they came into view. When they appeared at the far end of the intersection, Aquatania could see the uncanny precision in their swimming, no wasted motion, no natural adjustments for current or buoyancy, just mathematical efficiency that made them seem more like machines than living beings.

The moment they spotted Aquatania and Kieran, their trajectory changed with perfect synchronization, their bodies angling directly toward them with predatory intent.

"Now!" Aquatania commanded, her hands sweeping outward in a complex pattern.

The water responded instantly to her manipulation. Silt and organic particles that had settled on abandoned equipment suddenly lifted, swirling into a dense cloud that filled the entire intersection. Simultaneously, she created opposing currents that collided in the center of the space, generating a chaotic turbulence that would disorient any swimmer relying on conventional senses.

Kieran grabbed her hand and pulled her toward the service tunnel, both swimming with powerful strokes as the water behind them transformed into an impenetrable, churning mass. They slipped into the narrow passage just as alarmed vibrations passed through the water, the aliens attempting to communicate through the disruptive cloud.

The maintenance tunnel led them through the less glamorous infrastructure of Oceana Prime, waste reclamation systems, water purification chambers, and utility corridors that kept the underwater city functioning. Though clearly designed for human maintenance workers, these passages showed no signs of recent use, the emergency lighting crystal's dim glow revealing a layer of sediment undisturbed for weeks.

They eventually emerged into a completely different environment. The Kelp Forest Sanctuary spread before them in what should've been magnificent splendor. It was a carefully cultivated ecosystem where kelp stalks grew to ten times their natural size, creating an underwater forest that housed countless species. But something was wrong. The kelp, which should have been vibrant and golden-green, displayed patches of grayish discoloration. Many stalks had thinned significantly, their normally robust structures appearing brittle and sickly.

"This isn't from neglect," Aquatania said, swimming closer to examine a particularly affected section. "The water composition itself has changed."

She dipped her fingers into the liquid surrounding a discolored kelp frond, bringing them to her nose. A subtle metallic scent, almost imperceptible but distinct to her enhanced senses.

"It's similar to the alien blood we encountered in the laboratory," she observed. "But diffused, diluted, as if they're gradually introducing it into the water supply."

Kieran examined the dying kelp with grim assessment. "Terraforming," he concluded. "Or whatever their equivalent would be. Changing the environment to suit their biology rather than adapting to ours."

The implications sent a chill through Aquatania. It was environmental warfare on a scale that threatened every native species in their world.

They swam deeper into the sanctuary, following a meandering path between towering kelp stalks. Despite the disturbing signs of tampering, the forest still maintained its eerie beauty, shafts of filtered sunlight penetrating from the distant surface, creating dappled patterns across the ocean floor. Schools of small fish darted between the stalks, their movements suggesting they hadn't yet been affected by whatever was changing the kelp.

"There," Kieran said, pointing toward a clearing ahead where the kelp grew in a perfect circle around a depression in the seafloor.

The kelp dragons were immediately distinguishable from their reef cousins, more serpentine in form, with elongated bodies covered in overlapping scales that resembled kelp fronds more than traditional dragon armor. Their coloration ranged from deep gold to mossy green, providing perfect camouflage among the vegetation they called home. Where reef dragons bore coral-like growths, these creatures had developed filamentous extensions that mimicked kelp fronds, allowing them to blend seamlessly with their surroundings when stationary.

Unlike the calm dignity of the reef dragons, these creatures showed obvious signs of distress. Three adults circled the depression restlessly, their movements agitated, occasional bursts of speed sending them darting between kelp stalks before returning to their vigilant pattern. In the center of the clearing, two juvenile dragons huddled together, their normally golden scales dulled to a sickly yellow-gray.

"They're suffering from the water changes," Aquatania said, her heart aching at their obvious distress. "This is their home. They can't simply leave for cleaner waters."

She approached slowly, her hands extended in a non-threatening posture that communicated peaceful intent. The largest kelp dragon broke from its circular pattern to face her, its sinuous body coiling defensively between her and the juveniles. Unlike the reef dragons, this creature showed no immediate recognition or trust, only the wariness of a being whose environment had been violated.

"I need to gain its trust," Aquatania murmured to Kieran, who hovered a short distance behind her. "Stay back for now."

She focused inward, calling upon her sea dragon heritage more deeply than before. Scales shimmered across her forearms and neck, her eyes shifting slightly toward her draconic appearance, vertical pupils expanding in the dim light, irises taking on an iridescent quality. When she spoke, it was in the ancient draconic tongue, sounds that carried perfectly through water despite being designed for air.

The kelp dragon's defensive posture relaxed slightly, its head tilting in evident surprise at hearing the ancient language. Aquatania continued speaking, explaining their purpose, the threat to all species, and the need for samples that might save both human and dragon kind.

The dragon listened, intelligence evident in its amber eyes as it processed her words.

Finally, with obvious reluctance, it extended a foreleg toward her, revealing the collection point between its scales.

"Thank you," she said in both human and draconic language as she prepared her extraction equipment.

The blood of kelp dragons differed visibly from that of their reef cousins, a golden-green fluid that seemed almost to capture sunlight within its substance. As Aquatania carefully filled her collection vials, she noticed something else…tiny organisms swimming within the blood itself, symbiotic life forms that contributed to the dragon's remarkable adaptation to its environment.

"The aliens aren't just spreading disease," she realized as she secured the samples. "They're altering the environment itself. These dragons have developed symbiotic relationships with native microorganisms, relationships that would be destroyed if the water composition changes too dramatically."

She'd just finished collecting samples from the second adult when a low-frequency vibration passed through the water, not natural current movement, but a deliberate signal. Kieran was at her side instantly, his hand on her arm as he pointed toward the edge of the sanctuary where mechanical lights had appeared, sweeping methodically through the kelp forest.

"Alarm," he said tersely. "Our presence has been detected."

The kelp dragons scattered at the disturbance, disappearing into the forest with surprising speed despite their distressed state. Aquatania quickly secured the sample vials in her satchel as the sweeping lights drew closer, their mechanical precision confirming they belonged to alien patrols rather than legitimate Oceana Prime security.

Kieran pulled her behind a massive formation of coral and rock that had been cultivated as a natural feature of the sanctuary. They pressed themselves against its rough surface as searchlights swept through the water around them, the beams cutting through the murky distance with unnatural clarity.

"They're using some kind of detection technology," Kieran whispered, his body positioned protectively between Aquatania and the approaching lights. "Standard search patterns but with non-standard equipment."

The lights paused at the clearing where they'd just been collecting samples, focusing on the water where trace amounts of dragon blood might still linger. A signal passed between the lights, short pulses of altered frequency that Aquatania felt rather than heard. The message was clear. Evidence found, targets nearby.

"We need to move," Kieran urged, his eyes tracking the lights as they began a more concentrated search pattern.

"Now. Before they call for reinforcements."

Aquatania nodded, already calculating their next move. Two dragon subspecies sampled, one more to go. But with alien forces now actively hunting them, reaching the Phosphorescent Caves would require every skill and advantage they possessed.

The cooler embrace of the sea enveloped Aquatania as she dove deeper. Beside her, Kieran followed with practiced efficiency, his movements slightly constrained by the bandages beneath his diving suit. The temporary treatment for his wound had stabilized the alien toxin, but she could see the tightness around his eyes that spoke of lingering pain.

They descended toward the hidden entrance of the Phosphorescent Caves, the last location on their desperate quest for dragon blood components. The luminous dragons that dwelled within these ancient caverns held the final piece they needed, but with alien patrols now actively hunting them, reaching the creatures would test both her draconic abilities and Kieran's wounded strength to their limits.

"Stay close," Aquatania whispered, her voice carrying clearly through the water thanks to her sea dragon heritage. "The entrance shifts with the currents. Easy to miss if you don't know what to look for."

Kieran nodded, conserving his breath as he followed her precise movements through a seemingly solid wall of coral. Only when viewed from the exact right angle did the hidden passage reveal itself, a narrow corridor that twisted inward toward the heart of the underwater mountain range. As they slipped through, Aquatania noted the patrol markers embedded in the coral, small, bioluminescent tags placed by Oceana Prime's border guards. They hadn't been disturbed, which meant the aliens hadn't discovered this entrance. *Yet*.

Once inside the first chamber, Aquatania paused, gathering her concentration. She extended her hands, her palms facing outward, and focused on the water surrounding them. Gradually, the light passing through the liquid began to bend and refract differently, creating a shimmering distortion that wrapped around their bodies like a second skin.

"Water-light camouflage," she explained, her voice strained with the effort of maintaining such precise manipulation. "We'll appear as nothing more than shifting currents to anyone watching."

Kieran studied the effect with undisguised admiration. "I've seen military mages attempt similar illusions. None as effective as this."

"Not an illusion," she corrected, sweat already pouring from her forehead despite the cool water. "Actual manipulation of how light travels through water molecules. More science than magic."

They pressed deeper into the cave system, the natural blue of the seawater gradually giving way to the faint, ethereal glow that gave the Phosphorescent Caves their name. Ancient minerals embedded in the rock walls absorbed sunlight during the day and released it slowly throughout the night, creating paths of ghostly illumination that twisted through the darkness. The light cast strange, elongated shadows as they moved, their camouflaged forms occasionally visible as rippling distortions against the glowing backdrop.

"How much farther?" Kieran asked as they navigated a particularly narrow passage. The constricted space forced them close together, his shoulder brushing against hers as they angled their bodies to fit through.

"The inner chamber lies beyond the Shimmer Wall," Aquatania replied, her breathing becoming more labored. Maintaining the water-light camouflage demanded constant concentration, a steady drain on her energy reserves. "Half a mile deeper."

Kieran's eyes narrowed as he assessed her condition. "You're pushing yourself too hard," he warned, concern evident in his voice. "Your hands are trembling."

"I'm fine," she insisted, though the persistent throb behind her temples suggested otherwise. "We can't risk dropping the camouflage. Not with active patrols —"

Her response was cut short as they rounded a corner into a wider chamber and froze. Three figures hovered in the water ahead, their movements too fluid to be human. Though they maintained humanoid appearances, wearing the uniforms of Oceana Prime guards, their limbs moving with that distinctive wrongness Aquatania had come to recognize. An alien patrol was positioned directly between them and the path to the inner chamber.

Kieran's hand moved to the hilt of his underwater blade, the movement slow and deliberate to avoid creating telltale currents. The aliens hadn't spotted them yet. Their attention was focused on some kind of scanning device that emitted pulses of sickly green light.

"They're mapping the cave system," Aquatania whispered, making sure her voice was barely audible even to Kieran beside her. "Looking for the luminous dragons."

A sweat trickled down her temple despite the water, the strain of maintaining their camouflage while remaining perfectly still, taking its toll. They couldn't retreat because the passage behind them was too narrow to turn quickly, and any sudden movement would create water disturbances the aliens would surely detect.

The patrol leader raised its head suddenly, turning in their direction. Though its eyes appeared human, Aquatania could see the unnatural stillness in its gaze, the lack of natural blinking or movement. It had sensed something.

"Hold onto me," she whispered to Kieran, a decision made in an instant.

He gripped her arm without hesitation. Aquatania abandoned the camouflage, channeling that energy instead into a massive surge of water manipulation. With a sharp

111

thrust of both hands, she created a powerful current that slammed into the alien patrol with devastating force. The three figures catapulted against the far wall of the chamber, their disguises distorting with the impact as their limbs bent at impossible angles.

"Go!" she shouted, already propelling herself forward with powerful kicks.

Kieran drew his blade as he swam beside her, the silver metal gleaming with enchanted runes that activated in the water. The first alien recovered with unnatural speed, its form stretching as it launched itself toward them. Kieran met it with a slash, his weapon slicing through the creature's extended arm. Dark fluid dispersed into the water, momentarily creating a cloud that obscured their movements.

They raced through the next series of passages, Aquatania leading with unerring precision despite never having visited these specific caves before. Her sea dragon heritage provided an instinctive understanding of underwater geography, a primal memory passed down through generations of her mother's bloodline.

"The Shimmer Wall is ahead," she called back to Kieran, pointing toward a curtain of bioluminescent algae that hung across the widening passage. "The luminous dragons maintain it as a barrier. It analyzes intent. Those seeking to harm the dragons can't pass through."

"And those being pursued by shape-shifting aliens?" Kieran asked, glancing back at the darkening water behind them. The sounds of pursuit echoed through the caves, high-pitched clicking noises that resembled no earthly language.

"We're about to find out," she replied grimly.

They passed through the living barrier with a brief sensation of tingling warmth, the algae parting to allow them entry before sealing shut behind them. The chamber beyond stole Aquatania's breath despite her urgent mission. Vast and cathedral-like, its ceiling soared hundreds of feet above, dotted with stalactites that glowed with internal light. Pools of varying depths covered the chamber floor, each illuminated from within by the bioluminescent organisms that thrived in these protected waters.

And there, resting in the central pool, were the luminous dragons.

The sudden increase in clicking sounds from beyond the Shimmer Wall drew their attention. The barrier rippled ominously, dark shapes pressing against its translucent surface.

There's no time. You will need to return. For now, they cannot pass, the luminous dragon assured them. *But neither can you return that way.*

Kieran moved to Aquatania's side, his expression grim as he watched the barrier bulge inward under increasing pressure. "No, we won't make it back the way we came," he said, voicing what they both already knew.

The luminous dragon's ancient eyes settled on them with something like compassion. *There is another way*, it projected. *Though few have survived its passage.*

The maintenance shaft, the luminous dragon projected, its thoughts rippling through Aquatania's mind with crystalline clarity. *It channels excess water from the city's central reservoir out to the open sea.* The creature's light pulsed in patterns that conveyed both warning and guidance. *The current runs swift and merciless. Few survive its passage, but for one with your abilities...* The thought trailed off as the dragon's massive head turned toward a circular opening in the chamber's far wall, barely visible behind a cluster of glowing coral. Water rushed into it with hypnotic force, creating a swirling vortex that would crush ordinary swimmers against its walls.

Aquatania studied the opening, calculations running through her mind, water pressure, velocity, and distance. Her sea dragon heritage provided instinctive understanding of fluid dynamics that no human hydrologist could match.

Behind them, the clicking sounds grew louder as the aliens continued their assault on the Shimmer Wall. The barrier trembled under their relentless pressure, its bioluminescent fibers stretching thin in places.

"We need to move now," she said, securing the warded container with their precious samples against her body. The vials, sea dragon sapphire and fire dragon ruby, represented their best hope against the alien contagion. But they needed the third…

She grasped Kieran's arm, pulling him toward the maintenance shaft. "This way."

He resisted slightly, his eyes fixed on the powerful current. "The force will be too strong," he protested, his military mind assessing the risk with pragmatic clarity. "Even if we survive the initial surge, the pressure differential could crush our lungs before we reach the exit."

"Not for me," Aquatania replied with quiet determination. "Water is my element. I can manipulate its flow around us, create a pocket of stability." She met his eyes directly, willing him to understand what she wasn't explicitly stating, that using her abilities at this scale would exact a physical toll she wasn't certain she could withstand.

Kieran held her gaze, seemingly reading the unspoken message in her expression. His hand moved to cover hers where it gripped his arm, a gesture both reassuring and intimate. "How can I help?"

"Stay close. Don't fight the current. And trust me." The simplicity of her instructions belied the complexity of what she was about to attempt.

A resounding crack echoed through the chamber as the first breach appeared in the Shimmer Wall. A dark, fluid tendril pushed through the opening, its movement unlike anything in nature as it tasted the water beyond.

Go with the flow, the luminous dragon projected, its ancient mind touching theirs one final time. *Remember who you are, daughter of two worlds.*

Aquatania nodded gratefully to the ancient creature, then turned toward the maintenance shaft. With Kieran at her side, she kicked powerfully through the water, aiming directly for the swirling vortex. As they reached its edge, she felt him tense beside her, instinct fighting against the suicidal plunge they were about to take.

"Now!" she shouted, and together they surrendered to the pull of the current.

The force was immediate and overwhelming, a watery fist that grabbed them and hurled them into the shaft with crushing speed. Aquatania's body responded instantly, her draconic nature awakening to the challenge. She thrust her hands outward, her fingers splayed as she reached not with physical strength but with the innate connection to water that flowed through her dragon bloodline.

The rushing liquid responded to her call, molecules reordering themselves around their bodies. A bubble of calm formed within the raging torrent, not air, but water held in a different state, flowing around rather than against them. Kieran's eyes widened as he felt the difference, the devastating pressure suddenly reduced to a firm but manageable embrace.

"Remarkable," he said, the word forming bubbles that swirled away into the current.

Aquatania couldn't spare the concentration to respond. Every fiber of her being focused on maintaining the protective bubble as the shaft narrowed and twisted through Oceana Prime's infrastructure. The city had been built to harness water's natural power, channeling it through conduits like this one to generate energy and regulate temperature. What served as practical engineering for the city now became their desperate escape route.

They shot through a series of metal grates, the force of the water having long ago bent the barriers wide enough for

115

human passage. Each twist and turn of the shaft tested her control, requiring split-second adjustments to maintain their protective cocoon. Sweat mixed with the water on her face, her muscles trembling with the strain of such fine manipulation against such overwhelming force.

Kieran noticed her struggle, moving closer within their bubble. "You're bleeding," he said, his voice tight with concern.

Aquatania tasted copper on her lips, realizing blood had begun trickling from her nose. It was the physical manifestation of pushing her abilities beyond their limits. She couldn't spare the energy to answer, merely shaking her head slightly to indicate she would continue.

The maintenance shaft widened suddenly, emptying into a larger collection chamber where multiple conduits converged. The momentary reduction in pressure allowed her to catch her breath, to steady her concentration before the final push.

"Almost there," she said and gasped, wiping blood from her upper lip with the back of her hand. "The main outflow channel is ahead. Once we clear it, we'll be outside the city's outer wall, near the docking bays."

Kieran's hand found hers in the swirling water, a silent offering of strength. She accepted it, drawing not just comfort but actual energy from the contact, as if his human vitality could supplement her faltering reserves.

"Ready?" she asked, eyes fixed on the massive outflow tunnel ahead, its diameter easily three times the shaft they'd traversed.

"With you? Always," he replied, the simple phrase carrying weight beyond its words.

They surrendered to the current once more, Aquatania's control stretched to its breaking point as they hurtled through the final channel. The pressure built until her ears popped painfully, depths changing rapidly as they approached the exit. Light filtered through the water ahead, not the bioluminescent glow of the caves or the artificial illumination of the city, but natural sunlight diffused through seawater. They were nearly free.

With a final surge of power, Aquatania maintained the protective bubble as they shot from the outflow pipe like a projectile from a weapon. The sudden release of pressure sent them tumbling through open water, her concentration finally breaking as exhaustion claimed its due. The protective bubble dissolved, leaving them to right themselves in the calmer currents outside the city wall.

Kieran recovered first, orienting himself with a soldier's instinctive awareness of surroundings. He pointed toward a row of small vessels tethered nearby, the civilian docking area where they'd left their submersible hours earlier. Aquatania nodded, forcing her trembling limbs to cooperate as they swam toward the familiar outline of their craft.

As they drew closer, Kieran suddenly grabbed her arm, pulling her behind the cover of a mooring post. He pointed toward their submersible, where two figures that appeared to be dock workers moved with the too-fluid grace.

"Disguised aliens," he whispered. "They found our vessel."

Aquatania's heart sank. So close to escape, yet cut off from their only means of returning to Zephyria with the precious samples. She quickly surveyed the docking area, mind racing through possibilities despite her exhaustion.

"There," she indicated a control panel attached to the nearest mooring post. "It's connected to the emergency protocol system. Triggering an alarm would activate containment procedures, force fields, and security personnel."

Kieran understood immediately. "A diversion. I'll trigger it, draw them away from the submersible. You get aboard and prepare for immediate departure."

"They'll recognize you," she protested.

"They'll try to catch me," he corrected with grim confidence. "There's a difference."

Before she could argue further, he squeezed her shoulder once, then kicked away toward the control panel. Aquatania watched as he approached it casually, mimicking the movements of a dock worker going about routine business. His hand moved to the panel, his fingers dancing across the surface in a sequence that spoke of military override codes rather than civilian access.

Alarms blared instantly, lights flashing along the docking bay as emergency protocols activated. The disguised aliens' heads snapped toward the disturbance, their movements becoming less human as alert status disrupted their concentration on maintaining their forms.

Kieran was already swimming away from the panel, deliberately drawing their attention as both creatures abandoned their position by the submersible to pursue him.

Aquatania seized the opportunity, pushing her exhausted body through the water toward their vessel. She reached it in seconds, pressing her palm against the recognition plate that unlocked the hatch. The system acknowledged her with a soft click, the entrance sliding open to admit her to the craft's interior.

Her fingers flew across the control panel, initiating the startup sequence with practiced efficiency. The submersible hummed to life around her, systems engaging as she watched anxiously through the viewport for Kieran's return.

The aliens had nearly reached him, their pursuit hampered by the necessity of maintaining human appearance in the now-crowded docking area as other citizens responded to the alarm.

Kieran ducked between mooring lines and around other vessels, using the confusion to circle back toward their submersible. He reached the hatch just as Aquatania brought the engines to standby, slipping inside with barely a ripple in the water. His breath came in heavy gasps, a fresh stain of blood darkening the bandages beneath his torn diving suit.

"Go," he urged, securing the hatch behind him. "They've called for reinforcements."

Aquatania engaged the engines, the submersible pulling away from its mooring with gathering speed. Through the rear viewport, she saw the aliens reach their empty docking position, forms distorting in what could only be rage as their quarry escaped. One raised an arm that elongated impossibly, transforming into something that resembled a weapon more than a limb. Energy crackled at its tip.

"Brace!" Kieran shouted as the alien fired.

The blast struck their stern, rocking the submersible violently but failing to penetrate its reinforced hull. Aquatania pushed the engines to maximum power, the vessel responding with a surge of speed that pressed them back against their seats.

Within moments, they'd cleared the docking area and entered open water, diving deeper to put solid rock between them and any further attacks.

"We made it," she said and let out a deep breath, allowing herself a moment of relief as she patted the secured container holding their samples. "All components intact."

Kieran nodded, his expression grim despite their escape. "Don't celebrate yet," he said, pointing to the detection array on the control panel. "We've got company."

In the distance behind them, the sensors showed multiple vessels in pursuit, faster and more maneuverable than their scientific submersible. The danger was far from over.

Aquatania's fingers tightened on the controls. "Then we'll just have to be smarter," she said, adjusting their course toward a deep-sea trench that her dragon senses told her would offer protection. "These waters are my ancestral home. They don't know what they're chasing."

CHAPTER SEVEN

The royal submersible broke through a cloud of silver bubbles as it entered Oceana Prime's main transport canal, its enchanted hull adjusting to the change in pressure with a series of soft clicks. Aquatania guided the vessel with practiced hands, her fingers dancing across control crystals that responded to her touch with pulses of blue light. She glanced at Kieran, noting the tight line of his jaw despite his attempt to appear at ease. The samples from the reef and kelp dragons were secured in specialized containment vials at his side, each one a victory against impossible odds, but they both knew two subspecies wouldn't be enough.

"We lost the aliens at the kelp forest," Kieran said, answering her unspoken question. His hand absently moved to his side, where the alien wound was still healing. "For now. But they'll be watching the Phosphorescent Caves. We need a different approach."

"That's why we're here," she replied, guiding the submersible through a massive archway carved from living coral. "The Marine Sciences Institute has the equipment we need to analyze these samples immediately. And an old friend who might help us reach the third subspecies without detection."

Oceana Prime unfurled before them like a dream crystallized into reality — a vast underwater metropolis built within the skeletal remains of a giant ancient sea dragon. The creature's massive ribs, petrified over millennia, formed natural arches that supported entire neighborhoods. Bioluminescent algae had been cultivated along these structural bones, bathing the city in ever-shifting blues and greens that rippled with the water's movement. Between these organic frameworks, buildings of coral, glass, and enchanted stone created a city that appeared to have grown rather than been constructed.

Aquatania steered them through the outer districts, where the effects of the crisis remained largely invisible. Merfolk with tails in every color imaginable darted between buildings alongside humans wearing gill-enchantments. Water-breathing residents swam above walkways designed for those who preferred to keep their feet on solid surfaces. Enchanted bubbles carried conversations between swimmers, the magical spheres maintaining their integrity as they passed from person to person.

"It looks almost normal," Kieran observed, watching a group of children chase a school of glowing fish through a coral playground.

"The outer rings have been less affected," Aquatania explained, her voice tightening. "My father has kept the worst confined to the inner districts, hoping to contain the spread."

As they proceeded deeper into the city, the illusion of normalcy began to fray. A market square that should've been crowded with vendors now stood half-empty, abandoned stalls swaying gently in the current. Those merchants who remained called out their wares with forced cheerfulness, voices too loud in the unnaturally open space. Customers moved through the market with quick, purposeful movements, no longer lingering to socialize or haggle.

They passed a row of dwellings where crimson symbols had been painted across doorways—the universal sign for quarantine. Guards in enhanced armor stood at intervals along the street, their faces hidden behind helmets with enchanted visors that supposedly detected symptoms of the Red Death.

"Are you sure we weren't followed?" Aquatania asked, guiding the submersible into a less-traveled side canal. "After what happened at the kelp forest…"

"As sure as possible," Kieran replied, his eyes constantly scanning their surroundings. "But if they've infiltrated Oceana Prime as deeply as Zephyria, they won't need to follow us to know where we're going."

A sudden flash of movement caught Aquatania's attention—a medical team in flowing blue robes rushing toward a dwelling where the quarantine symbol glowed with fresh paint. A small crowd had gathered, held back by guards with crossed tridents. From the submersible, Aquatania could see a figure being carried from the home on a stretcher, the distinctive crimson patterns of the Red Death visible even at this distance.

"They're taking more victims somewhere," Kieran observed, his voice dropping to a whisper. "But where? And for what purpose?"

"That's what we need to find out." Aquatania guided their vessel away from the distressing scene, turning toward a massive formation that rose from the ocean floor at the city's heart.

The Marine Sciences Institute dominated the central district of Oceana Prime—a sprawling complex built into and around a living reef formation. Unlike the organic architecture of the surrounding city, the institute featured more deliberate design—perfect domes of reinforced glass, precision-cut coral walls inlaid with scientific runes, and observation towers that spiraled upward like frozen whirlpools. Enchanted lights outlined research chambers where scientists could be seen moving between workstations, their white robes billowing in the water.

"The foremost minds in marine science gather here," Aquatania explained as they approached. "Including experts in cross-species biology, which is exactly what we need to understand how dragon blood can be adapted for human use."

They docked their submersible at a small, private entrance

reserved for royal family members. As they exited the vessel, Aquatania noticed the security measures had been significantly enhanced since her last visit. Guards wearing enchanted armor that shifted colors to match their surroundings stood at rigid attention. Magical barriers shimmered across doorways, requiring specific authorization for passage.

"Identification and purpose," the lead guard demanded as they approached the entrance, his trident lowering to block their path. Though his face remained professional, Aquatania didn't miss how his eyes widened slightly at her appearance, recognizing her, yet protocol demanded formal verification.

"Princess Aquatania of the Twin Realms," she stated, touching her royal signet ring to the identification crystal he extended. The stone flared blue, confirming her identity. "I'm here to consult with Senior Researcher Marina on urgent matters related to the contagion."

The guard hesitated, his gaze shifting to Kieran. "And your companion?"

"General Kieran, military advisor to the crown," she replied, a hint of impatience entering her voice. "His presence is required for both security and consultation purposes."

The guard's posture stiffened. "Forgive me, Your Highness, but we have strict orders. No visitors to research facilities without advance clearance from the Science Council. Even for royal family members." He glanced nervously at his colleagues. "The contagion protocols—"

"Are necessary, yes," Aquatania cut in, stepping closer. She lowered her voice, forcing him to lean forward to hear. "But surely you understand that I wouldn't be here if it weren't of vital importance. We have samples that may lead to a treatment, samples that will deteriorate if not properly analyzed immediately."

The guard's eyes darted to the satchel at her side, then back to her face. She could see the conflict playing across his features, duty to follow protocols versus deference to royal authority.

"I can summon Senior Researcher Marina to verify my request," Aquatania offered, sensing his wavering resolve.

"That won't be necessary," a melodic voice called from behind the guards. The security formation parted to reveal a woman gliding toward them. Her lower body was a magnificent tail covered in iridescent scales that shifted between turquoise and violet with each movement. Her laboratory coat, specially designed for her physiology, floated around her torso like a cloud of white silk in water. "The princess's arrival was anticipated."

"Marina," Aquatania uttered, heaving a sigh of relief.

The mermaid scientist inclined her head respectfully, though her eyes sparkled with familiar warmth. "Your Highness. General." She turned to the lead guard. "I'll take responsibility for our guests. The proper authorization codes have already been transmitted to your superior."

The guard hesitated a moment longer, then stepped aside with a formal bow. "As you wish, Senior Researcher. Please ensure visitors remain within authorized areas only."

"Of course," Marina replied smoothly, gesturing for Aquatania and Kieran to follow her through the shimmering barrier. "The princess is quite familiar with our protocols."

As they passed through the magical threshold, Aquatania felt the subtle tingle of scanning enchantments washing over her, searching for contamination or concealed weapons. Kieran's shoulders tensed at the sensation, but he maintained his composed expression.

"You arrived just in time," Marina whispered once they were beyond the guards' hearing. Her playful demeanor vanished, replaced by urgent intensity. "Things are worse than your father knows. Much worse."

Marina led them through corridors where the walls themselves seemed alive, engineered coral that processed and purified the surrounding water while simultaneously housing delicate scientific instruments. Researchers in white coats moved purposefully between chambers, many offering quick, respectful nods to Marina as she passed. Unlike the outer sections of Oceana Prime, the institute hummed with focused energy, its personnel united by the urgency of their work against the contagion.

Aquatania felt a familiar sense of belonging among these scientists, remembering the years she'd spent in these very halls alongside Marina, both of them young researchers determined to unravel marine mysteries.

"They've converted half our marine genomics department to contagion research," Marina explained, her tail propelling her forward with graceful undulations. "The other half is studying unprecedented changes in ocean chemistry, changes that appear to be accelerating."

"The kelp forest," Aquatania said quietly. "We saw evidence of water composition alterations there."

Marina nodded grimly. "It's happening everywhere, though most noticeably in confined water systems. Whatever these creatures are, they're not just attacking our bodies, they're transforming our environment."

She guided them into a private laboratory at the end of a corridor marked with authorization runes that glowed at Marina's approach. The door sealed behind them with a soft pulse of magic, its security protocols automatically activating.

Aquatania took in the familiar chaos of her friend's workspace. The walls were lined with preservation tanks containing specimens from the deepest ocean trenches to the shallowest tide pools. Bioluminescent cultures bubbled in crystal containers, their soft glow fluctuating in hypnotic patterns. Holographic displays hovered above workstations, showing complex molecular structures rotating slowly in three dimensions.

"Your organizational system hasn't improved, I see,"

Aquatania remarked with a small smile, gesturing to the precariously stacked research journals and scattered collection vials.

Marina's laugh rippled through the water like music. "Some things never change. Including your perfect posture." She swam closer, the formality of their public greeting giving way to genuine warmth as she clasped Aquatania's hands in her own. "It's been too long, Tania."

"Nearly two years," Aquatania agreed, squeezing her friend's webbed fingers. "Not since that conference on cross-species pathogen transmission in the Eastern Archipelago."

"Which proved remarkably relevant, as it turns out." Marina's expression sobered. "Though none of us imagined the pathogens might come from beyond our world entirely."

Kieran had positioned himself near the doorway, his back to the wall, his eyes constantly sweeping the laboratory and its many shadowed corners. His hand rested casually on his weapon hilt, his stance relaxed yet ready for immediate action. Aquatania had noticed this habit, his instinctive positioning to maintain sight lines to all potential entrances while keeping her within protective range.

Marina glanced at him, one eyebrow arching elegantly. "Your guardian is thorough," she observed in a lower voice.

"We were attacked at our last collection site," Aquatania explained. "And in my laboratory before that. The infiltrators have identified us as a threat."

"Then you must be on the right track." Marina gestured to a specialized workstation surrounded by analysis equipment. "Show me what you've found."

Aquatania carefully removed the vials from her satchel, each one glowing with the distinctive colors of different dragon blood types. "Reef dragon and kelp dragon, both showing significant neutralizing effects against the pathogen. We'd planned to collect phosphorescent dragon samples next, but—"

"But the caves will be watched now," Marina finished, nodding as she gently took the vials. "Especially after your encounter at the kelp forest."

She placed the first sample, the deep blue blood of the reef dragon, into an analysis chamber lined with enchanted crystal. The machine hummed to life, projecting a magnified image of the blood's cellular structure into the water above them. Complex patterns of molecules danced in the projection, their movements revealing biochemical properties invisible to the naked eye.

"Extraordinary," Marina murmured, manipulating the projection with graceful gestures to isolate specific structures. "The cell membranes contain compounds I've never seen before, a unique lipid configuration that appears to repel foreign bodies while maintaining permeability for essential nutrients."

She inserted the kelp dragon sample into a second chamber, bringing up a comparative display. "And here...similar protective properties but achieved through completely different mechanisms. The kelp dragon blood contains symbiotic microorganisms that actively hunt and neutralize pathogens."

Kieran moved closer, his curiosity momentarily overriding his vigilance. "Can these properties be synthesized? Replicated for treatment?"

"That's the challenge," Marina replied, her webbed fingers dancing through the projection to highlight specific molecular chains. "The reptilian immunity factor is fascinating. It appears to function on both biological and quasi-magical levels simultaneously. But isolating it for human compatibility will be incredibly difficult."

She expanded a section of the projection showing the interaction between dragon blood and infected human cells. Where they made contact, the alien influence visibly retreated, geometric patterns dissolving as healthy cellular function was restored.

"The difficulty lies in the integration," Marina continued, her scientific mind fully engaged. "Human physiology rejects direct dragon blood transfusion. The magical elements cause severe reactions. We need to identify precisely which components provide immunity, then find a way to make them compatible with human biology."

"Which is why we need the third subspecies," Aquatania said. "The phosphorescent dragons evolved in deep-water caves with unique mineral compositions. Their adaptation to extreme pressure environments might provide the missing link."

Marina nodded, already manipulating her equipment to run additional tests. "The triple-helix structure here" — she indicated a twisting molecular formation in the reef dragon sample — "bears striking similarities to human DNA repair mechanisms. If we could isolate this and combine it with the adaptive properties from other subspecies..."

"We could create a treatment that works with human biology rather than against it," Aquatania finished, the excitement of scientific discovery momentarily outweighing the urgency of their situation.

Kieran cleared his throat softly, drawing their attention back to practical matters. "The Phosphorescent Caves will be heavily guarded now. How do we access the dragons there?"

Marina's lips curved into a knowing smile. "You don't need to go to the caves," she said, swimming to a secure storage unit embedded in the wall. She pressed her palm against its surface, whispering an incantation that caused the door to slide open with a soft click. "Because I have this."

She carefully removed a crystal containment vessel, its contents glowing with gentle, pulsing blue-white light. Inside floated what appeared to be a scale, translucent as the finest glass yet shimmering with internal luminescence.

"A phosphorescent dragon scale," Aquatania whispered,

recognition dawning. "From the research expedition to the Deep Trench last year."

"Precisely." Marina placed the vessel on her workstation. "Complete with preserved cellular material that should contain all the genetic information we need. I've been studying its unique properties for months, its ability to generate light without heat, to withstand crushing pressure, and most importantly"—she manipulated the analysis equipment to display the scale's internal structure—"its remarkable resistance to environmental toxins."

Aquatania stared at the projection, her mind racing through possibilities. "With this, we might be able to bypass the collection stage entirely and move directly to synthesis."

"It will still be challenging," Marina cautioned, already preparing extraction tools. "But yes, theoretically possible. Especially with two brilliant scientists working together." Her grin flashed, reminiscent of their academy days when they'd stayed up nights tackling seemingly impossible problems. "Just like old times, except with higher stakes."

"Will you join us, then?" Aquatania asked, though she already knew the answer from her friend's energized movements.

"Try to stop me," Marina replied, gathering specialized equipment and placing it in a case. "My expertise in marine adaptive biology is exactly what you need." Her expression darkened momentarily. "Besides, three of my research assistants have fallen ill. One disappeared from the quarantine ward last night. This is personal now."

Kieran had returned to his position by the door, but his posture had shifted subtly, a new tension visible in his shoulders. "How quickly can you be ready to move? We shouldn't stay in one location too long."

"Give me twenty minutes to gather what we need and secure my research data," Marina said, already moving efficiently between storage units. "There's someone else you should meet while you're here, a sky dragon diplomat who arrived yesterday for the emergency summit. He might provide valuable connections for your work."

"A sky dragon?" Aquatania exchanged glances with Kieran. "Here in Oceana Prime?"

"Unusual, I know," Marina agreed, securing vials of reagents in a specialized container. "But these are unusual times. His name is Zephyr, and he's been quite interested in cross-species research on the contagion." She hesitated, then added more quietly, "He also has access to restricted facilities across multiple kingdoms, access that even your royal credentials might not provide."

*

Marina's private office occupied a curved section of the institute's eastern dome, its transparent outer wall offering an uninterrupted view of Oceana Prime's central districts. Schools of enhanced messenger fish streamed past the window like ribbons of living light, carrying information between distant sections of the underwater metropolis. Aquatania stood before the curved glass, watching the city's pulse while they waited, her mind cataloging changes since her last visit—more guards at junction points, fewer civilians in open waters, medical transports moving with increasing frequency toward the quarantine zones. Behind her, she heard the office door slide open with a gentle hydraulic sigh.

"Your Highness," Marina announced formally, "may I present Zephyr, Diplomatic Envoy from the Sky Archipelago."

Aquatania turned to find herself facing a man of striking appearance. Tall and lean, with features that seemed carved from alabaster, Zephyr moved with the unmistakable grace of those who spent more time in the air than on solid ground. His hair fell in platinum waves to his shoulders, so pale it appeared almost silver under the office's crystal lights. Though he wore the formal attire of a diplomat, flowing robes in graduated shades of blue fastened with silver clasps shaped like clouds, Aquatania immediately recognized the subtle signs of his true nature…eyes with vertical pupils that caught and reflected light at odd angles, fingernails with the slight curve and hardness of talons, and an aura of contained power that no human form could fully disguise.

"Princess Aquatania," he said, his voice carrying the distinctive melodic quality of sky dragons, each word precisely formed yet flowing into the next like wind through mountain passes. He bowed with perfect diplomatic grace. "Your reputation extends far beyond the Twin Realms. It is an honor to meet the scientist-princess whose research might save us all."

"The honor is mine, Envoy Zephyr," she replied with equal formality, though her mind was already calculating the potential advantages of a sky dragon ally. "Your presence in Oceana Prime suggests the Sky Archipelago takes this crisis as seriously as we do."

"More seriously than some might believe." Zephyr moved to the viewing window, his reflection overlaying the city beyond as he gazed outward. "The contagion has reached even our highest settlements. Isolation offers no protection when the enemy can wear familiar faces."

Kieran remained near the door, his posture relaxed to casual observation but positioned to monitor both Zephyr and the office's entrance. Aquatania noticed how his eyes tracked the diplomat's every movement, missing nothing.

"Senior Researcher Marina tells me you've made significant breakthroughs," Zephyr continued, turning from the window to face them. "Dragon blood as a potential treatment. It's an elegant solution, bridging magical and biological approaches."

"We've confirmed the theory," Aquatania acknowledged.

"But practical application remains challenging. The transition from laboratory success to widespread treatment requires resources, facilities, and access that are increasingly difficult to secure."

Zephyr's lips curved into a confident smile. "Which is precisely where I might be of service. My diplomatic credentials can open doors that even royal authority might find locked." He moved to a small table where Marina had laid out refreshments, selecting a crystallized kelp delicacy with deliberate care. "The Sky Archipelago maintains research facilities in seven kingdoms, all with specialized equipment that could accelerate your work."

"Why offer this assistance?" Kieran asked, speaking for the first time since entering the office. His tone remained neutral, but Aquatania heard the underlying caution. "The Sky Archipelago isn't known for sharing resources without clear benefit."

Rather than taking offense, Zephyr nodded as if appreciating the directness. "A fair question, General. The answer is simple...survival. This contagion threatens all intelligent species. Our oracles predict extinction-level outcomes if it remains unchecked." He set down his untouched refreshment. "And frankly, your approach shows more promise than anything our own scientists have developed."

"You've been studying the disease as well," Aquatania observed.

"Since the first cases appeared in our western territories," Zephyr confirmed. "We've identified similar patterns, human vulnerability, reptilian resistance, and the mathematical progression of symptoms. But the treatment angle eluded us until reports of your research reached our High Council."

Marina, who'd been arranging her collected equipment near the door, joined the conversation. "Zephyr arrived yesterday with authorization to share the Sky Archipelago's research data, including their mapping of infection patterns across multiple regions."

The diplomat nodded, withdrawing a crystal sphere from his robes. He placed it on Marina's desk, then passed his hand over its surface. The sphere activated instantly, projecting a three-dimensional map of their known world into the water around them. Red points of light pulsed across the projection, each representing infection clusters.

"The spread isn't random," Zephyr explained, manipulating the display to highlight specific patterns. "The contagion appeared simultaneously in twelve major population centers, then expanded outward in perfect mathematical progression. This isn't natural transmission, it's coordinated deployment."

Aquatania studied the projection, her scientific mind immediately grasping the implications. "They're targeting communication and transportation hubs first, then government centers, then medical facilities."

"Precisely," Zephyr agreed. "A strategy designed to maximize chaos while minimizing effective response. Classic invasion tactics." He gestured toward the display. "But their pattern reveals a weakness…they're spreading their resources thin, trying to control too many regions simultaneously."

Kieran had moved closer to examine the projection, though he maintained a position between Zephyr and Aquatania. "If we could distribute a treatment to even a few of these key locations, we might disrupt their entire strategy."

"My thoughts exactly," Zephyr said with an approving nod to the general. "The Sky Archipelago has swift transport vessels that could deliver treatments once developed. What we lack is the treatment itself."

"Which is where our collaboration becomes essential," Marina concluded, securing the last of her equipment cases. "Zephyr's diplomatic credentials, my marine biology expertise, Aquatania's research foundation, and Kieran's strategic mind...together we might actually stand a chance."

Aquatania weighed their options, studying Zephyr with careful consideration. Sky dragons were known for their strategic thinking and long-term planning. They were valuable allies but rarely transparent about their full motivations. Yet his offer aligned perfectly with their needs, and time was running critically short.

"If we combine our resources," she said finally, "we could establish a secure laboratory at the boundary between water and air, perhaps in the Coral Citadel at the edge of Oceana Prime. It would allow us to work without requiring you to remain underwater, Envoy Zephyr."

"An excellent suggestion," Zephyr replied, deactivating the projection with a gesture. "The citadel also houses one of our diplomatic enclaves, which offers additional security measures."

They gathered around Marina's desk, discussing logistics, transportation routes, equipment needs, and security protocols. Kieran contributed tactical considerations, identifying potential vulnerabilities and suggesting countermeasures. Marina outlined the specialized equipment they would need to transfer. Zephyr offered access codes and diplomatic clearances that would smooth their passage.

As they finalized their plans, Aquatania noticed a subtle change in the office's ambient sounds. A faint clicking, almost imperceptible, emanated from the ventilation system overhead, a rhythm too regular to be a mechanical malfunction, too deliberate to be a water current.

Kieran noticed it in the same instant, his body tensing mid-sentence. Without warning, he drew his weapon, the silver blade gleaming under the crystal lights as he moved toward Aquatania.

"We're not alone," he whispered, his gaze fixed on the ventilation grate where the clicking had momentarily ceased, replaced by an unnatural silence more telling than any sound.

The ventilation grate exploded outward in a shower of metal fragments as Kieran lunged toward Aquatania, his body colliding with hers just as something dark and segmented shot through the opening. They tumbled behind Marina's desk as more crashes echoed through the office, the main door buckling inward, a section of the ceiling collapsing, and the transparent outer wall crackling with impact stress. Water swirled chaotically as pressure differentials created violent currents. Through the chaos, Aquatania glimpsed figures pouring into the room, some dropping from the ventilation system, others bursting through the compromised door, all of them moving with that distinctive, too-perfect synchronization that betrayed their true nature.

"Stay down," Kieran ordered, already rising to a defensive crouch, his sword drawn. The blade hummed to life in the water, the ancient dragon runes etched along its length beginning to glow with silver-blue energy.

The infiltrators shed their human disguises as they advanced, the transformation rippling across their bodies like oil spreading over water. Their true forms emerged in nightmarish segments, exoskeletons replacing skin, joints reversing direction with wet clicking sounds, faces splitting to reveal compound eyes that reflected the room's crystal lights in fractured patterns. What had appeared to be institute staff moments before now moved with insectoid precision, limbs elongating into segmented appendages tipped with serrated edges that cut through water with unnatural efficiency.

Marina darted toward a control panel on the far wall, her tail propelling her in a blur of movement. "Emergency containment protocols!" she shouted, slapping her palm against a glowing crystal. Alarm sirens wailed through the water as protective shields began descending over equipment stations and sample storage units.

An infiltrator intercepted her before she could complete the sequence, its partially transformed arm whipping forward to wrap around her tail. Marina twisted with remarkable agility, producing a small coral dagger from her coat sleeve and slashing at the appendage. The blade connected with a sound like a shell breaking, releasing a cloud of dark fluid that hung in the water between them.

Zephyr moved with unexpected speed and grace, placing himself between the injured creature and Marina. "Diplomatic defense techniques," he announced with incongruous formality, his hands flowing through patterns that seemed more dance than combat. Where his fingers traced through water, currents solidified momentarily into razor-thin sheets that sliced through the advancing infiltrator's limbs. "A necessity in my profession."

Aquatania had no time to marvel at the sky dragon's surprising abilities. Two infiltrators converged on her position, their movements coordinated with mathematical precision as they circled the desk from opposite directions. She reached out with her sea dragon senses, feeling the water around her, its weight, its potential, its hidden power waiting to be shaped by her will.

The laboratory tanks lining the office walls responded to her call, their glass enclosures shattering as she pulled the water forth in powerful tentacles that whipped through the air. The liquid constructs wrapped around the nearest infiltrator, constricting with crushing force. The creature's exoskeleton buckled with a series of sharp cracks, dark fluid pulsing from the fractures as it thrashed within her watery grip.

Kieran had engaged three infiltrators simultaneously, his sword moving in precise arcs that left trails of silver light through the water. Where the enchanted blade connected with alien flesh, the creatures recoiled as if burned, their segmented limbs spasming and retreating. He fought with economy of movement, each strike calculated for maximum effect while maintaining his position between the majority of attackers and Aquatania.

"They're trying to flank us!" he called out, parrying a strike that would've severed his arm at the shoulder. "Marina, watch your left!"

The mermaid scientist ducked just as a segmented limb slashed through the water where her head had been. She twisted again, jabbing her coral dagger into a joint between the creature's armor plates. The infiltrator emitted a high-frequency sound that vibrated painfully through the water.

Energy weapons materialized from what had appeared to be standard institute equipment, the infiltrators transforming tools into weapons as easily as they changed their own forms. Beams of sickly green light cut through the water, leaving superheated trails that scorched the walls and shattered remaining equipment. One blast struck a cabinet of chemical containers, which exploded in a cloud of bubbling reaction that spread across the ceiling in toxic patterns.

"The samples!" Marina cried as an infiltrator smashed through the protective shield over her workstation, reaching for the precious vials of dragon blood.

Aquatania released one water tentacle to form a pressurized jet that shot across the room, striking the creature with enough force to slam it against the outer wall. The transparent barrier, already compromised, developed a spiderweb of cracks from the impact. Water pressure differentials immediately widened the damage, the entire panel threatening to give way to the crushing force of the deep.

Zephyr abandoned his position to dart toward the threatened samples, snatching the case containing the precious vials moments before another infiltrator's blade-like appendage sliced through the workstation. "Secure the research!" he called, tossing the case toward Aquatania.

"Without it, none of this matters!"

She caught the case, clutching it to her chest as she redirected her water constructs to create a defensive perimeter. The infiltrators seemed to recognize the importance of what she held. Five of them immediately changed course, converging on her position with single-minded intent.

Kieran read the shift in their attack pattern instantly. "They're after the samples! Marina...emergency exit protocol!"

The mermaid scientist understood immediately, swimming to a different control panel and entering a rapid sequence of commands. A section of flooring beneath Aquatania's feet began to glow with activation runes.

"Maintenance tunnels," Marina explained breathlessly, fighting her way toward them through the chaos. "They run beneath the entire institute."

An infiltrator landed on the desk beside Aquatania, its compound eyes reflecting her terrified expression in dozens of fragmented images. Its jaw unhinged to reveal row upon row of needle-like teeth, then lunging for the case in her arms. She reacted instinctively, her free hand shooting forward as scales rippled across her skin. Her partially transformed fingers, now tipped with dragon talons, raked across the creature's eyes, releasing a cloud of dark ichor that hung between them like ink in water.

Kieran appeared behind the wounded infiltrator, his blade severing its head with a single powerful stroke. "Move to the exit!" he ordered, already turning to engage another attacker. "I'll cover your retreat!"

The floor panel had fully activated now, the runes forming a glowing circle large enough for one person at a time. Marina positioned herself beside it, continuing to input commands that would secure their escape route.

"Once you're through, you'll have thirty seconds before I

follow," she instructed Aquatania. "The tunnels will be dark. Follow the bioluminescent markers along the right wall. They'll lead to an emergency exit in the southeast quadrant."

Zephyr fought his way toward them, his robes torn and stained with both his blood and the darker fluid of the infiltrators. Despite his injuries, he moved with fluid grace, his diplomatic defense techniques proving remarkably lethal as he dispatched another attacker.

"They're communicating," he warned, joining their defensive circle around the escape hatch. "Calling for reinforcements. We have minutes at most."

An energy blast struck near Aquatania's head, superheating the water with a sound like steam escaping. Another hit Marina's control panel, shorting out the crystals in a shower of sparks. The mermaid hissed in pain as electrical discharge traveled up her arm, leaving a burn pattern across her scales.

"Now or never," she gasped, slapping the final activation sequence with her uninjured hand. The floor panel slid open, revealing a dark tunnel beneath. "Go!"

Aquatania hesitated, unwilling to leave her friends fighting alone. The laboratory lay in ruins around them, equipment shattered, specimens destroyed, the walls scorched by energy weapons. Three infiltrators lay in various states of dismemberment on the floor, their alien fluids mixing with water to create toxic clouds that drifted through the room. But more kept coming, their inhuman silhouettes visible through the damaged door and ventilation system.

"We can't lose the samples," Kieran reminded her, his voice steady despite the chaos. His gaze met hers for a brief moment, conveying strength and something more, a personal concern that transcended their professional relationship. "Go. We'll follow."

With the research case clutched tightly against her chest, Aquatania took a deep breath and plunged into the darkness below.

The maintenance tunnel swallowed Aquatania in cold darkness, the bioluminescent markers along the wall providing just enough light to reveal corroded pipes and ancient support beams overhead. She landed in knee-deep water. It was runoff from the institute's purification systems that had flowed through these passages for centuries. Clutching the case of precious samples against her chest, she moved forward as Marina had instructed, following the soft blue glow of markers embedded in the right wall. Behind her, she heard the sounds of battle continuing above, energy weapons discharging, the crash of breaking equipment, and beneath it all, that distinctive clicking communication of the infiltrators as they coordinated their attack.

A splash behind her announced the arrival of the first of her companions. Kieran dropped into the water, his sword still drawn and glowing with activation energy. Blood, both his own and the darker fluid of the infiltrators, streaked his face and arms in macabre patterns.

"Keep moving," he urged, scanning the darkness behind them. "Marina's right behind me."

They'd progressed perhaps ten meters when the mermaid scientist joined them, clutching a case against her chest. Despite her natural grace even in shallow water, Marina's movements betrayed exhaustion and injuries — one arm hanging awkwardly at her side and burns visible along her tail where an energy weapon had grazed her scales.

"I grabbed what I could," she gasped, indicating the case. "Research data, partial sequencing of the reptilian immunity factor, and preliminary treatment formulations."

"Zephyr?" Aquatania asked, noting the sky dragon's absence.

"Covering our retreat," Kieran replied tersely. "He said he'd find his own way out."

A distant explosion reverberated through the tunnel,

sending vibrations through the water around their legs. Dust and small fragments of stone drifted down from the ceiling. The sound of pursuit, that distinctive, too-perfect synchronized movement, echoed from the entrance they'd used.

"They're following," Marina whispered unnecessarily. "These tunnels branch in hundreds of directions. We need to move before they organize a proper search pattern."

They hurried forward, following the ancient maintenance passages that wound beneath Oceana Prime's foundations. The tunnels predated the city itself, carved by the earliest settlers who'd established the underwater colony generations ago. In places, the walls were lined with fossilized coral that emitted faint bioluminescence, providing just enough light to navigate by. In others, complete darkness forced them to move by touch and memory, Marina's familiarity with the institute's infrastructure guiding them through intersections and junctions.

"The main security forces will be monitoring all official exit points," Marina explained as they paused at a fork in the tunnels. "But these passages connect to natural cave systems that the founders incorporated into the city's design. Most have been forgotten or ignored for centuries."

She led them down the left passage, which descended at a steeper angle. The water deepened as they proceeded, rising from their knees to their waists. Aquatania felt the distinct change in current and temperature that indicated proximity to the open ocean beyond Oceana Prime's contained environment.

Behind them, the sounds of pursuit grew louder, methodical splashing and that unnerving clicking communication that seemed to carry through water with unnatural clarity. An energy weapon discharged in the distance, its green light briefly illuminating the tunnel behind them before plunging it back into darkness.

"They're gaining," Kieran warned, positioning himself at the rear of their group, sword at the ready.

Aquatania assessed their situation with scientific precision, three injured escapees with critical research materials, pursued by an unknown number of infiltrators in confined tunnels with limited visibility. The tactical disadvantages were severe. But water itself offered one advantage they could exploit.

"Keep moving forward," she instructed, stopping and turning to face the direction of pursuit. "I'll seal the tunnel behind us."

Marina hesitated. "Tania, the structural integrity of these passages—"

"Are already compromised by age and water erosion," Aquatania finished. "Exactly what we need." She handed the case of samples to Marina. "Take these. Don't wait for me. I'll catch up."

Kieran moved to her side, his stance clearly indicating he had no intention of leaving her. "What's your plan?"

"Controlled collapse." Aquatania extended her awareness into the water around them, feeling its pressure against the ancient tunnel walls, the microfractures in stone that had developed over centuries, and the natural forces that could be directed with proper application of her sea dragon abilities.

She began a series of fluid gestures, pulling water molecules into rapid circulation patterns that created localized pressure differentials. The tunnel walls groaned in response, ancient stone protesting as forces beyond its design tolerance pressed against weakened sections.

The first infiltrator appeared at the far end of the tunnel, a dark silhouette moving with that distinctive, too-perfect precision through knee-deep water. Its form had abandoned any pretense of humanity, elongated limbs propelling it forward with insectoid efficiency.

"Now would be good," Kieran suggested, raising his

sword as two more infiltrators appeared behind the first.

Aquatania completed her manipulation with a final, decisive gesture. Water responded to her command, rushing into the microfractures she'd identified and expanding with explosive force. The tunnel ceiling gave way with a thunderous crack, massive sections of stone plummeting into the passage. Water surged around the collapsing debris, creating a powerful current that threatened to sweep them off their feet.

"Run!" she shouted, grabbing Kieran's arm and pulling him backward as the collapse continued, spreading in their direction faster than she'd anticipated. They splashed through rapidly rising water, the current now working against their progress as more of the tunnel system failed under the strain of her manipulation.

They rounded a bend to find Marina waiting anxiously, clutching both sample cases. "This way!" she called, pointing to a narrow side passage barely visible behind a growth of ancient coral. "It leads to a maintenance access point in the outer reef!"

The three of them squeezed through the opening just as a rush of water and debris filled the main tunnel behind them. The side passage climbed steeply upward, eventually breaking the water's surface. They emerged into a narrow air pocket, a natural cavity in the reef structure where maintenance workers could rest and replenish air supplies.

"We should be safe here temporarily," Marina gasped, collapsing against a smooth stone ledge. "This maintenance node isn't on any current maps of the institute."

They sat in exhausted silence for several moments, the only sounds their labored breathing and water dripping from their clothes. The reality of what had just occurred settled over them, the precise targeting of their location, the coordinated attack, and the desperate escape that had nearly failed despite their combined abilities.

144

"They knew exactly where to find us," Kieran said finally, his voice quiet but heavy with suspicion. "Someone's tracking our movements."

"Or someone told them," Marina added, glancing toward the tunnel entrance as if expecting Zephyr to appear at any moment.

"He fought alongside us," Aquatania reminded them, though her own doubts gnawed at her. "Without his assistance, we might not have escaped at all."

Marina opened her case, carefully extracting crystal data storage devices and sample containers. "Most of the critical research survived," she confirmed after a quick inventory. "Enough to continue our work on the treatment formulation. The data on dragon blood properties is particularly valuable. It confirms your theory about combining elements from different subspecies to create a comprehensive immunity factor."

"We need a secure location to continue," Kieran said, wiping alien blood from his blade before sheathing it. "Somewhere defensible, with access to both research equipment and escape routes."

A soft scraping sound from the tunnel entrance drew their attention. All three tensed, Kieran's hand moving back to his weapon as a figure emerged from the water. Zephyr pulled himself onto the stone ledge, his platinum hair darkened with water and what appeared to be blood from a gash across his forehead. His diplomatic robes hung in tatters, revealing glimpses of a form that seemed to flicker between human and dragon aspects, scales appearing momentarily along his arms before receding beneath human skin.

"Forgive my delay," he said, breathing heavily. "I needed to ensure no one followed my exit route." Despite his disheveled appearance, he maintained that precise diction that marked him as a sky dragon diplomat. "The institute is lost. Infiltrators have control of the main research wings and are systematically searching all connected facilities."

"How did you find us?" Kieran asked, his tone neutral but his posture anything but relaxed.

"Marina mentioned emergency maintenance nodes during our planning," Zephyr replied smoothly. "This was the closest to our exit point." He surveyed their small group, his eyes lingering on the research cases. "You secured the critical materials. Excellent."

"We need a new base of operations," Aquatania stated, bringing them back to the immediate problem. "Somewhere we can continue our work safely."

Zephyr nodded, absently touching a cut on his arm that was already beginning to heal with unnatural speed. "I suggest the Coral Citadel," he said. "The diplomatic enclave there has independent security systems, research facilities that could be adapted to our needs, and multiple evacuation routes. Most importantly, it sits at the boundary between water and air, allowing each of us to work in our preferred environment."

As he spoke, Aquatania noticed something on his wrist, a device partially concealed by the torn sleeve of his robe. Not jewelry or a timepiece, but something that resembled a communication apparatus, its surface glowing with subtle patterns that pulsed in rhythmic sequence. When Zephyr caught her gaze, he smoothly adjusted his sleeve to cover the device, his expression revealing nothing.

"The citadel sounds ideal," Marina agreed, either not noticing the exchange or choosing to ignore it. "And it's only a short distance if we follow the outer reef line."

Aquatania nodded her agreement, but her mind was racing with new calculations. The precision of the attack, Zephyr's convenient appearance at the institute just before the infiltrators found them, the hidden communication device he seemed intent on concealing, none proved betrayal, but together they formed a pattern that her scientific mind couldn't ignore.

"We should move quickly," she said, gathering the sample case while maintaining a careful distance from Zephyr. "The treatment formula is too important to risk losing. Countless lives depend on our success."

As they prepared to leave their temporary sanctuary, Aquatania caught Kieran's attention. A silent message passed between them...heightened vigilance, shared suspicion, the understanding that their circle of trust had potentially narrowed even as their group had expanded. Whatever Zephyr's true motives might be, they would discover them soon enough. For now, they needed his resources and connections to continue their work.

The fate of their world depended on creating a treatment from the dragon blood samples. But first, they needed to determine who among them might be working against that very goal.

Chapter Eight

The Coral Citadel emerged from the murky depths like a forgotten dream, its massive spires of petrified coral and sea-worn stone reaching toward the distant surface. Aquatania led their small group through the outer reef formations, her eyes fixed on the ancient structure that had stood abandoned for centuries. Behind her swam Marina, clutching the precious research materials they'd salvaged from the institute, and Kieran, whose vigilant gaze constantly swept their surroundings for signs of pursuit. Zephyr had insisted on taking a separate route, citing diplomatic protocols, but promised to rejoin them inside the citadel, a convenient excuse that did nothing to allay Aquatania's suspicions about the sky dragon's true allegiances.

"The entrance should be through that archway," Marina said, pointing toward a massive coral formation that had once been carved into an ornate doorway. Time and ocean currents had worn away much of the detail, leaving behind a yawning mouth of shadows. "According to the old records, the library chambers lie at the heart of the structure."

Aquatania nodded, adjusting the waterproof satchel containing their dragon blood samples. "Stay close," she instructed the two junior researchers who'd joined them from Marina's team, a young man with gill implants and a woman whose webbed hands marked her mixed heritage. "The structural integrity is questionable after centuries of abandonment."

They approached the entrance with caution, the immensity of the citadel becoming more apparent with each stroke. What had appeared as spires from a distance revealed themselves as towering coral pinnacles, their surfaces etched with intricate patterns that told stories of sea dragon history. Between these natural columns, walls of fitted stone blocks created chambers and corridors, now partially collapsed from centuries of ocean pressure and seismic activity.

"It's magnificent," one of the junior researchers whispered, her voice carrying the distinctive musical lilt of those born in the deeper ocean trenches.

"And dangerous," Kieran added, moving closer to Aquatania as they neared the entrance. "Stay alert. These ruins offer too many hiding places."

The entrance loomed before them, a collapsed section of stone blocking most of the archway. Aquatania paused, extending her awareness into the surrounding water. She could feel the currents flowing through the structure, sense the weak points where walls had crumbled and supports had failed. With practiced concentration, she extended her hands toward the blocked entrance.

Water responded to her will, gathering into a concentrated stream that she directed at the debris. The pressurized jet carved through sediment that had accumulated over centuries, dislodging smaller stones and exposing the larger blocks beneath. When the water alone proved insufficient, she altered her approach, creating opposing currents that surrounded the largest stone block. The counterforces lifted the massive object just enough for her to guide it aside, clearing a passage large enough for them to enter single file.

"Impressive," Kieran murmured, close enough that only she could hear.

"Basic water manipulation," she replied, though the effort had left her slightly breathless. "Sea dragon children master this by their tenth year."

His lips curved in the half-smile that had become increasingly familiar. "Perhaps, but not with such precision or grace."

Before she could respond to the unexpected compliment,

Marina called from inside the cleared passage. "The main corridor is relatively intact! We should be able to reach the central chambers."

They swam through the narrow opening into a corridor lined with what had once been luminescent coral. Most of the organisms had died centuries ago, leaving only dark, empty skeletons where light should have bloomed. Kieran unclipped a crystal from his belt, activating it with a touch. The soft blue glow illuminated their immediate surroundings, revealing corridors branching in multiple directions.

"This way," Marina said confidently, consulting an ancient map she'd retrieved from her waterproof case. "The library should be through the grand hall and up the central spiral."

They proceeded cautiously, Aquatania periodically using her abilities to clear debris or reinforce unstable passages. In several places, she created supportive columns of pressurized water to hold crumbling ceilings while they passed beneath. Kieran remained at her side throughout, his hand occasionally steadying her when the effort of maintaining multiple water constructs threatened her balance.

The grand hall opened before them suddenly, a vast underwater cathedral where massive columns of petrified coral rose to support a dome of fitted stone blocks. Though much of the original decoration had been lost to time, hints of its former glory remained in fragments of mother-of-pearl inlay and etched patterns that spiraled around the columns. At the center of the hall, a wide staircase curved upward in a perfect spiral, its steps worn smooth by centuries of water flow.

"The ancient texts describe this as the Path of Ascension," Marina explained, her scientific detachment briefly giving way to genuine awe. "Sea dragon scholars would symbolically rise toward knowledge as they climbed to the library above."

They ascended the spiral, passing through a series of

smaller chambers where niches in the walls suggested display areas for treasured artifacts, now long since removed or decayed. At the top of the staircase, they faced a set of massive doors carved from a material that resembled neither stone nor coral, but something harder and more enduring. Intricate glyphs covered the surface—the ancient language of sea dragons that only the most educated scholars could still read.

She pressed her palms against the center of the doors, feeling for structural weaknesses. To her surprise, they began to move at her touch, swinging inward with only the faintest grating sound. Water currents that had been still for centuries rushed past them as pressure equalized between chambers.

What lay beyond stole the breath from Aquatania's lungs.

The library extended farther than their lights could penetrate. It was a vast chamber where shelves rose from floor to distant ceiling in concentric circles that mimicked the growth patterns of coral reefs. Upon these shelves rested the accumulated knowledge of sea dragon civilization, scrolls encased in preservation bubbles that had somehow survived the centuries, stone tablets etched with microscopic text, and most remarkably, crystalline memory orbs that still glowed with faint internal light despite their age.

"By all the ancient depths," Marina whispered, her scientific composure abandoned in the face of such discovery. "It's intact. After all these centuries, it's actually intact."

The junior researchers drifted forward in stunned silence, their hands reaching tentatively toward scrolls and tablets as if afraid they might dissolve at a touch. Aquatania moved deeper into the chamber, her heart pounding with the significance of what they'd found. Here, possibly, lay the answers they sought...ancient knowledge of diseases, treatments, and dragon biology that might hold the key to combating the alien contagion.

Kieran followed, activating additional light crystals and placing them strategically to illuminate the vast space. At one point, he shifted partially to dragon form, his hand transforming just enough to produce a controlled flame that cast warm light into the darkest corners. The brief display of his draconic nature seemed unconscious, a practical solution rather than a deliberate choice.

"We should coordinate our search," Aquatania said, pulling herself back to the urgent task at hand. "Marina, focus on biological texts and medical records. Look for anything resembling disease documentation or epidemic histories."

The mermaid scientist nodded, already moving toward a section where preserved specimens floated in crystal containers alongside what appeared to be anatomical diagrams etched on pale green tablets.

"The rest of us will divide the historical archives," Aquatania continued. "We're looking for any mention of plagues, contagions, or mass illnesses, particularly those affecting multiple species."

As the team spread out among the towering shelves, Aquatania found herself drawn to a section where particularly ancient scrolls were stored in sealed crystal tubes. Kieran stayed close, his presence a constant reassurance as she carefully extracted the first tube and examined its outer markings.

"Can you read all of these?" he asked, steadying a shelf that wobbled when she removed a particularly large scroll case.

"Most of them," she replied, gently opening the tube to reveal a scroll of material that resembled neither paper nor parchment, but some biological substance preserved through unknown methods. "Sea dragon script evolved over millennia, but the basic structures remained consistent."

He held a light crystal closer as she unrolled a small section, his face illuminated by its soft glow. The proximity brought his features into sharp relief, the angular jaw, the intensity of his eyes as he watched her work, and the lingering marks of their recent battle still visible as faint scratches across his cheek.

"What does this one say?" he asked, his voice low and intimate in the vastness of the library.

"It's a treatise on water manipulation techniques," she answered, carefully rewrapping the delicate material. "Useful, but not what we need right now."

As they moved deeper into the archives, Aquatania felt a growing sense of both wonder and urgency. The knowledge surrounding them represented centuries of draconic wisdom, preservation techniques, healing methods, and biological understandings that modern science had yet to rediscover. Somewhere in this vast collection lay the information they needed to combat the alien contagion and save countless lives. They just had to find it before the infiltrators found them.

Kieran reached across her to stabilize a teetering stack of stone tablets, his arm brushing against hers in the process. The brief contact sent an unexpected warmth through her that had nothing to do with water temperature or exertion. When she glanced up, she found his eyes on her face, his expression conveying something beyond their shared scientific purpose or military alliance, something personal that neither of them had acknowledged amid the crisis surrounding them.

"We'll find what we need," he said quietly, as if reading her thoughts. "And when we do, we'll stop them."

*

Hours passed in the silent depths of the ancient library, each researcher methodically working through their assigned section. Aquatania's eyes burned from strain, the faded glyphs of countless scrolls blurring together as she carefully unrolled and resealed container after container. Her determination hadn't wavered, but fatigue pulled at her limbs, the aftermath of their narrow escape from the institute

153

and the energy expended clearing their path to the citadel.

She reached for another crystal tube, this one marked with spiral patterns that indicated medical knowledge, according to the organizational system she'd gradually deciphered. Something about this container was different. The preservation seal glowed with faint bioluminescence despite its age, suggesting contents of particular importance.

"Kieran," she called softly, her voice barely disturbing the water around them. "Can you bring the light closer?"

He appeared at her side within moments, as if he'd been waiting for her call. The controlled flame he cupped in his partially transformed hand cast a warm glow over the crystal tube as Aquatania carefully examined the ancient seal.

"These markings," she murmured, tracing the etched symbols with her fingertip. "They're warning glyphs, used to indicate dangerous knowledge or information about contagious diseases."

Kieran leaned closer, his shoulder brushing against hers. "Exactly what we're looking for, then."

With practiced care, Aquatania manipulated the water molecules around the seal, creating a precisely calibrated pressure differential that caused the ancient lock mechanism to release with a soft click. The crystal tube opened, revealing a scroll encased in a thin membrane that resembled fish skin but possessed the transparency of finest glass. Unlike the other texts they'd examined, this scroll emitted its own pale light, pulsing faintly like a dying heartbeat.

"Bioluminescent ink," she explained, gently removing the scroll from its protective case. "Derived from deep-sea creatures and preserved through a process modern science hasn't rediscovered. The ancient sea dragons used it for their most important records. The light will never fade, even over centuries."

She carried the precious document to a flat stone table at the center of their research area, Kieran following with his light. Marina and the other researchers continued their work nearby, occasionally glancing toward Aquatania with hopeful expressions before returning to their own searches.

The scroll resisted as she carefully began to unroll it, centuries of stillness making the material stiff and uncooperative. She directed a gentle current of water across its surface, slowly rehydrating the biological components without damaging the delicate structure. Gradually, the scroll relaxed, revealing columns of densely packed glyphs that glowed with that same ethereal light.

"The Elder Weeping," she translated, her finger hovering above the first line of text. "A Treatise on the Great Plague of the Fifth Oceanic Age."

Kieran positioned himself at her shoulder, close enough that she could feel the warmth radiating from his body despite the cool water surrounding them. "Can you read it all?"

"The dialect is archaic, but decipherable," she replied, already scanning the opening passages. "It appears to be a comprehensive record compiled by the chief healer of the Abyssal Court during a widespread epidemic."

She fell silent as she absorbed the ancient account, her scientific mind cataloging symptoms and comparing them to what they knew of the current contagion. The familiar rhythm of academic concentration steadied her, transforming the overwhelming library into simply another research environment.

"The Elder Weeping began with fever and chills," she translated, her voice taking on the cadence of the ancient text. "Then came the markings upon the skin, crimson lines that followed the flow of blood through the body, spreading outward from the heart in patterns like coral branches or river deltas."

Kieran's sharp intake of breath mirrored her own realization. "Just like the Red Death."

"Exactly like it," she confirmed, fingers trembling slightly as she continued unrolling the scroll. "Listen to this... The affliction moved between species with unnatural speed, first appearing among surface dwellers, then spreading to the merfolk and finally reaching even the dragon enclaves. Those with greater dragon heritage showed resistance, some suffering only mild symptoms before recovery."

"That matches our observations precisely," Kieran said, leaning closer to study the glowing text. "Does it mention the cause? Or how they stopped it?"

Aquatania continued translating, scanning ahead through passages describing the epidemic's spread and the initial failures to contain it. Her heart rate quickened as she reached a section marked with distinctive healing symbols.

"Here," she said, excitement threading through her voice. "After conventional treatments failed, the healer describes a ritual developed by combining ancient dragon magic with emerging alchemical principles."

The text detailed a complex procedure involving blood from three distinct dragon subspecies — depths, shallows, and surface — combined with specific sea plants harvested during full moons. The mixture was then exposed to both moonlight and deep-ocean pressure in alternating cycles, creating what the text called the Balanced Elixir.

"The ritual was designed to balance opposing forces," Aquatania explained, her scientific mind already translating the ancient concepts into modern equivalents. "What they described as moonlight purification was likely exposing the compound to specific wavelengths of light that catalyzed biochemical reactions in the dragon blood components."

"And the pressure cycling?" Kieran asked, following her reasoning.

"Probably altered the protein structures in the blood," she replied, excitement building as she connected ancient wisdom with modern science. "Creating more stable compounds that could be tolerated by non-draconic physiology. We do something similar in our labs with pressure chambers, but never would've thought to combine it with specific light exposures."

She continued translating, her fingers tracing the glowing glyphs with increasing urgency. "According to this record, the elixir didn't just treat symptoms, it provided complete immunity to those who consumed it. The epidemic was contained within two lunar cycles once production reached sufficient scale."

"This is it," Kieran said, his voice low but intense. "This is what we've been searching for."

Aquatania carefully rolled the scroll to reveal the final sections, which contained precise proportions and preparation methods. "The sea plants they used still exist...crystal kelp, moon algae, and pressure ferns. We could harvest them from the deep trenches near Oceana Prime."

"And we already have blood samples from multiple dragon subspecies," Kieran added, referring to the precious vials they'd collected at such risk.

"With Marina's expertise in marine biology and modern equipment, we could adapt this ritual into a standardized medical treatment," Aquatania continued, her mind racing ahead through implementation steps. "The scroll even includes dosage recommendations for different species and body weights."

She looked up at Kieran, a smile breaking through her scientific concentration for the first time in hours. "This could work. It could actually work."

His hand moved to cover hers where it rested on the ancient scroll, the warm weight of his touch sending an unexpected tremor through her arm. "You found it," he said simply, his eyes holding hers with an intensity that transcended their shared purpose. "If anyone could understand both the science and the draconic elements, it

157

would be you."

Aquatania became suddenly aware of how close they were standing, the library's vastness seeming to contract around just the two of them. The scroll's bioluminescent glow cast soft light across Kieran's features, highlighting the strong line of his jaw and the unexpected tenderness in his expression.

"I should show this to Marina," she said, her voice softer than she'd intended. "Get her perspective on the biological components."

"Of course," he agreed, but neither of them moved.

His hand remained over hers on the scroll, his thumb brushing lightly across her knuckles in a gesture too deliberate to be accidental. Aquatania felt a flutter in her chest that had nothing to do with scientific discovery or the urgency of their mission…a purely personal response to his proximity that she'd been too busy to acknowledge until this moment.

"Kieran," she began, unsure what she intended to say.

"We'll find a way through this," he said quietly, his voice pitched for her ears alone. "Whatever happens, whatever we're facing…we'll find a way."

The simple assurance touched something deeper than her rational mind, a place where fear and doubt had lodged despite her scientific detachment. His confidence wasn't hollow optimism but the solid willpower of someone who'd faced impossible odds before and persevered.

She found herself leaning slightly toward him, drawn by something beyond conscious decision. Kieran's free hand moved to her arm, steadying her against the gentle current that flowed through the library. The scroll momentarily forgotten between them, their faces drew closer, the moment suspended in the silent, ancient library.

A distant rumble interrupted the stillness, vibrations passing through the water around them. Both froze, eyes moving to the library's vaulted ceiling where fine particles of coral dust had begun to drift downward from disturbances in

158

the upper structure.

"What was that?" she whispered, the intimate moment shattered by immediate concern.

"Nothing good," Kieran replied, his posture shifting instantly from tender to alert. He released her hand, though his eyes lingered on her face for a heartbeat longer than necessary. "We should gather the others. This structure has stood for centuries. Something significant would have to happen to disturb it now."

Aquatania carefully rewrapped the precious scroll, securing it in her satchel as another, stronger tremor passed through the water around them. Whatever had caused the disturbance, they couldn't risk losing this ancient knowledge, their best hope against the alien contagion that threatened their world.

The second tremor hit with greater force, sending ancient stone blocks tumbling from the library's vaulted ceiling. Dust clouds billowed through the water as support columns that had stood for centuries began to crack with sounds like breaking bones. The massive knowledge repository that had survived millennia was now coming apart around them, threatening to bury its rediscovered wisdom along with those who'd come seeking it.

"Everyone out! Now!" Kieran's voice cut through the chaos, carrying the unmistakable authority of military command. "Follow the route we came in. Stay together!"

Marina was already gathering the junior researchers, her tail propelling her through the swirling debris with remarkable agility as she corralled them toward the library entrance. Ancient scrolls and tablets tumbled from their repositories, centuries of knowledge lost in moments as preservation cases shattered against the stone floor.

Aquatania forced herself not to dwell on the tragic destruction. The Elder Weeping scroll was secure...the most critical piece of knowledge was saved. She swam toward the entrance, using directed water currents to push aside falling debris that threatened to block their path.

A massive crack appeared across the library floor, widening rapidly as the entire structure shifted. The two junior researchers found themselves suddenly cut off from the main group, trapped behind a shower of collapsing stone and coral. One called out in panic, her voice distorted by the churning water.

Without hesitation, Aquatania altered course, swimming toward the trapped pair. The ceiling above them was giving way, and massive blocks of petrified coral were descending with deceptive slowness through the water.

"Get back!" she shouted to Kieran, who'd moved to follow her. "I need space to work!"

Drawing on her sea dragon heritage, Aquatania extended both hands toward the failing section of ceiling. She felt the water around her respond, molecules aligning to her will as she shaped them into a dense, pressurized arch between the falling debris and the trapped researchers. The water construct solidified under her concentration, becoming almost as tangible as stone while remaining flexible enough to adjust as more debris came down.

The effort sent immediate pain shooting through her temples, her body straining against the unnatural manipulation of such a large volume of water. Sweat beaded on her forehead despite their underwater environment, her muscles trembling with the effort of maintaining the protective arch.

"I can't hold this long," she gasped.

Kieran assessed the situation in an instant, his military mind calculating risk and opportunity. "Keep it stable for ten seconds," he said, already moving toward the gap beneath her water arch.

He darted through the opening, powerful strokes carrying him to the trapped researchers. With efficient movements, he grabbed them both, one under each arm, and kicked hard toward the gap, timing his return perfectly as Aquatania's strength began to falter. They cleared the collapsing section just as her water arch gave way, debris crashing down behind them with a sound that reverberated through the entire structure.

"Exit route," Kieran demanded of Marina as he released the shaken researchers to her care.

"Same way we came in," the mermaid scientist replied, already guiding the group toward the spiral staircase. "It's our only option."

Another violent tremor shook the citadel, this one accompanied by a deep, groaning sound that seemed to emanate from the very foundation of the structure. The spiral staircase they had ascended earlier now displayed ominous cracks along its central column.

"One at a time," Kieran ordered as they reached the staircase. "Quickly but carefully. Test each step before putting your full weight on it."

Marina led the way, her tail giving her stability advantages as she guided the junior researchers down the deteriorating spiral. Aquatania and Kieran came last, both scanning the collapsing library behind them for any sign of pursuit or further danger.

"What caused this?" she asked as they began their descent, one hand pressed against her satchel where the precious scroll rested. "The citadel stood intact for centuries."

"Could be natural...seismic activity, structural failure," Kieran replied, though his tone suggested he believed otherwise. "Or it could be that we weren't the only ones interested in what this place contained."

The implication sent a chill through Aquatania despite the physical exertion warming her muscles. If the infiltrators had followed them here and deliberately triggered the citadel's collapse, it meant the ancient knowledge was even more

161

valuable than they'd realized...worth destroying rather than allowing it to fall into their hands.

They reached the bottom of the spiral just as the upper section gave way completely, stone steps collapsing into the grand hall below. The hall itself was transforming from majestic chamber to death trap, massive columns toppling like felled trees, walls buckling under pressures they were never designed to withstand.

"This way!" Marina called, pointing toward the corridor that would lead them back to the entrance. Her voice cut off abruptly as a section of decorative archway crashed down, missing her by inches.

Their escape became a desperate race against the citadel's accelerating destruction. Corridors that had been navigable hours earlier now presented new obstacles. Collapsed ceilings, floors split by widening cracks, and walls bulging inward from external pressure. Each new barrier required immediate action, with no time for planning or hesitation.

Aquatania and Kieran fell into a rhythm of teamwork that seemed almost choreographed, despite having never trained together. Where fallen debris blocked their path, she created focused water jets that cleared smaller obstacles or water cushions that allowed the team to push through. When structural elements threatened to collapse on them, Kieran's enhanced strength held supports in place long enough for everyone to pass safely.

"Your wound," Aquatania noticed with alarm as they paused at a junction, seeing fresh blood seeping through Kieran's bandages from the exertion.

"It's holding," he replied, dismissing her concern with a tight smile. "Focus on getting us out."

They were nearing the exit when disaster struck. A massive section of the outer wall collapsed inward, bringing with it a buttress of solid coral that completely blocked the final passage to freedom. The impact sent shockwaves through the remaining structure, accelerating the collapse of chambers behind them. There was no going back, and the way forward was sealed by tons of ancient coral and stone.

Marina tested the barrier with her hands, searching for weak points. "Too solid," she reported, fear finally breaking through her scientific composure. "And too massive to move."

Kieran stepped forward, his expression hardening with determination. "Stand back," he ordered, rolling his shoulders as if preparing for enormous strain.

Before their eyes, his form began to change, not the complete transformation to dragon shape, which would have been impossible in these confined spaces, but a partial shift that covered his skin with iridescent scales and altered his musculature. His arms and chest expanded with draconic strength, fingers extending into clawed hands capable of gripping the rough coral surface.

"I need pressure," he said to Aquatania, his voice deeper and rougher in this partial form. "Directed at the center point when I tell you."

She nodded, gathering her remaining strength to manipulate the water once more. Kieran positioned himself against the coral buttress, his scaled shoulders braced against the massive obstruction. His partially transformed muscles bunched and strained as he began to push, feet finding purchase against the stone floor.

She directed a powerful current against the same point where he focused his strength, water pressure building to levels that would crush ordinary materials.

For a moment, nothing happened. Then, with a sound like thunder, the coral barrier began to shift. Tiny fractures appeared across its surface, spreading outward from the point of their combined assault. Kieran growled with effort, scales gleaming in the dim emergency light as he pushed harder, veins standing out along his neck and transformed

163

arms.

"More pressure," he said and gasped. Aquatania responded by drawing on her deepest reserves, pulling water from everywhere around them and focusing it into a single, devastating stream.

The barrier gave way with a splintering crack, fragments shooting outward as their combined force finally overcame its resistance. Beyond the broken obstruction lay open water, dark but unobstructed, their path to escape finally clear.

"Go!" Kieran shouted to Marina and the researchers, who wasted no time swimming through the opening.

Aquatania maintained her water pressure long enough for Kieran to duck through, then followed, her exhausted limbs barely responding to her commands. They emerged into the open ocean just as the entire entrance archway collapsed behind them, sealing the Coral Citadel forever.

They kicked hard toward the surface, putting distance between themselves and the continuing destruction below. The ancient structure that had stood for centuries was returning to the ocean floor, its knowledge lost except for the single, precious scroll secured against Aquatania's chest.

As they ascended through increasingly lighter waters, Aquatania found Kieran swimming beside her, his form gradually returning to a fully human appearance. His eyes met hers, sharing a look that contained both triumph and something deeper.

She touched the satchel containing the Elder Weeping scroll, reassuring herself of its presence. The ancient citadel was lost, but they had rescued the knowledge most critical to their fight against the alien contagion. For the first time since the crisis began, she felt something beyond scientific curiosity or royal duty, a genuine hope that they might actually succeed.

Chapter Nine

Three days had passed since their narrow escape from the collapsing Coral Citadel. Three days of relentless work, translating the ancient text of the Elder Weeping scroll and preparing the laboratory for the delicate process ahead. Aquatania bent over a crystal microscope, her eyes fixed on the swirling patterns of luminous dragon blood that danced across the viewing plate. Without conscious thought, her fingers traced small circles in the air beside her, a tiny whirlpool of water forming and dissolving as her concentration ebbed and flowed with each new discovery.

"The phosphorescent blood shows remarkable adaptive properties," she murmured, adjusting the crystal lens to increase magnification. "Look at how the cellular structures reshape themselves when exposed to the human tissue sample."

Kieran moved from his workstation to stand beside her, his shoulder nearly touching hers as he leaned down to view the specimen. The warmth of his proximity sent a subtle ripple through the hovering water droplets she'd unconsciously gathered.

"They're not just reshaping," he observed, his voice soft yet precise. "They're creating protective barriers around the human cells while still allowing nutrient exchange." He pointed to the boundary where dragon blood met human tissue. "It's almost like they're teaching the human cells how to defend themselves."

Aquatania's laboratory occupied the highest tower of Zephyria's scientific academy, its circular design offering panoramic views of the floating city through windows of enchanted glass that adjusted their transparency with the changing light. Ancient sea dragon artifacts lined shelves between cutting-edge equipment—coral computing devices pulsed with stored data beside fossilized dragon scales mounted in preservation fields. A massive water tank dominated one wall, its contents glowing with cultivated bioluminescent organisms that provided both light and specialized research materials.

At the center of the room stood the Integration Chamber, a spherical apparatus suspended in a controlled gravitational field where the most delicate alchemical processes could be performed without interference from external forces. The chamber had been modified according to the Elder Weeping scroll's instructions, copper and silver conduits now wrapped around its circumference to direct moonlight and pressure in precise alternating cycles.

"The scroll mentioned balancing opposing forces," Aquatania said, straightening from the microscope. Her scales shimmered briefly beneath the skin of her forearms as she stretched, the iridescent pattern appearing and fading like light through water. "I believe they were describing what we'd now call biochemical equilibrium...stabilizing the dragon blood components so they remain potent while becoming compatible with human physiology."

She moved to a workstation where the three vials rested in a specialized cooling field. Each contained power beyond mere biological material, magic and science intertwined in their cellular structure.

She felt Kieran watching her work, his eyes tracking the graceful efficiency of her movements. Her hair, still carrying the faint scent of ocean depths despite days above water, fell across her face as she leaned forward to adjust the containment field, hiding her emotions.

"Your scales show when you're deep in thought," he said, handing her a precision pipette before she could ask for it.

Her fingers brushed his as she took the instrument,

sending a jolt of awareness through her. "A family trait," she replied, her voice betraying a slight catch. "My father says it means the sea dragon blood runs strong in me. Though he always showed more control."

"I wouldn't call it a lack of control," Kieran said, his eyes still on her face. "Just a harmony between your human and dragon natures."

They worked side by side, extracting precise quantities from each vial and combining them in proportions dictated by the ancient scroll. Aquatania manipulated water pressure within crystal containment spheres, simulating deep ocean conditions that activated specific properties in the reef dragon's blood. Kieran, drawing on his fire dragon heritage, regulated temperature with exacting precision, his fingertips occasionally glowing with suppressed heat as he touched the calibration crystals.

"The scroll mentioned a catalyst," Aquatania said, carefully unrolling the preserved document on a specially designed reading table. Water cushions supported the fragile material while preservation fields maintained optimal humidity. "A combination of crystal kelp and moon algae that must be harvested during the alignment of both moons."

"Which happens tonight," Kieran noted, glancing toward the windows where the first traces of evening were painting the sky in deepening blues. "The expedition team should return within hours with the specimens."

"If the weather holds," she added, concern coloring her voice. "The upper atmospheric currents have been increasingly unstable since the infiltrators arrived."

Kieran moved to a monitoring station, checking readings from weather sensors placed strategically around Zephyria's floating archipelago. "The patterns seem normal for now. We should have a clear night for the moonlight exposure phase."

Aquatania returned to the Integration Chamber, making final adjustments to the receptacle where the combined blood

167

samples would interact with the catalytic plants under precisely controlled conditions. Her fingers danced across the control panel, programming the sequence of pressure changes and light exposures that would mimic the ancient ritual described in the Elder Weeping scroll.

They reached for the same calibration tool simultaneously, their hands colliding with gentle force. Neither pulled away immediately, the brief contact stretching into a moment of connection amid the scientific intensity surrounding them. Aquatania felt the roughness of calluses on his fingertips. They were evidence of years of military training combined with scholarly pursuits, a duality that mirrored her own.

"We're making remarkable progress," she said softly, finally withdrawing her hand to continue the calibration. "Three days ago, I feared we'd lost everything when the citadel collapsed. Now we're closer than ever to a viable treatment."

"Thanks to you," Kieran replied, his voice carrying that same warmth she'd heard in the ancient library before chaos erupted. "Your understanding of both the science and the draconic elements is what's making this possible."

She shook her head, unwilling to accept sole credit. "It's our combination of knowledge. Your fire dragon understanding of thermal catalysis has been crucial for adapting the process to modern equipment."

They continued working as the afternoon faded into evening, the laboratory's artificial lighting adjusting automatically to optimal research conditions. Aquatania occasionally sent small currents of water through the air to retrieve tools from distant workstations, the liquid forming into hand-like shapes that carried instruments before dissolving back into suspended droplets.

"The infiltrators won't stop hunting for us," Kieran said as he carefully measured a neutralizing agent into a buffer solution. "They know what we're trying to accomplish."

"All the more reason to succeed quickly," Aquatania replied, determination hardening her features. "Once we perfect the formula, we can begin production immediately. Marina has already prepared the medical distribution networks in Oceana Prime. Your military contacts in the fire kingdoms have established secure transport routes."

"And the sky dragons?" Kieran asked, his tone carefully neutral.

"Still an unknown factor," she admitted. "After Zephyr's disappearance during the citadel collapse, I'm reluctant to trust their official diplomatic channels. But we have enough allies to begin without them."

They fell into comfortable silence, each focused on their tasks yet acutely aware of the other's presence. When Aquatania struggled to stabilize a particularly volatile reaction between blood components, Kieran steadied her hands with his own, lending his strength to her precision. When he needed to maintain a specific temperature for exactly seven minutes, she created a timing mechanism of water droplets that fell with perfect regularity, each one marking exactly fifteen seconds.

As they worked, a sense of cautious hope grew between them—not just for the cure they were developing, but for something more personal that neither had found time to acknowledge amid the crisis. The fate of kingdoms rested on their success, yet in the quiet moments between critical procedures, Aquatania found her thoughts drifting to possibilities beyond the immediate danger.

"I think we're ready for the final preparations," Aquatania said at last, straightening from her workstation with a small smile of triumph. "Once the expedition returns with the catalyst plants, we can begin the integration process."

Kieran nodded, his eyes meeting hers with shared purpose and something deeper that made her scales shimmer briefly beneath her skin. "Then we'll have our cure, and the beginning of the end for the infiltrators' plans."

"We should take a break." Aquatania's words surprised even herself as she straightened from the Integration Chamber, rolling her shoulders to release the tension that had built there over hours of meticulous work. "The expedition won't return for at least another hour, and we've done all we can until they arrive with the catalyst plants." Outside the laboratory windows, night had fully claimed the sky, the two moons of their world, one silver, one with a faint blue tinge, climbing slowly above the horizon.

Kieran looked up from the formula calculations he'd been reviewing, fatigue evident in the slight shadows beneath his eyes. "You're right. Fresh perspective might help us see something we've missed." He set down his crystal stylus, the instrument clicking softly against the translucent writing surface.

"There's a balcony off my private study," she said, indicating a door half-hidden behind a bookshelf filled with ancient texts. "The kitchen staff always leaves something for me during long research sessions."

The balcony extended from the curved side of the tower like the prow of a ship sailing through the night air. Unlike the utilitarian efficiency of the laboratory, this space reflected Aquatania's personal aesthetic. Living plants with bioluminescent blossoms grew from carved stone planters, their soft blue glow complementing the moonlight. A small table and two chairs of woven coral stood near the balustrade, and a covered tray was waiting as promised.

But it was the view that commanded attention. Zephyria spread below them, a constellation of lights suspended in darkness. The floating city's main island formed a crescent shape, with smaller platforms connected by graceful bridges that swayed gently in high-altitude winds. Enchanted lampposts lined thoroughfares and public squares, their warm, golden glow contrasting with the cooler blue lights of residences and gardens. Far below, nearly invisible at this height, the ocean stretched to the horizon, its surface reflecting moonlight in rippling patterns.

In the distance, other sky islands twinkled like earthbound stars, some stationary, others following predetermined paths through carefully plotted aerial currents. Each represented a different district of the kingdom, connected through elaborate transport systems of enchanted gliders and dragon-drawn aerial carriages.

"I forget sometimes how beautiful this world is that we're fighting to save," Kieran said softly as he took in the panorama.

Aquatania removed the cover from the waiting tray, revealing a simple meal of smoked fish, bread still warm from the ovens, and a carafe of chilled fruit nectar. "Especially at night, when you can't see the signs of the contagion's spread." She poured two glasses of the pale golden liquid, handing one to Kieran. "To progress," she offered.

"To hope," he countered, touching his glass gently to hers.

They ate in comfortable silence for a few minutes, the simple flavors a welcome respite from the intense concentration of the laboratory. The breeze carried the scent of night-blooming flowers from the royal gardens several platforms away, along with the faint mineral tang that always accompanied high-altitude air.

"Tell me about the calculations you were reviewing," Aquatania said eventually, breaking a piece of bread. "Did you find anything concerning?"

Kieran shook his head. "The opposite, actually. The pressure cycling sequence you developed should stabilize the combined blood components perfectly. The formula is sound. It's just a matter of proper execution now."

"And distribution," she added, her eyes drawn to distant lights of transport vessels moving between sky islands. "Even with a perfect cure, reaching everyone in time will be challenging."

"The military has already mobilized transport squadrons," Kieran said. "Once we confirm the treatment works, we can begin immediate distribution to the worst-affected areas."

The practical discussion of logistics gradually gave way to quieter, more personal conversation as the meal dwindled and the moons rose higher in the night sky. Aquatania found herself asking questions she'd been too busy to voice during their days of frantic work.

"How did you come to join the military?" she asked, watching as Kieran absently traced the rim of his glass with one finger. "Most fire dragons serve their own kingdoms exclusively."

A shadow passed across his features. "I didn't have a kingdom to serve, not really. My parents died during a border dispute when I was very young. I have almost no memory of them." He looked out at the night sky rather than meeting her eyes. "I was raised in various military orphanages, moving wherever my guardians were stationed. The army became my family, in a way."

"Yet you studied science as well as warfare," she observed. "That's unusual for military tracks."

A small smile softened his expression. "I was a difficult child with too many questions, too much energy. One commander recognized it as curiosity rather than defiance and assigned me to the research division as punishment for some minor infraction." His smile widened at the memory. "It backfired spectacularly. I found my second home among the scientists and strategists, combining military discipline with scientific inquiry."

"And rose through the ranks," she finished. "Until you became the youngest general in the Combined Kingdoms' history."

He shrugged, seeming almost embarrassed by the accomplishment. "I was in the right places at the right times.

And I understood the threats we faced better than some of my superiors."

"Including the current one," Aquatania said softly. "You recognized the infiltrators before anyone else connected the patterns."

"Not soon enough." His voice held a hint of the same self-recrimination she sometimes felt. "We could've been better prepared if I'd been more convincing earlier."

Aquatania moved to stand at the balustrade, looking out over the kingdom that was her birthright and her responsibility. The weight of that duty suddenly felt overwhelming in the quiet night air. "Sometimes I wonder if I'm strong enough to save them all," she admitted, the words escaping before she could reconsider them.

She sensed rather than saw Kieran join her at the railing, his presence solid and reassuring beside her. "What do you mean?"

"I'm neither fully human nor fully dragon," she said, watching a distant aerial transport cross between sky islands. "My father rules the human realms with political acumen I've never mastered. My mother's sea dragon heritage gave me abilities I'm still learning to fully control. I exist between worlds, never quite belonging to either." She turned to face him, vulnerability evident in her expression. "What if that divided nature means I lack the strength to lead when it matters most?"

Kieran studied her face in the moonlight, his gaze steady and certain. "Your strength isn't just in your powers, but in your heart," he said quietly. "I've seen you face impossible odds without hesitation. I've watched you work until exhaustion because others depend on you. That courage, that dedication, doesn't come from dragon abilities or human politics. It comes from who you are at your core."

The wind picked up, sending a strand of Aquatania's hair across her face. Before she could reach for it, Kieran's hand moved, gently brushing the wayward lock behind her ear. His touch lingered, his fingers tracing a path along her jawline with unexpected tenderness.

"Who we are matters more than what we are," he continued, his voice dropping to just above a whisper. "And who you are, Aquatania, is remarkable."

She became acutely aware of how close they stood, of the warmth emanating from his body despite the cool night air, of the way his eyes reflected moonlight like banked embers. The concerns that had occupied her mind moments ago receded, replaced by a different kind of awareness that had nothing to do with their mission and everything to do with the man before her.

"Kieran," she began, unsure what would follow his name.

He closed the small distance between them, one hand coming to rest at her waist while the other remained at her cheek. "Tell me to step away," he said softly, "and I will."

Instead of answering with words, Aquatania leaned forward, her lips meeting his in a kiss that started tentatively but quickly deepened as weeks of unacknowledged tension dissolved into something honest and undeniable. His arms encircled her, drawing her closer as she reached up to touch his face, her fingertips tracing the strong line of his jaw.

Around them, water droplets rose from the decorative fountain and the dewy surfaces of plants, responding to the surge of emotion coursing through Aquatania. The droplets caught moonlight as they swirled in a gentle spiral around the embracing couple, each one glowing with reflected silver and blue from the dual moons. Neither noticed this display of unconscious power, too absorbed in the discovery of each other after so many days of restraint.

When they finally drew apart, both slightly breathless, Aquatania saw the water dancing around them and laughed softly, a sound of genuine joy that seemed to brighten the night itself. "My powers have always been tied to my

174

emotions," she explained, somewhat embarrassed. "Though usually not quite so...demonstratively."

Kieran smiled, catching one of the hovering droplets on his fingertip. "It's beautiful," he said simply. "Like you."

She leaned into him again, resting her head against his chest as they looked out over the kingdom spread below them. For this brief, stolen moment, the weight of responsibility lifted, allowing something personal to flourish amidst the crisis that had brought them together.

The soft spiral of water droplets still danced around them, catching moonlight in miniature constellations, when the sharp rap of knuckles against the laboratory doors shattered their moment of peace. Three distinct knocks, the royal urgent summons pattern that Aquatania had heard too many times during her life at court.

She pulled back from Kieran's embrace, her eyes meeting his with sudden concern before she called, "Enter," her voice automatically assuming the authoritative tone of the princess rather than the woman who'd been in his arms moments before.

The water droplets fell in a gentle rain around them as her concentration broke, pattering against the balcony stones as the laboratory door swung open. A young woman in the blue and silver livery of the royal household stepped through, her face unnaturally pale in the laboratory's crystal lighting. Even from the balcony, Aquatania could see the messenger's hands trembling as she clutched a sealed scroll bearing the royal insignia.

"Your Highness," the messenger began, her voice strained with the effort of maintaining formal protocol despite her obvious distress. "I bring urgent tidings from the Royal Physicians' Council." She hesitated, visibly struggling with the weight of her message.

"Speak plainly," Aquatania commanded, already moving from the balcony into the laboratory, Kieran a half-step behind her.

The messenger swallowed hard. "It's His Majesty, King Poseidronus. He has fallen ill with the Red Death." Her professional composure finally cracked. "The symptoms appeared without warning during the evening council session. He...he collapsed while addressing the ministers. The progression is...unusually rapid."

The words struck Aquatania like a physical blow. For a moment, she couldn't breathe, couldn't think beyond the terrible implications. Her father...the seemingly indestructible pillar who'd guided multiple kingdoms through decades of challenges...now lay afflicted with the very contagion they'd been racing to cure. The irony was as cruel as it was terrifying.

"How advanced are the symptoms?" Her voice sounded strange to her own ears, hollow yet somehow steady.

"The crimson markings have already spread across his chest and throat," the messenger replied, extending the sealed scroll with a slightly steadier hand. "The royal physicians have enacted all known treatment protocols, but they report minimal effect. This contains their detailed observations and a formal request for your immediate presence."

Aquatania took the scroll but didn't open it, her mind already racing beyond its contents to necessary actions. The shock that had momentarily paralyzed her gave way to a clarity that crystallized her thoughts into precise, ordered steps. She moved to the Integration Chamber, her movements swift but controlled as she began adjusting settings on the control panel.

"Prepare two transport containers," she instructed Kieran, who'd already anticipated her needs and was moving toward the specialized storage units. "We'll need to bring the blood components separately and combine them at my father's bedside. The prototype stabilizer solution should allow us to transport the partially processed formula without degradation."

Her fingers flew across the chamber's controls, initiating an accelerated version of the treatment protocol they'd been refining. Without the catalyst plants that the expedition team was still collecting, they couldn't complete the final integration, but they could advance the preliminary stages to save crucial time once they reached the king.

"What about the pressure cycling?" Kieran asked, efficiently packing crystal vials into a reinforced carrying case. "The scroll specified alternating cycles over hours."

"I'll manipulate the water pressure manually during our journey," she replied, not looking up from her calibrations. "It's risky, but we don't have the luxury of following the traditional timing." Her scales flickered more prominently beneath her skin now, no longer mere shimmer but distinct patterns that rippled down her arms as her draconic nature responded to the crisis.

The messenger still stood near the door, awaiting formal dismissal. Aquatania looked up briefly. "Return to the royal physicians. Tell them we're coming immediately with treatment prototypes. Have them prepare a sterile environment with lunar exposure capabilities."

As the messenger departed, Kieran moved to Aquatania's side, briefly touching her shoulder in a gesture that conveyed both support and shared purpose. "We'll reach him in time," he said, his voice carrying the absolute certainty she needed to hear.

"We have to," she replied, sealing the chamber and initiating the extraction sequence that would transfer the partially processed formula into transport containers.

They worked in coordinated silence, gathering equipment and research notes with practiced efficiency. Aquatania retrieved the Elder Weeping scroll from its preservation field, carefully securing it in a case before adding it to her pack. The ancient knowledge that had guided their research was too valuable to leave behind, especially if they needed to reference specific passages while adapting the treatment to her father's condition.

"The king's sea dragon heritage should provide some natural resistance," Kieran noted as he packed specialized instruments they might need. "His symptoms may progress more slowly than in full humans."

"Or the infiltrators may have engineered a more aggressive strain specifically targeting the royal family," Aquatania countered, the thought having haunted her since hearing the news. "They're strategic enough to recognize that destabilizing leadership would accelerate chaos."

She paused in her preparations, her hands resting on the edge of a workstation as the personal reality of the situation suddenly pierced through her scientific focus. This wasn't just about curing a contagion or saving an abstract group of victims. This was her father...the man who'd taught her to swim before she could walk, who'd supported her scientific pursuits when court advisors pushed for a more traditional royal education, who still sometimes called her by childhood nicknames when they were alone.

Kieran was beside her instantly, his hand covering hers. "Aquatania," he said softly. "We will save him. Everything we've discovered, everything we've prepared...it was always leading to this moment."

She nodded, drawing strength from his certainty. "You're right." She straightened, reaching for the final transport container as the Integration Chamber completed its cycle. "We need to move quickly. Even with our fastest transport vessel, it will take hours to reach the king's palace."

"Not if we fly," Kieran said, his expression serious. "In dragon form, we could reach the palace in a fraction of the time."

The suggestion made immediate tactical sense, yet carried significant risks. "Transforming makes us visible targets," she pointed out. "The infiltrators have anti-dragon weaponry deployed around major cities."

"Speed outweighs the risk," he countered. "And between your water manipulation and my fire abilities, we can defend ourselves if necessary."

Aquatania considered the options rapidly, weighing probabilities against her father's deteriorating condition. "You're right," she decided. "We'll transform and fly directly to the royal residence."

With their essential materials secured in specialized packs designed to remain stable during transformation, they moved to the balcony where they would have sufficient space for the change. Standing beneath the dual moons, they faced each other for a brief moment.

Aquatania closed her eyes, calling forth the draconic essence that flowed in her blood. Beside her, Kieran underwent his transformation, his body expanding into the massive form of a fire dragon. Where her scales shimmered with oceanic hues, his gleamed with the colors of flame and ember, deep crimson and burnished gold that seemed to glow from within. His wings spread wider than hers, designed for soaring on thermal currents rather than navigating water depths. When the transformation was completed, his dragon eyes, vertical pupils surrounded by irises the color of molten copper, met hers with the same determination and connection they'd shared in human form.

They secured their packs between their shoulder blades, the specialized harnesses designed to remain stable during flight. Aquatania extended her awareness beyond the balcony, sensing air currents and pressure systems that would affect their journey. With a silent nod to each other, they launched simultaneously from the balcony, their powerful wings displacing air with enough force to scatter research papers across the laboratory behind them.

Rising above Zephyria, their massive forms caught the

moonlight on their outstretched wings as they banked toward the distant royal palace. Below them, citizens looked up in awe and speculation...the princess in her sea dragon form and the fire general flying in perfect formation was a sight unprecedented in recent memory, a clear signal that something momentous was occurring.

Aquatania pushed all other thoughts aside, focusing only on speed and the precious cargo they carried. Within her dragon heart burned twin flames...fear and determination...fear for her father's life, and absolute determination that they would reach him in time.

CHAPTER TEN

Aquatania bent over her workstation, her fingers trembling with exhaustion as she adjusted the calibration on the Integration Chamber. Three days had passed since her father had fallen ill, and though the treatment they'd administered had slowed the progression of the Red Death, he remained in critical condition. She'd left the royal physicians monitoring his vital signs while she returned to her laboratory to continue refining the cure. Her eyes burned from lack of sleep, her shoulders aching from the strain of maintaining water pressure manipulations for hours during the delicate treatment process. But she couldn't rest, not when thousands more fell ill each day, not when the final catalyst component remained just beyond her reach.

"The extraction rate is still too slow," she murmured, mostly to herself, though Kieran stood at a nearby workstation, reviewing data from the latest field reports. "If we can't accelerate the process, we'll never produce enough doses to—"

Every screen in the laboratory flickered simultaneously, the data displays vanishing in a wash of static. The soft blue lighting dimmed, then returned with an unnatural greenish tint that made Aquatania's skin crawl. She straightened, exchanging a quick glance with Kieran, whose hand had already moved to the hilt of his weapon.

"Something's overriding the communication systems," he said, crossing to the main monitoring station. "Not just here. Look."

Through the laboratory's panoramic windows, Aquatania could see the same disruption spreading across Zephyria. Public information displays in plazas and along

181

thoroughfares flickered with the same static. Transport beacons faltered, causing several aerial carriages to hover uncertainly between platforms. Even the enchanted navigation buoys that marked safe flight paths between sky islands pulsed with that same sickly green light.

The static resolved into an image that stole the breath from her lungs.

They stood nearly nine feet tall, their bodies segmented like those of massive insects, but with an unnerving intelligence shining from compound eyes arranged in clusters across their elongated heads. Their skin, if it could be called that, was translucent green, revealing internal structures that pulsed with fluid movements no creature possessed. Multiple limbs extended from their torsos, some ending in delicate manipulators with too many joints, others in what appeared to be integrated technological components.

"People of this world."

The voice that emerged from every speaker carried a distinct clicking undertone, as if the creatures struggled to form human sounds despite perfect linguistic understanding.

"We have lived among you, studied your weaknesses. Your planet is ours. Surrender now or face extinction."

Aquatania's hand found the edge of her workstation, gripping it until her knuckles whitened. Behind her, the Integration Chamber continued its work, vials of dragon blood components glowing faintly in their housing...their only hope against these creatures that now revealed themselves so boldly.

The broadcast continued, the camera pulling back to reveal dozens of the aliens standing in what appeared to be a control center. Screens behind them displayed maps of the Twin Realms and beyond, infection vectors marked in pulsing red patterns that matched the research data Aquatania had been collecting for weeks.

"Your attempts at resistance have been noted," the alien

leader continued, its head tilting at an angle that seemed wrong for its neck structure. "Your scientists' efforts to counter our contagion are futile. Observe."

The image shifted to footage that Aquatania recognized immediately…quarantine zones in major population centers. The floating hospitals of Zephyria, where patients covered in crimson markings lay in rows, were attended by exhausted medical staff. The underwater isolation chambers of Oceana Prime, where merfolk with scaled skin blotched by red patterns drifted listlessly in medicated waters. The fever tents of Aethoria, where fire kingdom residents burned with temperatures that would kill ordinary humans.

"You believe you understand our contagion," the alien continued, its voice emotionless yet somehow mocking. "You do not. Witness the true power at our disposal."

The broadcast shifted again, showing a bustling market square that Aquatania recognized as the Central Exchange in Zephyria's eastern district. The footage was live, citizens pointing upward at public screens displaying the very broadcast they were now a part of. Confusion and fear rippled through the crowd as they saw themselves appear on the screens.

From above the market, a small craft appeared, sleek and nearly invisible against the sky until it released a cloud of greenish mist that descended on the unsuspecting shoppers. The effect was immediate and horrifying. People collapsed where they stood, some managing a few stumbling steps before falling. Within moments…not days as with the original contagion…angry red patterns erupted across exposed skin, spreading visibly as the broadcast continued.

"No," Aquatania whispered, her scientist's mind comprehending the implications even as her heart rejected the reality. They'd weaponized the contagion, accelerated its progression from days to minutes.

The broadcast shifted between locations, showing similar

scenes unfolding across multiple regions. In Oceana Prime's underwater viewing domes, families who had gathered to watch the evening light displays now huddled together in terror, parents clutching children to their chests as they stared upward at the alien visages on the normally peaceful information screens.

"Your leadership remains divided," the alien observed with clinical detachment. "Inefficient. Emotional. We offer one opportunity for orderly transition. Surrender your major population centers within twelve hours, or we will release our enhanced contagion in all areas simultaneously."

The broadcast cut back to the alien leader, its compound gaze seeming to stare directly through the screen. "Twelve hours. The time for resistance has ended."

The screens across Zephyria flickered once more, then returned to their normal functions as if nothing had happened. But *everything* had changed.

For several moments, Aquatania couldn't move, the horror of what she'd witnessed paralyzing her usually quick mind. The implications cascaded through her thoughts...the aliens had been watching them all along, tracking their research, allowing them to believe they were making progress while preparing an even deadlier version of the contagion. Every step they'd taken might have been anticipated, countered before they even completed it.

"Aquatania." Kieran's voice broke through her spiraling thoughts. He stood beside her now, his presence solid and grounding. "We need to secure the laboratory. They'll target our research next."

His words snapped her back to the immediate reality. She straightened, drawing a deep breath as she turned to face the Integration Chamber where their incomplete cure continued its processing cycle. The vials glowed with subtle power, each containing elements of the immunity they desperately needed to replicate.

"Twelve hours," she said, her voice finding strength despite the tremor that still ran through her body. "They've shown their hand, revealed their true nature and capabilities."

"A mistake," Kieran noted, his tactical mind already analyzing the situation. "Arrogance made them reveal their methods and timeline."

Aquatania nodded, moving to the Integration Chamber with renewed purpose. "We don't need twelve hours. We need the catalyst plants the expedition was collecting." Her fingers flew across the control panel, accelerating certain processes while modifying others. "Even without the final component, what we have might be enough to counter their accelerated contagion, at least partially."

Outside the laboratory windows, the city had erupted into motion. Emergency response teams with enchanted protection gear streamed toward the eastern district. Aerial defense platforms that had remained dormant for generations now hummed with activated energy, rising from their docking stations to form a protective network around key infrastructure.

Through it all, Aquatania focused on the glowing vials that represented their only hope against extinction. Her knuckles whitened as she gripped the edge of her workstation, but her mind had cleared, determination replacing the initial shock.

"They think they've won," she said quietly. "They've calculated everything except what we're willing to sacrifice to survive."

Behind her, the Integration Chamber hummed, dragon blood components swirling in patterns that mimicked the eternal dance of their world's twin moons...light against darkness, hope against despair, life against the extinction that now threatened them all.

*

An hour after the broadcast, Aquatania's laboratory had transformed from research space to crisis command center. Holographic displays flickered around the circular room, each showing different aspects of the unfolding catastrophe — infection spread patterns, population density maps, transportation networks now operating at emergency capacity.

The Integration Chamber dominated the center of the room, its low hum providing an almost meditative counterpoint to the crisis unfolding beyond the laboratory walls. Aquatania moved between workstations with precise efficiency, her exhaustion temporarily forgotten as adrenaline fueled each decision, each calculation that might mean the difference between survival and extinction.

The laboratory doors slid open with a soft hiss, admitting Marina. The scientist had clearly traveled at a dangerous speed. Her normally immaculate scales showed stress patterns, and her breathing came in quick bursts despite the water-breathing adaptations Aquatania had installed throughout the laboratory for her friend's comfort.

"The emergency transport tubes are overwhelmed," Marina reported, dropping a waterproof case on the nearest workstation. "I had to use the military channels, and even those are operating at capacity limits."

"You made it...that's what matters," Aquatania replied, embracing her friend briefly before turning to the data Marina had brought. "What's the situation in Oceana Prime?"

"Total chaos in the outer rings. Partial containment in the central districts." Marina's webbed fingers danced across a control panel, uploading new data to the holographic display. A three-dimensional map of the underwater city materialized above the table, red indicators pulsing at infection hotspots. "The accelerated contagion they demonstrated hasn't been widely deployed underwater yet, but the regular version has reached critical levels in these sectors."

Kieran joined them, his movement slightly stiff as he favored his right side. The wound he'd sustained during their escape from the Coral Citadel had improved, but clearly still troubled him. He studied the holographic display with a general's tactical assessment.

"They're isolating transportation hubs," he said, pointing out what he observed of the pattern of red indicators. "Cutting off evacuation routes before deploying the accelerated version."

Aquatania nodded grimly, then gestured toward the Integration Chamber, where vials of processed dragon blood components glowed with subtle power. "This is where we stand. The chamber has completed seventy percent of the necessary integration cycles. Without the final catalyst from the moonlight algae, the formula remains incomplete, but what we have might slow the progression enough to buy time."

"Might," Marina repeated, the scientist in her seemingly uncomfortable with the uncertainty. "Without final testing, we can't be sure of efficacy or side effects."

"We don't have the luxury of certainty anymore," Kieran said, wincing slightly as he reached for one of the sample vials to examine. His movement pulled at his healing wound, a reminder of how much they'd already sacrificed to get this far. "How many doses can we produce with current supplies?"

Marina moved to a data pad, her fingers tapping rapidly as she ran calculations. "With all processed materials and accounting for minimal wastage during distribution..." She paused, rechecking her figures before looking up with a troubled expression. "Maybe enough for key population centers, but we'll need to prioritize. Even being generous, we're looking at coverage for perhaps twenty percent of critical zones."

The weight of that calculation settled over the room. Eighty percent of those in critical zones would receive nothing…an impossible mathematics of survival that would force them to decide who lived and who died.

Aquatania stared at the holographic map where millions of lives blinked as abstract data points. "Show me the highest density areas with the slowest evacuation potential."

Marina adjusted the display, highlighting sections across multiple kingdoms. "Oceana Prime's inner sectors are essentially trapped. The pressure gates were sealed after the first contagion wave to prevent further spread. Zephyria's lower platforms have limited aerial transport capacity. Aethoria's fever districts are under quarantine already."

"We need three parallel distribution strategies," Aquatania decided, her mind quickly organizing possibilities. "Marina, can underwater convoys reach Oceana Prime's inner sectors through the maintenance tunnels we used to escape?"

"Possibly." Marina traced a path through the holographic city. "With small vessels and proper codes, we could bypass the security lockdowns. The water itself could serve as a distribution medium once we're inside…introduce the treatment into filtration systems to reach maximum population."

Kieran nodded, already thinking ahead. "For the remote sky outposts and Zephyria's lower platforms, dragon couriers are the only option. They can navigate without the standard flight paths, avoid detection."

"And medical vessels for Aethoria," Aquatania added, moving to a different display showing the fire kingdom's geography. "Their defenses are designed for water-based attacks. They'll never expect medical aid from that direction."

They continued refining the plan, each contributing their specialized knowledge. Marina calculated dilution rates for water-based distribution, Kieran mapped courier routes that minimized exposure to alien detection systems, and

Aquatania developed modified versions of the formula for different physiologies.

"There's still the matter of the formula's incomplete state," Marina said finally, the concern they'd all been harboring finally surfacing. "Without the moonlight algae catalyst, we can't guarantee it will work as intended. Best case, it slows progression. Worst case..."

"What are the potential side effects?" Aquatania asked directly.

Marina hesitated, looking uncomfortable with speculation, but her scientific integrity demanded honesty. "Theoretically? Temporary immune suppression, possible neurological effects from the unbalanced draconic elements. The Elder Weeping scroll emphasized balance for a reason."

"And if we wait for the expedition to return with the catalyst?" Kieran asked.

"Assuming they return at all?" Marina replied. "We'd still need hours to complete the integration process. Well beyond the aliens' twelve-hour deadline."

Silence fell over the laboratory as the impossible choice crystallized before them. Distribute an incomplete cure that might help but could potentially harm, or wait for a complete formula that would come too late for thousands.

Aquatania moved to the Integration Chamber, placing her hand against its crystal housing. Inside, the combined blood components continued their slow dance toward stability, each molecule finding its proper alignment through carefully controlled pressure and energy fields. It was beautiful, precise, scientific...and tragically insufficient against the accelerating crisis.

"We distribute what we have now," she said finally, her voice steady despite the weight of the decision. "The risk of side effects is better than certain death."

She met Kieran's eyes across the room, seeing both concern and understanding in his gaze. Marina looked down at her calculations, her scientific caution warring with the desperate reality they faced.

"I'll begin modifying the formula for water distribution," the mermaid scientist said after a moment. She nodded in acceptance of the decision, even if Aquatania knew it was difficult for her to fully embrace it.

"I'll organize the courier network," Kieran added, straightening despite the pain it clearly caused him. "We'll need two dozen dragons minimum, with specialized training for combat evasion."

Aquatania nodded, grateful for their support even as she shouldered the ultimate responsibility for the choice. "I'll prepare the Aethoria expedition." She turned back to the Integration Chamber, adjusting settings to accelerate the final processing stage. "We have nine hours before the aliens' deadline. Let's use every minute."

The partial cure might save some, harm others, and leave many beyond help entirely. It was an imperfect solution to an impossible problem, a desperate gamble against an enemy that had calculated every move except, perhaps, how far they would go to save their world.

Her fingers traced the ancient symbols etched into the Integration Chamber's housing...sea dragon glyphs that translated roughly to *balance in all things brings healing*. They had no balance now, only desperate measures and the hope that sometimes, imperfect solutions were enough to change the course of fate.

*

The medical vessel's hull vibrated beneath Aquatania's feet as its enchanted engines powered up to maximum capacity. The sleek craft, designed for speed rather than comfort, sat poised at Zephyria's eastern launch platform, its cargo holds loaded with precious containers of the partial cure. Around her, the medical team moved with practiced efficiency, securing equipment and checking the specialized delivery systems they would use in Aethoria's fever districts. No one spoke beyond essential communication, the gravity of their mission reflected in tight expressions and precise movements. Aquatania secured the final container herself, her fingers lingering momentarily on the sealed lid as if her touch could somehow strengthen the incomplete formula within.

"Launch clearance confirmed, Your Highness," the pilot called from the open cockpit. "Weather patterns show unusual disturbances in the mid-altitude layers. Recommend immediate departure to avoid potential alien interference with atmospheric conditions."

"Proceed," she ordered, strapping herself into a seat as the launch countdown began.

The vessel shot forward with a force that pressed Aquatania back against her restraints, Zephyria's floating spires blurring as they accelerated away from the city. Within moments, they'd entered the first layer of clouds, the view outside the windows transforming into swirling white vapor streaked with occasional flashes of blue as they passed through pockets of enchanted air currents that ordinarily regulated weather patterns around the sky islands.

"Communication crystal stabilized," a technician reported, adjusting controls on a palm-sized device that glowed with internal light. "Connection established with both secondary teams."

Aquatania leaned forward as the crystal projected a small holographic display showing Marina's face, the image occasionally distorting as the connection wavered.

"Submersible convoy passing the outer reef boundary," Marina reported, her voice faintly echoing through the crystal's transmission. "Water conditions deteriorating. Unusual currents suggesting possible alien technology affecting ocean patterns. Adjusting course to compensate."

The projection shifted, revealing Marina's environment, the cramped command center of the lead submersible where she directed a small fleet of vessels toward Oceana Prime's sealed inner districts. Behind her, crew members monitored detection equipment and navigation systems, their movements economical in the confined space.

"Security barriers?" Aquatania asked, aware that Oceana Prime's defensive systems would have been fully activated after the alien broadcast.

"Bypassing using royal override codes," Marina replied, her fingers dancing across control panels out of view. "They've added new encryption layers, but nothing my team can't handle. We should reach the maintenance tunnels within forty minutes."

The image flickered as their vessel entered a denser cloud bank, the connection briefly destabilizing before reestablishing with a different location.

Now Kieran appeared in the projection, standing in Zephyria's highest messenger tower, where curved perches extended outward, allowing dragon couriers to land and launch without interference from the city's air traffic.

"First wave dispatched," he reported, his voice clipped and professional, though Aquatania noted the tension around his eyes. "Eight couriers heading to the northern outposts, six to the eastern platforms, ten to the southern archipelago."

Behind him, dragons of various sizes received waterproof pouches containing cure vials, the specialized containers secured to harnesses designed for maximum stability during high-speed flight. Each courier also carried defensive weaponry, not standard practice for messenger dragons, but necessary given the circumstances.

"Weather interference?" she asked, noting how the clouds outside their vessel had darkened to an unnatural greenish-gray.

"Increasing," Kieran confirmed, glancing at atmospheric

monitoring equipment beside him. "We're seeing pattern disruptions consistent with the aliens' technology. I've instructed the couriers to fly below standard routes, using terrain features for cover when possible."

Aquatania's medical vessel suddenly lurched, dropping altitude sharply before the pilots stabilized their course. She gripped her seat as alarms sounded briefly before being silenced.

"Atmospheric pocket," the pilot called back. "Natural or artificial, impossible to determine. Adjusting approach vector to Aethoria."

Aquatania returned her attention to the communication crystal, where Kieran's projection had been replaced by static. When the image reestablished, she immediately sensed something was wrong. The messenger tower appeared in disarray, dragons screeching in the background as figures moved with urgent purpose.

"Courier seven is under attack," Kieran's voice came through before his image appeared. "Infiltrator intercepted the northern route. Dispatching response team now."

The projection shifted, showing a distant aerial view captured by monitoring crystals…a messenger dragon wheeling through cloud cover as a smaller, faster shape pursued it. The courier attempted evasive maneuvers, diving and banking sharply, but the pursuing form matched each movement with unnatural precision.

"They've discovered the distribution plan," Aquatania said, her stomach tightening with dread. "How many routes are compromised?"

"Unknown," Kieran replied, his face reappearing in the projection. "I'm—" His words cut off as something crashed behind him. The image tilted wildly, then stabilized to show Kieran facing what appeared to be a tower guard but moved with the too-fluid grace that betrayed an infiltrator.

The alien shed its human disguise in a rippling

transformation, limbs elongating into segmented appendages tipped with blade-like protrusions. It lunged at Kieran with frightening speed, forcing him to abandon the communication crystal as he drew his weapon.

Aquatania watched helplessly as the crystal continued to transmit, its angle now showing only a partial view of the ensuing combat. Kieran moved with military precision despite his healing wound, his sword leaving trails of light as he parried the infiltrator's attacks. Each clash produced a sound like metal striking chitin, the alien's exoskeleton apparently resistant to normal blades.

Kieran feinted left, then dropped unexpectedly to sweep the infiltrator's legs. The creature jumped with inhuman agility, but Kieran had anticipated the move, his sword arcing upward to strike at the alien's midsection. Dark fluid sprayed from the wound, sizzling where it touched the tower's stone floor.

The alien countered with a series of rapid strikes, its limbs moving almost too fast to follow. One blow connected with Kieran's injured side, causing him to stumble momentarily. The infiltrator pressed its advantage, forcing him back toward the open edge of the tower where a sheer drop awaited.

With seemingly nowhere to retreat, Kieran did the unexpected...he stepped backward into empty air. The infiltrator lunged forward, only to meet empty space as Kieran's hand caught a support beam beneath the tower's edge. He swung himself around and up, coming back onto the platform behind the alien, his sword driving forward in one clean thrust.

The infiltrator collapsed, its form twitching before becoming still. Kieran stood for a moment, breathing heavily, then limped back to the communication crystal.

"Infiltrator neutralized," he reported, wiping dark fluid from his blade. "But we have confirmation. They know what we're doing. All courier routes are likely compromised. I'm accelerating the launch schedule for the remaining teams."

The projection split, now showing both Kieran and Marina simultaneously. The mermaid scientist's expression was grim as she absorbed the new information.

"We're approaching the maintenance access tunnels," she reported. "No direct interference yet, but unusual activity detected near our destination. Security protocols at the inner districts have been altered—the signatures don't match standard Oceana Prime encryption."

"They're taking control of the cities' defense systems," Aquatania realized, the implications sending a chill down her spine. "How much time until you reach the distribution point?"

"Twenty minutes if we maintain current speed," Marina replied. "But I've had to modify the formula again. The water samples show increasing contamination. Something's changing the basic chemistry of Oceana Prime's environment."

The medical vessel began its descent toward Aethoria, breaking through the final cloud layer to reveal the fire kingdom spread across volcanic mountains and ash plains below. Even from that altitude, Aquatania could see the evidence of crisis—evacuation caravans moving along mountain passes, quarantine zones marked by distinctive red barrier fields, and fever tents concentrated in valleys where steam vents could provide the extreme heat that fire kingdom natives required when they were ill.

"We're approaching Aethoria's central medical district," she informed both teams. "Heavy quarantine measures are visible. Estimated time to distribution point...twelve minutes."

"Courier teams report alien vessels appearing on Zephyria's horizon," Kieran said, his voice tight with urgency. "Large craft, unlike anything in our records. They're moving toward the city center. We're running out of time."

The communication crystal projected a final split image. Marina's submersible slipped into a narrow maintenance tunnel beneath Oceana Prime's outer walls while Kieran dispatched the final courier dragons as ominous shapes appeared in the distant sky. And from Aquatania's vessel, the fever tents of Aethoria came into sharp focus as they made their final approach.

Three fronts, three desperate attempts to distribute a cure that might not even fully work. Aquatania closed her fingers around the communication crystal, drawing strength from the connection to her companions even as the challenges before them multiplied. Outside her window, the red rashes of infected patients were visible even from the air, angry patterns spreading across bodies that might soon receive either salvation or false hope in the form of their incomplete cure.

The vessel's landing gear deployed with a mechanical whine as they began their final descent, the medical team already preparing distribution equipment for immediate deployment. Whether their efforts would prove sufficient, or timely enough, remained to be seen, but they'd committed to this course. There was no turning back now.

*

Heat pressed against Aquatania like a living entity as she moved between patients in Aethoria's main medical tent. Fire kingdom natives required temperatures that would scald human skin, the ambient air shimmering with thermal distortion that made the rows of afflicted patients seem to waver like mirages. Sweat beaded on her forehead and ran in rivulets down her back, her sea dragon heritage making her particularly sensitive to the oppressive environment. Yet she worked without pause, personally administering injections of their precious partial cure to the most critical cases, her movements precise despite her discomfort. The medical team had established an efficient system, triage, treatment, and monitoring, with Aquatania focusing on those whose crimson markings had progressed furthest toward their hearts.

"Injection complete," she murmured to an elderly man whose fiery orange eyes had dulled to ember-like resignation. The crimson markings of the Red Death had already traced most major blood vessels across his chest, creating an ominous roadmap leading to his heart. "Rest now. The treatment will take effect soon."

She moved to the next patient, a middle-aged woman whose fever burned so intensely that the air around her bed rippled with heat haze. Aquatania adjusted the dosage formula, adding stabilizing agents specifically designed for fire kingdom physiology before administering the injection directly into a vein where the red markings appeared brightest.

For three hours, she continued without rest, each dose precious, each patient another chance to prove that their partial cure could make a difference. The supply diminished steadily, forcing increasingly difficult choices about who received treatment and who must wait for later batches, if they survived long enough.

As she prepared to treat her thirty-seventh patient, Aquatania noticed something that made her pause. The elderly man she'd injected first was sitting up, speaking quietly with a medic. His movements remained weak, but the angry red markings on his exposed skin had stopped their ominous progression. When he turned his face toward the light, Aquatania saw that his eyes had regained some of their characteristic fire kingdom glow.

"Temperature readings are dropping across all treated patients," the chief medic reported, consulting a crystal data tablet. "Not to normal ranges, but below critical thresholds. The rash progression has slowed significantly in eighty-three percent of recipients."

Aquatania moved quickly to check other early recipients, confirming the pattern. The partial cure wasn't eliminating the contagion, and the red markings remained visible. However, it was slowing the progression dramatically, giving immune systems time to mount their defense. It wasn't a complete victory, but it was undeniably working.

"Continue monitoring for side effects," she instructed, knowing the incomplete formula carried risks they couldn't fully predict. "Watch particularly for neurological responses and immune system fluctuations."

She returned to her work with renewed energy, the evidence of even partial success fueling her. As she administered a dose to a young girl, perhaps seven years old, the child's hand suddenly reached out, thin fingers wrapping around Aquatania's wrist with surprising strength.

"Are you a water spirit?" the girl asked, her voice raspy from days of fever. The child's crimson markings had formed delicate patterns across her cheeks like macabre face paint.

"No," Aquatania replied gently, completing the injection. "Just someone trying to help."

The girl didn't release her grip. "My mother said water and fire together make steam that reaches the sky." Her fever-bright eyes fixed on Aquatania's face with unexpected clarity. "Are you making steam to fight the sky monsters?"

The innocent question...part fever-dream, part profound truth...caught Aquatania off guard. For a moment, the weight of their desperate gambit, of all they stood to lose, pressed down with crushing force. This child and countless others like her across multiple kingdoms depended on decisions made in haste, on incomplete solutions born of desperation.

"Yes," she answered finally, her voice thick with emotion she rarely allowed herself to display. "That's exactly what we're doing."

The girl nodded solemnly, as if this confirmed something

important, then released Aquatania's wrist and closed her eyes. Within moments, the child's breathing eased, the first sign that the treatment was taking effect.

Aquatania allowed herself five seconds, five precious seconds of relief and hope, before moving to the next patient. As she worked, her communication crystal activated, projecting Marina's image beside a portable treatment station.

"Distribution through Oceana Prime's water filtration system proceeding as planned," she reported, her image occasionally distorting as the signal passed through layers of water and stone. "We've managed to introduce the formula into all inner sector circulation systems. Early results show reduced symptom progression in exposed patients."

"Any sign of the side effects we feared?" Aquatania asked, preparing another injection as she spoke.

"Some neurological responses, disorientation, mild hallucinations, but nothing life-threatening," Marina replied. "The formula is performing better than expected given its incomplete state. I've adjusted concentrations to minimize side effects while maintaining efficacy."

The projection shifted, now showing Kieran in what appeared to be a transportation hub in Zephyria. His clothing showed signs of recent combat, torn in places, stained with both his blood and the darker fluid of the infiltrators, but his expression carried the calm certainty of a mission successfully completed.

"All courier deliveries confirmed," he reported. "We lost two dragons to alien interceptors, but the remaining teams reached their destinations. Distribution has begun in all outlying sky islands and Zephyria's lower platforms."

"And the alien vessels spotted approaching Zephyria?" Aquatania asked, the momentary relief she'd felt giving way to renewed concern.

"Holding position just beyond the defensive perimeter," Kieran replied. "They seem to be waiting for something, possibly reinforcements or simply the expiration of their twelve-hour deadline. Either way, we've successfully distributed the first wave of treatments before they could interfere directly."

The crystal expanded its projection field, now showing all three of them in a triangular configuration that allowed for a joint conference despite their physical separation across hundreds of miles. In this virtual space, they shared data, compared treatment responses, and calculated next steps with the focused efficiency of a team that had faced multiple crises together.

"The partial cure is working better than we dared hope," Marina summarized, reviewing combined data from all three locations. "Fever reduction, slowed progression, and some early signs of contagion retreat in patients with stronger immune systems."

"But it's not a complete cure," Kieran noted, ever the pragmatic strategist. "At best, we've bought time."

"Time we desperately needed," Aquatania agreed. "If the expedition returns with the catalyst plants, we can complete the formula and produce a true cure rather than just a delaying measure."

Before anyone could respond, a fourth projection appeared in their communication field, a harried-looking messenger in Zephyria royal guard uniform.

"Forgive the interruption, Your Highness," the guard began, formal protocol strained by obvious urgency. "An emergency report from Central Platform Security. A new outbreak has been detected in Residential Sector Seven."

"That's impossible," Kieran interrupted, his expression darkening. "Sector Seven is a sealed environment with enhanced security protocols. It was designated as a safe zone for vulnerable populations precisely because of its isolation capabilities."

"The outbreak appeared suddenly, sir," the messenger

continued. "And the progression pattern is...different. Medical teams report the contagion is following neural pathways rather than blood vessels. The red markings are spreading along nerve routes directly toward the brain instead of the heart."

Silence fell across their connected projections as the implications became clear. The aliens hadn't been idle during the twelve hours they'd given for their deadline. They'd already adapted their contagion again, developing a new variant that targeted different systems and likely wouldn't respond to the current treatment.

"Send all available data to my laboratory," Aquatania ordered, her mind already racing ahead to necessary modifications. "Full neural mapping of infected patients, progression rates, response to current treatment attempts."

As the messenger's projection disappeared, the three leaders exchanged grim looks, their momentary triumph overshadowed by this new development.

"They're always one step ahead," Marina said softly.

Aquatania turned to check on the young girl she'd treated earlier. The child slept peacefully now, her fever visibly reduced, the crimson markings no longer spreading across her delicate features. Similar scenes played out across the medical tent, patients showing improvement, medical staff allowing themselves cautious optimism, and family members embracing with tentative hope.

A temporary victory, but a victory nonetheless. Aquatania's fingers closed around a vial of their partial cure, the luminous liquid catching the harsh light of the fever tent.

"We've bought some time," she said, her features hardening as she turned back to the projection of her companions. "Now we need to find that catalyst before they strike again."

In her mind, she was already calculating modifications to the formula, planning countermeasures against this new neural-targeting variant. The aliens might be adaptive, might have planned for contingencies, but they'd underestimated one crucial factor...the relentless determination of those fighting for their world's survival.

Chapter Eleven

Aquatania pressed her palms against the crystal observation panel, the cool surface a welcome relief against her skin after forty-eight hours with minimal rest. Below, in the vast production chamber, three dozen technicians moved with practiced precision between integration units where the completed cure formula was being processed and sealed into distribution vials. The expedition had returned with the moonlight algae just in time, the precious catalyst allowing them to perfect the formula that now represented their world's best hope against both variants of the alien contagion.

She should have felt triumphant. Instead, unease crawled along her spine like ice water, her sea dragon senses picking up subtle disruptions in the laboratory's rhythm that her conscious mind couldn't yet identify.

The high-security facility occupied the uppermost level of Zephyria's scientific spire, its domed ceiling made of reinforced glass that admitted the combined light of the twin moons. This lunar illumination, essential for activating certain properties of the catalyst, bathed the chamber in silver-blue radiance that complemented the glowing integration units arranged in concentric circles. The air hummed with the synchronized vibration of pressure regulators maintaining perfect conditions for the delicate alchemical processes. Security crystals pulsed at regular intervals along the walls, their enchantments creating an invisible barrier against unauthorized entry.

Below, white-coated technicians checked readings, adjusted settings, and carefully transferred completed batches to cooling stations where the cure's components stabilized into their final form.

"Your Highness." Marina's voice pulled Aquatania from her observations. The mermaid scientist approached with a crystal tablet, her webbed fingers tapping urgently against its surface. The specialized breathing apparatus she wore for extended periods outside water emitted a soft hiss with each exhalation. "I've been reviewing the production logs from the night shift, and something doesn't add up."

Aquatania took the tablet, scanning the data displays with practiced efficiency. "What am I looking at?"

"Output discrepancies." Marina traced a pattern across the screen, highlighting fluctuating numbers. "These three integration units should have produced forty-two vials each during last night's cycle. Units seven and twelve recorded normal output, but unit nine shows only thirty-eight vials completed."

"Could be mechanical failure," Aquatania suggested, though her tone betrayed her skepticism.

"That's what I thought initially." Marina's gills fluttered with agitation beneath her breathing collar. "So I checked the system diagnostics. No failures reported. Then I found this." She adjusted the display to show inventory records. "Sixteen vials unaccounted for across three shifts. And these equipment logs show seven instances of unexplained power fluctuations in the secure storage area."

Aquatania's unease crystallized into cold certainty. She handed the tablet back to Marina. "Show me the affected equipment."

They descended to the production floor, where the hum of machinery intensified to a constant vibration felt through the soles of their feet. Technicians nodded respectfully as they passed, their eyes bloodshot from extended shifts and the strain of precise work. Marina led her to integration unit nine, where a technician was already removing the outer access panel.

Aquatania crouched beside the opened unit, her eyes

narrowing as she examined the exposed components. The central processing crystal — the heart of the integration system that regulated the combining of dragon blood elements with the catalyst — showed minute scratches around its housing that wouldn't be visible to anyone without enhanced draconic vision. She ran her finger along one scratch, feeling the deliberate precision of the mark.

"This wasn't accidental," she said quietly, gesturing for Marina to come closer. "See these marks? Someone recalibrated the crystal alignment, shifting it just enough to reduce efficacy without triggering failure alerts." She pointed to connections deeper in the unit. "And here…the pressure regulator's been adjusted. Subtle, but enough to compromise approximately ten percent of each batch."

Marina's scientific detachment momentarily faltered, her expression tightening with anger. "Sabotage."

"Sophisticated sabotage," Aquatania agreed, replacing the access panel. "Only someone with detailed knowledge of these systems could make adjustments this precise."

As they straightened, a technician in a senior supervisor's uniform approached, his posture communicating urgency despite his attempt at discretion. "Your Highness, if I might have a word in private?"

They moved to a small monitoring alcove away from the main floor. The supervisor, a man whose silver-streaked hair and steady hands spoke of decades of laboratory experience, checked to ensure they wouldn't be overheard before speaking.

"My security team completed the access audit you requested," he said, his voice barely above a whisper. "Someone entered the secure storage area at two hours past midnight last night using diplomatic override codes. The system identified the credentials as belonging to Envoy Zephyr."

Aquatania exchanged glances with Marina, the

implications hanging between them like a storm cloud. "Zephyr left for the Sky Archipelago diplomatic summit three days ago," she said carefully.

"Exactly, Your Highness." The supervisor's eyes reflected the gravity of this revelation. "Either someone has stolen his credentials, or…"

"Or Zephyr himself is involved." Aquatania completed the thought, years of political training preventing her from fully expressing her concern. "Thank you for your discretion. Please continue normal operations while I address this matter."

When the supervisor had returned to his duties, Marina moved closer. "If Zephyr is compromised —"

"Then our entire security protocol is at risk," Aquatania finished. "He has access to every aspect of our operation."

They were interrupted by Kieran's arrival. The fire dragon general entered through the main security checkpoint, his military posture unchanged despite evident fatigue in the shadows beneath his eyes. He crossed directly to them, immediately sensing the tension.

"What's happened?" he asked without preamble.

Aquatania quickly summarized their discoveries, the production discrepancies, the sabotaged equipment, and Zephyr's credentials being used during his supposed absence. Kieran listened without interruption, his expression hardening into the tactical focus she'd come to recognize when his military mind engaged with a threat.

"We need to identify exactly what was taken and who's responsible," he said when she finished. "But doing so openly will alert whoever's behind this."

"What do you suggest?" Marina asked.

Kieran's eyes met Aquatania's, something unspoken passing between them. "A trap. We mark certain vials with traceable compounds, completely harmless but distinctive enough to track. Then we create a security blind spot, a deliberate gap in surveillance that looks accidental."

"And wait to see who takes the bait," Aquatania nodded, already considering the logistics. "We'll need to maintain normal operations as cover. No one outside this circle can know what we're doing."

They spent the next few hours implementing their plan with careful precision. Publicly, production continued uninterrupted, technicians rotating through shifts as scheduled. Behind this facade of normalcy, Marina prepared specialized tracking compounds that would be undetectable without specific equipment, and Kieran adjusted security systems to create an apparent vulnerability in the monitoring network.

*

Night fell, the twin moons reaching their apex and flooding the laboratory with silver radiance that activated the cure's catalyst components. The day shift departed, replaced by a skeleton crew of night technicians, all vetted personally by Kieran and strategically positioned to observe without being obvious.

Near midnight, Aquatania dismissed her personal attendants, ostensibly retiring to her private chambers adjacent to the laboratory. Instead, she slipped back into the now-dimmed production floor, her sea dragon eyes adjusting instantly to the reduced light. She moved silently between integration units, extending her awareness into the water molecules that existed in the air, in the cooling systems, in the very walls of the facility.

Water responded to her call, gathering into invisible tendrils that extended her senses beyond normal range. She felt the vibrations of movement, the subtle changes in humidity and temperature that marked recent activity. Following these sensations, she was drawn to a section of wall near the secure storage area that appeared solid and unremarkable.

Placing her palm against the smooth surface, she sent water molecules seeking through microscopic spaces, mapping what lay beyond. Her eyes widened as she discovered a concealed compartment, expertly hidden behind seamless panels. With delicate precision, she manipulated the water pressure against specific points, triggering a hidden mechanism.

The panel slid aside silently, revealing a small space where sixteen missing vials rested in a specialized carrying case. Beside them lay something that confirmed her worst fears…a communication device of alien design, its surface covered with symbols no human language could produce. The technology pulsed with faint energy, transmitting information through channels that bypassed all standard security measures.

Aquatania carefully resealed the hidden compartment, leaving everything exactly as she'd found it. She retreated to the monitoring station where Kieran and Marina waited, their faces tense in the glow of surveillance crystals.

"I found them," she said, her voice steady despite the gravity of her discovery. "And I know how our enemies have stayed one step ahead. Now we wait to see who returns for their prize."

*

The laboratory's night cycle brought a stillness broken only by the soft hum of integration units and the occasional footsteps of security patrols. Aquatania remained motionless in the observation alcove, her body tense with anticipation as minutes stretched into hours. Kieran stood at her right shoulder, his presence warm even in silence, while Marina monitored security feeds through a crystal tablet, the screen's glow illuminating her features in the darkness. They'd waited for nearly four hours when the main entrance's security crystal pulsed with recognition, admitting a tall figure whose platinum hair caught the moonlight streaming through the dome above.

"Zephyr," Marina whispered, angling the tablet so the others could see the security feed.

The sky dragon diplomat moved with practiced grace through the laboratory, his formal robes replaced by simpler attire that wouldn't attract attention during the night cycle. He paused occasionally, appearing to check that his movements went unobserved, before continuing toward the secure storage area. His path was purposeful, without the hesitation of someone exploring unfamiliar territory.

"He knows exactly where he's going," Kieran noted, his voice barely audible.

Aquatania nodded, watching as Zephyr approached the section of wall containing the hidden compartment she'd discovered earlier. "He's not even trying to access the official storage units. He's going straight for the concealed section."

They observed in tense silence as Zephyr placed his palm against the seemingly solid wall, manipulating hidden mechanisms with the confidence of frequent practice. The panel slid aside, revealing the compartment where the stolen vials and alien communication device waited. As he reached inside, Aquatania gave the signal they'd agreed upon…three quick taps against her crystal pendant.

Kieran and Marina moved silently to predetermined positions, securing exit routes while Aquatania stepped from the shadows. She extended her awareness to the water molecules throughout the chamber, gathering them into an invisible cloud around her, ready to respond to her will.

"Working late, Envoy Zephyr?" Her voice cut through the stillness, causing the diplomat to freeze with his hand still inside the compartment. "The diplomatic summit must have

209

concluded earlier than expected."

Zephyr withdrew his hand slowly, turning to face her with the smooth composure that had served him so well in diplomatic circles. His features arranged themselves into an expression of mild surprise that would have been convincing if Aquatania hadn't been watching for the fractional delay in his response.

"Princess Aquatania," he greeted her, his melodic voice perfectly modulated. "I returned early when I received reports of production difficulties. As an official liaison between kingdoms, I felt obligated to offer whatever assistance I could."

"How considerate." Aquatania took several measured steps toward him, simultaneously sending a surge of water molecules racing across the floor and up the walls, forming a transparent barrier across the laboratory's exits. The water solidified into a shimmering wall that caught and refracted moonlight in hypnotic patterns. "Especially since no such reports were filed through official channels."

Something flickered behind Zephyr's eyes, too quick to name but distinct enough to confirm her suspicions. His posture shifted subtly, his weight redistributing as if he were preparing for sudden movement.

"There appears to be some misunderstanding." His tone remained pleasant, though a new intensity had entered his gaze. "Perhaps we should discuss this in more appropriate surroundings. The hour is late, and —"

"We found the vials, Zephyr." Aquatania cut through his carefully constructed explanation. "Sixteen missing doses. Along with an interesting piece of technology that doesn't match any design in our world's records."

Kieran emerged from his position near the main entrance, moving to stand at Aquatania's side. "Your credentials were used to access secure areas during times you were supposedly elsewhere. The equipment sabotage carries your signature, precise adjustments that only someone with your access and knowledge could accomplish."

Zephyr's diplomatic smile remained fixed in place, though it no longer reached his eyes. "These are serious accusations against a representative of the Sky Archipelago. I suggest caution before proceeding further." His gaze darted briefly to the water barrier blocking the exits. "Diplomatic immunity protects me from detainment."

"Diplomatic immunity," Marina said, joining them from her monitoring position, "doesn't extend to acts of sabotage during a global crisis." She held up the crystal tablet displaying surveillance footage of Zephyr's nighttime visits to the laboratory. "Or to espionage on behalf of hostile forces."

Zephyr's expression hardened, the charming diplomat vanishing like morning mist. "You have no idea what you're involving yourselves in," he said, his voice dropping to a register that sent involuntary shivers down Aquatania's spine. "This conflict was decided before your kind even became aware of it."

"Then why sabotage our cure?" Aquatania demanded, taking another step forward. "Why not simply destroy it completely?"

"Because total destruction would have alerted you too quickly." A strange ripple passed across Zephyr's features, momentarily distorting his perfect profile. "We needed to know the formula's components while ensuring it remained ineffective enough to fail in widespread application."

As he spoke, another ripple moved across his skin, more pronounced than the first. The smooth porcelain complexion briefly revealed something beneath, a greenish translucency where solid flesh should be. His fingers, gesturing to emphasize a point, momentarily elongated into jointed appendages too numerous and flexible for any dragon or human anatomy.

"We?" Kieran's hand moved to his weapon, though he didn't draw it yet.

Zephyr's smile returned, but it was wrong somehow, too wide, revealing teeth that seemed to shift position within his mouth. "Did you really believe I was a sky dragon?" The melodic quality of his voice faltered, harmonics splitting into discordant tones. "Your species' habit of trusting surface appearances made infiltration embarrassingly simple."

The diplomatic facade crumbled further as he spoke, his skin rippling like water disturbed by underwater currents. Patches of iridescent green showed through the human disguise, revealing the compound eyes briefly before the humanoid appearance reasserted itself with visible effort.

"You were never going to succeed," Zephyr continued, his voice now carrying that distinctive clicking undertone they'd heard in the alien broadcast. "We've known your plans from the beginning, every formula adjustment, every distribution route, every desperate attempt to counter our contagion."

Aquatania felt cold horror spreading through her veins as the truth crystallized. "You've been transmitting everything directly to them."

"Not just transmitting." The thing wearing Zephyr's appearance gestured toward the hidden compartment. "Providing samples. Your cure attempts have been tested against our contagion variants before you could even begin distribution."

With sudden violence, Zephyr lunged toward the nearest integration unit, his arm extending with unnatural speed to grasp a crystal control panel. "Enough talk. This facility has served its purpose in our research. It's now a liability to be eliminated."

His fingers transformed as they touched the control surface, splitting into wirelike appendages that penetrated the crystal housing. Integration unit alarms blared as critical systems began to overload, and pressure regulators failed as sabotage commands spread through connected systems.

Kieran reacted instantly, throwing himself at Zephyr. They collided with bone-jarring force, crashing into adjacent equipment. Glassware shattered, spilling chemicals that hissed against the floor. The two figures rolled across the laboratory in a blur of motion, Kieran's combat training meeting Zephyr's inhuman strength and flexibility.

"Marina, secure the samples!" Aquatania shouted above the chaos of alarms and struggle. She directed her gathered water into a powerful stream that separated the combatants long enough for Kieran to regain his footing.

Zephyr rose with unnatural fluidity, his disguise now failing in large sections to reveal the alien form beneath. Jointed limbs too numerous for his clothing extended from his torso, ripping through fabric as compound eyes gleamed in the moonlight.

"Your cure production data has already been transmitted," he said, the voice now barely recognizable as the diplomat they'd trusted. "Our adaptation protocols are already generating countermeasures. Your distribution networks are compromised, your leadership infiltrated at every level."

Kieran circled warily, blood streaming from a cut above his eye where Zephyr had struck him. "You won't leave this facility."

"I don't need to." Zephyr's partially transformed mouth formed something approximating a smile. "I merely needed to confirm our final data points. The primary objective is already complete."

He reached for the alien communication device in the hidden compartment, but Aquatania was faster. Water surged forward in a concentrated wave, freezing instantly around the device and Zephyr's extended limb. He hissed with pain or rage, the sound entirely inhuman.

Kieran seized the moment of immobility, tackling Zephyr again with enough force to break through the ice formation.

They crashed into a storage unit, sending vials and equipment cascading around them. The alien limb snapped with a sound like breaking chitin, dark fluid spraying across the floor.

Marina worked frantically at a control panel, overriding the sabotage commands to stabilize the integration units. Alarms continued to sound throughout the facility as security teams responded to the chaos, their footsteps thundering down corridors toward the production floor.

Aquatania gathered her water into a spherical prison, encasing Zephyr in a globe of liquid that hardened to crystal clarity while remaining flexible enough to contain his thrashing limbs. Through the water barrier, she watched as the last vestiges of the diplomat's appearance dissolved, revealing the alien creature that had lived among them, betrayed them, and nearly destroyed their last hope for survival.

*

Dawn light filtered through the laboratory's dome, illuminating a scene of calculated destruction. Broken glass crunched beneath Aquatania's boots as she surveyed the damage...integration units with their panels torn open, workstations overturned, chemical compounds drying in caustic pools across the floor. Security officers maintained a wary perimeter around the water sphere where Zephyr, or the creature that had worn his identity, remained contained, its alien form occasionally pressing against the flexible barrier as if testing for weaknesses. Marina knelt amid the wreckage of a sample storage unit, her webbed hands trembling slightly as she carefully transferred surviving vials into a preservation case.

"Forty-three intact samples," Marina reported without looking up, her scientific precision a defense against the horror they'd witnessed. "Another twenty-seven potentially salvageable if we can filter out the contaminants." Her breathing apparatus hissed with each stressed exhalation, the sound unnervingly similar to the clicking communication they'd heard from Zephyr's true form.

Aquatania moved to her friend's side, steadying Marina's hands as they reached for another vial. "You need rest."

"We all do." Marina's gills fluttered with agitation beneath her collar. "But the distribution schedule doesn't allow for it. The second contagion wave is spreading through Oceana Prime's outer sectors. These samples are already promised to transport vessels departing at midday."

Across the laboratory, cleanup teams worked to restore order, salvaging what equipment they could while documenting the destruction for security reports. The night's events had shaken the entire facility, not just physically, but at the core of their fragile trust. Staff who'd worked alongside each other for weeks now exchanged wary glances, each wondering what other infiltrators might be hiding behind familiar faces.

The undercurrent of suspicion found voice when the senior supervisor approached Kieran, who was conferring with security officers near the containment area. The supervisor's usually respectful demeanor had hardened into open accusation.

"You brought him into our inner circle," he said, loud enough for nearby staff to hear. "Vouched for his credentials when questions were raised about his access level. We trusted your judgment, General."

Heads turned throughout the laboratory, conversations faltering as attention focused on the confrontation. Kieran straightened, his expression carefully neutral despite the challenge.

"I did," he acknowledged, neither deflecting the accusation nor defending himself yet.

"How do we know you weren't working with him?" the

supervisor pressed, emboldened by the silent support of watching staff. "Convenient that *you discovered* the sabotage just when production was reaching critical mass."

Aquatania felt the accusation like a physical blow. The possibility had lurked at the edges of her thoughts since Zephyr's capture that Kieran's initial support for the sky dragon diplomat might have deeper, darker implications. He'd been the one to introduce Zephyr to their group, to advocate for his inclusion in sensitive discussions. The logical, analytical part of her mind couldn't dismiss the possibility entirely, even as her heart rejected it.

Kieran's eyes found hers across the room, something vulnerable and fierce passing between them before he addressed the gathered staff.

"I trusted him because he saved my life during the Aethoria mission," he said, his voice steady but stripped of its usual military formality. "When our transport was attacked by what we thought were rogue elements, Zephyr fought alongside me. He took an energy blast that would have killed me." His hand unconsciously moved to the wound at his side, the injury that still pained him, that she'd seen him favoring during their most difficult moments. "I never suspected that attack might have been staged precisely to earn my trust."

The laboratory fell silent as staff processed this revelation. Aquatania studied Kieran's face, searching for any hint of deception. She found only raw honesty and the same haunted look she'd seen in her own reflection, the recognition that they'd all been manipulated by an enemy whose capacity for strategic patience exceeded their own.

"We were all deceived," she said, her voice carrying the authority of both her royal position and scientific leadership. "Zephyr, or whatever its real designation is, was placed among us long before we understood the nature of the threat we faced. Blame serves no purpose now. Securing our work does."

She crossed to the containment sphere, water rippling beneath her approach as if recognizing its mistress. Inside, the alien creature had ceased its testing of the barrier, settling into a configuration of limbs that approximated sitting. Its compound gaze tracked her movement with unsettling precision.

"You will tell us what we need to know," she said, modulating the water pressure within the sphere to ensure the creature could hear her clearly. "Beginning with your true designation and the extent of your network within our governments."

The alien's response came with that distinctive clicking undertone, its mouth parts moving in patterns never meant for human speech. "Designation Vex-Seventeen, deep infiltration specialist, third wave." The words emerged with mechanical precision, as if reciting established protocol. "Primary objective, intelligence gathering on cure development. Secondary objective, controlled sabotage to ensure optimal data collection without alerting targets."

Aquatania felt Kieran's presence as he joined her before the containment sphere, his momentary ostracism apparently forgotten as staff returned to their duties. "How many infiltrators are embedded in leadership positions?" he asked.

The alien's attention shifted between them. "Sufficient numbers. Strategic placements. Some known to each other, most isolated for security." A sound like dry leaves rustling emerged from its speech apparatus…perhaps the alien equivalent of laughter. "You've captured one cell. The organism continues functioning."

Marina joined them, her scientific curiosity temporarily overcoming her revulsion. "The contagion variants, how quickly can your people adapt them to counter our cure formulations?"

"Adaptation protocols already initiated based on transmitted data," the creature replied. "Estimated countermeasure deployment, thirty-six hours. New variant targeting neural-respiratory junction rather than cardiac or primary neural pathways."

A chill passed through Aquatania at this clinical description of what amounted to a death sentence for thousands. "The attack schedule? The locations of your primary vessels?"

The compound gaze fixed on her face with disturbing intensity. "Information above my clearance. Deployment patterns are compartmentalized. Cell structure maintains operational security even under interrogation conditions."

Kieran's expression darkened. "You'll find we can be very persuasive when necessary."

"Biological persuasion techniques are ineffective against my physiology," the creature responded with that same mechanical precision. "Pain receptors can be voluntarily deactivated. Critical neural functions will self-terminate before security protocols can be breached."

Aquatania signaled the security officers to maintain their perimeter around the containment sphere. They would learn what they could from the captured infiltrator, but she recognized the limitations of this approach. The alien hierarchy had clearly been designed with capture contingencies in mind, each operative knowing only enough to fulfill their specific function.

She turned to address the assembled staff, who'd paused in their work to observe the interrogation. Faces looked back at her with varying degrees of fear, exhaustion, and uncertainty, scientists and technicians who'd worked beyond normal human endurance, only to discover that their efforts had been compromised from within.

"We've suffered a setback," she acknowledged, her voice steady despite her own fatigue. "But we've also gained critical intelligence. We now know how our enemy has stayed ahead of our efforts. We've confirmed that our formula works.

Otherwise, they wouldn't have expended such effort to sabotage it." She gestured to the integration units that remained functional. "We will rebuild what was destroyed. We will secure our production process with new protocols. And we will distribute this cure before their next variant can be deployed."

She moved among the workstations, personally assisting with the restoration of critical systems. Her actions spoke louder than words...the princess working alongside technicians, refusing to be defeated by either the physical destruction or the psychological blow of betrayal. Gradually, the laboratory's rhythm reestablished itself.

*

Hours later, with the immediate crisis contained and production cautiously restarted, Aquatania found Kieran alone on the small observation balcony overlooking the laboratory floor.

"You should have told me about Aethoria," she said quietly, joining him at the railing. "About how Zephyr supposedly saved your life."

"I should have," he agreed, his eyes still fixed on the activity below. "But it seemed...personal. A life debt is a serious matter among fire dragons. It clouded my judgment about his motivations."

"We all missed the signs," she said after a moment. "Even when we grew suspicious, none of us imagined the extent of the deception."

Kieran turned to face her fully, the sunset light catching the amber flecks in his eyes. "I need you to know that you can trust me, Aquatania. Whatever happens next, whatever we face, my loyalty is to you and this mission. Nothing else."

She studied his face, seeing beyond the general's composure to the man beneath, the person who'd fought

219

alongside her, who'd shared rare moments of connection amid constant crises. The doubt that had flickered briefly in her mind dissolved before the evidence of everything they'd been through together.

"I know," she said simply, her hand finding his on the railing. Scales shimmered briefly beneath her skin where they touched, her sea dragon heritage responding to the intensity of the moment. "And we have work to do."

Below them, the integration units hummed with renewed activity, as batches of completed cures moved through production cycles that would continue through the night. They'd lost time and resources to Zephyr's betrayal, but they had gained something perhaps more valuable, confirmation that their efforts truly threatened the alien invasion. Their cure worked well enough that the enemy had infiltrated their highest levels to sabotage it.

Chapter Twelve

The security door hissed shut behind Aquatania, sealing her inside the interrogation cell with the creature that had worn Zephyr's face. Moonlight filtered through a narrow window set high in the water-reinforced wall, casting rippling patterns across the floor that matched her unsettled thoughts. Before her, suspended in a crystalline sphere of water, her own creation, the alien infiltrator waited, its full attention tracking her movement with unsettling precision. She'd come seeking answers, but found herself momentarily frozen, suddenly uncertain if she truly wanted to hear them.

Four guards stationed outside the cell had tried to accompany her inside. She'd dismissed them with a simple gesture. This conversation required privacy, and if the being contained within her water prison attempted anything, she was far more capable of protecting herself than any guard.

"Your containment protocols are elegant," the creature said, its voice carrying that unsettling clicking undertone that no human vocal cords could produce. "Pressure modulation, molecular alignment, temperature gradients, all precisely calibrated."

The familiar face of Zephyr flickered over the alien's features like a poorly maintained illusion, revealing patches of translucent green exoskeleton beneath. The effect was more disturbing than if the disguise had failed completely.

"Spare me the observations," Aquatania replied, circling the water sphere slowly. She kept her voice level despite the revulsion crawling along her spine. "You didn't infiltrate our highest levels of government to admire our scientific techniques."

She paused directly before the sphere, where the creature's

compound eyes could focus fully upon her. With subtle concentration, she adjusted the water pressure around Vex-17, not enough to cause pain, but sufficient to remind the infiltrator who controlled this environment.

"Why our world?" she asked, her voice calm but carrying undeniable authority. "What do you really want?"

Vex-17's mouth parts moved in what might have been a smile, too many teeth, arranged wrong, glimpsed through the fading illusion of Zephyr's face. "Information above my clearance," it replied mechanically, repeating the same evasion it had offered in the laboratory.

Aquatania narrowed her eyes. The water sphere contracted slightly, pressure increasing just enough to make the creature's breathing more labored. "You're no simple operative. Your access to our governments, your knowledge of our research, you're a mission commander at minimum."

The alien's limbs shifted within the sphere, adjusting to the pressure change with discomfort evident in the stiffening of joints and the rapid blinking of its eyes. "Careful, Princess," it said, attempting to maintain its composure. "Damage me and you lose valuable intelligence."

"I know exactly how much pressure your physiology can withstand," she replied, loosening the sphere just enough to make her point. "We've been studying your biology since the Coral Citadel. You're not the only one who can gather intelligence."

The bluff worked better than she expected. Something like uncertainty flickered across the creature's features, the first genuine reaction she'd witnessed.

"Three more questions answered truthfully, and I'll consider adjusting your containment to more comfortable parameters. Refuse, and I'll see how much pressure is required to separate that exoskeleton from whatever serves as muscle beneath."

A tense silence stretched between them, broken only by the

soft sound of water molecules shifting within the sphere. Finally, the alien's head tilted in what appeared to be resignation.

"We are not invaders in the sense you understand," it said, the mechanical precision of its earlier responses giving way to something more conversational. "Not conquerors seeking resources or strategic positions."

"Then...what?"

"Colonists." The word hung in the air between them. "Your oceans...perfect composition...ideal for our species. A rare biochemical harmony we've found on only seven planets across multiple galaxies."

Aquatania felt her heart rate increase, the water sphere responding unconsciously to her emotional state with subtle ripples across its surface. "You're here to settle."

"To transform," the creature corrected. "Your world is...close to suitable. Not quite perfect. Requiring adjustment."

The implication hit Aquatania with physical force. "The contagion."

"Phase one of environmental preparation," Vex-17 confirmed, seeming almost relieved to finally speak openly. "Your understanding of it as merely a plague is...charmingly primitive."

She tightened the water pressure again, not bothering to mask her disgust. "Explain."

Vex-17 gasped but continued, perhaps recognizing that cooperation offered the only respite. "The contagion releases enzymes into your planetary water system. Microscopic terraforming agents that gradually alter chemical balances, salinity levels, and organic content." The alien's limbs shifted, gesturing despite their confinement. "The marking patterns you observe on infected subjects are merely...byproducts. Visual indicators of biochemical conversion already underway."

"Conversion to what?" Aquatania demanded, leaning closer to the sphere.

"Habitability for us. Uninhabitability for you." The creature's compound eyes caught the moonlight, reflecting it in fractured patterns. "Our vessels maintain atmospheric deployment systems targeting cloud formation and rainfall composition. Submersible platforms are already positioned at key deep-ocean convergence points to alter current patterns. And specialized agents have begun destabilizing your reef ecosystems to allow for our architectural requirements."

Aquatania's mind raced, suddenly connecting dozens of previously unrelated observations. The unexplained chemical shifts in water samples from infected regions. The strange degradation of coral formations near outbreak zones. The unusual weather patterns that had interfered with their distribution efforts.

"You're not trying to kill us," she whispered, the horror of comprehension washing over her. "You're transforming our entire planet's ecosystem to suit your species."

"An elegant solution," Vex-17 replied with what sounded disturbingly like pride. "Total conversion requires approximately twelve of your months. The contagion weakens resistance while simultaneously beginning chemical transformation. By the time your species realizes the full scope, adaptation will be impossible."

The water sphere trembled, responding to Aquatania's surging emotions. Scales darkened along her forearms, spreading in patterns that reflected her sea dragon heritage, asserting itself in response to the threat. Her control slipped momentarily, pressure fluctuating within the sphere and causing Vex-17 to writhe in discomfort.

"You would exterminate entire species, civilizations, for colonization?" Her voice had dropped dangerously, scales now visible across her throat and cheeks.

"We would create a new world," the alien corrected,

speaking through what appeared to be significant discomfort. "Your perspective is...limited by attachment to current conditions. The resulting ecosystem will support more diverse life than currently exists, simply not your forms of life."

Aquatania stepped back, forcing herself to breathe evenly as she regained control of the water sphere. Her scientific mind had already moved beyond shock to analysis, cataloging implications and potential countermeasures. If the contagion was actually an environmental transformation agent rather than simply a disease, their cure efforts would need radical reconsideration.

"You've miscalculated," she said after a moment, her voice steadier. "Knowing your true purpose changes everything about our response."

The alien's head tilted with what might have been curiosity. "How so?"

"You selected our world for its oceans," Aquatania replied, turning toward the door. "But you failed to understand who truly controls those oceans."

She left without another word, the water sphere maintaining its perfect integrity behind her. As the security door sealed shut, she was already mentally formulating new equations, new approaches that would target not just the symptoms but the environmental transformation itself. The weight of this knowledge pressed against her chest with each step...they weren't just fighting a disease...they were fighting for the continued existence of their entire planetary ecosystem.

Aquatania's footsteps echoed through the empty corridor as she sprinted from the interrogation cell, her mind racing faster than her body. The revelations from Vex-17 had transformed everything, shifted the entire paradigm of their understanding.

Not a contagion but terraforming.

Not an attack but preparation.
Not invaders but colonists.

Each thought crashed against her consciousness like waves during a storm, demanding immediate scientific recalibration of everything they'd worked toward.

She burst through the laboratory doors, barely registering the hiss of the security seal reengaging behind her. The Integration Chamber dominated the center of the room, its crystal housing humming with energy that pulsed in rhythm with the twin moons' light streaming through the dome above. The chamber's copper-silver conduits glowed with faint blue luminescence as they channeled specialized energy fields around the precious cure components.

Marina looked up from a workstation surrounded by vials of dragon blood samples, each glowing with distinct bioluminescent properties. The mermaid scientist's gills fluttered visibly beneath her breathing apparatus, registering Aquatania's agitated state before her expression could.

"What happened?" Marina asked, setting down a pipette labeled with a precisely measured drop of kelp dragon blood.

"It's not just a plague," Aquatania explained, her words tumbling out in a breathless rush as she moved to the central holographic display. "It's terraforming, preparation for colonization." Her fingers flew across the control surface, pulling up molecular diagrams of the contagion they'd been studying for weeks. "Everything we thought we understood was incomplete."

Marina abandoned her samples, moving to Aquatania's side with a swish of her tail. "Explain."

Aquatania grabbed a stylus and began sketching directly onto a transparent board, modifying the existing molecular structures with rapid, precise strokes. "The red markings, the fever, the respiratory symptoms, they're all secondary effects. The primary function is environmental modification."

She pulled up a new diagram showing the chemical

composition of water samples from infected regions. "Look at these pH shifts, these altered saline concentrations, we thought they were byproducts of the contagion's spread." Her stylus circled specific molecular chains. "They're actually the intended effect. The infected hosts are carriers for environmental transformation agents."

Marina's scientific mind engaged immediately, her initial shock giving way to analytical focus. "Carriers? Like walking terraforming devices."

"Exactly." Aquatania moved to a storage unit, removing several sealed containers of water collected from outbreak zones. "Each infected individual releases these compounds into their environment through respiration, perspiration, and eventually decomposition after death."

She placed a sample into a sensor array. The laboratory's detection systems immediately responded, holographic displays erupting with data as the water bubbled with previously unidentified enzymatic activity. The readouts showed rapid alteration of basic chemical properties, oxygen content decreasing, unknown mineral compounds forming, and organic materials breaking down into unfamiliar configurations.

"These enzymes aren't attacking hosts," Aquatania explained, pointing to a molecular chain restructuring before their eyes. "They're preparing environments. Changing our world's fundamental chemistry to match whatever their home world requires."

Marina's webbed fingers moved across another control panel, adding historical data from previous tests. "The molecular restructuring matches patterns we've observed in deep ocean samples near the earliest outbreak sites." Her scientific detachment briefly cracked, horror seeping into her voice. "Those areas have already become uninhabitable for native species."

"And we've been treating the symptoms while ignoring

the cause," Aquatania said, frustration evident in the sudden darkening of scales along her wrists. "Our cure addresses the contagion's effect on individual hosts but does nothing to counter the environmental transformation."

She pulled up another holographic display, this one showing their current cure formula, a complex integration of dragon blood components and the moonlight algae catalyst. "We need to modify everything. The cure needs to do more than heal. It *must* create resistance to their environmental weapons."

Marina studied the formula, her mind obviously already adapting to this paradigm shift. "What if we combine specific dragon blood proteins with native coral enzymes?" Her fingers traced patterns in the air above the display. "Coral reefs naturally resist chemical changes in their immediate environment, maintaining stable microclimates despite ocean fluctuations."

"Biological shields," Aquatania whispered, the concept taking shape in her mind. "Not just treating infected individuals but creating environmental resistance."

They moved with renewed vigor, their earlier exhaustion forgotten in the surge of scientific urgency. Aquatania adjusted the Integration Chamber's settings, modifying pressure parameters to accommodate new compound combinations. Marina retrieved preserved coral samples from specialized storage units, extracting enzyme complexes.

A warning alarm sounded from the monitoring station, the display flashing red as it tracked real-time data from the kingdom's borders.

"Another outbreak zone detected," Marina noted, not looking up from her work. "Southern reef sector. Spreading pattern consistent with deliberate deployment rather than natural transmission."

"They're accelerating their timeline," Aquatania said, measuring precise quantities of dragon blood components into a new testing chamber. "They know we've discovered their true purpose."

The laboratory hummed with frantic activity as they tested combination after combination. Pressure gauges fluctuated wildly as they subjected test samples to various environmental conditions, simulating ocean depths, atmospheric interface zones, and the specialized environments of different dragon habitats. The copper-silver conduits surrounding the Integration Chamber pulsed with increasing energy as they channeled moonlight into specific wavelengths required for catalyst activation.

"This combination is promising," Marina called, analyzing results from their seventh test protocol. "The reef dragon blood proteins bind with coral polyp enzymes, creating a stable matrix that resists chemical alteration."

Aquatania joined her, studying the holographic representation of molecular interactions. "But the duration is too short. The protection will break down after approximately twelve hours."

"What if we add luminous dragon blood as a stabilizing agent?" Marina suggested, already reaching for the pearlescent vial. "Its bioluminescent properties might extend the binding duration through continuous energy provision at the cellular level."

They adjusted the formula, the Integration Chamber humming at a higher frequency as it processed the new combination. Aquatania manipulated water pressure within the testing environment, creating alternating cycles that mimicked tidal patterns while Marina monitored real-time molecular stability.

The distant wail of emergency sirens penetrated even the laboratory's soundproofed walls, a stark reminder of the accelerating crisis beyond their scientific bubble. Another monitor flashed warning indicators, water composition in Oceana Prime's outer sectors showing rapid chemical alteration, atmospheric sensors detecting unusual particle concentrations above major population centers.

"Duration improved to thirty-six hours," Marina reported, analyzing the latest test results. "Still temporary, but significantly better."

"It'll have to be enough for now," Aquatania decided, initiating the final integration process. "We can refine it once we've distributed the first batch."

The Integration Chamber completed its cycle with a soft chime. Aquatania retrieved the resulting solution, a small test tube containing liquid that shimmered with pearlescent blue luminescence, catching and refracting the moonlight in hypnotic patterns. The formula seemed almost alive, subtle currents moving within the contained liquid even when held perfectly still.

"Preliminary analysis confirms it should grant temporary resistance to the environmental alterations," Marina said, reading data from the final scans. "Thirty-six hours of protection during which standard body processes should naturally flush the terraforming enzymes from the system."

Aquatania held the glowing vial up to the moonlight.. "We'll need to modify our distribution strategy completely. This isn't just about treating infected individuals anymore...it's about protecting entire ecosystems."

The emergency sirens grew louder, joined by the distinctive tone that signaled aerial defense systems activating across Zephyria. Time was running out as the aliens moved to counter their discovery.

"Begin production scaling," Aquatania instructed, securing the precious formula in a specialized containment field. "I need to brief Kieran on the new strategic requirements. This changes everything about our defensive approach."

Chapter Thirteen

Aquatania stood before the Integration Chamber, her gaze fixed on the swirling luminescence within the crystal housing. The copper-silver conduits pulsed with moonlight, channeling energy into the precious formula that represented their world's last hope. Every molecule, every carefully calibrated pressure cycle, every precisely timed light exposure...all culminating in this moment as the dragon blood components merged with the moonlight algae catalyst in a dance of science and ancient magic. She barely blinked, afraid to miss the telltale shift in color that would signal success.

Around her, the Integration Tower laboratory hummed with purposeful energy. Technicians moved with the precision of dancers in a well-rehearsed performance, checking pressure gauges, adjusting moonlight filters, and monitoring the formula's molecular stability on crystal displays. The air vibrated with the low thrum of power cycling through ancient conduits embedded in the tower's walls, technology that predated modern understanding but functioned with unerring reliability under her guidance.

Kieran stood at her right shoulder, his presence solid and reassuring despite the bandages visible beneath his partially open uniform. The wound from the Coral Citadel still troubled him. She'd noticed his slight wince when he moved too quickly, but he remained vigilant, his eyes constantly scanning the laboratory for potential threats. Zephyr's betrayal had left them all wary of shadows, seeing potential infiltrators in every corner.

"The luminescence is intensifying," Aquatania noted, leaning closer to the chamber. Indeed, the pearlescent blue glow had deepened, spreading through the formula like dawn light through morning mist. "The catalyst is fully integrating with the dragon blood components."

Marina approached from a monitoring station, her gills fluttering with excitement beneath her breathing collar. "Molecular stability at ninety-three percent and rising. The binding matrices are forming exactly as predicted."

Aquatania allowed herself a small moment of hope, cautious, fragile, but undeniably present. After weeks of desperate research, betrayals, and near-defeats, they stood on the precipice of success. The formula within the chamber wasn't just a cure for the alien contagion. It was a shield against their terraforming enzymes, a temporary defense that might give their world time to mount a more permanent resistance.

"Begin final pressure cycling," she instructed while her fingers adjusted controls. Water responded to her subtle manipulations, molecules aligning into perfect formation as pressure fields shifted within the chamber. "Thirty seconds at deep-ocean pressure, then fifteen at standard atmospheric."

The formula responded immediately, its glow intensifying with each pressure shift.

"Final integration cycle initiating," a senior technician announced, his fingers dancing across control crystals that pulsed in harmony with the chamber's glow. "Moonlight exposure at maximum intensity."

The twin moons had reached their apex above the tower's crystal dome, their combined light focusing through angled reflectors to bathe the Integration Chamber in silver-blue radiance. The formula within responded with a sudden flare of brilliance, causing several technicians to shield their eyes. Aquatania didn't look away, her sea dragon heritage allowing her to withstand the intensity as she searched for the critical color shift that would signal success.

There, at the heart of the swirling liquid, a pulse of pure

light, neither blue nor white but something transcendent, as if the formula had momentarily connected with some fundamental energy source beyond normal perception. The pulse expanded outward, suffusing the entire formula with a stable, even glow that shimmered with quiet power.

"Integration complete," Aquatania announced, unable to keep a note of triumph from her voice. "Begin extraction and vial preparation."

A cheer rippled through the laboratory, subdued, professional, but heartfelt after so many setbacks and false starts. Technicians moved to extraction stations as the Integration Chamber's housing began to open, releasing the precious formula into specialized collection apparatus. The air filled with the subtle scent of ocean depths and moonlight...an impossible combination that somehow perfectly described the formula's essence.

Kieran placed his hand briefly on Aquatania's shoulder, the warmth of his touch conveying what words could not in this moment of shared victory. "We did it," he said simply, his eyes meeting hers with quiet pride.

"The first batch, at least," she replied, though she allowed herself to return his smile. "Now we need to—"

The deafening wail of emergency sirens cut through her words, the laboratory's blue-white illumination suddenly replaced by pulsing red warning lights. The Integration Tower shuddered beneath their feet, a distant boom reverberating through its ancient structure with enough force to rattle equipment and send several unsecured items crashing to the floor.

"Security breach in outer perimeter," an automated voice announced through the laboratory's communication system. "Multiple hostiles detected. Defensive protocols activated."

Kieran's demeanor transformed instantly from quiet pride to battle-ready vigilance. "Secure the formula," he ordered, his voice carrying the unmistakable authority of military command. "Lockdown procedures! Now!"

Another explosion rocked the tower, this one closer than the first. Crystal displays flickered momentarily before emergency power systems engaged. Through the laboratory's dome, Aquatania glimpsed dark shapes moving against the night sky, vessels unlike any in their world's fleets, their surfaces gleaming with an oily iridescence that marked them as alien craft.

"They know," she said, the realization hitting her with cold certainty. "They know we've succeeded."

"And they're here to stop distribution before it starts," Kieran agreed, moving to a wall panel where emergency weapons were stored. He retrieved a long blade that glowed faintly with enchanted fire, the weapon seeming to come alive in his hands. "Technical team, secure those vials in pressure-resistant containers. Security detail, defensive formation at all entry points."

The laboratory erupted into controlled chaos. Technicians who'd been celebrating moments earlier now moved with frantic urgency, transferring the precious formula into specialized transport containers designed to withstand extreme conditions. Security personnel, too few, Aquatania realized with growing dread, took up positions near doorways and ventilation shafts, weapons ready.

Armored shutters slammed down over the dome and windows with reverberating finality, sealing the laboratory from external attack but also trapping them inside with whatever forces might breach their defenses. Emergency lights cast harsh shadows across faces now taut with fear.

Another impact shook the tower, close enough that fine dust drifted down from ancient ceiling joints. Cracks appeared in the laboratory's eastern wall, spreading like frost across glass.

"That section leads to the tertiary access corridor," Kieran noted, positioning himself between the weakening wall and the technicians still securing formula vials. "They're being strategic, avoiding the main defenses."

"How long until all vials are secure?" Aquatania asked the lead technician, her hands already moving to activate the distribution system that would transfer the cure to waiting transport vessels.

"Three minutes minimum," the woman replied, her fingers working with remarkable steadiness despite the chaos erupting around them.

"We may not have three minutes," Kieran said grimly as another impact sent larger chunks of material falling from the cracking wall. He raised his voice to address all personnel. "Everyone not essential to formula security, prepare for combat. We hold this position at all costs."

The wall exploded inward in a shower of stone and crystal shards, revealing dark shapes moving in the dust and smoke beyond.

The aliens poured through the breach like fluid, their movements unnaturally smooth as they emerged from the dust and debris. In the harsh red emergency lighting, their translucent exoskeletons gleamed with a sickly iridescence, compound eyes reflecting the chaos in fractured patterns. They carried weapons that seemed fused to their limbs, not held but integrated into their biology, pulsing with the same greenish energy Aquatania had witnessed during their broadcast.

The first guard to engage them disintegrated in a flash of that same energy, not even time for a scream as his molecular structure came apart.

"Defensive formation alpha!" Kieran shouted, his voice cutting through the initial shock that had frozen the remaining security personnel. "Three-point coverage, overlapping fields of fire!"

The guards snapped into action, arranging themselves in triangular formations that maximized their coverage while minimizing exposure. Kieran moved among them with the practiced efficiency of a veteran commander, positioning each fighter where their strengths would be most effective. His wounded side seemed forgotten in the heat of battle, adrenaline overriding pain as he unsheathed his glowing blade.

"Get the cure distribution online," he ordered Aquatania without looking back, his focus entirely on the advancing alien forms. "Nothing else matters now."

Aquatania forced herself to turn away from the unfolding horror, directing her attention to the distribution control station where the cure's deployment mechanisms awaited activation. Her fingers flew across crystal interfaces, initializing transport tubes and pressure systems designed to move the formula from the laboratory to waiting vessels throughout Zephyria's aerial docks. Each command sequence required precise calibration. Too much pressure would destabilize the formula's delicate molecular structure. Too little would cause transport delays that they couldn't afford.

Behind her, the battle erupted in earnest. Energy weapons discharged with high-pitched whines that hurt her ears, the air filling with the acrid smell of ozone and burning materials. Guards shouted commands and warnings to each other as they engaged the infiltrators, their conventional weapons seeming pitifully inadequate against the alien technology.

"System pressure normalized," she muttered to herself, adjusting final parameters as a technician handed her the first sealed container of the completed cure. "Distribution channels open and ready for loading."

The ground shuddered beneath her feet as something massive impacted nearby, another section of wall collapsing under alien assault. She glanced over her shoulder to see three more infiltrators entering through a new breach, their segmented limbs moving with that same unsettling fluidity that denied normal joint limitations. One guard fell, clutching a wound that smoked with unnatural green fire where alien energy had struck him.

Kieran met the new threat directly, moving with a speed that belied his injury. His sword flashed in tight, controlled arcs, the enchanted blade leaving trails of fire in the air as he engaged the nearest infiltrator. The alien's exoskeleton hissed and bubbled where the blade made contact, dark fluid spraying across the laboratory floor.

"Second wave incoming!" a guard near the primary breach shouted, his voice tight with controlled fear. "At least a dozen more!"

Aquatania turned back to her work, loading the first container into the distribution system with trembling hands that she forced to steady through sheer will. The cure glowed through the container's transparent sections, its pearlescent blue luminescence a stark contrast to the harsh red emergency lighting and the sickly green of alien weapons fire.

"Carrier one loading complete," the system in its calm, automated voice announced. "Commencing pressure equalization for transport."

A strangled cry drew her attention once more. A technician who'd been securing additional vials collapsed, his body convulsing as alien energy coursed through him. The infiltrator responsible advanced toward the remaining cure containers, its compound gaze fixing on the precious formula with predatory focus.

Kieran appeared suddenly between the alien and its target, his body shifting visibly as he called upon his fire dragon heritage. Scales erupted across his exposed arms and neck, glittering like burning copper in the emergency lighting. His eyes transformed, the pupils elongating into vertical slits surrounded by irises that glowed with internal fire.

"Get back!" he growled to the remaining technicians, his voice deeper and rougher in this partial transformation.

The alien fired its integrated weapon, the energy blast

striking Kieran directly in the chest. He staggered but didn't fall, the scales partially absorbing the impact that would have dissolved a fully human target. With a guttural roar, he exhaled a controlled stream of fire directly at the infiltrator, the flames hot enough to melt laboratory equipment several feet away.

The alien's exoskeleton blackened and cracked under the intense heat, its eyes bursting with sickening pops. It collapsed, limbs twitching in death spasms that sent its weapon discharging randomly across the ceiling.

Smoke filled the laboratory now, a mixture of chemical fires, alien fluids, and the acrid residue of energy weapons. Through the haze, Aquatania could see the remaining guards falling back toward the central area where she worked, their numbers diminished by half in the few minutes since the attack began. Kieran moved among them, his partially transformed state allowing him to engage multiple infiltrators simultaneously, breathing precisely controlled bursts of flame that created momentary barriers between the aliens and the cure.

"Carrier two loading complete," the distribution system announced. "Commencing pressure equalization for transport."

Two more containers to go.

Aquatania worked frantically, her sea dragon senses allowing her to maintain focus despite the chaos erupting around her. Water responded unconsciously to her heightened emotions, moisture in the air gathering into protective layers around the remaining cure vials.

A deafening explosion rocked the laboratory as the main entrance doors blew inward, the reinforced barriers that should have withstood any conventional attack yielding to alien technology. More infiltrators poured through the new breach, not the disguised forms they'd encountered before, but fully revealed in their alien biology. Multiple jointed limbs moved in complex patterns, some ending in delicate manipulators, others in integrated weapons that pulsed with deadly energy.

"They're flanking us!" a guard shouted, his voice nearly lost in the cacophony of battle. "We can't hold both breaches!"

Kieran assessed the situation in an instant, his partially transformed features hardening with grim determination. "Pull back to the inner ring! Protect the distribution system at all costs!"

The remaining guards retreated in good order, forming a final defensive perimeter around Aquatania and the cure. They fought with the desperation of those who knew retreat was impossible, each buying precious seconds with their lives. Three fell in quick succession as concentrated alien energy fire overwhelmed their positions.

"Carrier three loading complete," the system announced, seemingly oblivious to the life-and-death struggle surrounding it. "Commencing pressure equalization for transport."

One container left.

Aquatania's fingers flew across the controls, initiating the final loading sequence as the battle closed in around her. A stray energy blast struck the console beside her, components exploding in a shower of crystal shards that sliced her cheek. She barely felt the pain, her focus absolute as she secured the last container into its transport cradle.

"Aquatania!" Kieran shouted over the din, his voice strained as he engaged three infiltrators simultaneously. His scales glowed with intense heat as he channeled more of his draconic power, but even in his partially transformed state, the sheer numbers were overwhelming him. "Get the cure out! I'll hold them!"

"Final carrier loading sequence initiated," she called back, her fingers completing the activation protocol. "Thirty seconds to distribution launch!"

Kieran nodded once, understanding in his eyes as he redoubled his efforts, purposefully drawing the aliens' attention toward himself and away from her. He charged directly into the densest concentration of infiltrators, his blade whirling in complex patterns that created a momentary clearing around him.

"For our world!" he roared, fire erupting not just from his mouth but from his entire body as he pushed his transformation to its limits in this enclosed space.

The aliens converged on him like a tide of segmented limbs and glinting eyes, their weapons discharging in a focused barrage that even his enhanced form couldn't entirely withstand. He stumbled, one knee hitting the ground as energy blasts tore through the scales on his left side.

"Ten seconds to distribution launch," the system announced with maddening calm.

Aquatania watched in horror as Kieran was gradually submerged beneath the wave of alien attackers, his fire still burning but dimmer now as they systematically overwhelmed him. His eyes found hers across the chaos of the laboratory. He mouthed something she couldn't hear over the din—two words that might have been "Do it."

"Distribution launch sequence complete," the system announced. "Transport initiated."

The final container descended into the distribution tube with a soft pneumatic hiss, joining its companions on the journey to waiting vessels that would carry the cure to the furthest corners of their world. Aquatania stood frozen before the controls, watching as the aliens finally subdued Kieran, his transformed body disappearing beneath a mass of segmented limbs.

Aquatania's world narrowed to a single focal point…Kieran's body disappearing beneath the mass of alien limbs. Time seemed to slow, each heartbeat stretching into eternity as she watched him struggle one final time before

240

going still. Not dead…she could still see the rise and fall of his chest…but subdued, overwhelmed by sheer numbers. The aliens worked with clinical efficiency, producing energy cuffs that pulsed with the same sickly green light as their weapons. They bound his wrists and ankles, the specialized restraints immediately causing his partial transformation to recede, scales fading back into human skin as his fire dragon abilities were forcibly suppressed.

The distribution system hummed before her. Once activated, the distribution system would require her full attention for critical minutes of calibration as the cure entered transport vessels. By the time she could pursue, the alien ship would be gone. Kieran with it.

Her fingers hovered inches from the control, trembling with the weight of what should have been a simple action.

But it wasn't simple.

Not anymore.

The aliens hauled Kieran to his feet, his head lolling momentarily before he regained consciousness. Blood trickled from a fresh wound at his temple, matting his hair and tracing a crimson line down his face. Despite his injuries, despite the restraints that clearly caused him pain, he straightened as much as the alien grip allowed, refusing to appear defeated even in capture.

His eyes sought hers across the smoke-filled laboratory, finding her with unerring precision despite the chaos that separated them. In that shared gaze passed a universe of unspoken communication. A final infiltrator joined the group, restraining him, gesturing toward what appeared to be a transport vessel visible through the breached wall. They were taking him.

Aquatania felt her body responding to the realization with visceral intensity. Her heartbeat thundered in her ears, drowning out the continued sounds of battle as the few remaining guards fought their final, hopeless engagements.

Her lungs seemed to forget their purpose, breath coming in short, painful gasps that did nothing to clear the growing fog in her mind. A single tear escaped, tracking down her cheek where it mingled with the blood from her earlier injury, the salt stinging the open wound in a perfect metaphor for the choice before her.

Pull the lever, save the world, lose Kieran.

Or...abandon the lever, attempt a rescue, and risk everything they'd fought for.

The aliens began moving toward the breach, dragging Kieran with them. His eyes never left hers, intensity burning in their depths despite the pain evident in every line of his body. He mouthed something...silent words she had to strain to understand in the chaos.

"Do it."

Two simple words that contained the essence of who he was, the soldier willing to sacrifice himself, the man who understood what truly mattered beyond personal survival. In those two words lay his absolute trust in her to make the right choice, no matter the personal cost to either of them.

They feared the cure. They feared what it represented...not just biochemical resistance, but the possibility that their carefully calculated invasion might actually fail.

Kieran understood this. She understood this. Their personal connection, however profound, could not outweigh the survival of an entire world.

Her hand stopped trembling.

She grasped the lever firmly, meeting Kieran's gaze one final time across the diminishing space between them. "I will find you," she promised, words he couldn't possibly hear but might read on her lips. Then she pulled the lever down with a decisive motion that seemed to require all her remaining strength.

The distribution system engaged with a deep, resonant hum that vibrated through the laboratory floor. Status indicators flashed from amber to green as the cure began flowing through hidden conduits beneath the tower, racing toward transport vessels already prepared for immediate launch. Pressure gauges fluctuated, then stabilized as the system automatically adjusted to maintain optimal conditions for the formula's molecular integrity.

"Distribution activated," the system announced. "Transport vessels loading. Calibration required for optimal dispersal patterns."

Aquatania forced herself to turn toward the calibration controls, though every fiber of her being screamed to run after Kieran. Her hands moved across crystal interfaces, adjusting pressure parameters and flow rates with the precision of the scientist she'd trained her entire life to become. Each adjustment felt like a betrayal, each moment focused on the cure rather than pursuing another link in a chain of guilt that wrapped around her heart.

From the corner of her eye, she saw Kieran disappear entirely through the breach, the last glimpse of him a final, determined look that somehow conveyed both love and absolute certainty that she'd made the right choice. Then he was gone, pulled into the alien vessel whose hull sealed with a sound like wet flesh closing over a wound.

"Primary distribution complete," the system announced. "Transport vessels departing for designated coordinates."

Through the laboratory's shattered dome, Aquatania watched as smaller vessels launched from Zephyria's aerial docks, each carrying precious vials of the cure to different regions of their world. They streaked across the night sky like comets, trailing faint blue luminescence from their enchanted engines. Behind them, moving in the opposite direction, the angular form of the alien craft accelerated away from the Integration Tower, carrying Kieran toward an unknown fate.

Around her, the laboratory lay in ruins. Equipment shattered beyond repair, the Integration Chamber's crystal housing cracked and dark, the bodies of brave guards and technicians who'd given everything to protect their world's last hope. The alien attackers had withdrawn with their prize, leaving destruction and loss in their wake.

Aquatania stood amid the devastation, her body exhausted, but her mind suddenly, painfully clear. She bent to retrieve an object from beside a fallen guard…Kieran's weapon, dropped during his final desperate stand. The blade still glowed faintly with enchanted fire, responding to her touch as if recognizing a kindred spirit to its master.

She clutched it against her chest, the warmth of the blade a poor substitute for the man who'd wielded it. The cure was away, and their world granted a temporary reprieve from environmental transformation.

The princess had fulfilled her duty to her kingdom.

The scientist had successfully deployed her creation.

Now, another aspect of herself emerged from the ashes of the laboratory…the warrior who would not abandon one of her own to alien hands.

The dragon whose nature demanded justice and retribution.

The woman who'd found something worth fighting for beyond abstract duty.

"I will find you," she repeated, this time a vow spoken to the empty air where Kieran had stood. The blade pulsed brighter in her hands, as if acknowledging her oath.

Aquatania turned toward the breach, scales shimmering beneath her skin as her sea dragon heritage responded.

She would save their world from terraforming.

And then she would find the man she loved.

Chapter Fourteen

Dawn broke over Zephyria's main dock in streams of pale gold, illuminating vessels and couriers prepared for the day's critical mission. Aquatania stood at the edge of the platform, her shadow stretching long behind her as she surveyed the organized chaos of final preparations. Three days had passed since Kieran's capture, three days of relentless work distributing the cure to the nearest islands while preparing for the more distant journeys that would begin today. She hadn't allowed herself the luxury of proper rest, knowing that each hour spent in recovery was another hour the aliens could use to counter their efforts. The weight of the kingdom, of the entire world, pressed against her shoulders, but it was the absence at her side that threatened to break her composure.

"Your Highness, the final shipments are being loaded now," a dock supervisor reported, her uniform crisp despite the early hour. "Transport vessels report all systems functioning at optimal capacity."

Aquatania nodded, forcing her attention back to the immediate task. "And the submersible carriers? Have the pressure seals been reinforced as I requested?"

"Yes, Princess. Double-reinforced and tested to withstand depths exceeding Oceana Prime's lowest levels."

"Good. Proceed."

The supervisor bowed and returned to her duties, leaving Aquatania alone with her thoughts once more. Below the dock's edge, dragons in their full forms circled in a holding pattern, their scales catching the morning light in flashes of crimson, emerald, and sapphire. Each had been selected for this mission based on specific abilities, fire dragons for their endurance, forest dragons for their healing capabilities, and sky dragons for their speed. They wore specialized harnesses designed by Marina's engineering team, each fitted with compartments to safely transport the cure's delicate vials through varying atmospheric conditions.

Aquatania moved along the loading area, watching as human and shifter medical teams worked with practiced efficiency. They handled each case of the cure with reverent care, securing the containers in shock-absorbent housing before attaching them to dragon harnesses. The pearlescent blue liquid glowed faintly even through the protective casing, pulsing with the rhythmic energy that marked its successful integration.

"Three cases to Aethoria's central hospital," the head of the medical division instructed, checking items off a crystal tablet. "Seven to the Ventus distribution hub. Four submersible units for Oceana Prime's outer reefs."

Each dragon nodded in acknowledgment, understanding the gravity of their cargo. They'd all seen the devastation wrought by the alien contagion, friends and family marked with the telltale red patterns, entire communities reduced to quarantine zones. The cure represented their only hope against not just the disease but the environmental transformation it heralded.

Aquatania approached the final loading station where a special case waited, larger than the others, reinforced with additional protective layers. This contained the concentrated form of the cure, designed to be introduced directly into Oceana Prime's water filtration system. She reached for it personally, dismissing the attendant with a small gesture.

As her fingers closed around the handles, a tremor passed through her hands, subtle but unmistakable. The case wavered in her grip for a heartbeat before she steadied it. She stared at her own traitorous hands in momentary shock, unused to such physical betrayal of her emotions.

An image of Kieran flashed unbidden in her mind...his

246

final look of absolute trust as the aliens dragged him away. The weight of her choice pressed against her chest anew, stealing her breath and making the case suddenly seem impossibly heavy.

"Princess, are you well?"

The voice startled her from her memories. A young dragon shifter stood nearby, concern evident in his features. His scales hadn't fully receded from his recent transformation, iridescent blue patches still visible along his jawline and forearms. She recognized him as one of the newer recruits to the courier division, barely past his eighteenth year.

Aquatania straightened her shoulders immediately, forcing the tremor from her hands through sheer will. "We have no time for weakness," she replied, her voice firm but hollow even to her own ears. She secured the case to its designated transport vessel with precise movements that betrayed none of her inner turmoil.

The young shifter ducked his head respectfully but lingered. "I...I trained under General Kieran," he said hesitantly. "He spoke highly of your strength. Said you were the only one who could lead us through this."

The unexpected mention of Kieran's name sent a fresh wave of pain through her, but she nodded acknowledgment, unable to trust her voice for a moment. When she spoke again, her tone carried the authority expected of the royal heiress.

"Take your position. We depart in three minutes."

As the shifter moved away, Aquatania stepped to the edge of the dock where she would have space for her transformation. She closed her eyes, drawing deep breaths as she called forth her sea dragon nature. The change began as it always did, a tingling sensation that started at her core and radiated outward, her body remembering its alternate form with fluid grace.

Her skin shimmered, human flesh giving way to iridescent blue-green scales that caught the morning light in mesmerizing patterns. Bones elongated and restructured, her slender human frame expanding into the powerful musculature of a sea dragon. Wings erupted from her shoulders, membrane-thin yet strong enough to carry her through hurricane winds. Her face extended into an elegant muzzle, teeth lengthening into precise points designed for both combat and delicate manipulation. Within moments, where the princess had stood, now towered a magnificent sea dragon, regal in bearing despite the sorrow she carried.

She moved to the lead position with powerful strides, the dock trembling slightly beneath her transformed weight. The transport receptacle containing the special case was secured to her harness, its precious cargo now her direct responsibility. Around her, other dragons took flight in a synchronized ascent that spoke of military precision, Kieran's training evident in their perfect formation.

"All couriers report ready, Your Highness," the flight coordinator announced through a communication crystal embedded in Aquatania's harness. "Submersible vessels standing by for water dragon escort."

Aquatania unfurled her wings fully, the translucent membranes catching updrafts from the morning air. With a powerful downstroke that sent dock workers scrambling back, she launched into the sky, leading the formation with instinctive authority. The fleet followed in a V-pattern behind her, dragons carrying standard cure cases to the left, those with submersible receptacles for the underwater portions of their journey to the right.

They soared higher, breaking through the first layer of clouds into the clearer air above. From this altitude, Zephyria's floating spires looked almost peaceful, the morning light softening the evidence of alien attacks and hasty defenses. The wind streamed past her scales, carrying the familiar scents of home that would soon give way to the distinctive atmospheres of other islands.

As they leveled into cruising formation, Aquatania became acutely aware of the empty space beside her where Kieran would normally fly. In previous missions, his crimson-gold form had been a constant presence at her right wing, his fire dragon abilities complementing her water-based powers in perfect balance. Now that space remained conspicuously vacant, a physical manifestation of the loss that echoed through her heart.

She forced her gaze forward, focusing on the horizon where their first destination would soon appear. The cure would reach those who needed it. The world would resist the aliens' terraforming attempts. And when these immediate threats were addressed, she would fulfill her vow to find Kieran, wherever in the vast cosmos they'd taken him.

*

Aethoria appeared through a break in the clouds, the floating island no longer the vibrant metropolis Aquatania remembered from diplomatic visits past. Where ornate spires had once reached toward the sun, makeshift medical tents now sprawled across plazas. The famous floating gardens — once lush with rare flora that thrived in high-altitude air — had been converted to quarantine zones, their delicate ecosystem trampled by necessity. As they descended toward the central plaza, Aquatania's enhanced dragon vision caught the telltale patterns of red markings spreading across the exposed skin of citizens who stood in lines outside distribution centers, their faces turned upward at the approaching dragons with expressions that mingled desperation with fragile hope.

She led the formation in a wide arc over the city, allowing citizens to see their arrival, a deliberate choice to provide visible evidence that help had come. The fleet descended in concentric circles, landing in precise intervals across the designated area of the central plaza. Aquatania touched down with practiced grace despite her size, her claws finding purchase on stones worn smooth by generations of sky traffic.

Medical workers rushed forward before she'd fully folded her wings, their uniforms stained with evidence of endless shifts. Exhaustion lined their faces, dark circles beneath bloodshot eyes speaking of days with minimal rest. Some wore partial protective gear, masks, and gloves that had clearly been reused beyond recommended limits, while others had abandoned such precautions entirely, perhaps having decided that speed of treatment outweighed personal safety.

Aquatania transformed back to her human form, the change rippling through her body in waves of blue-green light. As her scaled form receded, she adjusted the simple flight bodysuit she wore beneath her harness, then immediately began unfastening the transport receptacle secured to what had moments ago been her dragon spine.

"Princess Aquatania." A woman approached, her medical director's insignia partially obscured by stains on her lab coat. Dark hair had been hastily secured in a knot at her nape, strands escaping to frame a face drawn tight with strain. "I'm Doctor Lyra. We...we weren't certain you would come."

The physician extended her hand in a formal greeting, inadvertently revealing a wrist where the cuff of her protective gear had pulled back. The beginning of the telltale red rash formed patterns along her veins despite her protective equipment, evidence that she continued working even after exposure.

Aquatania clasped the woman's hand firmly. "We came as quickly as possible. How many are affected?"

"We've lost thirty more since dawn," Lyra replied, her professional composure cracking momentarily, her voice catching on the words. She gestured toward the sprawling medical complex that had consumed what was once a civic celebration ground. "Nearly two thousand under treatment, with hundreds more arriving hourly. Our containment protocols failed three days ago. We simply ran out of space to isolate new cases."

Aquatania nodded grimly, turning to direct the unloading process. Dragon couriers transformed back to their humanoid forms, working alongside medical staff to transfer sealed cases to waiting hover-carts. She personally unsealed the first container, revealing rows of vials glowing with pearlescent blue luminescence.

"The cure requires specific administration techniques," she explained, gathering the medical team leaders around a makeshift demonstration table. Her fingers moved with practiced efficiency as she prepared a dosage, drawing the glowing liquid into a specialized injector. "Direct introduction to the bloodstream is most effective for advanced cases. For early-stage exposure, inhalation methods show promising results with larger population coverage."

She demonstrated the proper injection technique on a medical simulation crystal, the holographic patient displaying the optimal administration points where major blood vessels would carry the cure throughout the body most efficiently. Medical staff leaned forward, their attention absolute despite their exhaustion.

"For mass distribution to those with early-stage symptoms or preventative treatment for the exposed but asymptomatic, I recommend atmospheric dispersal." Aquatania moved toward an open area of the plaza, gesturing for the others to follow. "My abilities allow for a specialized delivery method that your teams can later replicate with mechanical dispersal units."

She closed her eyes briefly, extending her awareness to the water molecules present in the air around them. Her hands rose in a fluid motion, her fingers tracing complex patterns that seemed to draw moisture from the very atmosphere.

251

Water responded to her call, gathering into a swirling mist that hovered before her, growing denser with each subtle movement of her fingers.

"Add the diluted formula," she instructed. A medical technician carefully poured a prepared solution into the suspended water cloud, the cure's distinctive blue glow spreading throughout the mist like gentle lightning.

Aquatania began the final manipulation sequence, her hands guiding the medicated mist into an expanding spiral pattern designed to maximize coverage while maintaining proper concentration. The mist responded perfectly until a child's cry pierced the focused silence, a sound of such pure distress that it cut through her concentration like a blade.

The children suffer most, Kieran had said during their first observation of the contagion's effects. *They lack the physical reserves to fight it. We must prioritize their protection above all else.*

The memory struck without warning, Kieran's voice so clear in her mind that for a disorienting moment, she expected to find him standing beside her. The mist wavered, losing cohesion at its edges as her focus faltered. Aquatania drew a sharp breath, forcing her attention back to the task with visible effort. The mist stabilized, then expanded outward as she directed it toward the queue of waiting citizens, the fine droplets settling on skin and clothing, immediately beginning their protective work.

"The formula remains effective in mist form for approximately four hours," she explained, her voice steady once more. "After that, the molecular structure begins to degrade. Schedule your dispersals accordingly."

Lyra led them into the main treatment facility, once the grand hall where Aethoria's council had met for centuries, now converted into a ward packed so densely with patients that medical staff could barely navigate between beds. Many patients lay on simple pallets directly on the floor, the facility having exhausted its proper bedding days ago. The air hung heavy with the smells of sickness and antiseptic, punctuated by moans and labored breathing.

Aquatania moved among them, assessing conditions with the practiced eye of someone who'd witnessed the contagion's progression firsthand. Some patients displayed the advanced stages, angry red patterns covering most visible skin, spreading toward the heart in branching pathways that mimicked blood vessels. Others showed early symptoms, low fever, scattered red markings appearing at extremities, the characteristic shortness of breath that preceded systemic involvement.

A woman reached out as Aquatania passed, her fingers catching the hem of her lab coat with surprising strength given her condition. Red patterns already traced their way up her neck, disappearing into her hairline.

"My daughter, please…" she whispered, gesturing weakly toward a small form curled on a pallet beside her. The child couldn't have been more than six years old, her small body wracked with fever tremors, her dark hair plastered to her forehead with sweat. The red markings had just begun their journey across her chest, still contained to her upper torso, early enough for the cure to work effectively.

Without hesitation, Aquatania knelt beside the child, pulling a vial of the cure from the case she carried. "What's her name?" she asked softly, preparing the injection.

"Janna," the mother whispered, tears tracking down her marked cheeks.

Aquatania nodded, carefully turning the child's arm to find a suitable vein. "Janna," she said, her voice gentle, "this will help you feel better. A small pinch, then it's over."

The girl whimpered but remained still as Aquatania administered the cure with practiced precision. The blue liquid disappeared into her small vein, a faint glow briefly visible beneath her skin as it entered her bloodstream.

Aquatania remained kneeling beside them, monitoring the

initial response. Within minutes, the child's breathing eased, the labored gasps smoothing into more regular patterns. The angry red at the edges of her markings began to fade ever so slightly from crimson to pink, the first visible sign of the cure taking effect.

"Rest now," Aquatania told both mother and child, placing a cool hand briefly on the girl's forehead. "The medicine will continue working. You're going to be all right."

She rose, already looking for the next critical patient, aware that each vial required careful allocation when so many needed treatment. Behind her, the mother whispered words of gratitude that Aquatania barely registered, her mind already calculating distribution patterns, prioritizing cases, mapping the path through suffering that might lead as many as possible back to health.

*

Departure from Aethoria came with the weight of too many left untreated, too many whose desperate eyes followed their ascent into cloud cover. Aquatania led her depleted fleet eastward, having left nearly half their number behind to continue distribution efforts on the stricken island. The morning had aged into early afternoon, sunlight gleaming against dragon scales as they soared toward Ventus, the next sky island on their critical path.

Unlike Aethoria's broad, stable landmass, Ventus consisted of dozens of smaller floating fragments connected by enchanted bridges. It was a design that had made it a center for aeronautical research and wind-based magic. Aquatania remembered it as a graceful collection of spires and research platforms. As they approached the cloud bank that perpetually surrounded the island's perimeter, a sense of wrongness prickled along her spine, her scales rippling beneath her human skin in unconscious warning.

She slowed their advance with a raised claw, her eyes narrowing as she studied the clouds ahead. The formation was too uniform, too still, lacking the natural currents that should have stirred the vapor into ever-changing patterns. Something disrupted the normal air flow, creating an artificial stability that nothing in nature could maintain.

Her suspicion transformed to certainty as the first alien vessel emerged from the cloud cover, its hull gleaming with that unmistakable oily iridescence that marked it as non-terrestrial. The craft's angular form cut through the air with unnatural silence, followed by a second, then a third, until seven vessels formed a blocking line between her fleet and Ventus.

Defensive formation! Aquatania commanded, her voice carrying across the wind to the dragons behind her. Her wings snapped wide, catching an updraft that lifted her above the first energy blast from the lead alien craft.

The dragons scattered in practiced maneuvers, breaking their travel formation into smaller tactical groups as they'd drilled countless times under Kieran's instruction. Fire dragons banked sharply right, forming a protective screen around the carriers with the most critical cargo. Water dragons dove beneath the engagement zone, using cloud cover to conceal their approach vectors. Air dragons shot upward, gaining an altitude advantage that would allow them to dive-bomb the alien vessels if the opportunity presented.

Green energy weapons discharged from the alien crafts, sizzling through the air in deadly arcs. One blast passed close enough to Aquatania that she felt the heat against her scales, the air itself seeming to warp around the weapon's path. The dragons had faced these weapons before, had lost comrades to their molecular-disrupting properties, and knew that even a glancing blow could be catastrophic.

Aquatania circled higher, drawing moisture from the

surrounding clouds with her innate abilities. Water responded to her call, molecules gathering into a massive, undulating shield that she positioned between the main alien vessels and her most vulnerable carriers. The first energy blast struck her water shield with a hissing roar, the liquid momentarily glowing green before dispersing the energy in a shower of superheated steam.

Maintain spacing! she called to a young forest dragon who'd drifted too close to another carrier. *Remember your evasion patterns!*

She reinforced the water shield, drawing more moisture from the clouds as another volley of alien fire converged on their position. The constant manipulation taxed her strength, each molecular adjustment requiring precise concentration amid the chaos of aerial combat. Around her, dragons executed defensive maneuvers, spiraling dives, tight barrel rolls, and sudden altitude drops that made them difficult targets.

A bolt of green energy slipped past her shield, striking near her left wing joint. Pain lanced through Aquatania's body, the scales blackening where the energy had grazed her. She faltered mid-air, one wing momentarily failing to support her weight. The sensation of falling gripped her for three terrifying heartbeats before she regained control, forcing the injured wing to extend despite the burning pain.

In that moment of vulnerability, her mind flashed to Kieran, how he would've been there, covering her flank, his fire breath creating a counter-barrier against this exact attack vector. During previous engagements, they'd worked as a seamless unit, her water abilities complementing his fire in perfect balance. Now she compensated alone, adjusting her shield's position to cover the area he would have protected.

Second formation, break right! she ordered, pushing the thought away as she banked toward a trio of alien vessels attempting to outflank them.

Two courier dragons near the edge of the formation weren't fast enough to evade a concentrated barrage. Energy blasts struck one directly in the shoulder, sending him spinning downward with a roar of pain. The second took a glancing blow to her tail, the impact causing her to lose grip on the precious cargo harnessed to her back. Both specialized cases containing cure vials tumbled through open air, their contents moments from being lost.

Aquatania dove without hesitation, tucking her wings close to her body to increase speed. Wind screamed past her scales as she plummeted after the falling cases, extending her awareness to the water molecules in the air around them. With a flick of her thought, she formed a water tendril that snaked around the first case, then the second, securing them in a liquid grip that halted their descent.

She pulled up sharply, wings straining as she reversed her downward momentum, the water tendrils trailing behind her with their precious cargo. Pain flared anew in her injured wing, but she maintained altitude, bringing the recovered cases back to safer positions within the formation. A young air dragon swept in to take one case, while Aquatania secured the other to her own harness.

The aliens pursued relentlessly, their vessels maneuvering with mechanical precision that no living pilot could match. They seemed to anticipate standard evasion patterns, positioning their crafts to intercept dragons before they completed their defensive moves.

They're predicting our tactics. Aquatania had the realization as she watched another energy blast narrowly miss a carrier who'd followed standard protocol.

New pattern! Chaotic response, individual discretion!

Her dragons adapted immediately, abandoning the formations they'd drilled in favor of unpredictable, improvised movements. The shift confused the alien targeting systems just long enough for Aquatania to gather massive amounts of moisture from the surrounding clouds.

All carriers, prepare for visual impairment, she warned, then released her control in a specific pattern.

The gathered water exploded outward in all directions, instantly forming a dense fog bank that engulfed both dragons and alien vessels. Visibility dropped to near zero, the thick mist obscuring everything beyond a wingspan's distance. The aliens' energy weapons discharged wildly into the fog, finding no targets as the dragons navigated by instinct and the innate directional sense that all their kind possessed.

Descend to surface level, Aquatania commanded through the communication crystal embedded in her harness. *Maintain fog coverage until landfall.*

They dropped lower, the fog moving with them as Aquatania maintained her concentration on the water molecules. Occasional bursts of alien energy fire lit the mist from within, creating eerie green flashes that illuminated nothing. When they finally broke through the cloud bank surrounding Ventus, the sight below stole what little breath remained in Aquatania's lungs.

The island burned, not with natural fire, but with the same sickly green energy that powered alien weapons. Several of the smaller floating platforms had broken free from their enchanted tethers, drifting aimlessly with structures ablaze. Citizens ran through streets choked with debris, some helping the injured, others simply fleeing from unknown terrors. The central research spire, once the proud heart of wind magic innovation, tilted at a precarious angle, its upper third sheared away completely.

They landed amid this chaos, touching down on what remained of the main plaza. The stone beneath Aquatania's claws still felt warm from recent energy discharges. Around them, buildings smoldered, windows shattered, and evidence of both conventional explosives and alien weaponry was visible in the destruction patterns.

"They knew we were coming," a lieutenant said. He was a water dragon whose scales bore fresh scorch marks from their aerial engagement. He'd transformed back to his humanoid form, but telltale blue patches remained along his neck and forearms, evidence of stress inhibiting complete transformation. "This wasn't random. This was a targeted strike against a known distribution point."

Aquatania nodded grimly, her own transformation flowing over her as she shifted back to human form. The pain in her shoulder, where the wing joint had been damaged, translated to a deep burn that made her left arm hang slightly askew. "Our plans have been compromised. Again."

"How could they have known our route?" another courier asked, frantically checking her cargo for damage. "We only finalized the distribution sequence yesterday."

"They have more infiltrators than we realized," Aquatania replied, scanning the skies for signs of returning alien vessels. "Or they've managed to access our communication systems." Her jaw tightened as she watched citizens approaching from partially collapsed buildings, their faces showing the familiar mix of fear and desperate hope. "It doesn't matter. They're getting desperate. We're winning."

The lieutenant looked skeptical, gesturing to the destruction around them. "This doesn't look like winning, Your Highness."

"They wouldn't commit resources to stopping us if the cure wasn't working," she explained, already moving toward the approaching medical teams. "Every attack confirms our success. Now, secure the remaining cargo. We distribute immediately, before they can regroup for another assault."

As the distribution began under makeshift shelters, Aquatania maintained a constant vigil toward the sky, her senses extended to the water in the clouds above, ready to detect the first sign of returning alien vessels. The burning in her shoulder faded to background awareness, unimportant compared to the task at hand. Every vial delivered, every citizen treated was another small victory against an enemy that grew more desperate with each passing hour.

*

The transition from air to water had always been Aquatania's favorite part of any journey. That moment when gravity's hold loosened, when the world transformed from sharp edges to fluid curves, when sound dampened to that peculiar underwater resonance that felt more like home than anything above the surface.

Today, that transition brought no joy. As her sea dragon form sliced cleanly into the ocean's embrace, Aquatania was met not with the vibrant underwater world she remembered, but with a dimmed, sickened version that confirmed their worst fears about the aliens' terraforming progress. The waters surrounding Oceana Prime, once crystal clear and teeming with life, had developed an unnatural greenish tinge, visibility reduced to mere dozens of yards where once she could see for miles through the pristine depths.

Behind her, a formation of specialized submersible vessels followed her descent. Their sleek, bubble-shaped hulls contained non-water dragons and human medical personnel who lacked the ability to breathe underwater naturally. Each vessel had been reinforced against the increasing pressure of deeper waters, enchanted seals glowing with the soft blue light of protection spells. Through the transparent sections, Aquatania could see her team members monitoring gauges and checking the secure containers holding precious vials of the cure.

She led the underwater convoy with powerful sweeps of her tail, her sea dragon form perfectly adapted to this environment despite its degraded state. Gills along her neck filtered oxygen efficiently from the water, while specialized membranes protected her eyes from the increasing irritants present in what should've been a clean ocean. Her scales, iridescent blue-green that normally caught and reflected the sun's rays penetrating from above, seemed dulled in the murky conditions, their natural luminescence working harder to provide visibility for those following.

They passed through what had once been thriving coral neighborhoods, underwater communities where reef dragons and merfolk had lived in harmonious tandem with the living coral structures. Now these areas stood abandoned, the once-vibrant coral formations bleached white or stained with the same sickly green that permeated the water. Delicate branches that had taken centuries to grow now crumbled at the slightest touch, releasing clouds of particulate matter that further degraded visibility.

A pearl farm drifted into view, its perfectly aligned cultivation beds now in disarray. Thousands of oysters lay open and empty, their precious contents apparently harvested in haste before the farmers fled. Tools remained scattered across the sandy bottom, evidence of work abandoned mid-task when the contamination reached this area. Aquatania's heart ached at the sight; this particular farm had supplied the royal jewelry crafters for generations, and its unique pink-silver pearls had been a symbol of her family's connection to the sea.

Most disturbing were the schools of affected fish that occasionally drifted past, their movements sluggish and uncoordinated. The same red patterns that marked human victims spread across their scales in telltale branching structures. Some floated lifelessly, while others swam in disoriented circles, bumping mindlessly into obstacles they normally would've avoided with ease. The contagion, or rather, the terraforming agent, had adapted to affect multiple species across different biological kingdoms, further evidence of its designed nature.

The great domes of Oceana Prime finally appeared through the murky water, massive crystalline structures that housed the underwater kingdom's major population centers. Even from a distance, Aquatania could see the damage. Cracks spider-webbed across sections of the protective barriers, emergency forcefields pulsing with strained energy as they maintained water pressure against structural failure. Some smaller domes had collapsed entirely, their broken shells lying in glittering shards across the ocean floor.

She adjusted their approach vector, leading the convoy toward an access point that still appeared intact. Her enhanced senses detected unusual currents surrounding the city, not the natural flow patterns that had once been carefully cultivated to provide fresh water circulation, but erratic movements that suggested damaged infrastructure and compromised water management systems.

Security checkpoints had been established at all remaining entry points, merfolk guards in full battle armor scrutinizing every approach. Their weapons, tridents and spears enhanced with water magic, remained at ready position even as they recognized Aquatania's distinctive dragon form. Protocol had clearly been amended in response to infiltration concerns.

"Identification and purpose," the lead guard demanded, his voice carrying through the water with the distinctive harmonic resonance of merfolk speech. His gills flared with tension, his eyes narrowed behind his helmet visor.

Aquatania transformed partially, maintaining her dragon head for underwater communication while shifting her forelegs to arms that could present the royal insignia embedded in her scales. *Princess Aquatania with medical convoy. We bring the cure.*

The guard's posture changed instantly, weapon lowering as he signaled frantically to his companions. "Clear the entry channel! Royal medical priority!" His eyes, when they returned to Aquatania, held desperate hope barely contained behind his professional demeanor. "We...we feared you wouldn't reach us, Your Highness. The alien blockade has turned back three supply vessels this week."

They were ushered through with unprecedented speed, the normal decontamination protocols abbreviated to the bare minimum required for safety. Inside the main dome, the devastation proved worse than external appearances had suggested. Entire sections had been flooded, and emergency barriers were hastily erected to contain water pressure breaches. The displaced population crowded into remaining habitable areas, creating dangerous density in structures designed for half their current occupancy. Temporary breathing apparatuses had been distributed to those unaccustomed to water immersion, citizens floating in remaining air pockets with expressions of frightened resignation.

"Aquatania!" The voice, half spoken, half sung through water, came from a flooded side corridor. Marina swam toward them with the powerful undulating motion unique to merfolk, her tail propelling her through water with grace that even Aquatania's dragon form couldn't fully match. The chief scientist's appearance shocked Aquatania. Marina's usually vibrant scales had dulled to a matte finish, and stress lines marked her face beneath her breathing apparatus. "We thought you wouldn't make it. The aliens have blockaded most routes."

Aquatania shifted to her human, and they embraced briefly, the formal protocol that usually governed their public interactions abandoned in the face of their shared crisis. Marina's hands gripped Aquatania's shoulders with surprising strength, as if confirming she was truly present rather than another false hope.

"We found an unmonitored approach through the Deep Trench," Aquatania explained as they separated. "My sea

263

dragon senses detected unusual current patterns. They're using some kind of underwater propulsion system that disrupts normal water flow. We followed the disruption gaps."

Marina nodded, already turning her attention to the submersible vessels as they docked at the remaining functional platforms. "Your timing is critical. Our internal filtration system is failing. The alien contaminants have begun breaking down the purification crystals."

They moved with practiced efficiency toward the city's central water processing hub, a massive crystal structure that normally glowed with blue-white energy as it purified and distributed water throughout Oceana Prime's complex network of domes and tunnels. Now the crystal pulsed erratically, sections darkened completely where systems had failed.

"The terraforming agents target our purification technology specifically," Marina explained as they navigated through narrow maintenance corridors designed for emergency access. "It's as if they studied our infrastructure's vulnerabilities before deploying their contagion."

Aquatania nodded grimly. "They did. The infiltrators have been gathering intelligence for longer than we realized."

They reached the main injection chamber, a specialized interface where treatments could be introduced directly into the filtration system for distribution throughout the city. Medical teams followed with the concentrated formula designed specifically for water-based delivery, the sealed containers glowing with intense blue luminescence that stood in stark contrast to the sickly green tinge that had infiltrated even the supposedly clean water within the dome.

Working together, Aquatania and Marina calibrated the injection system, adjusting pressure parameters to accommodate the cure's molecular structure. Aquatania extended her awareness into the water itself, sensing its compromised state at the molecular level. With careful concentration, she began manipulating the water's basic properties, creating optimal conditions for the cure to disperse evenly through the filtration network.

"The cure should reach all connected sections within four hours," Marina noted, monitoring distribution patterns on a crystal display. "Unconnected areas will require direct delivery." She hesitated, then added more softly, "We've lost the eastern dome completely. The structure collapsed yesterday after prolonged exposure to the alien contaminants. Three hundred casualties at minimum."

Aquatania absorbed this information with outward calm, though each death added to the weight she carried. Her hands continued their precise work, guiding water currents through the filtration system to maximize distribution efficiency. The injected cure created beautiful spiral patterns as it entered the main water supply, its luminescence temporarily overpowering the greenish tinge of contamination.

In a quiet moment while waiting for the first distribution cycle to complete, Marina turned to Aquatania with the question she'd clearly been holding back. "Where's General Kieran? I expected him to lead the military escort for a mission this critical."

Aquatania's hands froze mid-gesture, water droplets suspended in air around her fingers as her concentration shattered. The question, asked innocently, without knowledge of what had transpired, pierced through her carefully maintained composure. For a heartbeat, she couldn't speak, couldn't breathe, couldn't move as the full weight of memory crashed through her professional detachment.

"Captured," she finally answered, the single word carrying the weight of her guilt and grief. The suspended water droplets fell in a gentle rain around her hands, her control momentarily abandoned.

Marina's expression shifted from confusion to horror as

understanding dawned. She reached out as if to offer comfort, then hesitated, recognizing the public setting and Aquatania's position. "When?" she asked simply.

"During the laboratory attack." Aquatania forced her hands back into motion, resuming the distribution process with mechanical precision. "He held them off while I launched the cure." The facts, stated plainly, without the emotional context that threatened to overwhelm her if given voice.

Marina said nothing more, but her presence shifted subtly closer, offering silent support as they continued their work. Around them, the filtration system hummed with renewed energy as the cure began counteracting alien contaminants, the water gradually regaining some of its natural clarity. First steps toward healing, for the city if not for Aquatania's private wounds.

*

Marina's private laboratory felt like a sanctuary after hours of coordinating cure distribution through Oceana Prime's compromised systems. Tucked away in a corner of the science dome, the small space remained untouched by the chaos that had consumed most of the underwater city. Specimen tanks lined the walls, rare aquatic plants gently swaying in filtered currents. Instruments of crystal and pearl lay in precise arrangements on workbenches, each tool a testament to Marina's methodical nature. Aquatania had always admired this space, had spent countless hours here during her scientific training, learning the principles of molecular water manipulation under Marina's patient guidance. Now she allowed herself to sink onto a bench beside a bubbling tank of luminescent coral, the weight of exhaustion finally claiming its due.

The laboratory's specialized environment was maintained

at precise humidity and temperature levels to accommodate both merfolk and air-breathers. Marina adjusted her breathing apparatus, switching to the minimal setting that allowed her to survive in the partially air-filled laboratory while maintaining comfortable speech. She moved to a cooling unit, retrieving a flask of pale liquid that she offered to Aquatania without comment.

"You need hydration. Your cellular structure shows stress patterns."

Aquatania accepted the flask, the scientist in her recognizing the specialized formula designed to replenish trace minerals lost during prolonged water manipulation. As she drank, she caught her reflection in one of the specimen tanks. Dark circles shadowed her eyes, and her cheeks had hollowed noticeably, giving her face a haunted quality she barely recognized. When had that happened? The days since Kieran's capture had blurred together in a haze of constant movement, planning, and distribution efforts.

"I left him," she whispered, the words escaping before she could reconsider them. She slumped against the wall, her eyes fixing on a point somewhere beyond the laboratory's confines. "I chose the cure over him."

The admission hung in the air between them, the first time she'd voiced the choice aloud. Marina settled beside her on the bench, her tail curling beneath her in the posture merfolk adopted when preparing for extended conversation. She said nothing, allowing Aquatania the space to continue or retreat as needed.

"He wanted me to," Aquatania continued, her voice barely audible. "I could see it in his eyes as they dragged him away. He knew what the cure meant, knew it was more important than any single life, even his own." Her fingers tightened around the flask until her knuckles whitened. "I pulled the lever. I watched them take him. I did nothing."

Marina placed a hand on Aquatania's shoulder, the touch

gentle but firm. "And he would have made the same choice," she said. "Kieran has always understood the larger battle we face. He never would have forgiven you for sacrificing our world's chance for his survival."

Aquatania nodded, not entirely convinced but finding a measure of comfort in Marina's certainty. Her hand moved to her throat, her fingers finding the slender chain partially hidden beneath her flight suit. She pulled it free, revealing the small locket crafted from iridescent shell and silver. With a delicate touch, she opened the clasp, exposing what lay within, a single scale, deep crimson with gold flecks, that caught the laboratory's light with a faint, pulsing glow.

"One of Kieran's," Marina observed, leaning closer to examine the scale. "From his transformation pattern, yes?"

"He gave it to me before the Coral Citadel mission," Aquatania explained, her finger gently tracing the scale's edge. "A fire dragon tradition, offering a scale to someone who…" She hesitated, the words still difficult to form aloud. "To someone who matters. It creates a connection, allows a general sense of the other's well-being across distances."

Marina's eyes widened with scientific interest despite the emotional context. "A biological tether? I've read theoretical texts on such connections, but never observed one in practice."

"It's more than theory," Aquatania admitted, her gaze fixed on the faintly glowing scale. "I can feel him sometimes. Not thoughts or specific locations, just…presence. Emotional states. Physical condition." Her voice dropped lower, almost breaking. "He's in pain, but fighting. They're trying to extract information, I think. But he's still alive, still resisting."

The scale's glow pulsed slightly as she spoke, as if responding to her focus on the connection. Marina watched with fascination, her scientific mind clearly cataloging the phenomenon even as she maintained compassionate presence for her friend.

"The connection grows stronger sometimes at night," Aquatania continued, closing the locket gently. "When I'm less guarded, less focused on immediate tasks. It's like a thread stretched across a vast distance, vibrating with a frequency only I can sense."

"This connection," Marina began carefully, "could it potentially help locate—"

A sharp chime interrupted her question, the sound emanating from a crystal communication sphere that suddenly glowed red with priority signaling. Both women straightened immediately, the private moment shattered by the unmistakable indicator of urgent official communication.

Aquatania crossed to the workbench where the sphere pulsed with increasing intensity. She passed her hand over its surface, activating the message it contained. Light erupted from the crystal, coalescing into the projected image of her father, King Poseidronus. Even in the small projection, his imposing presence commanded attention, the monarch's scaled features set in the grave expression she'd seen only during the kingdom's most dire crises.

"Daughter, return immediately," King Poseidronus commanded, his voice carrying despite the projection's small size. "Our scouts report the aliens are amassing their forces. They plan to strike Zephyria directly, to end us once and for all."

The projection shifted, showing aerial reconnaissance images of what could only be described as an enormous alien mothership. Unlike the smaller vessels they'd encountered before, this craft dwarfed even Zephyria's largest defensive platforms. Its surface rippled with that distinctive oily iridescence, but at this scale, the effect became almost hypnotic, a visual distortion that made focusing on the vessel's true dimensions difficult and disorienting.

"Our defenses cannot withstand direct assault from a vessel of this magnitude," the king continued, his voice grim.

"We require your expertise and the remaining cure stockpiles. Whatever final strategy we implement must happen before this vessel reaches striking distance."

The projection displayed the mothership's projected course, a direct line toward Zephyria's central spires, with an estimated arrival time of less than eighteen hours. Smaller alien craft surrounded the massive vessel like remoras accompanying a shark, their formation suggesting coordinated attack capabilities that far exceeded previous encounters.

"Return with all haste," the king finished. "Council convenes at first light." The projection flickered once, then dissolved back into the crystal, which dulled to its normal transparent state.

Aquatania stood motionless for a moment, absorbing the implications of what she'd seen. The private vulnerability that had briefly emerged in Marina's sanctuary receded, replaced by something harder, more focused. Her posture straightened, her shoulders squaring as if physically taking on the weight of this new threat.

"Prepare the remaining cure for transport," she ordered Marina, her voice finding the clear authority of command once more. "And ready your warriors. This ends now."

Marina nodded, already moving toward her communication panel to alert Oceana Prime's military contingent. "What's the plan?" she asked, fingers hovering over crystal controls.

Aquatania's hand went briefly to the locket containing Kieran's scale, drawing strength from the connection it represented. "They think they're launching a final assault on us," she said, her eyes narrowing. "Instead, they're finally bringing their command structure within our reach."

She moved toward the laboratory exit, her body already beginning the partial transformation back to her sea dragon, her scales shimmering beneath her skin in anticipation. "I made a vow to find Kieran," she said, more to herself than to Marina. "The mothership is where they would take valuable prisoners. We'll deliver the cure, save our world, and reclaim what they stole from us…all in one strike."

Chapter Fifteen

Aquatania soared through cloud banks tinged orange by the setting sun. Below her, Zephyria's floating islands came into view, a sight that should have filled her with comfort but instead tightened something in her chest. The once-proud spires of her home reached toward the sky like broken fingers, their elegant architecture marred by scorched sections and hastily assembled scaffolding. Defense platforms that had stood for generations now listed at precarious angles, their enchanted cannons silent or missing entirely. This was not the homecoming she'd imagined when she'd left on her distribution mission merely days ago.

She banked left, circling lower to assess the damage more thoroughly. The eastern quadrant had suffered the worst of it. Three residential platforms had been severed from their tethering spells, their edges raw where magical anchors had once bound them to the main island. Emergency barriers pulsed with strained energy, holding the atmosphere for the citizens who remained. Workers crawled across the damaged sections like ants, their spelled construction harnesses glowing faintly as they attempted repairs that would typically take months to complete.

The grand market district, once alive with vendors from every kingdom, stood nearly deserted. Canopies that had sheltered exotic goods from across the world hung in tatters, their vibrant fabrics reduced to ashen scraps. A single food stall remained operational near the central fountain, a small queue of citizens waiting patiently for what appeared to be thin soup ladled from an enormous pot. Their faces turned skyward as her shadow passed over them, a mixture of recognition and desperate hope replacing momentary fear.

Aquatania felt each wound to her city as a physical pain. She'd been born here, had learned to fly among these spires, had studied in academies whose crystal domes now lay shattered across plazas where she'd played as a child. The aliens' strategy became clearer with each passing moment. They'd systematically targeted Zephyria's infrastructure while avoiding complete destruction. This was not annihilation but weakening, a deliberate effort to leave the kingdom vulnerable for the final assault her father had warned was coming.

The palace rose before her, its central spire relatively intact, though scorched along its western face, where defense spells had clearly repelled a direct attack. The floating gardens that usually surrounded the upper levels had been stripped bare, their specialized soil beds repurposed for growing emergency medicinal herbs rather than ornamental blooms. Military vessels docked at platforms designed for diplomatic gatherings, their hulls bearing the marks of recent combat.

She descended toward the main receiving terrace, her wings creating gentle whirlwinds that stirred fallen debris into small cyclones. Guards stationed at the corners snapped to attention as she approached, their spears raised in formal salute despite the visible fatigue in their postures.

As her claws touched down on the marble surface, Aquatania noted how few they were, perhaps a dozen where normally thirty would stand. More concerning was their youth...at least half appeared barely old enough for formal training, their armor adjusted with extra bindings to fit frames not yet filled out.

The transformation began at her core, scales receding in waves of blue-green light that rippled outward from her center. Wings folded inward, dissolving into her shoulder blades as her massive dragon form contracted into human proportions. The process, normally fluid and painless, sent unexpected waves of discomfort through her limbs, a reminder of how much energy she'd expended over the past few days. Her legs trembled slightly as she completed the change, standing now as a woman rather than a dragon, though faint scales still shimmered beneath the skin of her forearms where exhaustion had left the transformation incomplete.

"Your Highness." The head guard stepped forward, his fist pressed to his heart in a formal salute. The symbol of Zephyria on his breastplate was dented, his left pauldron missing entirely and replaced with leather strapping. "Welcome home."

"Captain." She acknowledged him with a nod, recognizing a senior officer who'd previously commanded an entire battalion. That he now led a palace guard detail spoke volumes about their depleted forces. "Status report?"

"Holding, Princess. The cure distribution has turned the tide of the contagion. Citizens recovering from the Red Death volunteer daily for defense training." His eyes betrayed what his formal report did not...pride in their resilience, fear of what was coming, exhaustion beyond measure.

Before she could question him further, the palace steward emerged from the grand entrance, his normally impeccable appearance disheveled in ways that would've been unthinkable in peacetime. The ceremonial staff he carried, a symbol of his office for three decades, now served a dual purpose as physical support for his limping gait. Red markings, faded but still visible, traced patterns along his neck where his high collar failed to cover them.

"Princess Aquatania." He bowed as deeply as his recovering body would allow. "His Majesty awaits you in the throne room. He has summoned the war council." The steward's voice carried a note of reverence that caught her attention. "The King stands again."

Relief washed through her with unexpected force. When she'd left Zephyria, her father had been bedridden, the Red

Death advancing despite their initial treatments. His recovery was one victory among many desperately needed. Yet the steward's emphasis on her father standing suggested his recovery remained incomplete.

"How long has he been up?" she asked, falling into step beside the steward as they moved toward the palace interior.

"Since yesterday, Your Highness. The cure reached him four days ago. He refused to remain abed once he could stand without assistance." The steward's tone carried equal measures of exasperation and admiration. "He insisted on overseeing defense preparations personally."

Aquatania's lips curved in a ghost of a smile. Her father's stubborn nature, so often a source of conflict between them in diplomatic matters, now manifested as the determination they all needed. As they passed through corridors lined with portraits of ancestors who'd faced their own crises, she straightened her shoulders despite her fatigue. The sea dragon royal line had never broken before enemies, not in two thousand years of recorded history. It would not break now, not under her watch, not while she drew breath.

"Then we shouldn't keep him waiting," she said, quickening her pace toward the throne room where decisions that would determine their world's fate, awaited.

*

The throne room doors swung open, their ancient hinges groaning under the weight of carved seafoam marble. Aquatania stepped through, her eyes immediately finding her father at the far end of the hall.

King Poseidronus stood before his throne rather than sitting upon it, a deliberate choice that spoke volumes. Though he leaned slightly on a trident staff—enchanted prongs glowing with subdued power—his posture carried the unmistakable authority that had defined his five-century reign. The azure scales along his forearms had regained their healthy luster, no longer dulled by the Red Death that had nearly claimed him. Relief flooded through Aquatania at the sight, momentarily washing away the exhaustion of her journey.

"Father." The word escaped her lips before protocol could contain it. Court formalities seemed trivial now, with their world balanced on the edge of extinction.

King Poseidronus's eyes, the same shade of deep ocean blue that she'd inherited, crinkled at their corners as his stern expression warmed. He extended his free arm toward her, abandoning centuries of formal court greeting.

"My daughter." His voice carried the resonant depths that could command armies or calm troubled waters with equal effectiveness. "Come."

Aquatania crossed the distance between them with measured steps that accelerated into an almost childlike rush as she reached him. His embrace was firm, his scales warm against her cheek as she pressed her face against his shoulder. For a heartbeat, she wasn't the princess, the scientist, or the warrior who'd distributed cures and commanded forces…she was simply a daughter relieved to find her father standing when she'd feared to find him fallen.

"The cure worked," he murmured against her hair, pride evident in his tone.

"Of course it did," she replied with a hint of her old confidence. "I made it."

He released her with a chuckle that faded quickly as he gestured toward the massive war table dominating the center of the throne room. "And not a moment too soon."

Aquatania turned, taking in the assembled advisors who'd maintained a respectful distance during their reunion. She recognized General Tidus of the naval forces, his uniform bearing a new insignia that suggested a consolidated command structure. Beside him stood Commander

Wavebreaker, her silver-streaked hair pulled back severely from a face lined with recent strain. Half a dozen other military leaders and council members formed a semicircle around the table, their expressions ranging from relieved to skeptical as they regarded her.

The war table itself was a marvel of magical engineering, a three-dimensional representation of Zephyria and surrounding territories rendered in living crystal that pulsed with real-time updates. Colored lights indicated troop positions, defensive emplacements, and supply caches. Too many positions glowed red, the universal indicator for critically understaffed.

"The cure worked," Poseidronus repeated, moving to the table's edge with careful steps that betrayed lingering weakness. "But we've lost nearly half our forces to the contagion before it could reach them. Another quarter remains too weak for combat roles."

Aquatania studied the deployment charts hovering above the table's surface. The outer defensive rings showed alarming gaps, with inexperienced recruits, indicated by pulsing yellow markers, positioned at critical junctures that seasoned veterans would normally hold. Supply lines stretched thin between platforms, many routes showing complete interruption where connecting bridges had been destroyed.

"Our air cavalry is at thirty percent strength," General Tidus reported, his weathered finger tracing a formation near the northern approach. "Dragon shifters were hit hardest by the second form of Red Death, something about their dual nature made the contagion spread faster through their systems."

"The cure reaches them slower for the same reason," Aquatania noted, memories of her distribution observations surfacing. "Their transformative abilities fight the cure initially, seeing it as another invasion rather than treatment."

She leaned closer to the tactical display, her mind already reconfiguring defense patterns with the efficiency of a chess master seeing twelve moves ahead. Without asking permission, she reached for the control crystals embedded in the table's edge, her fingers dancing across their facets with determined commands. The deployment indicators shifted in response, their positions reorganizing as she implemented changes.

"Move the remaining dragon shifters to staggered positions here, here, and here," she instructed, the markers relocating at her command. "They shouldn't form our first line, their value is in mobility and strike capability. Place human archers with enchanted arrows at these forward positions instead."

Commander Wavebreaker frowned. "That leaves our western approach vulnerable to direct assault."

"No," Aquatania countered, adjusting another formation. "It channels them into a calculated funnel. We don't have the numbers to form an impenetrable wall, so we create a trap instead." Her fingers manipulated the crystal controls again, and a simulation played across the table, showing alien craft following the path of least resistance directly into crossfire zones.

"The recovery wing reports three hundred fighters returning to duty by dawn," a medical officer offered, whose insignia marked him as the head of palace healing. "But they'll be at reduced capacity."

Aquatania nodded, incorporating this information without breaking her focus. "Position them as support units behind these veteran squadrons. Paired fighters, one at full strength, one recovering, provide better sustained defense than individual combatants spread thin."

She continued reorganizing the defensive strategy, addressing supply vulnerabilities by consolidating routes and establishing secondary caches at critical junctions. Her hands moved with increasing confidence despite the fatigue still evident in the faint tremor of her fingers when they briefly paused.

"The civilian volunteers?" she asked, looking up at a council member who oversaw community defense.

"Nearly two thousand," the woman replied, surprise evident in her tone at Aquatania's awareness of this resource. "Mostly untrained, but willing."

"Assign them to evacuation coordination and medical support. Any with maritime experience should be diverted to underwater shelter preparation." Aquatania tapped a sequence that illuminated cave systems beneath Zephyria's floating islands. "If we can't hold the surface, we retreat below, not outward."

A murmur ran through the assembled advisors, some nodding in appreciation of her foresight, others exchanging glances that questioned her authority to remake their defensive strategy so completely. One elder councilor cleared his throat, the sound carrying his disapproval more effectively than words.

"Princess, with respect, these changes contradict weeks of planning by experienced military leaders. General Kieran himself approved our current deployment before his..." He hesitated, uncomfortable with naming the general's capture.

"Before he was taken," Aquatania finished for him, her voice steady despite the pain that flashed through her at Kieran's name. "And circumstances have changed since then. The aliens adapt, so must we."

"The princess is correct," King Poseidronus interjected, his deep voice silencing further objections. He moved to stand beside her, his presence lending weight to her authority. "Our enemy brings a mothership capable of destroying everything we've built over millennia. Convention will not save us."

He surveyed the room, his gaze meeting each advisor's eyes in turn. When he spoke again, his tone carried the unmistakable command of a monarch who'd ruled through multiple crises.

"My daughter will oversee our final preparations. Her scientific knowledge, combined with her direct experience confronting these invaders, provides perspective none of us possess." His hand came to rest on Aquatania's shoulder, scales shimmering in response to her own. "The aliens will find Zephyria ready, under her command."

The proclamation settled over the room like a spell, resistance fading as the king's will became clear. Aquatania straightened under her father's touch, the mantle of leadership settling more firmly across her shoulders. She returned her attention to the war table, already calculating the next sequence of preparations as advisors moved to implement her initial changes.

"Send word to Marina in Oceana Prime," she instructed. "We'll need her water manipulation specialists integrated with our air defense squadrons." Her finger traced the projected path of the approaching mothership. "And prepare the ancient communion chamber beneath the palace. There are resources there we haven't yet accessed."

As the council dispersed to execute her orders, Aquatania remained at the table, her father a steady presence beside her.

*

Zephyria's central plaza had once hosted grand celebrations where enchanted fountains danced to celestial music and merchants from a dozen kingdoms offered exotic delights. Now, scaffolding embraced damaged buildings like desperate lovers, and temporary medical stations occupied corners where children had once played. The fountain at the plaza's heart stood dry, its intricate pipes redirected to supply emergency water purification systems nearby. Before it stood Aquatania, facing a sea of faces that reflected the city's battered but unbroken spirit. Hundreds had gathered, humans and shifters alike, many still bearing the fading red patterns of the contagion that had nearly claimed them. They pressed together in the afternoon light, their expressions a mixture of desperate hope and barely contained fear as they looked to their princess for guidance.

Aquatania surveyed them from her position atop the fountain's edge, noting how thin many appeared, how their clothes hung loose on frames that had lost weight during illness. Some leaned on makeshift crutches, others on friends and family, determined to attend despite lingering weakness. Parents clutched children close, protective despite the cure that now flowed through their veins. Elderly citizens whose faces she recognized from council meetings and festivals stood shoulder to shoulder with young recruits barely into their second decade. This was Zephyria, not its spires or enchanted bridges, but its people, gathered in defiance of an enemy that had tried to transform them into extinction.

She raised her hands slowly, deliberately, drawing the crowd's attention to her movement. Without speaking, she extended her awareness to the moisture in the air around them, calling water molecules to her command. They responded instantly, gathering from the atmosphere into a sphere that hovered above her outstretched palms. The water gleamed in the afternoon light, catching sunbeams and refracting them across the assembled faces. A soft murmur rippled through the crowd as the sphere grew larger, more defined, until it floated at eye level between Aquatania and her people.

"The cure flows through your veins," she announced, her voice carrying across the hushed gathering without need for magical amplification. "It protects you from the contagion that sought to transform not just our bodies, but our entire world."

With precise gestures, she shaped the hovering water into

a miniature version of Zephyria, its spires and platforms rendered in liquid crystal detail. The crowd's murmur grew appreciative as they recognized landmarks, some pointing to identify their homes among the watery structures.

"But the aliens who brought this plague have not surrendered their plans." Her fingers moved again, and the water-city transformed, reshaping itself into a shield that rotated slowly before them. "They bring a mothership capable of destroying everything we've built. Our strength against such force lies not in our walls or weapons, but in our unity."

The shield separated into smaller components that began to move in coordinated patterns, demonstrating defensive formations. Some members of the crowd leaned forward, eyes narrowed in concentration as they followed the liquid choreography.

"Humans and shifters, working together, create defenses greater than either could manage alone," Aquatania continued, the water components moving faster, more intricately. "I need volunteers to demonstrate these techniques."

A hesitant silence fell. Eyes dropped, gazes shifted sideways. The crowd, eager to listen, seemed suddenly reluctant to participate. Aquatania waited, maintaining the rotating water components with steady concentration despite the drain on her already depleted energy reserves. She'd expected this, fear masked as deference, uncertainty presenting as respect.

Movement near the front caught her attention. A young human girl, perhaps nine or ten years old, stepped forward. Her dark hair had been hastily braided, and fading red marks still traced patterns along her exposed forearms. Despite her small stature, she held herself with surprising dignity as she looked up at Aquatania.

"I'll help," she said, her voice clear though her hands

trembled slightly at her sides.

Beside her, a teenage boy shifted uncomfortably before also stepping forward. The subtle elongation of his canines and the amber tint to his eyes marked him as a wolf shifter, though he remained in human form. His posture suggested reluctance tempered by determination not to be outdone by someone half his age.

"As will I," he added, voice cracking on the final word.

Aquatania acknowledged them with a nod, releasing the water demonstration to hover nearby as she stepped down from the fountain's edge. "What are your names?"

"Lina," the girl answered.

"Reth," the boy offered, standing straighter as Aquatania approached.

"Lina and Reth," she repeated, ensuring the crowd heard them clearly. "Today, you represent all of Zephyria in our first public demonstration of unified defense." She turned to address the gathered citizens. "What they learn, you will learn. What they demonstrate, you will practice in your neighborhoods tonight."

She guided the young volunteers to stand several paces apart, positioning herself between them. The water sphere she'd maintained divided into smaller droplets that began circling all three of them, creating a visual boundary for the demonstration.

"Humans possess creativity and adaptability that can distract even the most focused enemy," Aquatania explained, nodding to Lina. "Shifters possess strength and sensory advantages that allow for precise strikes." She turned to Reth, who straightened further at her acknowledgment. "Together, they create opportunities neither could achieve alone."

She moved Lina to stand at the demonstration area's center, instructing her in a simple sequence of movements designed to draw attention. The girl followed with surprising grace, her small hands weaving patterns that Aquatania enhanced with trailing water droplets to make the movements more visible to the crowd.

"When an opponent focuses on the obvious threat," Aquatania continued, now positioning Reth at the peripheral edge of their demonstration space, "they become vulnerable to the unseen one."

She guided Reth through a flanking approach, teaching him how to use Lina's distracting movements as cover for his own advance. His initial awkwardness faded as he grasped the concept, amber eyes brightening with understanding.

"Now together," Aquatania instructed. On her signal, Lina began her distraction sequence while Reth circled behind where an imaginary opponent would stand. The water droplets followed their movements, creating glimmering trails that illustrated the technique for the watching crowd.

As the young volunteers completed their maneuver, Reth lunged forward in a precise strike while Lina completed her diversion, a spontaneous cheer erupted from the gathered citizens. The sound swelled across the plaza, echoing against damaged buildings with unexpected force. Aquatania allowed herself a small smile as she nodded approval to her volunteers, who stood breathless and flushed with accomplishment.

"Again," she called, "but this time, I'll be the opponent."

The demonstration evolved, Aquatania playing the role of an alien infiltrator while Lina and Reth executed their strategy with growing confidence. Each repetition brought greater coordination between the unlikely partners, their movements becoming fluid where they'd been stilted, certain where they had been hesitant.

"Who else will learn to defend Zephyria?" Aquatania asked as the demonstration concluded.

Hands rose throughout the crowd, first a few, then dozens, then hundreds. Citizens stepped forward, some still bearing the physical marks of recent illness but all carrying the unmistakable determination of those who'd faced extinction and refused its claim. Aquatania directed them to form small practice groups, with experienced guards and soldiers dispersing through the crowd to provide guidance.

The plaza transformed from a gathering of frightened citizens into a training ground where humans and shifters worked side by side, learning the defensive techniques she'd demonstrated.

Aquatania moved among them, correcting postures, demonstrating movements, offering encouragement where it was needed most. Her water droplets multiplied, providing visual guides for dozens of practice groups simultaneously.

Each manipulation of water drew from her dwindling reserves of energy. The pain behind her eyes intensified with each passing minute, the slight tremor in her hands becoming more pronounced when she thought no one was watching. She hadn't fully recovered from her distribution mission, had not allowed herself the luxury of rest before assuming command of Zephyria's defenses. Now she paid the price in silent suffering, masked behind a leader's confident exterior.

A senior guard approached, offering a flask of fortified water infused with strengthening herbs. He'd served in the palace since she was a child and recognized the signs of her exhaustion better than most.

"The people draw strength from your example, Princess," he said quietly as she accepted the flask. "But they need you whole for what comes tomorrow."

Aquatania nodded, taking a careful sip that replenished some small measure of her depleted energy. "And they will have me whole," she promised, already turning back to her duties. "After they have what they need today."

The sun began its descent toward the horizon, bathing the training plaza in golden light that softened the edges of damaged buildings and cast long shadows across practiced defensive maneuvers. In those lengthening shadows,

Aquatania saw not what Zephyria had lost, but what it might yet become…a unified force prepared to defend their world against impossible odds.

*

The palace corridors fell away behind Aquatania as she followed a path few living souls had walked in centuries. Royal guards stationed at regular intervals nodded respectfully as she passed, none questioning her destination, though curiosity flickered in their eyes. When she reached a simple wooden door set into the wall behind the throne room, the guards positioned there exchanged glances before stepping aside without challenge.

Beyond lay a spiraling staircase carved directly into the living rock of Zephyria's foundation stone, descending into darkness broken only by torches set in ancient sconces. Blue flames flickered to life as she approached, responding to her sea dragon bloodline with ancestral recognition. Each step took her deeper into the heart of Zephyria's oldest secrets, away from the chaos of preparation above and into a silence heavy with accumulated power.

The staircase wound counterclockwise, each turn revealing ancient carvings that chronicled the sea dragon dynasty's history. Here, a relief showed the first sea dragons emerging from primordial waters, their elongated forms more serpentine than their modern descendants. There, an intricate scene depicted the great alliance formed between dragons and humans during the Maelstrom Wars, scales and skin interwoven in patterns that symbolized their blood oath. Further down, Aquatania paused before a particularly detailed carving of sea dragons manipulating vast ocean currents to raise the first floating islands that would become Zephyria, their combined power lifting entire landmasses from the depths.

Her fingers traced the carved outline of a dragon whose features bore a striking resemblance to her own, her great-grandmother, Queen Thalassia, who'd been the last to perform the communion ritual Aquatania now sought. The stone felt warm beneath her touch, as if the memory of Thalassia's power lingered in the very rock that bore her image.

With each descending spiral, the air grew thicker with moisture, salt-laden and heavy in her lungs. Droplets condensed on the walls, catching blue torchlight and refracting it in prismatic patterns across the ancient carvings. The familiar scent of deep ocean currents, a fragrance no surface dweller could identify but every sea dragon recognized instinctively, strengthened with each step. Aquatania felt her gills stirring beneath the skin of her neck, responding to the increasing humidity, though she maintained her human form.

After what seemed both moments and eternities, the staircase ended, opening into a vast underground cavern whose true dimensions were lost in shadow. The blue torchlight extended only so far, illuminating the immediate area while leaving the ceiling and distant walls shrouded in darkness. At the cavern's center lay a perfectly circular pool, its surface unnaturally still despite the subtle currents that should disturb any body of water. Unlike normal water, this pool glowed with an inner phosphorescence that pulsed in slow, rhythmic waves, almost like heartbeats, sending ripples of blue-green light across the surrounding stone.

Aquatania approached reverently, her footsteps echoing in the immense space. The stone floor beneath her boots gave way to finely crushed shells and sand that whispered with each step, creating a sound like distant tides. Standing at the pool's edge, she looked upward, following the central column of the cavern to its apex where a crystal dome had been set into Zephyria's foundation. Though they were deep beneath the floating island, the dome somehow captured moonlight from above, focusing it into a single beam that pierced the darkness to touch the pool's center.

This was the sacred communion, the hidden heart of Zephyria where sea dragon royalty had connected with their ancestors since the kingdom's founding. Few records existed of its use. The ritual was passed through oral tradition rather than written text, deemed too powerful for casual documentation. Aquatania knew the procedure only through stories her great-grandmother had told her during childhood, before age and injury had taken Thalassia beyond the veil.

With deliberate movements, Aquatania began removing her outer garments. First, the formal overtunic with its royal insignia, then the protective leather vest she'd worn beneath it during the day's public appearances. Her boots and suit followed, placed neatly at the pool's edge. She stood in a simple white shift that reached her knees, her feet bare against the pearl-soft sand. The air against her skin felt alive, currents moving with purpose rather than random circulation.

From a small pouch at her waist, the only item she'd retained, she withdrew the ritual components. Each had been carefully selected and prepared in the brief private moments she'd claimed between council meetings and public duties. She knelt at the pool's edge, arranging them in the precise pattern the ritual demanded.

First, a scale from her first transformation, iridescent blue-green, preserved in a crystal vial that had been sealed the day she first shifted to dragon form at age seven. The scale represented her individual power, her unique connection to the sea dragon lineage. She placed it at the northern point of an invisible circle she created around herself.

Next came a vial of seawater collected from the specific deep-ocean trench where she'd been born. Sea dragon royalty traditionally returned to ancestral birthing waters for delivery, maintaining a connection to the primal forces that had shaped their evolution. This water, collected by her father after her birth, contained trace elements of her first contact with the world outside her mother's body. She positioned this vial at the eastern point, where the path of rebirth began in ancient dragon mythology.

At the southern point, she placed a small crystal that had been passed through generations of sea dragon queens. Veined with colors that shifted depending on the angle of observation, the crystal had absorbed the magical signatures of every royal who'd held it during similar rituals. It hummed faintly against her palm before she set it down, as if recognizing her bloodline and responding to her intent.

The western position, representing transition and transformation in dragon lore, remained empty for now. That space awaited water from the sacred pool itself, to be collected during the ritual.

Aquatania closed her eyes briefly, centering herself despite the exhaustion that pulled at her limbs and thoughts. The day's efforts had depleted her considerably, maintaining water constructs for hundreds of citizens while projecting unwavering confidence had taken more energy than she could easily spare. Yet the coming battle would demand even more. Without the ancient knowledge and power this ritual might provide, she feared her current strength would prove insufficient against the alien mothership.

Her hands moved with practiced precision despite her fatigue, arranging the components in slight adjustments until they aligned perfectly with the moonbeam striking the pool's center. The water's phosphorescence intensified in response, pulses of light growing stronger and more frequent as if the pool itself anticipated what was to come.

The ritual required complete immersion, physical and spiritual surrender to the ancestral memories carried in the sacred waters. With steady breaths, Aquatania prepared herself for communion with forces not accessed for generations, uncertain what wisdom or power she might find but knowing with bone-deep certainty that Zephyria's survival might depend on what she discovered beneath those glowing waters.

Aquatania stepped into the sacred pool with deliberate reverence, the water embracing her ankles with a warmth that defied the cavern's cool depths. Unlike ordinary water, it seemed to possess awareness, curling around her feet in a gentle greeting rather than mere displacement. The shift's white fabric darkened as it absorbed moisture, clinging to her legs as she waded deeper. When the water reached her waist, she paused, extending her arms palm-down upon the surface. The ancient words of ritual came to her lips unbidden, as if the pool itself supplied forgotten knowledge to her conscious mind.

"*Thalassa mer'vorith, dracon'seri valu,*" she intoned, her voice adopting the melodic cadence of the sea dragon tongue, syllables flowing like tide against shore. The language felt primordial in her mouth, each word carrying weight beyond its sound. "*Mem'vorath scalin, vorthis mer'draconum.*"

The water responded immediately, its phosphorescence intensifying around her submerged body. Currents that shouldn't exist in a contained pool began to circle her, creating intricate patterns across the surface that mirrored the carvings on the cavern walls. The moonbeam striking the center seemed to widen, its silver light diffusing through the moving water in fractal patterns that danced across Aquatania's upturned face.

"Ancestors of scale and tide, I seek communion," she continued, translating the ritual language into common tongue as tradition required. "Blood of my blood, memory beyond memory, I offer myself as a vessel."

The currents quickened, spiraling up her torso in ribbons of luminescent water that defied gravity's pull. Each ribbon followed the pathways where scales would emerge during her transformation, tracing the hidden patterns of her draconic heritage beneath human skin. The pool's glow pulsed in rhythm with her heartbeat now, the two falling into perfect synchronization.

Aquatania drew a final deep breath, then submerged completely, allowing the sacred waters to close over her head. Beneath the surface, sound transformed into the peculiar muffled resonance of underwater space, but overlaid with whispers that seemed to come from everywhere and nowhere, countless voices speaking in fragments of ancient sea dragon dialect. Her body responded to the complete immersion with instinctive transformation, not to full dragon form but to a liminal state between human and dragon. Scales erupted along her limbs in flowing patterns of iridescent blue-green, each one catching and amplifying the pool's inner light. Her eyes shifted, pupils elongating into vertical slits while the irises expanded, encompassing more of the visible spectrum as her vision adapted to underwater conditions.

The gills along her neck opened fully, allowing her to breathe the sacred water directly. With each breath, knowledge entered not just her lungs but her consciousness, memories that were not her own flooding through neural pathways like tidal forces. She experienced them not as distant observations but as lived moments, each one visceral and immediate despite occurring centuries before her birth.

She was Queen Meristra in the Third Maelstrom War, manipulating ocean currents to sink an enemy armada that threatened the first fragile settlements of Zephyria. The complex water manipulation techniques flowed into Aquatania's understanding, not just the physical movements but the precise mental focus required to affect water at molecular levels, creating pressure differentials that could shatter reinforced hulls.

She was King Coralus during the Deep Treaty negotiations, using subtle water vibrations to detect deception in rival delegates' heart rates and breathing patterns. The technique revealed in exquisite detail...how to extend awareness through water molecules touching another being, reading physiological responses that betrayed hidden intentions.

She was Princess Tideweaver during the first alien incursion five centuries past, a historical event Aquatania had never seen documented in royal archives. The memory showed beings similar to their current invaders, though their technology had evolved significantly in the intervening years. Tideweaver had discovered their weakness then, a vulnerability to specific frequencies of sound transmitted through water that disrupted their neural functions. The precise frequency pattern imprinted itself in Aquatania's mind, along with the specialized water manipulation technique required to generate and direct it.

Memory after memory cascaded through her consciousness, battle strategies from forgotten wars, diplomatic resolutions to ancient conflicts, scientific discoveries about water's properties that had been lost to modern understanding. Each added layers to her knowledge, expanding her capabilities beyond what formal training had provided. The weight of accumulated wisdom should have been overwhelming, yet the sacred pool supported her consciousness, integrating each memory with care rather than flooding her mind destructively.

The water around her grew increasingly luminescent, the blue-green glow intensifying until it seemed as if she was floating in liquid light rather than water. The disparate memories coalesced into a coherent understanding, forming connections between seemingly unrelated techniques and knowledge. Aquatania felt her own power expanding, not through external enhancement but through deeper connection to abilities that had always existed within her lineage, dormant until awakened by the communion.

As the ritual reached its crescendo, the water before her

shimmered, molecules reorganizing with purpose rather than random motion. A form materialized within the luminescent currents, first indistinct, then resolving into clear definition. Translucent scales caught the diffused moonlight, creating rainbow patterns across a draconic form that was both physically present and impossibly ethereal.

Queen Thalassia, her great-grandmother, appeared as a spectral dragon whose features Aquatania recognized from both palace portraits and childhood memories. Although physically smaller than a full-grown sea dragon, the spectral form radiated power that made the entire cavern feel suddenly confined.

No words passed between them in a conventional sense. Instead, knowledge was transferred directly — concepts and techniques flowing from ancestral consciousness to a living descendant through the sacred water that connected them. Aquatania suddenly understood why this ritual had been preserved only through oral tradition. The experience transcended language, rendering written description not merely inadequate but almost sacrilegious in its limitation.

Thalassia's spectral form circled her slowly, translucent tail and fins moving through water with fluid grace that seemed to bend physical laws. Where the spectral form touched Aquatania's partially transformed body, knowledge transferred with greater intensity, battle techniques refined through centuries of sea dragon evolution, water manipulation methods that combined science and innate magic in ways modern practitioners had forgotten, secrets of molecular control that allowed water to maintain complex structures independent of constant concentration.

Most precious was the knowledge of water armor, the ability to maintain dragon-scale immunity while in human form by bonding water molecules directly to skin in patterns that mimicked draconic protection. The technique had been considered legendary even in Thalassia's time, mastered by only a handful of sea dragon royalty throughout history. Now it unfolded in Aquatania's understanding with crystalline clarity, each mental and physical component precisely detailed.

As this knowledge was integrated into her consciousness, Aquatania's body responded with visible transformation. Her scales took on a deeper luster, the iridescent patterns growing more pronounced and complex. The water surrounding her body began bonding at the molecular level, forming an almost imperceptible second skin that enhanced rather than obscured her natural scales. Her movements became more fluid, as if the boundary between body and water had blurred, allowing her to extend her physical presence beyond conventional limitations. The golden runes that were always etched into her skin glowed more vividly now, their intricate lines unfolding like living calligraphy. They pulsed in resonance with the voice of her great-grandmother, the inheritance of a lineage that had never left her. In their shimmer was both memory and presence—an eternal reminder that she carried her ancestor's strength and wisdom in every breath, every motion, every flicker of light upon her skin.

Thalassia's spectral form completed its circuit around her, coming to face Aquatania directly. The ghostly dragon's eyes, vertical pupils surrounded by irises that contained every shade of ocean from shallow reef to abyssal trench, gazed into her descendant's with ancient wisdom and unmistakable pride. A final transfer of knowledge flowed between them, not techniques or memories this time, but something more fundamental, the underlying truth of water's nature that connected all sea dragon magic.

The spectral queen's form began to dissipate, returning to the sacred pool from which it had coalesced. As it faded, a final message resonated not through words but through direct understanding, imprinting itself in Aquatania's consciousness with gentle but undeniable authority…

The water remembers what we forget. Trust in both your science and your heritage.

The meaning expanded within her understanding, the recognition that her unique strength lay in the integration of scientific knowledge with ancestral magic, the empirical with the mystical. Neither alone would defeat the alien threat, but together they formed a power the invaders couldn't anticipate or counter.

As Thalassia's form dissolved completely into shimmering currents, Aquatania remained suspended in the sacred pool, her partially transformed body absorbing the final echoes of ancestral connection. The ritual neared completion, having delivered exactly what she'd sought, though in forms she couldn't have imagined before experiencing them directly. Knowledge, power, and heritage flowed through her veins now, not as separate currents but as a unified tide that would carry her, and through her, Zephyria, into the coming battle.

Aquatania broke the pool's surface with a gentle ripple, water cascading from her shoulders as she rose to stand. With the sacred communion complete, she found herself transformed in ways both visible and intangible. Where the water should've streamed away from her body, it instead clung like a second skin, not dripping but flowing around her limbs in continuous patterns that caught the cavern's blue light. Her shift, now transparent with saturation, revealed scales that hadn't receded with her emergence, iridescent patches that formed protective constellations across her skin rather than the full coverage of her dragon form. She extended her arms before her, observing how the water moved with her movements, responding to intentions she hadn't yet fully formed into conscious thought.

Stepping onto the pearl-soft sand surrounding the pool, she marveled at how the water continued to embrace her rather than falling away. It maintained perfect cohesion, forming a translucent armor that flowed like liquid glass over her partially scaled skin. When she focused on her hand, the water there thickened slightly, hardening into a gauntlet-like protection without any verbal command or elaborate gesture. The control felt effortless, requiring merely the direction of attention rather than the concentrated will her previous water manipulation had demanded.

"Show me," she whispered to the living water, curious about the extent of this new connection.

In response, the water coating her right arm extended outward, forming a crystalline blade that caught the moonlight in hypnotic patterns. The construct maintained perfect molecular alignment without her conscious focus, something she'd never achieved before, even with years of practice and scientific understanding of water's properties. She'd always needed to maintain constant concentration to hold water in complex forms...now the liquid seemed to remember her intentions, maintaining structure independently.

Aquatania extended her awareness further, calling to the sacred pool itself. Water rose in a sinuous column, separating from the main body to hover before her at eye level. With mere thought rather than elaborate manipulation, she shaped it into a perfect replica of Zephyria's central spire, complete with miniature defensive platforms and delicate architectural details she'd never been able to render with such precision before. The structure remained stable, requiring no ongoing concentration to maintain its complex form.

"Defense," she murmured, testing another aspect of her new ability.

The water armor covering her body thickened momentarily, scales beneath it brightening as if activated by her command. She reached for a ritual dagger she'd left with her clothing, an ornamental blade carried by sea dragon royalty during ceremonial functions. With deliberate motion, she drew the blade across her forearm where the water armor flowed.

The dagger's edge never reached her skin. The water hardened instantaneously at the point of contact, becoming momentarily solid as crystal before returning to its fluid state once the blade moved away. Not a drop of blood was drawn, not a scale disturbed beneath the living protection. She understood the full implication immediately. Her great-grandmother's final gift allowed her to maintain her dragon's immunity to conventional weapons while in human form, through this water armor that responded to threats faster than conscious thought.

Aquatania turned her attention to more complex applications, drawing again from the knowledge that had been transferred during communion. She extended both hands toward the pool, envisioning not just shapes but purpose. Water rose in response, forming humanoid figures that stood at attention before her, sentinels composed entirely of liquid yet maintaining perfect cohesion and form. She imbued them with simple directives, and the constructs began moving independently, circling the pool in patrol patterns she'd merely conceived rather than explicitly commanded.

"Guard," she instructed, curious if verbal commands would enhance the connection.

The water sentinels responded with immediate adaptation, their forms becoming more defined, developing shield-like appendages and spear-like extensions. They moved with increased purpose, positioning themselves at strategic points around the cavern as if assessing potential threats and optimal defensive positions. The level of autonomous function far exceeded anything she'd previously achieved with water manipulation.

As she continued experimenting, Aquatania realized the true nature of her great-grandmother's gift, not merely enhanced water control, but a fundamental shift in her relationship with the element. Where before she'd commanded water as an external force, now she communed with it as an extension of her own being. The molecular memory inherent in water, the property scientists had theorized but never fully utilized, was now accessible to her conscious direction. Water remembered the shapes she gave it, the purposes she assigned, maintaining them without constant reinforcement.

For Zephyria's defense, the implications were profound. Water sentinels could fight alongside their depleted forces, following complex tactical directions without requiring her constant focus. Defensive water shields could protect vulnerable structures, responding to threats autonomously while she directed her attention elsewhere. Even her personal combat capabilities had transformed, the water armor allowing her to engage enemies directly while maintaining draconic protection in a more maneuverable human form.

The spectral presence of Queen Thalassia had fully dissipated, returning to the ancestral memories contained within the sacred pool. Yet Aquatania felt her great-grandmother's influence lingering in the very water that embraced her, in the knowledge that now flowed through her consciousness like tidal currents. The final message resonated with deeper meaning as she explored these new abilities.

The water remembers what we forget. Trust in both your science and your heritage.

She understood now what Thalassia had meant. Her scientific understanding of water's molecular properties provided the framework for precise manipulation, while her draconic heritage supplied the intuitive connection that brought those manipulations to life. Neither alone would have granted this level of mastery; only their integration created power sufficient to counter the alien threat.

Aquatania dissolved the water sentinels with a thought,

returning them to the sacred pool with gentle respect. She gathered her ritual items from where they remained arranged at the pool's edge, the scale from her first transformation, the vial of birthwater, and the ancestral crystal now glowing with renewed energy after the communion. Each seemed to pulse with significance as she returned them to the small pouch at her waist.

Her white shift had dried against her skin, though the water armor continued to flow over it in protective layers. She dressed deliberately, donning her suit with measured movements that allowed the water to adjust and integrate with each garment. By the time she'd pulled on her boots and secured her formal overtunic with its royal insignia, the water armor had adapted perfectly, nearly invisible to casual observation yet present in the subtle gleam that followed her movements, in the faint ripple of protection that covered every inch of exposed skin.

Aquatania turned toward the spiral staircase, her steps steady and purposeful where fatigue had dragged at them hours earlier. The ritual had not just granted new abilities but had restored her energy, replacing exhaustion with the vibrant power of her full heritage. As she began ascending toward the palace above, blue torches igniting at her approach, her mind worked through applications of her new capabilities, integrating them into defensive strategies already taking shape in her tactical planning.

The water armor flowed with each step, adapting to her movement without resistance or distraction. A subtle blue glow emanated from her skin, visible only in the darkest sections between torches, a physical manifestation of the power she now carried. The sacred communion had transformed her from princess and scientist into something her people needed more urgently, a warrior queen prepared to defend her kingdom with powers the aliens couldn't have anticipated.

She emerged from the simple wooden door behind the throne room to find the palace in continued preparation for tomorrow's confrontation. Guards snapped to attention as she passed, their eyes widening slightly at her transformed appearance. Something in her bearing had changed, a fluid grace that transcended her normal movement, a subtle authority that radiated from her like heat from flame. They seemed to recognize their princess, but sensed the ancestral power she now carried within and around her.

Chapter Sixteen

Dawn broke over Zephyria in streaks of amber and gold, illuminating Aquatania as she stood at the highest point of the central spire. The water armor from her sacred communion flowed over her skin like liquid crystal, catching the first light of day in rippling patterns that accentuated the sea dragon scales still visible beneath. She felt the power from the ancient ritual thrumming through her veins, a steady pulse that matched the rhythmic movement of the water embracing her form. Below, stretched across multiple floating platforms connected by bridges of light, the combined forces of sky and sea gathered, thousands of dragons in both their natural forms and human shapes, their eyes turned upward toward their princess and the looming shadow that slowly eclipsed the morning sky.

The alien mothership had appeared just as their scouts had predicted, emerging from the cloud banks like a grotesque leviathan of metal and pulsing organic matter. Its surface rippled with that distinctive oily iridescence that marked all their alien technology, but at this scale, the effect was hypnotic and disorienting. The vessel dwarfed Zephyria's largest defense platforms, its underside stretching so far that it cast the eastern quadrant of the floating kingdom into premature dusk. Aquatania studied it with narrowed eyes, her scientific mind automatically calculating dimensions, identifying potential weaknesses despite the knot of dread that formed in her stomach at its sheer enormity.

She shifted her focus to the forces assembled below. Sea dragons dominated the central platforms, their iridescent scales shimmering in shades of blue, green, and violet that mirrored the deep ocean currents they commanded. Many

301

bore the royal crest on specialized battle harnesses, elite guards who'd trained under her father for centuries. Among them stood her father himself, his massive sea dragon form now fully recovered from the Red Death, his scales gleaming with renewed vigor as he organized formation groups with sweeps of his powerful tail.

On adjacent platforms, sky dragons gathered in formations that utilized their unique abilities. Their bodies were more streamlined than their sea cousins, with feathered wings that spanned twice their body length when fully extended. Lightning crackled occasionally between their extended talons as they communicated in the ancient draconic tongue, the air around them charged with potential energy. Fire dragons occupied the western platforms, their crimson and gold scales radiating heat that created visible distortion in the air above them. Forest dragons had taken up positions near the remaining gardens, their earth-toned scales helping them blend with the vegetation they would use to heal the wounded during battle.

Aquatania's hand moved unconsciously to the locket containing Kieran's scale. Through their connection, she sensed he still lived, his presence a distant pulse of determination and pain. The aliens hadn't broken him, despite whatever methods they'd employed to extract information. She drew strength from his continued resistance, just as she had when making the impossible choice to prioritize the cure over his immediate rescue.

"Today," she began, her voice carrying across the assembled forces without need for magical amplification, "we face an enemy that came not as honest conquerors, but as insidious transformers of all we hold sacred." The water armor around her throat vibrated slightly with each word, adding resonance that helped project her voice to the farthest platforms. "They sought to change our world molecule by molecule, to remake it into something that would sustain them while extinguishing us."

She gestured toward the looming mothership. "They believed their science superior to ours, their understanding of transformation more advanced than creatures who have embodied that principle for millennia." A murmur of agreement rippled through the assembled dragons. "They underestimated not just our resistance, but our adaptability, the very essence of what it means to be a dragon."

Aquatania raised her arms, calling to the water molecules present in the morning air. They responded instantly, gathering from the atmosphere into visible mist that swirled around her elevated position. Unlike her previous manipulations that required intense concentration, the water moved as a natural extension of her will, responding to intentions barely formed into conscious thought.

"Our strategy must utilize the strengths of each dragon lineage," she continued, the mist forming into a three-dimensional representation of the mothership that hovered before her. "Sea dragons will provide defensive shields and pressure attacks against their outer hull." The water model showed formations of sea dragons generating massive water barriers while others directed concentrated jets at specific points on the alien vessel.

"Sky dragons will neutralize their fighter craft and create electromagnetic disruption around their weapon systems." The model shifted, showing winged forms weaving between smaller alien vessels, lightning strikes disabling propulsion systems. "Fire dragons will focus on creating superheated breaches at these specific points." Several locations on the water model glowed brighter, marking vulnerability points their intelligence had identified.

The assembled dragons watched with growing confidence as the detailed battle plan unfolded before them, water shifting to illustrate each phase with precision impossible in conventional briefings. Aquatania felt their energy changing, fear giving way to determined purpose as they recognized the thought behind each tactical element.

"General Kieran is being held captive aboard this vessel," she said, her voice softening slightly despite her efforts to maintain an even command tone. The water model highlighted a section near the ship's center. "Intelligence suggests he is in their central laboratory, likely with other captured subjects. A specialized extraction team will focus on this objective once primary breaches are established."

She paused, allowing the water model to dissolve back into mist that circled her position in increasingly complex patterns. "Now, witness what the sacred communion has granted us, what the ancestors have returned to aid our defense."

With a thought that required no external gesture, Aquatania extended her awareness to the ocean far below Zephyria's floating islands. The response was immediate and unprecedented; massive columns of water rose from the distant surface, defying gravity as they spiraled upward toward the assembled forces. Dragons shifted nervously as the enormous water constructs approached, but held position at her father's commanding roar.

The columns reached their level and began transforming, molecular structures rearranging at Aquatania's direction. Some formed into perfect spherical shields twenty feet in diameter, their surfaces rippling with defensive energy. Others shaped themselves into spears and tridents of liquid crystal, edges honed to molecular precision. The most impressive transformed into water dragons three times the size of their living counterparts, their features detailed down to individual scales, their eyes glowing with the same phosphorescence as the sacred pool.

"These constructs will fight alongside us," Aquatania explained as the water dragons performed an aerial maneuver in perfect unison. "They require no constant control, maintaining form and purpose through the ancient memory of water itself."

To demonstrate, she directed a water dragon to intercept a simulated attack, then deliberately turned her attention elsewhere. The construct continued its defensive pattern independently, adjusting to changing conditions without further input. Gasps of appreciation rose from the assembled forces, particularly from elder sea dragons who recognized abilities long thought lost to their lineage.

"Today we fight not just for our world, but for every species that calls it home," Aquatania declared, the water armor around her body brightening with the intensity of her conviction. "For the coral reefs and floating forests, for the deepest trenches and highest spires, for every child who will inherit what we protect this day."

She raised her hand toward the alien mothership, and every water construct mirrored her gesture in perfect synchronization. "For Zephyria! For our world!"

The answering roar from thousands of dragon throats shook the floating islands, a battle cry that carried challenge and defiance toward the alien vessel that had dared threaten their existence. As the echoes faded, dragons began moving into attack formations with practiced precision, the water constructs taking positions among them like ancient guardians returned from legend to fight alongside their living descendants.

Aquatania looked to her father, who nodded once in solemn approval before lowering his massive head in invitation.

The time for words had ended.

The time for action had come.

Aquatania leapt from the spire with practiced grace, her body arcing through the morning air before landing perfectly on her father's waiting back. King Poseidronus's sea dragon form dwarfed even the largest warriors in their assembly, his ancient scales shimmering with deep azure that darkened to midnight blue along his spine. She positioned herself just behind his massive head crest, her legs finding secure purchase in the natural ridges of his armor. The water flowing over her body adjusted instantly, forming additional anchoring points that would keep her stable through even the most violent aerial maneuvers. With a resonant roar that signaled the attack's commencement, Poseidronus launched himself skyward, thousands of dragons surging after them in a living wave of scales, wings, and focused fury.

They ascended in tight formation toward the alien mothership, its underbelly looming larger with each powerful stroke of her father's wings. The vessel's surface seemed to shift and ripple like disturbed water, making it difficult for Aquatania to maintain visual focus on any single point. Her water constructs flanked their approach, massive liquid dragons and shields positioned to intercept the first wave of alien defenses. The air grew noticeably thicker as they approached, charged with unfamiliar energy that made the fine scales along her forearms rise in instinctive warning.

"Ready yourselves!" she called to the formation leaders flying nearest. She felt her father's muscles tense beneath her, his ancient warrior instincts sensing the imminent engagement before their eyes could confirm it.

The attack came with sudden ferocity, panels along the mothership's underside sliding open to disgorge hundreds of smaller craft. Unlike conventional vessels, these fighters emerged in unnatural synchronization, their movements suggesting hive-mind coordination rather than individual pilots. Their hulls bore the same oily iridescence as their parent ship, but in motion, the effect created visual distortion that made tracking their trajectories difficult.

Defensive formation! King Poseidronus pushed his thought command, his mental voice carrying the unmistakable authority that had led armies for centuries.

The sea dragons responded instantly, positioning themselves in overlapping patterns that allowed their combined water manipulation to create a multi-layered barrier. The first alien energy weapons discharged, sickly green beams that left trails of unnatural light hanging in the air like toxic smoke. They struck the water shields with hissing fury, converting liquid to steam on contact but failing to penetrate the continuously replenished barriers.

Sky dragons launched from behind this protection, their sleeker forms accelerating with stunning speed. Lightning crackled between their extended talons before discharging in blinding forks that connected with alien craft, causing their propulsion systems to falter. Where lightning struck, the oily iridescence briefly crystallized, revealing vulnerability in the otherwise seamless hulls.

Aquatania's perception expanded as battle adrenaline sharpened her senses. She directed her independent water constructs with mere thought, sending them to reinforce areas where the defensive line threatened to buckle under concentrated alien fire. Around her, the sky erupted into chaos, dragon fire illuminating clouds in brilliant orange bursts, lightning strikes creating spiderweb patterns across the battlefield, alien energy weapons leaving ghostly green trails through the morning air.

"Their weapons target water molecule coherence," she shouted to nearby commanders, her mind analyzing the effects even amid battle. "Double-layer your shields, outer dispersal, inner cohesion!"

Sea dragons adjusted their defensive techniques, creating dual-layered barriers where the outer water absorbed and scattered energy while inner layers maintained structural integrity. The adaptation worked immediately, their shields holding longer against sustained enemy fire. Aquatania felt a momentary surge of pride at their quick implementation before returning her focus to the larger battle.

Her father maneuvered with surprising agility for his size, evading concentrated enemy fire while maintaining their trajectory toward the mothership's underside. The water armor covering Aquatania's body responded to each sudden movement, keeping her firmly anchored while protecting against energy discharges that occasionally penetrated their immediate defenses. One blast passed close enough that she felt its heat against her cheek, the water armor instantly thickening to absorb the thermal impact.

Through the chaos of battle, her eyes caught a subtle irregularity in the mothership's otherwise seamless underside. Where most of the surface flowed in smooth curves, this section featured more defined edges, a recessed area approximately half a kilometer wide where the alien metal formed what appeared to be interlocking panels.

"There," she said, pointing toward the anomaly. Her father banked slightly, bringing them close enough to confirm her suspicion. The recessed area housed what could only be a docking mechanism, currently sealed but designed to open for returning fighter craft. "That's our entry point."

King Poseidronus's rumbled acknowledgment vibrated through his scales. With a mental command enhanced by centuries of water manipulation experience, he summoned a massive pressure wave that rippled outward, signaling the nearest squadron leaders to converge on their position. Twenty elite sea dragons broke from the main defensive formation, bringing their specialized water constructs with them.

"Concentrated pressure assault on those panels," Aquatania instructed, gesturing toward the docking area. "Sky dragons, electromagnetic pulse to disrupt their locking mechanisms."

The coordinated attack began with accuracy born from generations of training. Sea dragons positioned themselves in a perfect circle around the target area, each directing pressurized water jets at specific points where panel seams were visible. Sky dragons circled above this formation, gathering atmospheric charge until lightning danced between their wings like living coronas. At Aquatania's signal, they released their combined electromagnetic pulse, a blinding flash of blue-white energy that struck the center of the sea dragons' target.

The alien panels shuddered visibly, seams that had been nearly invisible now glowing with disrupted energy. Sea dragons intensified their pressure assault, water jets narrowing to needle-thin streams that found the weakened connections with surgical precision. A groaning sound penetrated the battle noise, alien metal straining against forces it hadn't been designed to withstand.

Their momentum broke suddenly as a new wave of alien fighters emerged from previously hidden launch bays. These crafts were larger than the first wave, their weapons systems more substantial. They converged on Aquatania's strike team with a singular purpose, green energy lancing out in concentrated barrages that overwhelmed individual water shields.

Evasive pattern! King Poseidronus roared mentally, banking sharply to avoid a direct hit.

The maneuver separated them from half their strike force as alien fighters deliberately divided their formation. Through the chaos, Aquatania saw several dragons take direct hits, their scales blackening where alien energy disrupted their natural armor. Water constructs moved to provide covering fire, but the sheer number of enemy craft made maintaining formation impossible.

The attacking force split in two, one group driven back toward Zephyria's main defensive line, the other, including Aquatania and her father, pushed closer to the mothership. Communication crystals embedded in her battle harness flickered with distress signals and fragmented tactical updates as the separation widened.

Aquatania assessed their position with the rapid calculation of a battle commander. Their strike had damaged the docking mechanism, creating a potential entry point, but they now had less than half their planned insertion force. Retreat would mean losing their momentum and giving the aliens time to reinforce the vulnerability they'd discovered. Pressing forward meant continuing with insufficient numbers against unknown interior defenses.

Her fingers touched the locket containing Kieran's scale briefly. The connection felt stronger now, his presence more defined...they were close. To retreat meant potentially losing this proximity, perhaps forever if the aliens withdrew with their prisoner once they recognized the attack's true purpose.

"We press forward," she decided, her voice carrying absolute certainty despite the tactical risks. "Signal those who can still maneuver to form on my position. We've created our opening, now we use it."

King Poseidronus growled his agreement, already gathering the nearest intact squadrons with commanding sweeps of his massive tail. Eight sea dragons, five sky dragons, and three fire dragons managed to break through the alien fighter screen to rejoin them, a mere fraction of their original strike force, but each a veteran warrior with centuries of battle experience.

"That's our way in!" Aquatania shouted over the din of continued combat, pointing toward the damaged docking mechanism where panels now hung askew, revealing glimpses of the interior beyond. "Concentrated attack, create a breach large enough for full dragon entry!"

The elite team converged on the target, combining their elemental attacks in a synchronized assault that the alien defenses couldn't counter effectively. Fire dragons superheated the already damaged panels, sea dragons followed with sudden cooling that caused structural

310

fractures, and sky dragons delivered pinpoint lightning strikes to the weakened areas. Under this coordinated elemental barrage, the alien docking bay began to crumble, their entry to the mothership's heart opening before them.

The breach yawned open like a wound in the mothership's side, edges of alien metal curled outward where their combined elemental assault had torn through the docking bay doors. Aquatania slid from her father's back as he landed on the threshold, her water armor flowing more thickly around her body in anticipation of unknown threats. The atmosphere that escaped from the opening carried unfamiliar scents, something metallic yet organic, like blood mixed with machine oil.

She stepped into the area first, her enhanced senses scanning for immediate dangers as her elite team followed, the last few sealing the breach behind them with strategic ice formations that would slow any pursuers. The docking bay stretched before them, its dimensions distorted by the unnatural architecture that seemed to reject conventional geometry...angles that should've been straight curved subtly, surfaces that appeared solid rippled with barely perceptible movement, as if the ship itself breathed.

"The corridors ahead will be too narrow for most dragon forms," Aquatania observed, studying the openings that led deeper into the vessel. "We need mobility and stealth now, not raw power."

King Poseidronus nodded, his massive form already beginning the transformation. Scales receded in waves of blue light as his draconic mass condensed into human shape, leaving a regal warrior with midnight-blue scale patterns still visible along his forearms and neck. Around them, other dragons followed suit, their transformations filling the docking bay with brief flashes of colored light as they assumed their humanoid forms.

"Talon, Riptide, Ember," Aquatania addressed three

smaller dragons—a sky dragon barely past adolescence, a sea dragon known for reconnaissance skills, and a forest dragon with exceptional healing abilities. "Remain in dragon form. Your size allows maneuverability, and we may need your natural abilities without the delay of transformation."

The three dragons acknowledged her command with dips of their heads, positioning themselves among the transformed warriors like living weapons to be deployed at strategic moments.

They moved deeper into the ship in tight formation, passing through an antechamber where alien craft in various stages of repair hung suspended in unknown energy fields. The walls here confirmed Aquatania's first impression…they weren't simply decorated with organic patterns but were partially alive, pulsing with subtle movement that sent ripples across the surface. Conduits that might have been technological or vascular ran through the walls, carrying luminescent fluids in rhythmic pulses.

"The atmosphere is denser here," one of the sky dragons whispered, his heightened sensitivity to air composition making him unusually perceptive. "Higher oxygen content, but something else, too. Something…wrong."

Aquatania nodded, having noticed the slight resistance when breathing. Each inhalation felt too thick, as if the air contained microscopic particles suspended in it. Her scientific mind catalogued possibilities, spores, chemical compounds, and microscopic machines, while her warrior instincts remained alert for immediate threats.

They reached a junction where three corridors branched outward, each identical in appearance save for subtle variations in the pulsing patterns of the wall conduits. Strange symbols glowed on panels at each entrance, their forms shifting slightly even as Aquatania studied them.

"These aren't static markings," she murmured, approaching one panel carefully. "They're changing in response to our presence."

Before she could examine the symbols more closely, movement registered in her peripheral vision. From the central corridor, three alien guards emerged, their segmented forms moving with that unsettling fluidity that defied normal joint limitations. Unlike the infiltrators they'd encountered previously, these wore no disguises to approximate human appearance. Their true forms were fully revealed, elongated limbs with too many joints, torsos segmented like insects but with translucent sections where internal organs could be glimpsed pulsing in unnatural rhythms, and heads that featured compound eyes surrounding what might have been sensory organs or weapons.

The aliens registered the intruders immediately, their limbs extending what looked to be specialized appendages that began glowing with the familiar sickly green energy of their weapons systems. The first one discharged before Aquatania could shout a warning, the energy blast streaking toward the nearest sky dragon warrior.

Without conscious thought, Aquatania extended her awareness to the moisture in the air, significantly more abundant in this alien atmosphere than she'd initially realized. Water molecules responded instantly, coalescing into a shield that intercepted the energy blast. The water hissed and boiled at the point of impact, but it dissipated the energy rather than allowing it to reach its target.

"Engage!" King Poseidronus commanded, already drawing his ceremonial trident that crackled with ancient sea magic.

The corridor erupted into close-quarters combat, dragons moving with the coordinated precision of warriors who'd trained together for centuries. Sky dragons utilized their superior speed, darting past alien defenses to strike at vulnerable joint connections. Fire dragons channeled controlled bursts of flame through specialized weapons

313

designed for interior combat, the concentrated heat causing alien exoskeletons to crack and bubble.

Aquatania's combat style had transformed completely since her communion with the sacred pool. Where once she'd maintained distance as a water manipulator, now she engaged directly, her water armor providing protection equivalent to full dragon scales. She extended her awareness to all moisture within twenty feet, giving her precise knowledge of enemy positions even when the direct line of sight was obscured.

An alien guard lunged toward her, multiple limbs extending with unnatural speed. Aquatania stepped into the attack rather than retreating, water flowing from her armor to form a blade that sheared through two of the alien's appendages with molecular precision. The creature emitted a high-pitched sound that might have been pain or rage, its compound gaze fixing on her with predatory focus.

Its remaining limbs reconfigured, forming what appeared to be specialized acid delivery systems, droplets of corrosive fluid spraying toward her face. Aquatania's water armor responded without conscious direction, thickening instantly to intercept the acid. Where the two liquids met, she manipulated the molecular interaction, neutralizing the corrosive compounds through perfect pH balance before they could penetrate her defenses.

"Their nervous systems are distributed throughout their bodies," she called to her teammates, scientific observation guiding her next strike. "No central brain, target junction points between segments!"

She demonstrated by forming a water spear that pierced precisely where the alien's torso connected to its lower body, disrupting the coordination between the upper and lower limbs. The creature's movements became erratic, limbs working at cross purposes as neural control fragmented. A final thrust of water, flash-frozen at the moment of impact, shattered the weakened junction point completely.

With their superior combat techniques guided by Aquatania's scientific insights, the dragon team dispatched the alien guards efficiently. King Poseidronus approached a glowing panel that appeared to be a control interface, its surface rippling with the same strange symbols they'd observed earlier.

"Can you make sense of this?" he asked her, recognizing her superior analytical abilities.

Aquatania studied the interface, noticing patterns within the seemingly random shifts of the alien symbols. "These aren't just markings," she realized. "They're responsive, changing based on input and environment." She extended her hand cautiously, not quite touching the surface but allowing her water armor to interact with the field it emitted.

The interface reacted immediately, symbols reorganizing in what appeared to be a response to the water's molecular structure. Aquatania adjusted the composition of her water armor slightly, changing mineral content and electrical conductivity in subtle increments. The symbols shifted again, some stabilizing into fixed positions while others continued to flow.

"It's a map," she announced as comprehension dawned. "Not visual as we understand it, but chemical, information encoded in molecular structures." Her scientific background allowed her to interpret the patterns where others saw only random movement. "The ship maps itself through chemical markers, like how insects navigate by pheromone trails."

With careful manipulations of her water armor's composition, she coaxed more information from the alien interface. The map expanded in her understanding, revealing the mothership's internal structure through patterns rather than conventional visual representation.

"Here," she said, pointing to a section where symbols pulsed with particular intensity. "This is their central laboratory. The molecular patterns match research and biological containment signatures." Her finger moved to another location directly above. "And this...this must be their command center. The patterns suggest communication hub functionality and decision-tree algorithms."

"Where would they keep prisoners?" King Poseidronus asked. The question was laden with unspoken concern for Kieran.

Aquatania studied the chemical map further, her water armor absorbing and analyzing molecular signatures from the interface. "The laboratory," she concluded with certainty that made her heart constrict. "They wouldn't separate valuable test subjects from their research facilities." She didn't voice what this implied about Kieran's treatment during captivity, but her jaw tightened visibly.

"We have two objectives then," her father said. "Rescue our people and confront the alien leadership."

The elite team gathered around as Aquatania transferred her understanding of the ship's layout to a more conventional tactical display using water constructs. The liquid formed a three-dimensional representation of critical pathways and potential hazard zones, hovering in the air between them.

"We split into two teams," she decided, strategic necessity overriding her desire to keep their already reduced force united. "One team to the command center to disrupt their leadership and communication systems, one team to the laboratory for extraction."

King Poseidronus studied the water map with the experienced eye of a military commander. "I will lead the strike on their command center," he stated, his tone allowing no argument. "Six warriors should be sufficient with proper elemental balance."

Aquatania nodded, already selecting the team composition in her mind. "I'll lead the extraction team to the laboratory." She paused, meeting her father's eyes directly. "Kieran is there. I can feel it through our connection." Her hand touched the locket briefly, confirming the strengthened sense of his presence.

For a moment, she saw concern flash across her father's features, not questioning her decision but recognizing the emotional complexity it carried. "Be mindful of your duty to all prisoners, not just one," he said quietly.

"I am," she answered with equal softness. "But I'm also the most qualified to understand whatever research they're conducting. If they've developed countermeasures to our cure, I need to see it firsthand."

The logic was sound, providing rational justification for what her heart had already decided. Her father must have recognized both the strategic validity and the personal necessity in her choice, giving a single nod of approval.

They divided their forces with quick efficiency, balancing elemental abilities between the teams. As they prepared to separate at the junction leading to their respective targets, King Poseidronus clasped Aquatania's shoulder briefly.

"The water remembers," he said, echoing her great-grandmother's wisdom from the sacred pool.

"And so do we," she completed the ancient saying, water armor flowing between them in momentary connection before they turned toward their separate paths into the heart of the alien vessel.

The corridors narrowed as Aquatania led her team deeper into the mothership's scientific sector, each junction bringing stronger resistance from alien guards. These defenders fought with increasing desperation, their tactics suggesting not just military discipline but fanatical protection of what lay beyond. She noticed subtle changes in the environment, the organic components of the walls pulsing faster, the air growing even thicker with unfamiliar particles that her water armor automatically filtered from each breath.

The temperature dropped noticeably, condensation

forming on metallic surfaces that provided her with additional water sources to weaponize. Whatever the aliens protected in their central laboratory, they had created ideal conditions for a sea dragon's combat abilities, a tactical error that Aquatania exploited with ruthless efficiency.

"They're concentrating forces ahead," a seasoned fire dragon warrior said, his scales still partially visible along his jawline despite his human form. "More than standard security protocols would justify."

Aquatania nodded, processing this tactical anomaly. "They're protecting something of critical value, something they fear we might understand." She formed water daggers between her fingers, the liquid hardening to crystalline sharpness as she prepared for the next engagement. "Stay tight. Conservation formation until we breach their inner security."

They encountered another squad of alien guards at the next junction. These were equipped with more advanced weaponry than the previous defenders. The aliens had adapted their tactics, focusing concentrated fire on water-users first, evidence they'd identified the particular threat Aquatania's abilities posed. She responded by creating layered water shields that absorbed and dissipated their energy weapons while her team circled to attack from multiple angles.

A young sky dragon darted past alien defenses with blinding speed, electricity crackling between her fingertips as she targeted neural junction points Aquatania had identified in earlier encounters. A sea dragon veteran created localized pressure differentials that disrupted alien communication devices, isolating individuals from their hive-mind coordination. Working in perfect harmony, they neutralized the defenders efficiently, though not without cost...two warriors sustained injuries that limited their combat effectiveness.

"Continue," Aquatania ordered the wounded pair. "But shift to defensive support. Conserve your strength."

Beyond the junction lay a curved hallway lined with transparent chambers, not holding cells, but observation tanks filled with viscous fluid that glowed with the same sickly green energy as alien weapons. Aquatania approached the first tank cautiously, her water armor thickening protectively as she peered through its crystal-clear surface.

The horror within froze her momentarily, a partially formed creature suspended in nutrient solution, its features a grotesque hybrid of dragon and alien biologies. Scaled limbs ended in segmented appendages, a reptilian spine fused with exoskeletal components along its length. Most disturbing were the half-formed wings, draconic in structure but veined with alien tissue that pulsed with an unnatural rhythm.

"Ancestors preserve us," one of her team whispered, voice thick with revulsion. "What are they doing?"

Aquatania moved from tank to tank, her scientific mind analyzing the progression of experiments despite her visceral disgust. Each chamber contained a different iteration, some emphasizing draconic traits, others favoring alien physiology, all disturbing failures of forced hybridization. Her eyes catalogued developmental stages, genetic incorporation techniques, and chemical enhancement systems with clinical detachment that barely contained her growing rage.

"They're trying to create hybrids," she explained, her voice tight with controlled fury. The markings surged across her arms and throat like molten lightning, the runes etching themselves in sharp clarity. They burned brighter than before, as though feeding on the storm inside her, a warning sigil written by something older and far stronger than her will. "Creatures that combine dragon transformation abilities with alien environmental adaptations." She pointed to specific features visible in the most developed specimens. "These respiratory structures, they're designed to process both our atmosphere and whatever toxic environment they intend to create through terraforming."

The implications struck her with sudden clarity. "They don't just want our world, they want our abilities. They're trying to incorporate our transformation genetics into their own species."

A sea dragon warrior growled, his hand moving to his weapon. "Should we destroy them? These abominations?"

Aquatania shook her head, though the same instinct had flared within her. "Not yet. They may contain information crucial to understanding their broader plans." Her eyes hardened as she turned away from the tanks. "Besides...Kieran first. Then we can decide what knowledge to preserve or destroy."

They pressed forward with renewed urgency, past more experimental chambers containing progressively more advanced hybrid attempts. At the end of the corridor stood a massive sealed doorway, clearly the entrance to the central laboratory. Unlike other barriers they'd encountered, this featured multiple locking mechanisms and was constructed of substantially thicker materials.

"Standard breaching won't work," Aquatania assessed, studying the door's composition. "This is designed to contain catastrophic experimental failures." Her mind worked through possible approaches, calculating material strengths against available resources. "We need a combined elemental assault, precisely coordinated."

She positioned her team strategically, fire dragons at the corners where locking mechanisms connected to the frame, sea dragons at center mass where pressure points would create maximum structural stress, and sky dragons at electronic control panels where electrical manipulation might override security protocols.

"On my mark," she instructed, gathering moisture from

the surrounding air into a compressed sphere between her palms. The water responded to her enhanced abilities, molecules aligning in patterns that would maximize penetrative force when released. "Simultaneous assault, maintained for fifteen seconds regardless of initial results."

At her signal, they unleashed their combined elemental powers. Fire dragons generated concentrated heat that approached metal's melting point, focusing on locking bolts recessed within the frame. Sea dragons, following Aquatania's lead, directed pressurized water jets at structural weak points she'd identified. Sky dragons sent precise electrical surges through control panels, disrupting security protocols with calculated overloads.

Aquatania's contribution merged science and ancestral magic. The water between her palms transformed into superheated steam under molecular compression, then was directed through microscopic imperfections in the door's surface. Where the steam penetrated, she manipulated its expansion with devastating precision, creating internal fractures throughout the barrier's structure.

The door groaned under their assault, seams appearing where none had been visible before. Alarm systems activated, warning lights pulsing along the corridor as the laboratory's defenses registered the breach attempt. With a final concentrated effort, the combined elemental forces overcame engineered resistance, the massive door buckled inward, locking mechanisms shearing from their housings as the barrier collapsed.

Aquatania moved through the opening first, water armor flowing around her in combat readiness. The sprawling laboratory beyond was arranged in alien disarray, equipment of unknown purpose placed in patterns that defied conventional scientific organization. Containers of luminescent fluid lined the walls, connected by pulsing conduits to central examination stations. Data interfaces flickered with the same shifting symbols they'd encountered previously, information streaming in patterns too rapid for even her enhanced perception to track completely.

In the chamber's center stood an elevated examination platform surrounded by diagnostic equipment. Strapped to its surface by translucent restraints that pulsed with energy, lay Kieran.

Her heart seized at the sight of him. His body appeared intact but altered. Patches of scales were visible across his torso, where his transformation ability had been artificially stimulated. Monitoring devices were attached to these areas with fiber-thin connections that penetrated beneath the scales themselves. Tubes ran from his arms to collection chambers filled with crimson fluid flecked with gold, fire dragon blood being harvested for its transformative properties. His eyes were closed, his face drawn with exhaustion, but the steady rise and fall of his chest confirmed he lived.

"Secure the perimeter," Aquatania ordered, her voice betraying none of the emotion that threatened to overwhelm her scientific detachment. "Check for other prisoners and watch those access points."

As her team moved to establish defensive positions, she approached the examination platform, water armor flowing from her fingertips to analyze the restraint technology. The alien energy fields responded to her molecular probes, fluctuating in patterns that revealed their operational parameters. With precise manipulation, she created counter-frequencies in her water constructs, disrupting the fields enough to weaken their cohesion.

"Kieran," she said softly, one hand moving to his face while the other continued working on his restraints.

His eyes opened immediately, his pupils contracting sharply before focusing on her face. Recognition flooded his features, followed by an emotion too complex to name, relief and pain, and something deeper that made the water armor around her heart ripple in response.

"I knew you'd come," he said hoarsely, his voice rough from disuse or screaming, she couldn't bear to consider which. "Though your timing could use improvement." A ghost of his familiar wry humor surfaced through evident suffering.

"The cure had to reach distribution first," she explained, though the justification felt hollow now, facing the direct consequences of her choice. "I couldn't —"

"You made the right decision," he interrupted, his eyes holding hers with surprising strength despite his weakened state. "I would have made the same."

The restraints finally yielded to her counter-frequencies, dissolving into harmless particles that dissipated into the laboratory atmosphere. She carefully removed monitoring devices from his scaled patches, using her water armor to seal puncture points and minimize further fluid loss. His body was dangerously depleted, both blood and energy harvested by alien experiments that had clearly sought to understand the biological mechanisms of dragon transformation.

He sat up with her assistance, wincing as dormant muscles protested the movement. "They've been thorough in their research," he noted with grim professionalism. "They understand our transformation abilities better than we do in some respects. That's why they wanted me specifically…fire dragons manifest the most dramatic physical changes during transformation."

Aquatania supported him as he swung his legs over the platform's edge, noting how carefully he moved to minimize pain. Her water armor flowed over his injuries automatically, providing cooling relief to inflamed tissue and structural support to weakened muscles.

The moment of relative calm was shattered as alarms suddenly blared throughout the laboratory, not the security breach warnings from earlier, but a deeper, more ominous tone that pulsed in perfect synchronization with red lighting that flooded the chamber. The alien interfaces along the walls shifted to uniform patterns, all displaying the same urgent symbols in crimson illumination.

"That's their extinction protocol," Kieran said, recognizing the alarm pattern. "I've heard it during simulations they ran. They're scuttling the ship."

Automated announcements began echoing through the laboratory in the aliens' clicking, multi-toned language. Though incomprehensible to most, Kieran had clearly been exposed to it enough to grasp its meaning.

"They're initiating complete molecular destabilization," he translated, pushing himself to stand despite obvious pain. "The command structure has ordered self-destruction rather than risk capture."

"How long?" Aquatania asked, already calculating evacuation routes through her water-constructed map of the ship.

"Twenty minutes until critical cascade begins. Another three before complete structural failure." His eyes met hers with grim certainty. "They'd rather destroy all their research than let us access it."

Aquatania nodded, immediately activating the communication crystal in her battle harness. "Father, status report," she called, praying the signal could penetrate the ship's internal interference.

King Poseidronus's voice returned fragmented but audible.

"Command center... Resistance... Aliens initiating... protocols..."

"Self-destruct is active," she confirmed. "Twenty minutes to critical. We have Kieran and are withdrawing. Meet at breach point."

She turned to her team, already reorganizing their formation to accommodate wounded members and their primary extraction target. "Defensive withdrawal, maximum speed. Talon, advance scout the return path. Riptide, rear guard with countermeasures active."

As her team prepared for immediate evacuation, Aquatania's gaze returned to the experimental tanks visible through the laboratory's inner chambers. The horror they contained represented critical intelligence about alien intentions, biological evidence that might prove invaluable in understanding and countering future threats.

"Ember," she addressed the small forest dragon who'd remained in draconic form. "Memory scales." She pointed toward the most advanced hybrid specimens. "Record everything. We need evidence of what they've attempted here."

The forest dragon nodded, special membranes in her eyes capturing detailed images that would be stored in specialized scales...a biological recording system unique to her subspecies that skilled healers and scientists could later access.

Kieran stood beside her now, steadier though still requiring her support. His eyes held understanding of both her tactical and scientific priorities despite their desperate situation. "The central data core is there," he indicated a pulsing column in the laboratory's far section. "It contains their complete research database, including terraforming formulas."

The timing was impossible. Extracting such data would require minutes they couldn't spare with the self-destruct counting down. Yet leaving it meant losing crucial information that might save lives in future confrontations.

The decision crystallized in her mind with sudden clarity. "Riptide, Ember, extraction team with Kieran, begin withdrawal immediately." She straightened, water armor flowing into more specialized configurations around her body. "I'll extract critical data and follow within five minutes."

Kieran's hand caught her arm, his weakened grip still conveying urgent concern. "Aquatania, there's no time—"

"Trust me," she replied, the water armor between them rippling with the connection that transcended physical touch. "I didn't come this far to lose you again."

Understanding passed between them, not acceptance, but recognition of her authority and capabilities. With evident reluctance, he nodded, allowing the extraction team to support him toward the exit.

As her team began their withdrawal, Aquatania turned toward the alien data core, water armor forming specialized interfaces along her fingertips. The self-destruct countdown continued its ominous progression, each pulse of the alarm marking precious seconds lost.

CHAPTER SEVENTEEN

The alien data core pulsed with sickly luminescence as Aquatania approached, her fingers extending into liquid filaments that probed its surface. Water from her armor flowed like living mercury, seeking interface points among the strange geometries of alien technology. The self-destruct countdown continued its ominous progression, each crimson flash marking seconds lost. She'd sent her team ahead with what they believed was Kieran, but something felt wrong...the connection through his scale remained undiminished, as if they hadn't found him at all.

Her water tendrils penetrated the core's outer membrane, encountering resistance that felt like pushing through thick gel rather than solid matter. The alien technology responded to her intrusion with a series of rapid pulses, data streams accelerating as if attempting to transfer vital information before destruction. Patterns flowed through her water armor, translated from alien code into sensations her mind could interpret, not quite images or sounds, but impressions that formed coherent concepts in her consciousness.

The first impression hit her with sickening clarity...deception. The being they'd rescued wasn't Kieran. A cold weight settled in her stomach as the data confirmed what her instincts had whispered. The aliens had created a simulacrum, a biological duplicate with surface-level memories but without the quintessence that made Kieran himself. Her team was escorting an empty shell, perhaps even a trap.

Aquatania's hand moved to the locket containing Kieran's scale. It pulsed against her skin with unmistakable warmth, a resonance that had never diminished despite the *rescue*. The connection remained unbroken because Kieran was still here, somewhere deeper in the ship. She closed her eyes, focusing on the subtle directional pull she'd always sensed but never fully trusted until now. Northwest, several levels below her current position, that's where the real Kieran waited.

"Riptide," she whispered into her communication crystal, "the extraction is compromised. What you have is not Kieran. Secure it for study, but treat it as hostile."

Static answered her, the ship's self-destruct protocols already interfering with communication. Seventeen minutes remained before the molecular cascade would render the entire vessel unstable. She had to move quickly.

Abandoning the data core after extracting what critical information her water armor could absorb, Aquatania turned toward a service shaft indicated in the ship's schematics. The organic-iridescent walls pulsed faster around her, as if the ship itself sensed her intentions and sought to impede them. Her water armor flowed around obstacles, creating streamlined patterns that reduced resistance as she moved with increased urgency.

The locket grew warmer against her skin with each correct turn, cooler when she veered off course. Following this primal compass, she navigated through maintenance corridors where the ship's organic components were more exposed, vein-like conduits pulsing with luminescent fluids, membrane walls that breathed with subtle movements. The alien architecture became increasingly biological as she descended, less mechanical and more visceral, as if approaching the living heart of the vessel.

A junction opened before her, revealing a corridor lined with translucent panels that glowed with internal light. The locket burned against her chest, its heat almost uncomfortable through her water armor. Kieran was close, perhaps behind one of these panels. She extended her awareness through the moisture in the air, sensing two distinct heartbeats beyond the corridor's end, both alien, their rhythms too rapid and arhythmic to be anything else.

Guards. She'd expected as much. If they held the real Kieran, they would protect him with their most capable defenders.

Aquatania flattened herself against the organic wall, feeling it pulse against her back as she observed the guards' movements. They stood with mechanistic precision on either side of a sealed chamber, their segmented limbs holding weapons that hummed with stored energy. Unlike the guards she'd encountered earlier, these moved with subtle fluidity that suggested higher functioning...elite protectors rather than standard security.

She formed water blades along her forearms, molecular-thin edges hardening to crystalline sharpness. Surprise would be her advantage; once they sounded an alarm, extraction would become exponentially more difficult. Taking a deep breath, she propelled herself forward with a thought, water jets at her heels accelerating her movement to blur-inducing speed.

The first guard registered her approach a fraction of a second too late. Her water blade sliced through its communication appendage before it could activate, the second blade piercing the junction between thorax and head. The alien collapsed in near silence, only a soft chittering sound escaping as its systems failed.

The second guard proved more alert, its weapon discharging a burst of green energy that would have dissolved standard armor on contact. Aquatania's water shield absorbed the impact, superheated molecules converting instantly to steam that she directed back at her attacker. Temporarily blinded, the guard failed to track her as she circled behind, water blades reforming after their brief vaporization. With surgical precision, she severed its primary neural pathways where they clustered at the base of its skull-analogue. The guard dropped without raising an alarm, limbs twitching in disconnected spasms.

The sealed chamber door confronted her next, a massive barrier of unknown alloy interwoven with the same organic fibers that composed much of the ship. No control panel offered conventional access. This room was designed for absolute isolation. Aquatania placed her palms against the door's surface, extending her awareness through her water armor to detect vibrations and thermal variations that might reveal its mechanism.

She found no electronic lock to override, no mechanical system to force. Instead, the door responded to specific biological signatures. The guards' unique molecular patterns granted access through direct contact with the organic components. With clinical detachment, she severed a sensory appendage from the nearest guard, her water armor preserving its neural activity long enough to maintain its biological signature.

Pressing the still-living tissue against the door's organic interface, she felt the barrier respond, fibers relaxing as recognition protocols activated. The massive door peeled open like separating flesh, revealing the chamber beyond.

The room blazed with harsh white light that contrasted sharply with the organic reds and greens of the outer ship. Clinical and sterile, it resembled a laboratory more than a prison cell. In its center stood a raised medical platform, to which Kieran was secured by translucent restraints that pulsed with energy. Monitoring devices surrounded him, their displays flickering with real-time data collected from sensors embedded in his skin.

Kieran's head turned at the sound of the door, his eyes narrowing against the corridor's relative darkness before recognition dawned. Despite obvious exhaustion and pain, his lips curved into a weak smile.

"Took you long enough, Princess," he managed, voice

raspy from disuse.

Aquatania rushed to the platform, water tendrils already extending to analyze the restraint technology. "I got a bit sidetracked with your impersonator," she replied, fingers hovering over the monitoring equipment as she assessed which could be safely removed.

"They made a copy?" Kieran winced as her water sliced through the first restraint, blood flowing back into his numbed limb. "Flattering, I suppose."

Her water tendrils worked with precise efficiency, cutting through his bonds while simultaneously sealing the puncture wounds left by alien monitoring devices. His skin was unnaturally pale, marked with geometric patterns where samples had been extracted for analysis. Beneath these surface wounds, she sensed deeper damage, cellular disruption consistent with forced transformation attempts.

"Can you shift?" she asked urgently, knowing their escape would be considerably easier with his dragon form's natural weapons and defenses.

Kieran closed his eyes, concentration evident in the tension of his jaw. Scales briefly shimmered beneath his skin before fading, the transformation stalling before it could complete. He exhaled shakily, disappointment and frustration evident in his expression.

"They've been injecting me with something," he explained, his eyes opening again to meet hers. "Some compound that interferes with the transformation trigger. It's temporary, but effective."

Aquatania helped him to a sitting position, her water armor flowing partially around him to support muscles weakened by prolonged restraint. As he swung his legs over the edge of the platform, ship alarms suddenly blared to life, bathing the chamber in pulsing red light.

"That would be the welcoming committee," Kieran remarked dryly, gripping her shoulder as he tested his weight on unsteady legs. "Please tell me you have an exit strategy."

"Several," Aquatania confirmed, already forming water shields around them both. "None particularly pleasant."

The chamber door began to close, organic components responding to the security alert. Through the narrowing opening, she glimpsed movement in the corridor beyond, reinforcements approaching at speed. Time had just become their most precious and limited resource.

Aquatania thrust her hand toward the closing door, water surging from her armor in a pressurized jet that forced the organic components apart just enough for them to slip through. She supported Kieran's weight against her side, his arm draped across her shoulders as they stumbled into the corridor. The alien guards she'd dispatched earlier lay motionless on the floor, their strange bodily fluids pooling beneath segmented limbs. Alarms continued their urgent pulsing, the ship's crimson emergency lighting casting everything in blood-tinted shadows.

"Left," Kieran rasped, his breathing labored but controlled. "Service conduit thirty meters ahead. Less security."

She adjusted their course, noting how he carried himself with deliberate movements that minimized pain while maximizing efficiency, the discipline of a warrior even in his weakened state. His body felt unnaturally warm against hers, fever heat radiating through the thin medical garment the aliens had left him in.

"They've been studying our immunity," he explained between careful breaths as they moved. "Not just to the Red Death, but to all diseases. Dragons in particular." His fingers tightened momentarily on her shoulder as they navigated around a junction. "They're trying to modify the contagion to affect dragons in all forms, targeting the transformation mechanism directly."

Aquatania processed this information even as she maintained vigilance for approaching threats. The implication was clear...if successful, such a modified contagion would eliminate their greatest advantage against the terraforming process. Dragons would become as vulnerable as humans, their natural resilience compromised at the cellular level.

"How close are they to succeeding?" she asked, pausing at an intersection to scan for movement.

"Too close." Kieran's mouth set in a grim line. "They've achieved temporary suppression, as you can see." He attempted to summon flame to his fingertips, producing only the faintest flicker before it extinguished. "They were extracting transformation enzymes from my blood to isolate the trigger mechanisms. Using me as their primary research subject."

Her water armor rippled with barely contained rage, responding to emotions she kept from her face. Instead of responding verbally, she extended her armor around him, the living water flowing partially across his torso and limbs. The molecular structure adapted instantly to his unique biological signature, supporting weakened muscles while providing a cooling barrier against his fever-hot skin.

Kieran exhaled softly as the water made contact, relief evident in the slight relaxation of his features. "That's...remarkably helpful," he admitted. "Your control has improved."

"Sacred communion," she explained briefly, guiding them toward the service conduit he'd indicated. "We have much to discuss when we're not fleeing with fourteen minutes left until molecular destabilization."

The service conduit proved to be a narrow passage where the ship's organic and mechanical components were more exposed, vein-like tubes carrying luminescent fluids alongside conventional power conduits. The ceiling hung low, forcing them to duck as they navigated between pulsing organic masses that resembled internal organs more than machinery. The space smelled of ozone and something sweeter, almost medicinal.

"Secondary security node ahead," Kieran warned, his steps growing steadier as they progressed. The water armor appeared to be accelerating his recovery, providing hydration and stability his depleted body desperately needed. "Two guards are usually stationed, and automated sensors are in the flooring."

Aquatania nodded, already extending her awareness through ambient moisture to confirm his intelligence. "Three life signs," she corrected. "They've increased security since your...extraction."

Kieran's expression darkened. "After my copy went missing, no doubt." He studied the corridor ahead, tactical assessment evident in his narrowed gaze. "We need an alternate route. Main ventilation is two junctions back, but it's monitored. Waste disposal conduits below us would be unpleasant but likely unguarded."

"Or," Aquatania suggested, "we take a more direct approach." She gestured toward an organic seam in the corridor wall where two sections of the living ship material joined. "The ship's internal barriers are semi-permeable here. Designed for emergency fluid exchange between sections."

Kieran raised an eyebrow. "You can penetrate that?"

"The water remembers," she replied, a cryptic reference to her communion that nevertheless conveyed her confidence.

Without waiting for further discussion, she pressed her palm against the seam, water flowing from her armor into the microscopic spaces between cell-like structures. The organic material resisted initially, then yielded as her water manipulated its chemical receptors, mimicking the signals that would naturally trigger expansion. The seam widened gradually, organic fibers parting to reveal a narrow passage into an adjacent maintenance shaft.

They slipped through just as distant footsteps echoed

down the corridor, reinforcements responding to security alerts. The organic seam sealed behind them, leaving no evidence of their passage. The maintenance shaft was dimly lit by bioluminescent nodules that pulsed with the ship's natural rhythm, providing just enough light to navigate by.

"Command center?" Aquatania asked, knowing they needed to reach the ship's control systems to have any hope of preventing the self-destruct sequence.

"Three levels up," Kieran confirmed. "But we'll need to cross the central atrium. No avoiding it if we want direct access."

They moved through the maintenance shaft with increasing speed, Kieran's strength visibly returning with each passing minute. The water armor continued to support him, but he relied on it less as his own body recovered from the immediate effects of his captivity. His breathing evened out, his movements becoming more fluid and deliberate. Whatever the aliens had used to suppress his transformation abilities was metabolizing out of his system faster than expected.

Their progress halted abruptly as they reached the shaft's end, finding themselves at a junction overlooking a broad corridor where a patrol of four alien guards moved in precise formation. Unlike the guards they'd encountered earlier, these carried more sophisticated weapons...crystalline devices that hummed with stored energy. Taking cover behind a protruding organic growth, they observed the patrol's movements, waiting for an opportunity.

"We can't avoid them," Kieran whispered, his assessment matching her own. "They're guarding the only approach to the central atrium."

Aquatania nodded, already forming water spears that hovered silently beside her, molecular edges honed to perfect sharpness. She glanced at Kieran, noting the color returning to his face, the increased steadiness in his hands.

"Can you manage any flame yet?" she asked quietly.

In response, Kieran extended his palm, concentration evident in the tight line of his mouth. A small flame flickered to life, dancing weakly above his skin, not the roaring blaze he could typically produce, but fire nonetheless. He looked up, meeting her eyes with a hint of his old confidence.

"Just like Coral Citadel?" he asked, referencing a previous mission where they'd faced similar odds with limited resources.

The memory flashed between them, a desperate extraction from an underwater fortress, her water and his fire combining to create a steam cover while they rescued captured allies. The tactics had been improvised in the moment, yet executed with perfect synchronization born from absolute trust in each other's abilities.

"Just like Coral Citadel," she confirmed, the water spears shifting formation as she prepared.

On her signal, they launched their coordinated attack. Aquatania's water spears shot forward, two finding their marks in vital connection points between alien body segments. The creatures collapsed instantly, their neural systems severed by the molecularly sharp edges. The remaining guards turned toward the threat, weapons rising.

Kieran moved with surprising speed for his condition, the small flame in his palm expanding as he channeled his returning energy. The fire wasn't powerful enough to damage the aliens directly, but that wasn't his intention. He directed it toward Aquatania's remaining water constructs, instantly creating a dense cloud of steam that filled the corridor with impenetrable white fog.

The aliens fired blindly, energy beams cutting through steam in random patterns that missed their targets entirely. Moving through the cover they'd created, Aquatania and Kieran closed the distance. Her water blades materialized through the fog, finding vulnerable points with deadly accuracy. Kieran, though still unable to transform, utilized his combat training effectively, striking pressure points that immobilized alien limbs long enough for Aquatania to deliver finishing blows.

In less than twenty seconds, the patrol lay neutralized, not a single alarm triggered. The steam dissipated gradually, revealing the corridor beyond now clear of obstacles. Kieran stood straighter than before, his breathing quick but controlled, a light of satisfaction in his eyes despite the exertion.

"Effective as ever," he noted, glancing down at his hand where the flame had grown noticeably stronger. "I'm recovering faster than expected."

"My water armor is accelerating your natural healing," Aquatania explained, already moving toward the atrium entrance. "Cellular repair at the molecular level."

Kieran followed, his gait steadier with each step. "Remind me to thank your ancestors when we survive this."

As they approached the central atrium, the ship's architecture changed dramatically, organic components giving way to more conventional alien technology. The corridor widened, the ceiling soaring upward into a vast open space that served as the mothership's primary transit hub. Multiple levels rose above them, connected by energy bridges that pulsed with the same sickly green light as the alien weapons.

"The command center is there." Kieran indicated a heavily fortified structure on the uppermost level, its entrance guarded by what appeared to be elite warriors. "The commander oversees all operations personally, including my *examinations*." His voice hardened on the final word, a glimpse of controlled fury beneath his professional demeanor.

Aquatania studied the defenses, calculating approaches, and vulnerabilities with tactical precision. The self-destruct countdown continued its relentless progression, twelve minutes remaining before the molecular cascade would render escape impossible. Her gaze shifted to Kieran, noting his improved condition, the increasing steadiness in his movements, the dangerous gleam returning to his eyes as small flames now danced continuously between his fingers.

"Ready for a proper fight?" she asked, water armor flowing into more aggressive configurations around her limbs.

Kieran's lips curved into a smile that contained no humor, only determination and the promise of retribution long delayed. "I've been ready since they first strapped me down."

Together they moved toward the atrium, their steps synchronized in the familiar rhythm of warriors who'd faced countless battles side by side. The water flowed. The fire burned. And between them, an unspoken promise, the aliens would pay for every moment of suffering they'd inflicted.

The central atrium of the alien mothership stretched above them like the inside of a mechanical cathedral, energy bridges connecting multiple levels in glowing green lattices. Aquatania and Kieran pressed against a curved bulkhead, studying the defenses that guarded their approach to the command center. Security drones hovered at regular intervals, their crystalline sensors sweeping in predictable patterns across open areas. Where the organic components of the ship had felt almost primitive, this section hummed with advanced technology, force fields shimmered almost imperceptibly around critical access points, and scanning beams periodically swept the walkways.

"Direct approach is suicide," Kieran murmured, his gaze focused on the uppermost level where energy conduits converged around a massive doorway. "Those drones detect molecular disruption. They'll identify your water armor instantly."

Aquatania nodded, having already reached the same

conclusion. "Alternatives?"

Kieran's eyes tracked the movement of the security systems, analyzing patterns with the practiced expertise of someone who'd been forced to observe them for weeks. "There." He indicated a barely visible seam in the curved wall approximately twenty meters to their right. "Maintenance shaft. I watched repair drones emerge from there during system recalibrations. It bypasses the main entrance."

"And takes us where exactly?"

"Antechamber adjacent to the control center." His expression darkened, his jaw tightening. "The commander will be inside. Nasty piece of work, watched all my *examinations* personally."

The clinical term couldn't disguise the reality it represented. Aquatania's water armor rippled with barely suppressed fury, responding to emotions she kept from her face. She'd seen enough of his injuries to understand what those *examinations* had entailed, systematic biological exploitation disguised as scientific inquiry.

"Tell me about this commander," she requested as they calculated their approach to the maintenance shaft, her tone deliberately neutral despite the anger simmering beneath.

"Larger than the others. Enhanced exoskeleton with integrated technological components." Kieran's description remained professional, though a muscle jumped in his cheek. "Multiple specialized limbs, at least eight that I observed. Communicates directly with the ship through neural interfaces. Refers to itself as Evolution Director in their language."

He paused, his eyes momentarily unfocused as if seeing something beyond their immediate surroundings. "It took particular interest in fire dragon physiology. The temperature thresholds…and the transformation trigger mechanisms. Seemed almost…fascinated by the process."

Aquatania absorbed this intelligence, cataloging it

alongside her existing knowledge of alien hierarchy. This commander wasn't merely a military leader but a specialized researcher, directly involved in developing the modified contagion that threatened dragon immunity. The personal nature of Kieran's captivity wasn't coincidental. It had been the targeted extraction of a specific dragon subspecies.

They moved along the perimeter of the atrium, using structural supports for cover as they approached the maintenance access. Timing their advance between drone sensor sweeps required precise coordination, each movement calculated to exploit blind spots in the security network. Kieran's intimate knowledge of the patterns proved invaluable, and his experience as their prisoner now turned against his captors.

The maintenance shaft entrance consisted of an oval panel that blended almost seamlessly with the surrounding wall. No conventional locking mechanism secured it. Instead, Kieran indicated a specific pattern of pressure points that needed to be activated simultaneously.

"Drone access sequence," he explained. "Observed it seventeen times during captivity."

Aquatania extended water tendrils from her armor, the liquid filaments pressing against the designated points with precise pressure. The panel responded with a soft hissing sound, organic components relaxing to create an opening just large enough for them to slip through single file.

The shaft beyond was cramped and uncomfortably warm, designed for mechanical drones rather than humanoid bodies. They crawled through the narrow space, surrounded by pulsing conduits that carried energy and information throughout the ship's nervous system. Occasional junction points offered glimpses into other sections of the vessel, engineering compartments where repair drones worked on damaged systems, communication hubs where data streams flowed in luminescent rivers.

"Self-destruct sequence can only be aborted from the command center," Kieran whispered as they navigated a particularly tight bend. "Manual override requires the commander's biological signature."

"Then we'll just have to borrow it," Aquatania replied, her water armor shifting slightly in anticipation.

They reached the terminus of the maintenance shaft after several minutes of careful navigation. A small observation grille provided visual access to the antechamber beyond, a rectangular space serving as the final security checkpoint before the command center proper. Four elite guards stood at attention, their forms substantially different from standard alien soldiers. These creatures wore integrated armor that seemed fused with their exoskeletons, their weapons not carried but embedded in specialized limbs that ended in crystalline energy projectors.

"Elite Protectors," Kieran said quietly on a breath, recognition and wariness evident in his tone. "Genetically enhanced, neurally linked to the commander. They react to threats before conscious recognition occurs."

Aquatania studied their positioning, noting the perfect symmetry of their formation, each guard angled to cover the others' vulnerable areas, creating overlapping fields of protection with no exploitable gaps. Standard tactics would fail against such disciplined defenders.

"Thoughts?" she asked, already forming her own strategy but valuing his insight.

"They anticipate conventional attacks," Kieran replied, flames now dancing more confidently between his fingers as his body continued purging the suppression compounds. "Their neural enhancements let them predict standard combat patterns."

A silent understanding passed between them. They would need to be unpredictable, abandoning formal training for improvisation that no algorithmic prediction could anticipate.

Aquatania extended her hand, water flowing from her armor to form a small model of the antechamber between them, highlighting guard positions and potential approaches.

Kieran nodded, understanding without words. He placed his palm near the water construct, the heat from his gradually returning powers causing steam to rise from specific points marking primary and secondary targets in their coordinated strike. The wordless planning was completed in moments — communication achieved through the intimate knowledge of each other's combat styles.

Aquatania dissolved the water model, redirecting the liquid to form specialized weapons along her arms and legs. She glanced at Kieran, raising an eyebrow in silent question.

He answered by producing a flame that, while not yet at full strength, burned significantly brighter than before, enough for their purposes. His nod confirmed readiness.

She placed her palm against the maintenance shaft's exit panel, water flowing into its operating mechanism to trigger release protocols. The panel slid open with surprising quietness, giving them the moment of surprise they needed.

Aquatania moved first, water propelling her forward with an explosive force that carried her directly into the center of the guard formation. Rather than attacking immediately, she created a spherical water barrier that expanded outward in all directions, momentarily separating the four guards from each other. The unexpected tactic, defense used as offense, confused their predictive algorithms long enough for Kieran to make his move.

He launched from the maintenance shaft opening, fire trailing from his hands in controlled arcs that targeted not the guards themselves but the environmental systems above them. Heat sensors triggered emergency protocols, activating suppression systems that released chemical retardants from ceiling panels. The falling particles created a momentary visual barrier while simultaneously introducing variables that the guards' prediction systems couldn't process effectively.

The elite guards recovered quickly, specialized limbs reconfiguring to compensate for the environmental changes. One fired a concentrated energy burst that struck Aquatania's water shield, the liquid absorbing and dispersing the energy rather than shattering as expected. Another guard launched itself toward Kieran, multiple limbs extending to immobilize the perceived weaker target.

Aquatania's water armor flowed into offensive formation, forming twin blades that sliced through the nearest guard's weapon arm before it could discharge a second blast. The alien hissed in pain or rage, acidic fluid spraying from the severed limb. Her armor hardened instantly where the acid made contact, neutralizing it before it could reach her skin.

Kieran ducked beneath the attacking guard's grasp, his smaller flame concentrated into a precise cutting tool that severed neural connectors visible at the creature's joint sections. Not powerful enough to kill, but sufficient to disrupt the specialized limbs' coordination. The guard's movements became erratic, and its systems were attempting to compensate for the sudden loss of missing neural inputs.

The battle collapsed into brutal close-quarters combat, alien guards pressing their numerical advantage while Aquatania and Kieran exploited their superior coordination and adaptability. Energy weapons discharged in erratic patterns, green beams cutting through the air close enough that Aquatania felt their heat against her water armor. Acid spit hissed against her shields, each molecular attack countered by automatic adjustments in her water's composition.

Kieran fought with the efficiency of a warrior, conserving limited resources, each flame precisely targeted to disrupt rather than destroy. What he lacked in raw power, he compensated for with intimate knowledge of alien physiology, striking vulnerable connection points that their standard armor left exposed.

The guards' prediction algorithms failed against their unpredictable attack patterns. Their enhanced reflexes were countered by Aquatania's water manipulation, altering the physical environment in real-time. She created momentary platforms of ice that shifted gravity dynamics, sudden currents that pushed or pulled combatants in unexpected directions, and density variations that absorbed or redirected energy weapons.

One guard fell to coordinated assault, Kieran's flame heating its exoskeleton to vulnerable temperatures while Aquatania's water blade found the softened section. Another went down when its predictive systems suffered a cascading failure after receiving contradictory sensory inputs from manipulated environmental conditions.

The third guard proved more adaptable, its systems learning from its fallen companions. It adjusted tactics, maintaining distance while firing sustained energy bursts that forced Aquatania to concentrate on defensive shields rather than offensive strikes. The fourth circled behind, seeking advantage against Kieran's position.

"Switch!" Aquatania called, an established command from countless previous engagements.

They moved in perfect synchronization, positions reversing in a fluid motion that confused the guards' targeting systems. Aquatania's water shield expanded to cover Kieran's previous position while his flame arced toward the guard that had been focusing on her. The unexpected tactic created a momentary opening that they exploited.

Water jets propelled Kieran upward, giving him an angle advantage over the nearest guard. His flame, though still not at full power, concentrated into a narrow beam that severed the creature's primary neural cluster. Simultaneously,

Aquatania formed water spears that penetrated the final guard's visual sensors, temporarily blinding it long enough for a decisive strike to its command centers.

The battle ended as suddenly as it had begun, four elite guards neutralized in under a minute of intensive combat. Aquatania and Kieran stood breathing heavily in the center of the antechamber, surrounded by disabled alien technology and the acrid scent of superheated exoskeleton.

"Efficient as ever," Kieran noted, a ghost of his old confidence returning despite the evident exertion. Sweat beaded on his forehead, but his hands remained steady, flames dancing between his fingers with increasing strength.

Aquatania nodded, water armor already reforming into combat configuration after the expenditure of the battle. "Your recovery is progressing faster than expected."

"Turns out rage is quite the metabolic accelerator," he replied, eyes fixed on the massive door that separated them from the command center and the alien who'd overseen his torture. "Ready?"

She formed twin water blades along her forearms, the liquid hardening to molecular sharpness that could slice through almost any material. "Let's end this."

Kieran nodded, dangerous anticipation gleaming in his eyes as small flames danced between his fingers with growing intensity. "I've imagined this moment through every *examination*. Don't disappoint me, Princess."

Together they approached the final barrier, the countdown to molecular destabilization ticking relentlessly in the background. Nine minutes remained to confront the commander and stop the self-destruct or escape the vessel before it tore itself apart at the atomic level. The door to the command center awaited, and behind it, the architect of Kieran's suffering.

The command center door responded to the elite guards' biological signatures, interpreting their proximity as authorization despite their incapacitated state. It slid open with a pneumatic hiss, revealing a vast chamber with architecture that defied conventional design principles. Curved surfaces flowed into angular structures without a logical transition, creating a space that disoriented human perception. Multiple control stations surrounded a raised central dais where the alien commander stood, larger than its subordinates, with an exoskeleton that gleamed with integrated technological enhancements. Its multiple limbs manipulated holographic controls that pulsed with data streams, creating ghostly green projections that circled its elongated form like orbiting satellites.

The commander turned as they entered, its compound gaze aimed in their direction. Unlike the other aliens they'd encountered, this one's exoskeleton featured iridescent scales that shifted colors with its movements, creating hypnotic patterns that drew and confused the eye. A neural crown encircled its upper segments, pulsing with the same rhythm as the ship's core systems.

"The princess and her pet," the commander hissed, its voice a discordant blend of mechanical translation and organic clicking that sounded like grinding metal. "How predictable."

The familiarity with which it identified them confirmed Aquatania's suspicion that the aliens had been studying Zephyria's leadership structure extensively. This wasn't merely an invasion; it was a calculated operation based on intimate knowledge of their society.

"I expected you sooner," the commander continued, limbs still moving across control interfaces without looking at them. "The extraction of my research subject should have prompted immediate rescue attempts. Your delay suggests emotional detachment…unusual for your species."

Aquatania and Kieran exchanged a brief glance before moving in opposite directions, instinctively spreading out to divide the commander's attention. Water armor flowed around her limbs in combat readiness while Kieran's hands emitted controlled flames that cast flickering shadows across the chamber's uneven surfaces.

"The cure took priority," Aquatania responded coolly, her gaze scanning the room for defensive systems and vulnerabilities. "Unlike your kind, we value collective survival over individual rescue."

The commander's head tilted in what might have been amusement or curiosity. "A surprisingly logical approach for emotional beings. Perhaps there's more to study before your extinction." Its primary limbs moved in a specific pattern across the control interface. "Unfortunately, that study must be conducted elsewhere."

Wall panels throughout the command center slid open, revealing recessed compartments housing robotic sentries. Sleek, insectoid machines with crystalline weapons integrated into their chassis. They emerged in synchronized movement, positioning themselves in defensive formation around the commander's dais.

"Your species is doomed," the commander declared, stepping back from the control interface to retrieve an energy staff that had been resting against the dais. The weapon activated at its touch, green energy crackling along its length in patterns that matched the neural crown on its head. "The contagion is merely the beginning. Your world will be remade at the molecular level, optimized for our biology while preserving those elements of your species we find…useful."

The sentries advanced, their movements precise and coordinated as they closed in from multiple angles. Aquatania reacted instantly, water shields expanding to intercept the first volley of energy fire. The liquid absorbed and dispersed the energy, and steam rose where molecular bonds were temporarily overloaded.

"Kieran!" she called, already moving to engage the nearest

group of sentries. Water formed into specialized weapons, some hardening into ice projectiles that shattered crucial joints, others forming whip-like tendrils that wrapped around mechanical limbs to restrict movement.

Kieran focused on a different cluster, his returning powers still limited but expertly applied. Rather than attempting to destroy the sentries with raw force, he targeted environmental systems, superheating coolant lines that ran beneath floor panels, creating localized temperature spikes that confused thermal sensors. The machines' targeting systems faltered, firing at phantom heat signatures rather than actual combatants.

"Your dragon form was particularly fascinating," the commander called to Kieran, observing the battle from its elevated position. "The cellular transformation process of reorganizing matter without loss of consciousness or memory. Such technology would revolutionize our expansion capabilities."

Kieran's expression hardened at the casual discussion of his captivity. "Did your research note the particular resilience of fire dragon memory?" he asked, his voice deceptively calm as he disabled another sentry with precise flame application to its control circuits. "How we recall every detail, every face, every procedure?"

He ducked beneath a sentry's attack, rolling to position himself behind a control station. "Did it mention how I memorized your research protocols while you thought I was sedated? How I identified the critical data nodes in your systems?"

The commander's movements stilled momentarily. Its attention focused on Kieran with new intensity.

"Your research data is compromised," Kieran continued, satisfaction evident beneath the strain of combat. "I sabotaged classification protocols during the seventeenth examination cycle. Your molecular formulas, transformation analyses, contagion modifications, all corrupted with false parameters that your verification systems won't detect until application."

Rage transformed the commander's posture, its limbs extending to full length, iridescent scales flushing with darker patterns that pulsed in rhythm with its neural crown. "Impossible!" it hissed, abandoning its observational position to descend from the dais with surprising speed.

"Entirely possible," Kieran countered, flames intensifying with his focused anger. "You were so fascinated by dragon transformation that you never considered dragon intelligence. Fatal oversight."

The commander charged directly toward him, the energy staff raised in multiple limbs that allowed for attack patterns impossible for bipedal combatants. The weapon discharged concentrated bursts that left scorched craters in the floor and walls where Kieran had stood moments before.

Aquatania shifted her focus from the sentries to the commander, recognizing the greater threat. Her water constructs reformed into specialized configurations, some continuing to engage remaining sentries while others prepared offensive capabilities. The self-destruct countdown continued its relentless progression...seven minutes remaining before the molecular cascade would render escape impossible.

"The control console," Kieran called to her between evasive maneuvers. "Neural interface at the primary station requires the commander's biological signature to abort self-destruct!"

She nodded understanding, already calculating approach vectors through the chaos of combat. The commander stood between them and the primary console, its multiple limbs providing omnidirectional attack capability that would make direct assault prohibitively dangerous.

Instead of attacking directly, Aquatania sent water tendrils snaking across the floor, the liquid almost invisible against the dark surface. While the commander focused its rage on Kieran, her water infiltrated control systems throughout the chamber, seeking vulnerabilities in the environmental regulators. Finding what she sought, she compressed water into the ventilation system with explosive force, causing overhead conduits to rupture.

Coolant fluid cascaded from ceiling panels, creating momentary confusion that allowed Kieran to gain distance from the commander's relentless assault. The liquid provided Aquatania with additional resources, her power amplifying as she incorporated the coolant into her water armor with molecular precision.

"You cannot stop what we have begun," the commander declared, recovering quickly from the environmental disruption. "The transformation of your world progresses regardless of this vessel's fate. Our seed ships have already deployed across your continents."

"Then we'll destroy them, too," Aquatania replied, water forming into offensive configurations around her body. "Starting with you."

The battle expanded across the command center, Kieran using his knowledge of the ship to short-circuit systems that controlled defensive capabilities, Aquatania manipulating water with unprecedented precision to counter the commander's multiple attack vectors. The alien proved formidable, its enhanced exoskeleton resistant to standard attacks, its neural crown allowing it to interface directly with the ship systems even while engaged in physical combat.

"Predictive algorithm engaged," it announced, compound eyes pulsing with data analysis. "Your combat patterns analyzed. Defeat is imminent."

The claim proved immediately false as Aquatania and Kieran abandoned conventional tactics, their movements becoming deliberately chaotic, attacks originating from unexpected angles. Kieran created fire barriers that restricted the commander's movement options, herding it toward positions where Aquatania had prepared molecular-thin water blades beneath floor panels. When it attempted aerial advantage using mechanical enhancements, Kieran superheated air currents to disrupt lift capabilities while she created ice projectiles that damaged flight mechanisms.

Their coordinated assault gradually pushed the commander back toward the primary control console, exactly where they needed it to be. The alien recognized the strategic positioning too late, attempting to pivot away only to find retreat options eliminated by exactly placed elemental barriers.

"Your species' resistance is admirable but futile," it hissed, the energy staff sweeping in wide arcs that forced them to maintain distance. "Even now, your atmosphere absorbs our transformative agents. Within one planetary cycle, the process will be irreversible."

"Unless we distribute the cure globally," Aquatania countered, her water shields absorbing another energy discharge. "Which requires your ship's transmission technology."

Understanding flashed across the commander's alien features. They weren't just fighting to escape or disable the self-destruct. They intended to repurpose the mothership's systems to distribute the cure worldwide in one synchronized broadcast.

With renewed fury, the commander launched a final desperate assault, multiple limbs attacking simultaneously from different angles. The energy staff crackled with increased power, drawing directly from the neural crown's connection to ship systems. Green lightning arced between control consoles, creating a lethal web of energy that restricted movement options.

Aquatania met the attack head-on, water armor flowing into specialized configurations that absorbed and redirected energy rather than simply blocking it. She formed a primary water blade that engaged directly with the commander's staff, the two weapons locking in a crackling stalemate as molecular structures contested for dominance.

"Kieran!" she called, maintaining the engagement through intense concentration. Sweat beaded on her forehead as the water blade held against overwhelming energy, the liquid's molecular structure constantly adapting to prevent disruption.

Understanding her intention immediately, Kieran circled behind the commander while it focused on the direct confrontation with Aquatania. She noticed that his flame had grown significantly stronger throughout the battle, rage and exertion burning through the suppression compounds in his system faster than the aliens had calculated possible. Fire coalesced in his hands, not as unfocused flame but as a perfectly shaped blade that mirrored Aquatania's water construct.

The commander sensed the flanking maneuver too late, its secondary limbs moving to intercept as Kieran closed the distance. Its compound eyes registered the threat, calculating response options even as it maintained pressure against Aquatania's water blade. The energy staff locked against her liquid construct, crackling with power that would have disintegrated standard matter on contact.

In that frozen moment of perfect balance, water and energy suspended in impossible equilibrium, Kieran positioned himself for the strike that would end the commander's threat permanently. His fire blade glowed with concentrated heat that would penetrate even the enhanced exoskeleton, aimed precisely at the neural crown that connected the alien to the ship's systems.

"For every examination," he said softly, eyes reflecting the fire he controlled. "For every sample extracted. For every moment of pain inflicted in the name of your evolution."

The fate of their world hung in the balance as water held energy at bay, as fire prepared to sever the connection between alien intelligence and the technology that threatened all they protected.

The self-destruct countdown continued its relentless progression, five minutes remaining before the confrontation would become irrelevant in molecular annihilation.

CHAPTER EIGHTEEN

Kieran's fire blade sliced through the neural crown with surgical precision, severing the connection between the alien commander and the ship's systems. The iridescent scales along the creature's exoskeleton darkened instantly, its multiple limbs convulsing as neural feedback cascaded through its enhanced biology. Aquatania maintained her water blade's pressure against the energy staff, preventing the commander from redirecting its failing systems against them in its final moments. The alien's compound gaze fixed on them with hateful intelligence even as its body failed, mandibles clicking in what might have been a curse or a final command.

"Your extinction is merely delayed," the commander rasped, its voice distorting as connections failed between organic and mechanical components. "Others will complete what we began."

The energy staff went dark in its failing grip, the green glow fading as Aquatania's water blade dissolved its final resistances. The commander collapsed in segments, jointed limbs folding inward like a dying spider. Its eyes dimmed section by section until they resembled nothing more than dead glass, reflecting the emergency lights that continued to pulse throughout the command center.

Kieran stood over the fallen commander, flames still dancing between his fingers, though his breathing came in ragged bursts. The exertion had clearly cost him, pushing his recovering body beyond reasonable limits. Yet satisfaction burned in his eyes, tempering the exhaustion that threatened to overwhelm him.

"The self-destruct sequence," Aquatania reminded him,

moving quickly to the primary console. The display flashed alien symbols in accelerating patterns, the countdown continuing its relentless progression. Four minutes and thirty seconds remained.

Kieran joined her, the flames receding as he focused his remaining energy on the task at hand. "We can't abort it," he concluded after studying the controls. "Not without the commander's neural signature, which died with it." His hands moved across the interface with surprising familiarity, navigating alien systems with the knowledge gained during his captivity. "But we can redirect it."

"Redirect how?" Aquatania asked, water armor flowing in nervous patterns across her skin, responding to her heightened alertness.

"The core chamber," he explained, indicating a pulsing symbol at the center of the display. "During my examinations, they discussed it, the heart of their ship's power systems. It's what generates the energy for their terraforming technology and powers their seed vessels." His fingers traced a path through the alien interface. "If we overload it, we don't just destroy this ship. We create an energy cascade that will disable their entire network."

Understanding dawned in her eyes. "Including the seed ships they've already deployed."

"Exactly." He manipulated the console further, revealing a schematic of the ship's interior. A pulsing route illuminated, showing their path to the core chamber. "We need to move. Now."

They navigated the ship's interior with desperate urgency, following emergency evacuation routes that alien crew members had already used, leaving the corridors eerily empty. Occasional automated defenses activated as they passed, but these proved easy to neutralize compared to the living guards they'd faced earlier. The ship shuddered periodically, the early stages of molecular destabilization beginning to affect non-critical systems.

Aquatania supported Kieran when necessary, his strength flagging then surging in unpredictable waves as his body continued purging the alien suppressants. Her water armor flowed between them during these moments, providing cooling relief to his overheated muscles and stability when his steps faltered.

"There," Kieran indicated as they rounded a final corner. A massive security door blocked their path, its surface inscribed with warning symbols that required no translation. Unlike previous barriers, this one featured multiple redundant systems, genetic scanners, neural interfaces, and mechanical locks designed to prevent unauthorized access to the ship's most critical component.

"Can we breach it?" Aquatania asked, studying the imposing barrier.

"Not conventionally." Kieran placed his palm against a section of wall adjacent to the door, feeling for something beneath the surface. "But during my captivity, I observed the commander accessing emergency protocols. There's always a bypass..." His fingers found what they sought, pressing against a nearly invisible seam. A panel slid open, revealing a secondary control system. "For exactly this scenario."

His hands moved across these controls with practiced efficiency, entering sequences that seemed random to Aquatania but clearly followed a pattern he'd memorized during his imprisonment. The massive door responded with a series of metallic groans, security systems disengaging in a cascading sequence.

"They never expected a prisoner to pay such close attention," he explained, a grim smile touching his lips as the final lock disengaged. "Or to survive long enough to use what they learned."

The security hydraulic doors parted down the middle, sections retracting into the walls. Beyond lay the core chamber, a massive spherical room that seemed to exist in defiance of the ship's otherwise angular architecture. Blue-green light pulsed from its center, emanating from a towering crystalline structure that rose from floor to ceiling. The light it cast threw strange, shifting shadows across curved walls lined with control panels and monitoring stations. Energy conduits extended from the central crystal-like veins from a heart, carrying power throughout the vessel's systems.

Aquatania stepped through the doorway first, her water armor thickening automatically in response to the intense heat radiating from the core. The temperature differential was immediate and severe, at least thirty degrees warmer than the corridors they'd navigated. Steam rose where droplets of moisture encountered superheated surfaces, creating a thin haze that added to the chamber's otherworldly atmosphere.

Kieran followed, his fire-attuned physiology better suited to the extreme heat, though his weakened state made him stumble slightly at the threshold. Aquatania caught him, her hand steady against his arm as her water armor flowed between them, providing cooling relief where their skin touched.

"You feel it?" he asked, his voice hushed despite the absence of alien crew.

She nodded, understanding immediately. The core emanated not just heat and light, but a subtle vibration that resonated in her chest like distant thunder. Something about it felt almost alive, a sensation more intuitive than scientific.

Their entry triggered automated responses throughout the chamber. Alien symbols flashed across curved control panels, warning systems activating in response to an unauthorized presence. A countdown sequence was initiated, displayed in pulsing red characters above the main control station, separate from but synchronized with the ship's overall self-destruct timer.

"Three minutes and forty seconds," Kieran noted, moving

toward the main control panel with Aquatania close behind. His steps grew steadier as they approached, as if proximity to the core somehow strengthened his fire dragon physiology.

The control panel spread before them in alien complexity, a curved interface featuring both physical components and holographic projections that shifted in response to their proximity. Kieran studied it with intense focus, recognition dawning in his eyes.

"This is it," he said, his fingers hovering over specific sections. "During my examinations, they discussed the core's function extensively. Not just power generation, but the source of their terraforming technology." He indicated energy junctions where conduits connected to the central crystal. "We need to overload it, reverse the energy flow back into the core itself instead of out to the ship's systems."

"Creating a cascade failure," Aquatania concluded, scientific understanding matching his explanation.

"Yes." His eyes met hers, honesty overriding whatever comfort he might have offered. "It'll destroy the ship completely, and the energy release will disable their seed ships through quantum entanglement. Their entire invasion ends with this core."

"But?" she prompted, sensing the unspoken conclusion.

Kieran didn't look away, though something in his expression softened. "But we won't survive the overload." He didn't elaborate further, didn't need to. The implication hung between them with perfect clarity — saving their world would require their ultimate sacrifice.

Aquatania's expression shifted, determination warring with the sudden, sharp awareness of all they would lose. Not just their lives, but the future they'd never quite allowed themselves to imagine together. Her water armor rippled across her skin, responding to emotions she kept from her face as she processed this information.

"Then we'd better make it count," she said finally, turning

toward the control panel.

The control panel's alien symbology shifted beneath Kieran's fingers, responding to commands he'd memorized during weeks of captivity. Aquatania stood at his side, following his lead while extending her awareness through her water armor to analyze the core's molecular structure. The countdown continued its relentless progression, three minutes and twenty seconds remaining before the ship's automated self-destruct would render their efforts meaningless. Whatever they accomplished needed to happen before that terminal moment.

"These control junctions redirect energy flow throughout the ship," Kieran explained, his voice tight with concentration. His hands moved across the interface, though Aquatania noticed the slight tremor in his fingers, lingering effects of his ordeal that determination alone couldn't entirely overcome. "We need to reverse the polarity at these seven points simultaneously."

She nodded, positioning her hands over the designated sections. The controls responded differently to her touch than to Kieran's, the alien technology seemingly calibrated to recognize specific genetic markers. Where his inputs registered immediately, hers required additional pressure, as if the system resisted her commands.

"It's rejecting my inputs," she noted, frustration edging her voice as precious seconds ticked away.

"The system's designed for their biology. They infused me with enough of their DNA that it responds to me," Kieran confirmed, not pausing in his work though sweat now beaded along his hairline from the chamber's intensifying heat. "Try using your water as a conductive medium."

Aquatania extended tendrils of water from her armor, allowing the liquid to flow over the control surfaces she needed to manipulate. The water responded to her commands, its molecular structure shifting to mimic the electrical conductivity patterns the alien technology expected. The interface flickered briefly, then accepted her inputs as the water served as a translator between her biology and the alien system.

"It's working," she confirmed, water tendrils spreading across additional control surfaces, multiplying her effectiveness. "Tell me exactly what we need to modify."

Kieran guided her through the process, his instructions revealing the depth of knowledge he'd accumulated during his captivity. "These energy conduits normally channel power outward from the core to the ship's systems," he explained, indicating glowing pathways on a holographic display that hovered above the control panel. "We need to reverse that flow, force energy back into the core beyond its containment parameters."

Together, they manipulated the alien controls, Kieran's fire-honed intuition complementing Aquatania's methodical water manipulation. Where circuits threatened to overload, she cooled them with an application of water, allowing them to push systems beyond their design specifications without premature failure. When control surfaces grew too hot for direct contact, Kieran's fire resistance allowed him to maintain physical connection where she couldn't.

The core responded to their alterations, its blue-green luminescence shifting gradually toward amber, then crimson as energy patterns reversed. The pulsing accelerated, rhythms becoming erratic as containment systems struggled with the unnatural energy flow. The temperature in the chamber rose dramatically, the air shimmering with heat distortion that made distant control stations waver like mirages.

"Two minutes remaining," Aquatania noted, the countdown display reflecting red against her water armor. The liquid responded automatically to the rising heat, forming cooling currents across her skin that prevented immediate distress but couldn't entirely counter the oppressive temperature.

Kieran nodded acknowledgment, his attention fixed on critical energy junction points where their sabotage needed to be precisely coordinated. His face glistened with sweat that evaporated almost instantly in the superheated air, yet his hands moved with increasing steadiness, the extreme heat seemingly burning away any remaining traces of alien suppressants from his system, restoring his natural fire dragon resilience.

"The core's approaching critical threshold," he announced, monitoring fluctuations in the energy readings that flashed across holographic displays. "Once we cross that line, the process becomes irreversible."

Aquatania extended additional water tendrils to cooling systems throughout the chamber, preventing premature shutdown of the control systems they still needed. Where her water contacted superheated metal, steam hissed upward in twisting columns that added to the chamber's hellish atmosphere. The moisture in the air was rapidly depleting, making each extension of her power more demanding as she pulled water molecules from increasingly dry surroundings.

The core's crimson light intensified, casting their shadows in sharp relief against the curved walls. Energy conduits connected to the crystal structure began to glow with dangerous luminescence, the material visibly straining to contain the reversed power flow. Small fractures appeared along the crystal's surface, releasing thin jets of pure energy that scored black lines across nearby equipment.

An automated voice suddenly echoed throughout the chamber, the alien language translated by embedded systems into a distorted approximation of human speech.

"Core destabilization imminent. Evacuation protocols initiated. All personnel proceed to the emergency craft."

"They still think someone's left to evacuate," Kieran noted, a grim smile touching his lips. "Little late for that."

The ship's internal communication continued, dispassionate warnings underscored by alarms that pulsed in time with the core's increasingly erratic rhythm. The alien symbols on the control panel flashed urgent warnings, as some sections shut down, automated safety protocols attempting to prevent what they were deliberately causing.

"One minute forty seconds," Aquatania reported, her water armor thinning as ambient moisture levels continued to drop. The liquid concentrated around her vital areas, prioritizing core body temperature regulation as the chamber approached temperatures that would damage human tissue within seconds of exposure.

Kieran made a final series of adjustments. The holographic display above the control panel stabilized briefly, confirming the changes they'd implemented. Energy flow diagrams showed the unnatural reversal now locked into the system, power feeding back into the core in a self-reinforcing loop that would inevitably lead to catastrophic failure.

"We've done it," he announced, stepping back from the control panel with weary satisfaction. "The overload sequence is locked in. We have three minutes before total core collapse." His eyes met hers across the shimmering heat between them. "Nothing they can do to stop it now."

As if responding to his declaration, the ship shuddered violently, the first major structural failures beginning as energy systems throughout the vessel suffered cascading overloads. The movement threw them off balance, sending them colliding into each other. Kieran's arms instinctively wrapped around Aquatania, steadying them both against the control panel as aftershocks rippled through the chamber.

For a moment, they remained locked together, his body unexpectedly solid against hers after weeks of separation and the uncertainty of rescue. Her water armor flowed between them, providing cooling relief where they touched without creating a barrier to the human contact they both suddenly seemed to need. The countdown continued its merciless advance, their successful sabotage now ensuring their own destruction along with the alien vessel.

Kieran didn't release her even after the shuddering subsided. Instead, his arms tightened slightly, his face close enough that she could see flecks of gold in his eyes, the dragon's fire that always burned just beneath the surface of his human form. Something in his expression shifted, the tactical focus giving way to a more personal urgency as the reality of their situation crystallized between them.

"Tania," he said softly, using the private diminutive very few dared. His hands found hers, fingers intertwining with gentle pressure despite the chaos surrounding them. "There's something I need to tell you before..." His voice faltered briefly, determination warring with emotions he rarely displayed so openly. "I love you. I think I have since the moment we met."

The confession hung between them, simple words carrying the weight of unspoken feelings. Around them, the core pulsed with increasingly unstable energy, the ship's structure groaned with imminent failure, and the countdown marched toward their seemingly inevitable end. Yet in that moment, with death approaching on multiple fronts, his eyes held only the quiet certainty of finally speaking truth too long left unsaid.

Aquatania's eyes widened at Kieran's confession, the words she'd never expected to hear resonating through her despite the core's dangerous rumbling. Time seemed to slow in that moment, the countdown's relentless progression fading to background noise as she processed what he'd said. His face remained open, vulnerable, a stark contrast to the guarded expressions he typically maintained. She recognized the cost of that vulnerability for someone like him, someone who'd built walls of duty and discipline around his heart just as she had around her own.

"I love you, too," she admitted, her voice steady despite the chaos around them. The truth of it washed through her with surprising clarity, as if naming the feeling stripped away years of careful denial. "I think I've been fighting it since our first mission together." A small smile touched her lips, remembering their initial clash of wills that had gradually transformed into something deeper, more essential.

Kieran's expression softened with wonder, as if he'd expected rejection even in these final moments. His hands tightened around hers, the heat of his skin providing an anchor amid the chamber's intensifying instability. The ship shuddered again, more violently this time, forcing them to brace against each other as structural supports throughout the core chamber began to fail.

The countdown display flashed ominously, two minutes remaining before complete core collapse. Around them, the alien technology responded to the imminent destruction with surging shutdowns, emergency systems activating too late to prevent the sabotage they'd successfully implemented. The crystal core had transformed from crimson to blinding white at its center, fractures spreading across its surface as containment fields struggled to manage the building energy.

"We've come too far to wait for the end," Aquatania said, reluctantly pulling back from their brief connection, though her eyes held his with newfound openness. "We should finish this ourselves."

Kieran nodded, understanding immediately. They'd always communicated most fluently through action rather than words, their combat synchronization reflecting a deeper harmony that transcended verbal expression. "What do you suggest?"

Her mind clicked into overdrive, analyzing the core's condition and their available resources. The water armor flowing across her skin had thinned considerably as ambient moisture evaporated in the extreme heat, but what remained had concentrated into its purest form, responsive to her commands with unprecedented molecular precision.

"We need to combine our powers," she suggested, the water armor rippling with energy as the idea crystallized. "My water control and your fire breath, together…they might create enough energy to trigger the final overload."

He raised an eyebrow, the tactical implications registering immediately. "Steam expansion at the molecular level." His eyes tracked to the core, assessing vulnerabilities in its remaining containment structure. "If we target the fracture points simultaneously from opposite directions…"

"The pressure differential would create a chain reaction," she confirmed, completing his thought with the ease of partnership. "Collapsing the containment field from multiple vectors rather than waiting for systematic failure."

"Taking control of our end," he added quietly, the deeper meaning clear between them. Not just hastening destruction, but choosing their final act rather than passively awaiting it.

Kieran straightened, summoning his remaining strength. Fire flickered along his forearms now without conscious effort, scales shimmering beneath his skin as his dragon nature responded to the imminent threat. He wasn't fully restored; weeks of captivity and experimentation had taken a toll that no quick recovery could erase.

"We'll need to position ourselves on opposite sides," Aquatania instructed, already moving toward the eastern quadrant of the spherical chamber. "Maximum effect requires perpendicular force application."

Kieran nodded, taking position in the western section where structural supports had already begun to buckle under heat stress. Between them, the crystal core pulsed with increasingly unstable energy, the fractures along its surface now emitting thin jets of pure power that scored black lines across the chamber walls.

Aquatania closed her eyes briefly, extending her awareness

to the rapidly diminishing moisture in the chamber. What remained had retreated to corners and crevices, condensation clinging to cooler surfaces in defiance of the overwhelming heat. She called to these scattered molecules, drawing them to her with the enhanced control her sacred communion had granted. Water responded from distances that would have been impossible before, molecules separating from their hiding places to join the swirling vortex that formed around her outstretched hands.

The effort cost her considerably, sweat beading on her forehead as she compressed the gathered moisture into an increasingly dense formation. The water spun faster, molecular bonds aligning in patterns that would maximize explosive force when released. She opened her eyes to see Kieran across the chamber, his stance widened for stability as he summoned his dragon fire.

Unlike his earlier flames, the weakened manifestations of recovering power, this burned with increasing intensity, his mouth opening slightly as fire gathered at the back of his throat. The dragon within him responded to a final need, pushing past physical limitations to provide what survival required. Golden light shone from within him, scales erupting across his chest and face as a partial transformation granted access to deeper reserves of power.

The countdown reached one minute, symbols flashing urgent warnings across all remaining operational displays. Structural supports throughout the chamber groaned under thermal expansion, exceeding their design parameters, as the floor plating began to warp where energy leakage from the core contacted the metal directly.

Aquatania met Kieran's eyes across the chamber, no words needed for what came next. They'd fought together, protected each other, and denied their feelings. Now, with the truth finally acknowledged between them, they would complete their final mission with the same perfect synchronization that had defined their relationship from the beginning.

"Now!" she called, the single word carrying complete understanding of timing and intent.

They unleashed their powers simultaneously, Aquatania directing her compressed water vortex in a pressurized jet toward the core's eastern fractures, Kieran exhaling dragon fire in a concentrated stream toward western vulnerabilities. The opposing forces converged at the crystal's surface, water and fire colliding in a spectacular reaction that shattered physics at the molecular level.

Steam exploded outward in a superheated cloud, but that represented only the visible manifestation of a deeper reaction. Where fire and water met at precisely calculated angles, energy multiplied rather than merely combined, creating localized pressure that exceeded the core's remaining structural tolerance. Fractures widened instantly into chasms, containment fields collapsing in a rolling sequence that released pure energy into the chamber.

The core absorbed their combined assault, its brilliance intensifying beyond visual tolerance. Aquatania squinted against the painful brightness, her water armor automatically forming protective layers across her eyes. Through this filtered vision, she witnessed the crystal's transformation, from merely damaged containment structure to actively destabilizing power source. White-hot energy coursed through previously controlled channels, overloading safeguards and melting conduits designed to regulate its flow.

Critical alarms blared throughout the chamber, their alien wailing taking on an almost organic quality, as if the ship itself recognized imminent death. The floor beneath them began to buckle and collapse, structural integrity failing as power meant to be distributed throughout the vessel concentrated in the core chamber. Metal plating tore along stress lines, revealing substructures that glowed red-hot beneath.

Aquatania maintained her water jet despite growing difficulty, pushing her power to its limits as the core responded to their attack. Across the chamber, Kieran's fire continued unabated, his dragon nature fully engaged in this final act of destruction. Between them, the crystal core had become a miniature sun, its containment failing in precisely the manner they'd intended. Their combined assault had accelerated the overload sequence, making the countdown now irrelevant as the core's destruction progressed beyond automated measuring systems.

The chamber floor gave way beneath Aquatania's feet, forcing her to create an instant water platform to avoid falling into the structural abyss opening below. Kieran similarly leapt to a more stable position, never interrupting his fire stream despite the deteriorating environment. The ship's death throes had begun in earnest, systems failing throughout its massive bulk as the poisoned heart at its center destabilized beyond recovery.

What they'd started couldn't be stopped. What they'd sacrificed wouldn't be wasted. The alien invasion would end here, in fire and water. Their eyes met once more across the chamber's disintegrating space, unspoken understanding passing between them, pride in what they'd accomplished, regret for time lost to duty and restraint, acceptance of the end they now faced as one.

The chamber continued to disintegrate around them, metal and crystal alike surrendering to forces they were never designed to contain. Aquatania fought to maintain her footing on the unstable platform her water had created, the liquid constantly reforming beneath her as sections collapsed into the growing abyss below. Thirty seconds remained according to the countdown display, though the core's condition suggested even that brief time might be optimistic. Energy discharges lashed outward from the crystal's fractured surface, scoring molten paths across remaining structures and blocking potential escape routes with superheated debris.

Kieran faced similar challenges across the chamber, balanced on a section of flooring that had partially detached from its supports. He'd ceased his fire assault, conservation instincts finally overriding attack protocols as survival became momentarily more pressing than hastening destruction already assured. His eyes sought hers through the chaos, wordless communication passing between them despite the distance and danger separating their positions.

Aquatania extended her water platform, creating a precarious bridge across the widening gap between them. The effort strained her depleted reserves, moisture now so scarce in the superheated chamber that she drew from her own body's hydration to maintain the construct. She moved across this liquid pathway with desperate focus, each step requiring conscious adjustment as structural collapses sent shock waves through the chamber.

"Kieran!" she called, extending her hand as she neared his position. An energy discharge from the core flashed between them, momentarily blinding her with its intensity. When her vision cleared, she saw him leaping toward her, trust overriding caution as he abandoned his failing perch.

They collided in mid-air, her water platform expanding instinctively to catch them both. The liquid flowed around them as they tumbled together, protecting vulnerable skin from contact with superheated metal as they rolled to relative safety against what remained of the chamber's outer wall. Her water armor automatically redistributed, extending partial coverage to Kieran where their bodies pressed together.

"We did it," she shouted over the deafening roar of the collapsing core. The chamber had become a maelstrom of energy and destruction, the countdown now irrelevant as the ship's death throes progressed beyond predictive modeling. "The invasion is over."

Kieran nodded, his face illuminated by the core's blinding brilliance. His arms tightened around her, providing an anchor against the violent shuddering that threatened to separate them. "Not exactly how I imagined our first date," he managed, the joke strained but genuine.

Aquatania laughed despite everything, the sound quickly lost in the chamber's cacophony. Even now, facing imminent destruction, his essential nature remained intact, the irreverent humor that had first pierced her carefully maintained professionalism. She pressed closer, her face against his neck where she could feel his pulse racing beneath skin that radiated dragon heat.

They braced for the end, holding each other tightly as the countdown reached its final seconds. The core had become something beyond physical description, a rupture in reality itself, contained only by failing alien technology never designed to restrain such forces. The wall that they sheltered against groaned with structural fatigue, its molecules vibrating with sympathetic resonance to the core's escalating destabilization.

Ten seconds.

Aquatania closed her eyes, focusing on the sensation of Kieran's arms around her rather than the destruction encircling them. If these were her final moments, she would fill them with something other than fear or regret.

Nine seconds.

The chamber's remaining supports gave way entirely, gravity asserting dominance over alien engineering as the ceiling began its final collapse.

Eight seconds.

A familiar ripple of turquoise light cut through the destruction, so unexpected that Aquatania initially dismissed it as a hallucination born from oxygen deprivation and acceptance of death.

Seven seconds.

The ripple expanded into a vertical tear in reality itself, edges shimmering with distinctly non-alien energy that pulsed in patterns she recognized from childhood lessons. A portal, not of alien design, but of ancient sea dragon magic.

Six seconds.

Marina appeared through the shimmering portal, her mermaid form briefly visible, the scales gleaming with deep ocean iridescence, her fins extended for stability, before she shifted to human, her feet touching the disintegrating chamber floor with surprising grace. Her expression registered shock at the destruction surrounding her, eyes widening as she took in the core's critical condition.

"I saw this moment," Marina called out, extending her hands toward them, her voice carrying despite the chamber's roaring death throes. Her eyes glowed with the same turquoise light as the portal, pupils elongated to vertical slits that revealed her divination trance had not fully dissipated. "Come now!"

Five seconds.

Aquatania's scientific mind stuttered over impossibilities, Marina's presence, the divination that had allowed her to find them, the portal technology that should not function in proximity to the alien core's energy signature. Yet survival instinct overrode analysis, her body already moving in response to the offered salvation.

"Kieran!" she shouted, pulling him toward Marina's portal. His eyes reflected the same disbelief she felt, but his body responded automatically to her urgency, battlefield trust overcoming rational skepticism.

Four seconds.

They stumbled toward the portal together, Aquatania's water armor flowing ahead to test whether the energy field would accept their passage. The liquid passed through unhindered, confirming compatibility despite the chaotic environment.

Three seconds.

Marina's hands reached for them, her expression shifting from determination to alarm as the core's brilliance intensified behind them. "Quickly!" she urged, half-stepping back through the portal while maintaining its stability with evident effort.

Two seconds.

Aquatania pushed Kieran ahead of her, ensuring his weakened body would reach safety first. His protestations died unspoken as another structural collapse sent a shower of molten debris between them, forcing her to dive forward or be separated.

One second.

They reached the portal's threshold together, Marina's hands grasping their outstretched arms to pull them through the dimensional tear. The core reached critical mass behind them, the countdown's final digit overwhelmed by reality's surrender to forces beyond containment.

Zero.

They dove through the portal just as blinding white light engulfed the chamber. The energy wave followed them through the dimensional opening, its leading edge singeing their heels before Marina sealed the connection with a gesture of desperate finality. The portal collapsed behind them, cutting off the alien ship's death throes with abrupt silence that seemed almost more shocking than the preceding chaos.

They emerged in waters near Zephyria, the transition from superheated destruction to cool ocean depths so sudden that Aquatania's body spasmed in shock. They surfaced together, gasping and disoriented, eyes adjusting to natural sunlight after the core's artificial brilliance. Marina floated nearby, her form already shifting back to mermaid as she recovered from the energy expenditure of creating and maintaining the portal under such extreme conditions.

"How?" Kieran managed, the single word encompassing

countless questions as he treaded water beside Aquatania. His body showed the strain of their ordeal, burns along his forearms where the protection had failed, exhaustion evident in the hollows beneath his eyes, yet wonder dominated his expression as he processed their unexpected survival.

Before Marina could answer, the sky above them erupted with distant light, a flash of blinding white followed by expanding rings of force that rippled through cloud formations. The alien mothership's destruction, visible even from their position, confirmed the success of their mission despite their unanticipated escape from its consequences.

"I saw it in the tides," Marina explained, her voice carrying the musical quality of her mermaid heritage. "The moment of destruction, but also the possibility of salvation. The currents showed a path between moments, a door that could open for exactly three seconds before the energies became incompatible."

Aquatania stared at the dissipating energy rings above them, scientific understanding warring with bone-deep relief. The mission had succeeded, the alien threat eliminated through their actions, yet somehow they'd survived to witness the results. Her hand found Kieran's beneath the water, their fingers intertwining with familiar pressure that carried new meaning after confessions exchanged in what they'd believed were final moments.

"Thank you," she said simply to Marina, words inadequate for the gift they'd been given, but all she could manage as the reaction continued to process through her system.

Marina nodded acknowledgment, her expression suggesting she understood all that remained unspoken. Her eyes turned toward Zephyria's floating islands visible on the horizon, where distant dragons could be seen circling in apparent celebration of the alien ship's destruction. "Your father will be waiting," she noted, beginning to swim in that direction with the effortless grace of her natural form.

Aquatania and Kieran followed more slowly, their human forms less efficient in water, though her lingering water armor assisted their movement. The physical demands of swimming provided a welcome focus as they processed what had happened, the mission, the confessions, the unexpected survival that now required them to live with truths spoken when death seemed certain.

"So," Kieran said after several minutes of silence, his voice finding something of its normal rhythm despite evident exhaustion. "About what I said in there..."

Aquatania turned to face him, treading water as she met his uncertain gaze. "I meant what I said, too," she confirmed, pre-empting whatever qualification or retreat he might have been considering. "Near-death clarity, perhaps, but no less true for it."

Relief softened his expression, the guard that typically masked his emotions temporarily abandoned in the aftermath of all they'd endured. "Good," he replied simply. "Because I'd hate to have survived certain death only to die of embarrassment."

She laughed, the sound startling in its normalcy after the extremes they'd just experienced. Her hand found his again beneath the water, connection reestablished with quiet certainty that required no further words. Above them, the last visible evidence of the alien mothership's destruction faded from the sky, leaving only ordinary clouds against Zephyria's eternal blue.

CHAPTER NINETEEN

Night settled over Zephyria like a velvet cloak, stars emerging as pinpricks of silver against deepening indigo. Hundreds of figures converged on the central pool, their paths illuminated by bioluminescent crystals that lined walkways in soft blue radiance. Each person carried a small illumination crystal, the combined effect creating rivers of light that flowed toward the ceremonial gathering. Aquatania stood at the pool's northern edge, ceremonial robes of sea-silk and silver flowing around her form in layers that caught and reflected the gentle illumination. The water armor beneath had transformed for this occasion, no longer a protective shield but a living connection between her body and the sacred waters that had granted her enhanced abilities.

The central pool itself had been restored to its pre-invasion glory, its circular basin lined with mother-of-pearl that shimmered beneath the surface. Ancient inscriptions along the rim, some predating even the oldest dragons' memories, glowed with subtle phosphorescence activated by proximity to water. Three moons hung in perfect alignment overhead, their reflected light creating overlapping rings on the pool's still surface, a celestial conjunction that occurred only once every seventy years. The timing had not been coincidental; this ritual had been planned to coincide with this rare astronomical event that symbolized the convergence of separate worlds into a harmonious whole.

Kieran approached from the eastern side, his formal dragon guard attire replaced by ceremonial robes that complemented hers, deep crimson fabric with gold and amber embroidery that evoked flame without directly depicting it. Fire dragons traditionally avoided water rituals, their elemental nature at odds with the ceremony's focus. His presence represented more than a personal connection. It symbolized the integration of previously separated dragon lineages into a cohesive whole.

Their eyes met across the pool's diameter, silent communication flowing between them with the ease of those who'd moved beyond needing words for core truths. Around the pool's perimeter, King Poseidronus and eleven senior dragons, three from each elemental lineage, took positions at equal intervals, forming a living circle that contained the gathered witnesses. Each wore ceremonial attire representing their element...flowing blues for sea dragons, cloud-white for sky dragons, ember-red for fire dragons, and earthy greens for forest dragons.

The crowd settled into respectful silence as King Poseidronus raised his ceremonial trident, moonlight catching on its triple points. "We gather beneath three moons to witness waters united," he intoned, the traditional opening of ancient rituals now carrying new significance. "As separate streams join to form mighty rivers, so too do separate peoples join to form mighty civilizations."

At this signal, Aquatania extended her hands toward the pool's center, her fingers spread in the ritual gesture passed down through generations of sea dragon royalty. The water responded immediately, rising in a perfect column that defied gravity to hover ten feet above the pool's surface. Her communion-enhanced abilities made the manipulation effortless, water molecules obeying her will with joyful eagerness rather than reluctant compliance.

The column took form slowly, shaping itself into a spiraling vortex that captured moonlight and scattered it in prismatic patterns across the gathered faces. Where once she might have created traditional sea dragon imagery, tonight she shaped the water into something new — an intertwined double helix that represented the fundamental molecular structure underlying all living beings present, regardless of species or origin.

"From the depths of sea to heights of sky," she proclaimed, the ritual words flowing from memory while their meaning transformed through recent experience. "From the heart of flame to roots of earth. Water connects all, carries all, remembers all."

Across the pool, Kieran extended his hands toward the water column, accepting his role in a ceremony traditionally closed to fire dragons. A murmur moved through the crowd as flames appeared above his palms, not the aggressive blaze of combat but controlled, reverent fire that reached toward the water spiral without threatening its integrity.

In the space between them, fire and water met without opposition. Steam formed where the elements touched, but rather than dissipating randomly, it coalesced into shapes guided by their combined will, dragons in flight, humans with arms upraised, merfolk emerging from waves, and even the multi-limbed forms of their former enemies now turned allies. These steam sculptures held their forms just long enough for recognition before dissolving into the next image, a continuous flow of representation that included every species present.

"From the depths of crisis, we have forged new bonds," Aquatania's voice carried across the gathered witnesses, water armor flowing visibly now across her exposed skin, no longer hidden beneath ceremony but integrated into ritual itself. "The waters that connect us all now carry not contagion, but cure...not division, but unity."

The water column expanded outward, thin tendrils extending toward the circle of senior dragons. Each reached forward to touch a tendril with bare hands, establishing a connection to the central element. Through these living conduits, the water flowed in continuous circuit, gathering essence from each elemental tradition before returning to the main column, now pulsing with combined energy that shifted through color spectrums representing each dragon lineage.

Witnesses around the pool raised their illumination crystals in unison, the gesture releasing stored light in controlled bursts that merged with the central water column's radiance. The combined effect transformed the ceremonial space into something between reality and dream—solid forms softened by luminescent mist, distinct boundaries blurred by shifting light that connected rather than divided.

"Join hands," King Poseidronus instructed, his voice carrying ancient authority tempered by newly earned wisdom. "As waters join, so must we."

Throughout the gathered crowd, hands reached across species divisions, scales touching skin touching membranes in a living demonstration of the unity they now sought. Human fingers clasped dragon talons, merfolk webbing entwined with both, and even the segmented appendages of reformed aliens integrated into the living circuit. Where traditional ceremonies had separated observers by species and rank, this ritual deliberately intermingled all present.

The water column responded to this unified connection, its light intensifying until it rivaled the moons overhead. Aquatania felt the collective energy flow through her water armor, thousands of individual experiences and perspectives merging into a consciousness larger than any single being could contain. The sacred communion she'd undergone alone now expanded to include all present, limited not by species but by willingness to connect.

"Water remembers," she stated, the ritual phrase now carrying weight beyond tradition. "And so do we, both what divided us and what united us."

At this culminating moment, she and Kieran moved simultaneously from opposite sides, stepping into the pool with deliberate, measured movements. The ceremonial robes floated around them as they waded toward the center where the water column originated. Steam rose where Kieran's naturally elevated body temperature met the cool water, creating a misty halo that surrounded them both as they approached each other.

They met at the pool's center, hands extending to connect beneath the hovering water column. Where their fingers touched, tiny flashes of light sparked, fire and water communicating at a molecular level that transcended conventional opposition. Around them, the water glowed with increasing intensity, responding to the symbolic union of elements traditionally considered incompatible.

"As water and fire find harmony," Kieran said, his voice pitched for her ears alone despite the hundreds witnessing their every movement, "so too do duty and desire."

Aquatania's heart quickened at the unscripted addition to the ritual, her fingers tightening around his. "Balance, not opposition," she responded, water armor flowing from her skin to dance briefly across their joined hands before returning.

Their embrace came with natural inevitability, the public ceremony momentarily condensed into a private connection as his arms encircled her waist, and hers linked behind his neck. Their kiss, witnessed by thousands yet somehow intimate as if they stood alone, sent ripples outward across the pool's surface, concentric circles expanding to touch every edge of the ceremonial basin.

The water column above them responded with spectacular transformation, splitting into twin spirals that intertwined in complex patterns while maintaining distinct identities. One glowed with cool blue luminescence, the other with warm amber light, separate elements unified without losing their essential nature.

As they separated slightly, still connected by their hands at the waist and shoulders, their dragon aspects manifested briefly through their human forms. Her scales shimmered in blue-green patterns across her cheekbones and temples, while his scales were in amber and gold along his jawline and brow. The transformation remained a partial, controlled demonstration of the duality they both contained, human and dragon, civilization and nature, science and instinct in continuous balance.

They emerged from the pool together, water streaming from ceremonial robes now saturated with ritual significance. The gathered witnesses erupted in sound that transcended mere applause, dragons rumbling in traditional approval, humans voicing celebration, merfolk producing harmonic tones that vibrated through water and air alike. Even the reformed aliens participated, their compound eyes shifting through color patterns that indicated recognition of a significant transition.

As they rejoined the ceremonial circle, where King Poseidronus waited with an uncharacteristic display of emotion evident in his expression, Aquatania felt a sense of completion that extended beyond the ritual itself. The journey from a desperate scientific princess fighting alone against contagion to a leader of united peoples had transformed her as thoroughly as her communion with ancestral waters.

Beside her, Kieran moved with the confident grace of a warrior who'd found purpose beyond battle, his protective instincts now channeled toward building rather than merely defending.

The water column gradually subsided, returning to the pool with gentle movement that left lingering luminescence across the surface. The three moons continued their rare alignment overhead, celestial witnesses to the terrestrial transformation.

CHAPTER TWENTY

Aquatania stood at the edge of the ceremonial terrace, her fingers lightly tracing the carved stone balustrade as she watched the final preparations unfold below. Three months had passed since the water ritual beneath the triple moons, three months of rebuilding, of healing, of forging connections between species that had once viewed each other with suspicion or outright hostility. Today would formalize what those months had begun to create…a new Zephyria, united, not despite their differences but because of them.

Wind lifted the edges of her sea-silk gown, the fabric rippling like water against her skin. Unlike the heavy ceremonial regalia of previous formal occasions, she'd chosen something that honored tradition while embracing transformation. The gown's subtle water-runic patterns pulsed beneath the surface of the fabric, ancient symbols of her lineage interwoven with newer designs that represented healing and unity. When she moved, the patterns shifted, some glowing faintly with the same blue luminescence as her water armor, which now flowed in delicate rivulets beneath her skin rather than forming external protection. The communion with her ancestors had permanently altered her connection to her element—water responded to her not as a tool to be wielded but as an extension of herself.

Below, the plaza had transformed from a battlefield to a celebration ground. Banners representing every species and settlement hung from newly erected poles, their colors vibrant against the restored limestone and crystal architecture. Sea dragon emblems in blues and greens fluttered alongside fire dragon standards in crimson and gold. Wave patterns on white backgrounds represented human settlements, while sky dragon banners rippled highest of all, catching updrafts that made them dance against the cloudless blue. Most striking were the newest additions — iridescent spiral patterns on banners representing the reformed aliens who'd chosen to remain and assist in rebuilding what their kind had nearly destroyed.

The crowd gathered in patterns that would have been unthinkable six months earlier. Dragon representatives moved among the assembly, their scales catching sunlight in elemental colors — sea dragons with blue-green iridescence, fire dragons with amber and crimson patterns, earth dragons with forest and moss tones, sky dragons with silver-white shimmer. Some maintained fully human forms with only subtle scale patterns visible at temples or wrists, while others displayed partial transformations with wings or tails manifested as visible statements of their dual nature.

Human dignitaries had arrived from coastal settlements and inner territories alike, their formal attire incorporating elements borrowed from dragon culture — fabrics that mimicked scale patterns, jewelry that represented elemental affiliation. They moved with growing comfort among larger dragon forms, the former hesitation replaced by emerging familiarity.

Perhaps most remarkable were the alien refugees clustered near the eastern fountain. Their exoskeletons had dulled slightly in Zephyria's atmosphere, adapting to new environmental conditions with the same evolutionary efficiency that had once made them formidable enemies. They'd abandoned the mechanized enhancements of warfare, their natural forms revealing surprising beauty when not obscured by weapons and armor. Several assisted with final adjustments to sound amplification crystals, their multi-jointed limbs allowing precision that human hands couldn't achieve.

"They still make me uneasy," King Poseidronus said,

materializing beside her with the quiet dignity that had only strengthened since his recovery. His crown, rebuilt with coral sections recovered from destroyed sections of the palace, caught sunlight in patterns that matched the healthy iridescence of his scales. "But I cannot deny their contributions to our reconstruction."

Aquatania smiled at her father, noting how completely he'd recovered from the Red Death that had nearly claimed him. "They understand redemption better than most," she replied. "Having come so close to destroying what they now help to rebuild."

He nodded, eyes reflecting wisdom earned through near-death and recovery. "Your mother would be proud of what you've accomplished," he said, rare emotion coloring his typically measured tone. "She always believed connection would prove stronger than conflict."

Before Aquatania could respond, movement at the terrace entrance caught her attention. Kieran approached, his dragon-guard dress uniform transformed from purely military garb to something that acknowledged both his warrior status and his diplomatic role. The deep blue fabric, traditional for Zephyrian formal wear, now featured flame accents along the collar and cuffs, subtle golden embroidery that shifted like living fire when he moved. The scars from alien captivity remained visible at his wrists where his sleeves ended, no longer angry red marks but silvery reminders carried without shame or concealment.

His eyes found hers immediately, warmth replacing the guarded expression he maintained for others. Three months of recovery had restored him completely, the lingering effects of alien suppression compounds finally purged from his system. The steady confidence in his stance, the clear focus in his gaze...these were the tangible signs of healing that meant more to her than any formal medical report.

"Ready to change the world?" he asked, offering his arm

with formal correctness that did nothing to disguise the intimate understanding beneath the gesture.

Aquatania felt the familiar flutter of nerves that preceded any major public address, intensified by the historic significance of this particular speech. The water armor flowing beneath her skin responded automatically, cool currents soothing heated skin with the internal equivalent of a calming touch.

"As ready as I'll ever be," she replied, accepting his support as she placed her hand on his arm. The contact sent a small wisp of steam rising where her naturally cool skin met his fire-dragon warmth, a physical manifestation of their elemental difference that had become a private symbol of their connection.

King Poseidronus nodded approval before moving ahead to take his position on the ceremonial dais. Aquatania and Kieran followed more slowly, their measured pace allowing her time to center herself before facing the assembled crowd.

"The security contingent reports no concerns," Kieran murmured as they descended the terrace steps. "All planetary defense systems remain at normal status. The outer islands confirm peaceful conditions continue."

She appreciated his attention to these details, understanding they represented not lingering paranoia but the vigilance of someone who'd learned through painful experience that peace required protection. "And the former alien outposts?"

"Final decommissioning completed yesterday," he confirmed. "Useful technology salvaged and repurposed according to council specifications. Weapons systems permanently neutralized."

They reached the bottom of the steps, the full expanse of the gathered crowd now visible before them. Thousands of faces turned toward them, expectation and hope visible in expressions across species and origins. The weight of responsibility pressed against Aquatania's shoulders, momentarily overwhelming despite months of preparation for this moment.

Kieran's hand covered hers where it rested on his arm, a brief pressure that conveyed complete understanding without words. "They're ready," he said simply. "You've shown them what's possible. Now you're just putting words to what they already believe."

Aquatania drew strength from his confidence, from the unity displayed in the gathering before them, from the water flowing through her veins with the collected wisdom of ancestors who'd navigated their own periods of transformation.

They walked toward the dais, toward the moment when celebration would become covenant, when victory would transform into vision for whatever future they would build from the ruins of conflict.

*

The highest peak of Zephyria caught the day's final light, turning stone to burnished gold beneath their feet. Aquatania stepped closer to the edge, the wind lifting her hair in gentle ripples that mimicked the ocean currents far below. From this vantage, their world unfurled in all directions, the vast seascapes with their hidden depths, the floating islands suspended like emerald jewels against the deepening sky, the boundaries between realms now connected rather than divided. She felt Kieran move beside her, his presence as familiar to her now as her own water armor that flowed in delicate patterns around her wrists and neck.

"I never tire of this view," she said softly, her gaze tracking the intricate paths of reconstruction visible even at this distance, as coral structures rose from once-devastated reefs, repurposed alien technology now serving as connection points between underwater communities and surface settlements. "Every time we come here, something new has been rebuilt."

Kieran's shoulder brushed against hers as he joined her at the precipice, his warmth radiating through the thin fabric of her ceremonial attire. The sunset painted his profile in amber and gold, highlighting the strong lines of his face and the pale scars at his temples that remained from his captivity. Those marks, like the more prominent ones at his wrists, had faded from angry red to silvery white but would never disappear completely. Aquatania had come to see them as maps of their journey, topographies of survival etched into his skin.

"The eastern quadrant is fully restored now," he noted, pointing toward a cluster of floating islands where new bridge systems caught the fading light in crystalline flashes. "The hybrid technology the reformed aliens developed is proving more effective than even your most optimistic projections."

She smiled at the precision of his observation, his military training transformed to peaceful purpose, but retaining its attention to detail. "Science and necessity finding common ground," she replied. "Much like fire and water."

As if summoned by her words, the fire-glow beneath his skin intensified slightly, sending ripples of amber light across his forearms and neck. Since his complete recovery from the alien suppression compounds, this manifestation of his dragon nature had become more pronounced during moments of strong emotion, joy as often as concern, wonder as frequently as wariness.

Far below, the crystal dome of Oceana Prime caught the sunset's reflection, sending rainbow fractals dancing across the water's surface. Aquatania could just make out the distinctive patterns of submarine traffic flowing through newly established routes, merfolk transports alongside reformed alien vessels, sea dragon couriers pacing human trade ships. The World Constitution, which they'd ratified three months earlier, had transformed theoretical unity into practical cooperation with surprising speed.

"Do you remember the first time we stood here together?" Kieran asked, his voice carrying the quiet intimacy they allowed themselves only in rare private moments.

Aquatania's water armor rippled in response to the memory, tiny currents flowing faster around her wrists. "Before the invasion. When we were just colleagues consulting on water purification systems." She turned toward him, finding his gaze, pale amber like distant flame, fixed on her face with an intensity that still made her heart race despite all they had shared. "You kept a professional distance of exactly two feet at all times."

His laugh surprised a nearby sky hawk into flight, the bird's startled cry carrying across the peak. "Protocol for military personnel assigned to royal protection," he admitted, reaching for her hand with the natural confidence that had replaced that early formality. "Though I suspect I was protecting myself as much as observing regulations."

Their fingers intertwined with practiced ease, the familiar wisp of steam rising where her naturally cool skin met his fire-dragon warmth. This physical manifestation of their elemental difference had become a private symbol of their connection, opposing forces creating something new rather than canceling each other out.

"From scientific colleagues to reluctant allies," she mused, watching the steam curl between their joined hands. "From allies to friends, from friends to lovers, from lovers to leaders of a unified world."

"A journey I couldn't have imagined when I was first assigned to your laboratory," Kieran acknowledged, his thumb tracing gentle patterns against her palm. "The serious scientific princess and the suspicious military commander, not exactly a promising beginning."

The sunset deepened around them, painting the sky in vibrant streaks of orange and purple that reflected in the scattered clouds. As the light shifted, it caught in Kieran's eyes, transforming the pale amber to molten gold. Aquatania found herself transported momentarily to the alien mothership, that desperate moment when similar light had illuminated his face as he placed himself between her and certain death. The memory sent an involuntary shiver through her despite the evening's warmth.

"What is it?" he asked immediately, attuned to the subtle shifts in her emotional state after months of shared life.

"Just remembering," she replied, her free hand rising to touch his cheek where a thin scar curved along his jawline. "The moment I realized I couldn't bear to lose you. When you intercepted that energy pulse meant for me aboard the mothership."

His expression softened, the fire-glow beneath his skin intensifying to match the sunset's deepening hues. "I was operating on instinct," he admitted. "My mind caught up with my heart somewhere between pushing you aside and absorbing that blast."

The directness of his words sent a rush of emotion through Aquatania so powerful that her sea dragon nature responded automatically. Iridescent scales shimmered briefly beneath the skin of her forearms and across her cheekbones, blue-green patterns appearing and vanishing like lightning beneath the surface of a stormy sea. The involuntary transformation had become more frequent during moments of heightened feeling, her dragon responding to emotional currents her human composure might otherwise conceal.

Kieran noticed immediately, his eyes tracking the patterns with quiet appreciation. His fingers released hers to trace the fading scale outline at her temple. "Your father mentioned that happened to your mother, too," he said softly. "The scales appearing when she felt something deeply."

"Did he?" Aquatania hadn't known that particular detail. Her father rarely spoke of her mother, the pain of loss still evident decades after her death. "When did he tell you that?"

"After our water ritual beneath the triple moons," Kieran replied, his hand sliding to cup her cheek with gentle pressure. "He said seeing your scales appear when we kissed reminded him of his first years with her, how her dragon nature would show itself despite her royal composure."

The revelation touched something deep within her, connecting her to a mother she'd barely known through this unexpected shared trait. Her water armor responded by flowing in more complex patterns around her throat and wrists, the liquid catching the sunset's final light in a prismatic display.

They stood silhouetted against the vibrant sky, their forms merging into a single shape from a distant perspective. Rulers of a unified world taking a rare moment to be themselves, their dragon natures partially concealed in human forms but never truly hidden from each other. Below them, lights began to appear across settlements as darkness approached, pinpricks of illumination that represented the thousands of lives connected through their leadership and vision.

"We've come so far," Aquatania whispered, leaning into his warmth as the first stars appeared in the eastern sky.

"With so much further yet to go," Kieran completed, his arm encircling her waist.

The twilight deepened around them, stars emerging in greater numbers as the last bands of purple faded from the western horizon. Aquatania took a deep breath. The moment she'd been waiting for finally arrived with perfect synchronicity, their world at peace, their position as leaders established, their bond unquestionable. She reached for Kieran's hand, her water armor parting to allow skin-to-skin contact as she guided his palm to rest against her abdomen. The subtle changes were imperceptible to anyone but her scientific awareness, yet they represented the most miraculous transformation she'd ever documented.

"According to my calculations," she said, her voice steady despite the thunder of her heart, "we'll be welcoming a little hybrid dragon in about seven months."

Kieran went perfectly still, his palm warm against her still-flat abdomen. She watched the progression of emotions across his face with scientific fascination and loving attention, shock widening his eyes, confusion furrowing his brow as he processed her words, realization dawning in the slight parting of his lips, and finally, joy illuminating his features from within. The fire-glow beneath his skin intensified dramatically, spreading from his core outward until his entire body radiated golden light that pushed back the gathering darkness.

"A baby?" he whispered, the words carrying both question and wonder. "Our baby? A hybrid..."

"Sea dragon and fire dragon," she confirmed, allowing her scientific mind to temper the emotion threatening to overwhelm her voice. "The first confirmed case in recorded history. Marina has been helping me monitor the cellular development. The genetic integration is remarkable. Both elemental traits appear to be expressing without conflict."

Kieran laughed suddenly, the sound pure and unburdened in a way she'd rarely heard from him. "Only you would describe our miracle in terms of cellular development and genetic integration." His free hand rose to cup her cheek, thumb brushing where scales had briefly shimmered moments earlier. "How long have you known?"

"Six weeks, three days," she admitted. "I wanted to be certain before telling you. The early stages of interspecies pregnancy can be volatile, especially with elementally opposed parents."

His expression shifted subtly, the joy tempered by concern. "Are you all right? Is there a risk to you?"

The question warmed her more than any congratulations could have. Even in his shock, his first thought was for her well-being. "I'm perfectly healthy," she assured him. "The water armor actually assists in maintaining optimal conditions for development. Marina theorizes it's acting as a mediator between the opposing elements."

Kieran's hand remained on her abdomen, his touch gentle yet somehow protective already. The fire-glow beneath his skin pulsed in rhythm with his heartbeat, visible evidence of emotion too profound for words alone. "A child," he murmured. "Our child."

"Half diplomat, half warrior," Aquatania said with a smile. "Half scientist, half strategist."

"Wholly miraculous," Kieran completed, drawing her closer until their foreheads touched. The connection sent pleasant warmth cascading through her, her water armor responding with flowing patterns that harmonized with his fire glow.

She closed her eyes, allowing the moment to exist without analysis or projection. Yet memories surfaced unbidden, crystallized moments from their journey together that had led to this unprecedented future.

"Do you remember our first kiss?" Kieran asked softly, as if reading her thoughts.

Aquatania smiled against his shoulder. "In the laboratory. I was extracting fire enzyme samples for the cure's stabilization compound."

"You were so focused on the extraction process you didn't notice I was in pain," he recalled, no accusation in his tone, only fond remembrance.

"Until you flinched and I realized the extraction needle had penetrated too deeply." She traced the almost invisible mark on his inner wrist where her inexperience with fire dragon physiology had caused unintended harm. "I was horrified at my carelessness."

"And I was so desperate to show it didn't matter that I grabbed your hand to reassure you—"

"Creating our first steam cloud when my water armor reacted to your fire-touch," she finished. "I was so startled I dropped the collection vial."

"Which I caught," he continued, the shared memory unfolding between them like cherished text. "And when I handed it back—"

"I kissed you instead of taking it," Aquatania completed. "Completely unprofessional behavior for a scientific princess."

They laughed together at the memory, the sound carrying across the peak and down into the valleys below. Yet other memories waited their turn, not all holding the same lightness.

"I still dream about the mothership sometimes," Kieran admitted, his voice dropping to a near whisper. "Those final moments when the core was destabilizing. The countdown."

Aquatania nodded against his chest, her own memory of those moments razor-sharp despite the year that had passed. "Ten seconds, and we thought we were facing the end together."

"I remember being grateful, even then," he said, surprising her. "Grateful that if I had to die, it would be holding you. That my last sensation would be your heart beating against mine."

Her water armor rippled with emotion, flowing more rapidly around her wrists. "And then Marina appeared through that impossible portal. I still don't understand how her divination allowed her to find that exact moment, that precise location in space and time."

"Seven seconds left," Kieran recalled. "Her eyes glowing with that turquoise light. Her hands reaching for us."

"We dove through the portal just as the core reached critical mass," Aquatania continued, the memory so vivid she could almost feel the energy wave singeing her heels as they escaped. "And emerged in waters near Zephyria, disoriented but alive against all probability."

They fell silent, both remembering those who hadn't been so fortunate — the dragon scouts lost during early reconnaissance missions, the human settlements decimated before the cure could reach them, the reformed aliens executed by their own command structure for choosing peace over conquest. Their victory had come at tremendous cost, each life lost was a thread severed from the fabric they now worked to strengthen.

"What does this mean for us?" Kieran asked finally, his hand still resting protectively over the new life growing within her. "For our duties, our positions?"

Aquatania appreciated the practical question, so characteristic of his approach to even the most emotional situations. "Politically, it represents the ultimate symbol of unity," she said, the analyst in her never fully dormant. "The first child born of elemental opposition, carrying both fire and water heritage."

"I wasn't asking about the politics," he corrected gently.

She met his eyes, finding them soft with understanding. "I know," she acknowledged. "Personally...everything changes. Our priorities, our decisions, our view of the future. We're no longer building a world just for others, but for our own child."

"A child who will carry the legacy of everything we've accomplished," Kieran said, his hand moving in a small circle over her abdomen. "And everything we've survived."

"A child who will never know a world where dragons remain separate by element, where humans and merfolk live in isolation, where difference means division." The thought filled her with fierce hope that momentarily overwhelmed her scientific detachment.

Kieran noticed immediately, his smile deepening as scales

shimmered briefly across her cheekbones, her dragon nature responding to emotion too powerful for her human form to contain completely. His thumb traced the vanishing pattern with familiar tenderness.

"Your father will be ecstatic," he noted. "The first royal grandchild."

"I can't wait to tell him."

"And I imagine Marina is already designing specialized monitoring equipment and planning research studies on hybrid dragon development."

"Complete with underwater observation chambers and thermal regulation systems," Aquatania said, confirming with a smile. "Though she's been remarkably restrained about the scientific opportunities this presents."

The stars now filled the sky above them, the peak illuminated only by Kieran's fire-glow and the gentle bioluminescence of Aquatania's water armor. They stood together at the highest point of their world, future parents contemplating a possibility that had never existed before, a child born from elements that once opposed each other, now finding harmony in new life.

"Shall we fly?" Kieran suggested, his voice carrying the quiet certainty of one who knew exactly what she needed. The stars had fully emerged now, pinpricks of silver against deepening indigo, while below them Zephyria's lights twinkled in peaceful constellation. Aquatania felt the familiar yearning rise within her, the sea dragon's desire for movement unrestricted by human form, the pure freedom of wings cutting through air and fins trailing through the clouds. They'd maintained human forms for weeks during the diplomatic missions, propriety requiring suppression of their dragon natures except during formal demonstrations. Now, alone on the peak with only stars as witnesses, they could embrace their true selves completely.

"Yes," she answered, already moving toward the widest

section of the plateau where transformation would be unimpeded. "The baby is perfectly protected during shifting. Marina confirmed the amniotic sac develops enhanced elasticity in hybrid pregnancies."

Kieran smiled at her characteristic blend of emotion and science. "I wasn't worried," he said, though the subtle relief in his eyes suggested otherwise. "Your body knows how to protect what's precious."

They stood facing each other in the center of the stone circle, their formal attire moving in the gentle night breeze. The transformation was most harmonious when begun in synchronicity, their opposite elements finding balance in simultaneous change. Aquatania extended her hands palm upward, Kieran's coming to rest palm downward above hers without touching. The space between vibrated with potential energy, water, and fire, communicating without contact.

"Let's do this," she whispered, the words both a statement and an invitation.

They regarded each other with dragon eyes that saw beyond the visible spectrum, perceiving energy signatures and thermal patterns alongside physical form. Communication shifted from verbal to multisensory, subtle movements of wing and tail conveying meaning, pheromonal signals carrying emotional content, micro-expressions readable only to those who shared their dual nature. Despite their elemental opposition, they'd learned each other's dragon language through months of practice, finding common ground between water currents and flame patterns.

Without the need for spoken agreement, they moved to the edge of the peak in perfect coordination. Aquatania felt the night air caress her wings, the currents testing membrane strength and flexibility. Beside her, Kieran's body temperature elevated in preparation for flight.

They launched simultaneously, powerful hind legs propelling them from stone to air in explosive movement that sent loose pebbles cascading down the mountainside. The first wingbeats created temporary separation as they each established individual flight patterns, adjusting to air currents and finding optimal altitude. Aquatania's sea dragon form cut through the darkness with fluid grace, her wings catching moonlight in translucent beauty while the water element flowing around her fins left a momentary trail of luminescent particles.

Kieran's fire dragon form ascended through different flight mechanics, his wings beat less frequently but with greater power, while heat generated from his core created rising thermal that added lift beyond pure muscular effort. The effect made him appear to glide upward as if carried by invisible hands, his scales gleaming from within like captured starlight.

They circled the peak independently once before their flight paths converged into a coordinated dance, demonstrating perfect balance between their elements. Aquatania banked sharply left while Kieran spiraled right, their trajectories creating double helix patterns as they climbed higher through thinning air. Where their paths crossed, brief contact between wingtip and tail sent sparks of elemental energy trailing behind them, steam wisps where water met fire, visible evidence of opposition finding harmony.

The higher they flew, beyond the boundary where human settlements could observe, into a realm where dragons had traditionally maintained separate territories by element. Sea dragons had claimed coastal airways, fire dragons the volcanic thermals, sky dragons the highest currents, and forest dragons the canopy spaces. Now they flew together through all domains, a physical embodiment of the unity they'd helped forge in diplomatic chambers.

Their aerial dance evolved into more complex patterns, Kieran's fire creating updrafts that Aquatania rode with minimal effort, her water element cooling air around them to create pressure differentials that enhanced their combined movement.

They spiraled around each other in ancient courtship patterns that predated civilization itself, instinctive choreography encoded in their dragon nature that human consciousness merely accompanied rather than directed.

Finally, they ascended above cloud level, breaking through a vapor ceiling into a clear starscape where moonlight turned everything to silver and shadow. Their wingbeats slowed as they found a stable position hovering together, energy expenditure reduced through complementary positioning that allowed his heat to create lift they both utilized.

Kieran's wing curved around her in a protective gesture that acknowledged without words the precious cargo she carried, their child, future embodiment of elemental harmony, the first of a new generation that would never know a world divided.

Aquatania's dragon senses detected the subtle changes already occurring within her, cellular structures developing that contained both fire and water affinities, an impossible combination made viable through the love that had transcended elemental opposition. Her awareness extended momentarily to this new life, sensing its dragon nature already forming alongside human potential, both aspects equally vital to the unprecedented being they'd created.

About the Author

Gabriella Bradley lives amidst rugged mountains. She more often than not has a grizzly in her yard searching for food and breaking into her garbage tote. Other critters that visit on a regular basis are cougars, coyotes, squirrels, and raccoons.

Gabby's hobbies include graphic art, gardening, swimming, sewing, embroidery, and knitting. Favorite movies are old timers like Gone with the Wind, Spartacus, etc. She is an avid Trekkie, loves series like Lost, Fringe, The 12 Monkeys, and Shadowhunters. Her favorite music is Abba.

Visit her website at: http://www.gabriellabradley.com